2
THE INFIDEL BOOKS

THE

GRIM
ALLIANCE

ANGELA R. WATTS

THE GRIM ALLIANCE

THE INFIDEL BOOKS - 2

ANGELA R. WATTS

Published by Revelation Way Publishing. All rights reserved. Cover design
by miblart.com. All rights reserved.

All Scriptures are from the King James Version (KJV) version: King James
Version, public domain.

This is a work of fiction. All names, characters, locations, places, incidents,
and so forth are either the product of the author's imagination or used in a
fictitious manner. Any similarities to people, living or dead, and actual
events, are entirely coincidental.

Printed in the United States of America.

First edition: 2020 by Angela R. Watts

Second edition: 2021 by Angela R. Watts

ISBN: 978-1-7332495-3-9

Contents

ALSO BY ANGELA

WHISPERS OF HEAVEN

Seek

ANTHOLOGIES

Run from the Dead

LIFE

The Depths We'll Go To

PRAISE FOR THE INFIDEL BOOKS

"Fresh, fast, and almost too timely for comfort, The Divided Nation is a gripping thriller from an authoritative new voice on the thriller scene. Angela Watts can really, really write." – Ryan Steck, The Real Book Spy

"Superior novel by the talented author Ms. Angela Watts. Action, adventure, general badassery? Oh yes!" – Lt Col USMC (Ret.) H. Rip Rawlings, New York Times and USA Today bestseller of RED METAL

"I highly recommend this book. It is packed with everything a good thriller should have - action, memorable characters, a plot that flies by, emotion, light & darkness, and more action." – Stuart Ashenbrenner, Best Thriller Books reviewer

TO THE FIGHTERS.
MAY OUR EVERY BREATH BE A WAR CRY.

GANGSTERS

George Johnston: United Nations politician, businessman, and ganglord of his own large army that controls large portions of the UN across the globe.

West Johnston: gangster son of George Johnston, the Johnston heir.

Kaleb Savage: ganglord and close ally of George Johnston. Father of Nate Savage and uncle of Jack Savage.

Jack Savage: gangster son of Hunter Savage.

Hunter Savage: ex-special operative, assassin that works for George.

Nate Savage: gangster son of Kaleb. Best friends with Simon.

Jordan Bucks: ganglord and close ally of George Johnston's. Father of Simon Bucks.

Simon Bucks: gangster son of Jordan Bucks.

Gideon Hochberg: close ally of George Johnston. Best friends with Alex Thompson.

Alex Thompson: gangster in George's gang. Comrade of Gideon Hochberg.

Percy & Preston Royal: brothers in Gideon's group.

Spencer Anderson: gangster in George's group. Friends with West and Jack. Older brother of Randy Anderson.

Ty Brooks: gangster in George's gang, close friend to West.

FISHER FAMILY

Burl Fisher and Kay Fisher: parents of the Fisher family and leaders of Springtown, Kentucky.

Rene' Fisher: daughter of the Fisher parents. Friends with Simon.

Lee Fisher: son of the Fisher parents.

Brian Jones: Union Army General. Husband and father. Birth son of Kay Fisher.

Terri Brewer and Howie (Henry) Brewer: daughter and son-in-law of the Fisher parents, and their five kids, Dax, Jaycee, Paisley, Lily, and Aiden.

OTHER

Keegan Black: a new ally to Springtown and Gideon Hochberg. In secret, he aids small townships by paying enemies to leave them alone. Brother of Brett Black.

Philip & Danny Dunnham: brothers that fled George's group and abide in Springtown.

CHAPTER ONE

September 14th, 2027

A WARRIOR FOUGHT FOR what must be. The world changed, technology advanced, and the goals of society evolved, but war remained. And as long as there was war, there were warriors. West Johnston, son to one of the world's most powerful ganglords, was one of those warriors, and the weight of what was burdened him daily. It was up to him to end the madness and he couldn't do the dirt work if his head was in the clouds, wondering what the world might be one day when the Second Civil War ended.

West sipped his piping hot black coffee, sifting through the morning newspaper. The Johnston estate, a well-secured mansion in Michigan, received news coverage in forms of electronic holograms, news articles, and newspapers. West preferred beginning his mornings with the papers and finishing with the far more detailed hologram coverage.

George, his father, had brought him up to be the Johnston heir—ruler of the empire that George had fought for decades to build. George had practically nudged the United States into division before the 2024 election. He had caused leaders to stumble, wicked men to rise into power, and innocent lives to be lost. All in the construction of the forthcoming Johnston empire.

Before the nation's hope of redemption is lost, I have to kill George. West tossed the paper aside. The Civil War hadn't slowed since September 11th, when the conservative Confeds won over D.C. The government was off its rocker and had every right to be outraged—the Union had failed to protect the nation's capital. The war was practically over.

But it wasn't. The Union would fight back dirty.

Over the past few months, West had done the unfathomable: left his comrade—practically his brother—Jack, his group of gangsters, and submitted to George. George had given him a long leash over the years but recently cut it short. West had chosen to become his father's perfect prodigy, but it was a sham. Or, it was a sham as long as he could pull it off. George was one of the world's greatest ganglords, politicians, and businessmen, with millions of followers: even if West had a plan, he stood the chance to be killed by security detail after the drastic deed was done.

Killing George and getting killed in return sounded worth it to him. But Jack wouldn't like the plan, so West had to be smarter.

West downed the rest of his coffee and leaned back into the hard wooden chair, glancing around. The room he'd grown up in now stood bare, with only a few pieces of furniture and nothing of sentimental value. He'd had less room in his old apartment, but at least then he'd been close to Jack, Spencer, and the gangsters who would have followed him into hell and back.

On his father's estate, he played by George's rules and he played them well. George was clueless as to his precious prodigy's true motives.

West scrolled on his tablet and pulled up a few hologram newscasts. The Union was scrambling to retaliate but without D.C., the government leaders had been forced to sanctuary. The Confeds had a crucial upper hand and had locked down the capital. President Larry, of the Confederates, had asked President Kaden, of the Union and previous US, to surrender.

President Kaden had responded, "When hell freezes over."

West hadn't met President Larry, but he knew President Kaden well enough. He met the pompous man often at meetings and briefings alongside his father. West knew many of the United Nations leaders and disliked most of them: most of them had no care for human lives and didn't care what it took to get rich or gain power. The few men and women who loved their people and worked to protect them were snuffed out and overruled. Sometimes, they were killed.

It couldn't go on. The US would have no chance of reformation if the war didn't end soon.

The holograph broadcast live news feed of the walls outside of D.C. where people rioted. In the US, there were few kinds of people: the rich, who still had lives that resembled "normal"; the middle class who, if they abode by the Union's rules, could barely get by; and the outcasts, which were a mix between the ones too far from the government to follow rules and get help, or those too poor to do so. Many of the outcasts fell through the cracks and fell away from the Union's well-bred, well-monotonized society. They either became homeless, died in caravan attacks, or were sold into the human trafficking cartels.

West watched the footage closely. People screamed and threw various little bombs at the D.C. capital's wall, but the Confeds did not open fire at them. The Union and the Confeds had done their share of pillaging innocent townships that hadn't been destroyed by gangs and the lack of US government, but now, it seemed the Confeds were trying to keep the media on their side by not striking down the attackers.

West rubbed his hairy, broad chest in frustration before tossing the tablet onto the table. He got up, heading over to his closet. George had a morning meeting with one of his right-hand ganglords, Kaleb Savage. West would be accompanying him.

West grabbed a clean pair of jeans and a long-sleeved t-shirt, throwing them on. He sent another encrypted text to Jack, hoping he'd reply.

Jack spent most of his time in North Carolina with his girlfriend, Mels. He'd been visiting her before West left, and if Jack wasn't with her, he was working jobs with some of George's best men for cash and supplies. Jack was inches away from marrying Mels—it was up to West to protect Jack's chance.

Of course, Jack wasn't always good at following plans, and he hadn't been too happy with West leaving to play martyr. But none of the men had been foolish enough to try stopping him. They all struggled to survive and make George happy.

West headed into the hallway, locking his bedroom door behind him with a code only he knew, and went down the giant, mahogany stairs. The mansion was the perfect location for a horror film—big, richly furnished, with secret passages that only the Johnston family knew about. There was even a huge underground system but it was top secret. West used to get lost in the halls, but it'd usually been on purpose. He never wanted to be near his parents.

"Good morning, son," George smiled softly as West entered the enormous dining room. The servants finished serving breakfast and stepped away.

"Good morning," West said courteously.

"See the news?"

"Yessir." West sat beside his father, across from his mother, Cindy, who methodically slathered butter onto a biscuit. Her Southern belle habits died hard.

"What do you think?" George asked. He wore a suit, as he so often did, and stirred some sugar into his coffee, a real picture-perfect mafia man.

Knowing it was a question with hidden motives, West spoke calmly, "I believe that the Union will fight even dirtier, but with Brian Jones leading his group, they have a solid chance of winning D.C. back."

"Kaden's awfully irritated," George chuckled. "He hates going into hiding."

"Most of the UN leaders haven't the slightest clue what hardships are," West said.

"So you think Jones will lead the Union to this victory? Why not another government leader or General?"

"Jones has thorough training and unlike most of the Union generals and spies, he isn't afraid of risks." West sipped his water, studying his father. "*Calculated* risks. And so far, it has paid off."

"Why hasn't he acted then? It's been three days since the government lost D.C." George challenged.

"The Confeds are in tip top shape. It will take multiple attacks to wear them out. Jones is probably planning out every last detail. That's how soldier boys roll."

"Until they throw the plan to the wind and change tactics," George mused. "Men like you and I, West, we are always in control. Be sure you maintain that. A man without control is—"

"—a man without reason," West finished, voice cool.

George chuckled and lifted his coffee mug. "It took a few years of rebellion, but you've done nothing if not make me proud of how fast you've come to see the light, boy."

Because you killed Ed, my friend, my comrade, when I kept fighting. You took a life to claim mine. West smiled slightly. "Of course."

"This legacy is yours, West. Do not forget that."

"It is if I am able to pass your test, father." West hated calling George *father* but it was all part of earning his

7

trust, even if he despised the process.

"In due time. Never be too eager for a fight that could end you." George winked. They ate in silence for a short while, which gave West time to think, something he did far too often.

George never spoke of the Test he gave select few—and only his gang leaders—and no one talked much about it. The gang leaders who worked directly with George had two paths if they wanted to make it with the big dogs. First, in the most basic of examples, they did their jobs well, had men who followed them, and earned George's trust. If they pulled that off, they might receive George's branding—a J carved into their back—and have more freedom to do as George bid them too. Most men stopped there and didn't want to push further, but George had elites who were almost his equals. These men had to pass a test which combined pyshcical and mental torture, but that was the extent of West's knowledge.

Kaleb Savage, Jack's uncle, had survived the test, but Jack's father had not. Hunter Savage had been a great man —a SEAL, practically a hero back when West and Jack had been kids—and George had let him die during the test. While West didn't think of it often, it was something that drove him to end his father's legacy.

There's no climbing up the ranks for me. George won't give me the mark. He says a ruler cannot be branded, but can be tested. George wants to make sure I'm fit for his role and he won't cut me slack. West finished his eggs. He knew plenty of men with scarred J's on their backsides. Gideon Hochberg, for example, was one of the finest gang leaders West had the displeasure of working with, but the man had been branded shortly after West returned to George. Gideon probably wasn't fully healed yet, though he wasn't a man to sit around and rest. He kept busy, like West. Together, they could do some real damage. Or fixing, depending on the viewpoint.

More was going on in the US than what met the news coverage, and West needed help to deflect the powers that be.

"HE'S OVER AN HOUR late," George grunted, drumming his fingers along the table. George had plenty of safehouses and secure warehouses around the nation, but this warehouse was one of his favorites, with a full bar and lounging area. They were alone in the dimly lit room, with plenty of trained security guards outside. George always had bodyguards with him. No one could snipe him without being shot down first.

"Kaleb likes to push his limits." West poured George some rum.

"The whole Savage family loves to push buttons," George scoffed.

West pictured Jack, the man who'd had West's back no matter the dire situation, from shootings to burning buildings to things in between. He smirked. "They do."

George watched him, most likely knowing the sarcasm behind his words. "You are better off detaching yourself from him."

"I have."

George hummed softly. "You have come a long way, son, but you have not stopped loving people. That must change."

The door to the warehouse pushed open and the familiar, rough voice of Kaleb echoed in the large, empty room: "I need a drink."

"The drunkard needs a drink?" George laughed, leaning back in his chair as he watched Kaleb come over. "You're late... Do explain why."

Kaleb sat down heavily, covered in blood that most likely wasn't his own, a few scratches along his arms. He snatched the bottle of whiskey from West and chugged a few swallows before meeting George's gaze. "Just a little job."

"That's a lot of blood for a little job." George mused, sipping his own drink.

West gulped. *He killed Dickerson and Reynolds... he fell for George's trap...* Only a week earlier, Kaleb's only son, Nate, had taken a job Kaleb gave him and a few others. The job was simple—scare two old men into submitting to George's rules again. The old men were unruly and always had been, but they'd been close to Kaleb, and he hadn't expected the job to go bad. The men had pulled one over on Nate and his friends, injured Nate, and gotten away with it. Or they had until Kaleb caught up with them.

"You like games, I don't," Kaleb said coolly. "So let's cut the chase. You hired Dick and Rey to psyche my boys out. You made 'em hurt Nate without killing him so you could remind me who's boss. And you knew I'd hunt my old friends down and take them out." He held the bottle close to his lips, never breaking his gaze.

George smirked. "I'm not the one who pulled the trigger.""No, you never are." Kaleb's lips turned upward. His gray eyes grew bitter. "And I didn't pull a trigger." He gestured at his bloodied jacket and SOG pants. "Family friend or arch nemesis, men who harm my family all die the same way."

West looked between them quietly. He knew Kaleb was a terrible drunkard of a father, but he was a good leader. He would've shot himself dead if it meant Nate survived.

Man's terrible at showing that, though, even though Hunter never struggled to show his compassion.

"A pity," George said easily. "You put such effort into protecting Nate, yet, he still hates you."

"Every man has a right to hate the man who gave him life." Kaleb chuckled. "Nate's a valuable part of my group and his emotions don't change the fact that he listens well."

"He's as reckless and temperamental as you," George said.

"Better rage than remorse. We get the job done." Kaleb leaned in close to George, voice cool as ice. "But if you ever hire someone to hurt my flesh and blood again, you'll be the one screaming for God to save you. Clear?"

"As a spring blue sky." George set his drink down and West refilled it. "Let's talk business."

West sat down. He forced a few sips of his whiskey, but it burned too much and he didn't feel like grabbing a beer from the fridge. He listened to George explain the situation of the Union.

Kaleb waved him off midway. "Don't pacify me, I know the updates. What do you need from me?""Men," George said simply. "The Union will need spies, moles, people on the inside of the Confederate army. The Union will need foot soldiers, as well."

Kaleb leaned back into his seat and crossed his well-muscled arms across his chest. "You want me to send the gov canon fodder?" he asked coldly.

"You have men to spare. New recruits, weak links, just people who can pull the trigger a few times before getting blown up." George didn't look away. "This is war, after all."

"If the Union wants to get their men blown up, I won't stop them. But I refuse to send my own into a war that has no winning side." Kaleb slammed the whiskey bottle down. "The Union can handle this alone, freezing temperatures or not, because they've got funding from the UN. They've got food, clothes, men, ammo—I won't toss men just to toss men. The Confeds won't hold D.C. or any other city they've claimed forever because they're freezing to death. They're dying behind their lines like flies, and you want me to pity either side? One is weak and hopeful, one is strong and demented."

"I didn't ask to hear your political views, Kaleb," George said firmly. "You will do this."

"Ain't got a need to. I've done your dirty work a thousand times over but this is stupid." Kaleb shook his head, light brown hair tousled and streaks of dried blood showing. "You know that."

"I do, but the President requires thugs, as he so humbly calls them. It would be best to pacify him, don't you think?" George raised his eyebrows. "If the president wants a paci, I'll put a gun in his mouth. I ain't sending anyone to the battle grounds."

"Your men aren't trained with moral codes as the Army boys are, Kaleb. Your men stand a solid chance at surviving and helping the Union win. Think of this. You've known it has been coming. Isn't it why you've been so hard on your boy? Your son dying alone in an alley doesn't scare you—he knows the rules of the gangs. But him dying on a bloody battlefield is different, and that scares you, that he'll die hearing—"

"Don't try getting inside my head, George, I don't have room." Kaleb lifted a calloused hand. "I've known you'd ask me for thugs. You've squeezed other gangs dry for extra men, for fodder, for scapegoats, and I've watched them lie down and roll over. But I'm not. My men aren't going. Go ask someone else." A pause. "And don't bother asking Jordan. He stands with me." Jordan Bucks was Kaleb's comrade, practically his brother, which was saying a lot since Kaleb despised people in general. Jordan was also Simon's father, and Simon and Nate were two peas in a pod.

George pushed his empty glass away. "This is not something I will reinforce, but I recommend it. Even a few hundred men, men outside your HQ, would be sufficient."

"Answer is still no. I'll tell the president that myself if you'd like."

"Stay away from President Kaden." George rolled his eyes.

"One bullet—"

"Believe me, Kaleb, I've pictured many ways of how he could breathe his last, but I'm a man of politics, war, and business. I wear many hats," George chuckled wryly, "and none of them allow me to vocalize such things as freely as you do."

Kaleb lifted his bottle. "My men stay with me, away from the fields. You knew that before you asked."

"I was hoping you'd be wiser than you used to be."

"Hope is the thing with chains that binds the soul and sings the cries without the words and never stops at all." Kaleb finished the rest of his whiskey with one long drought.

"You don't seem the type to twist a poet woman's words around. I'm impressed." George pulled a small chip from his suit pocket. "There are more matters to discuss."

"Shoot." Kaleb glanced at West and smirked.

"Brian will be attacking D.C. during winter."

"Not sending my men," Kaleb said in a dry sing-song voice.

George ignored him and briefed him of the situation of the UN. "Jones will be leading an attack on D.C. shortly, and I suggest all of our gangs remove anyone nearby. We don't want ugly fire—if our men aren't with the Union they'll be shot down."

"No duh, Holmes." Kaleb got up. "I know the updates with the little UN's fear mongering tactics and the media coverage making the Confeds into baby killers—mind if I head out?"

"You need to be alert, Kaleb. I protect you, we are allies, but if you refuse to benefit the Union, it might bite you back." George didn't bat an eyelash at Kaleb's gruff nature. He'd grown accustomed to it over the years.

"I help the Union. I help them more than I help the Confeds!" Kaleb snarled. "I scratch their back, they stab mine. What else do you want, George? These are hellish times and none of you big wigs with lush homes and security deposits are out here bleeding for anything."

"Consider sending five hundred, Kaleb, and President Kaden will continue to trust us as alliances. Trust from the UN leaders is crucial," George said smoothly.

Kaleb threw tantrums plenty of times with George, and George didn't prefer dealing with them, but he didn't bash Kaleb's head in. Kaleb was vital for the gangs to work together—his temper was maintainable when George played his cards right. West, however, was not only used to the Savage men's tempers, but found Jack's frustration oftentimes amusing.

Kaleb headed to the door. "Anything else I need to know?""Besides Brian's plan, the president's request, and the fact the Confeds will be getting close to Paradise this winter, but you probably know that—"

"They try to take my HQ, they die. Union boys or Confeds, my territory is my own, government ain't taking it." Kaleb smirked slightly, picking up another large bottle of whiskey from the shelves. "See you, George." He left the warehouse without another word.

"Seems to be mellowing with age," West said dryly.

"He's a good leader. I don't put up with drama for nothing." George stood up and smoothed his suit. "When you have valuable members like that, it doesn't hurt to meet them in person every once and awhile, even when you know the answer to your requests. It reminds them you're tangible... and unstoppable."

"So you think Kaleb will send the men?"

"He's done far worse for the Union." George nodded. "His tantrum doesn't change the fact he would sacrifice five hundred men if it meant Nathan was withheld from the gunfire."

West studied George for a long moment. "Why do you think Kaleb's more afraid of Nate entering a civil war, when Nate's in gang wars all the time?"

"You'd have to ask him. His motivations might be more than that. But so long as he follows my instructions, I don't care what keeps him up at night. He took care of Dickerson and Reynolds, but threatened my life—I'll give him some room to breathe for a while..." George chuckled and headed for the door. "Let's go meet the president."

CHAPTER TWO

September 15th, 2027

GIDEON HOCHBERG SAT AT a tiny kitchen table with his holographic tablet. He hadn't rested much since the battle of Springtown—which was after his brutal marking—where he had buried over thirty men. About one-third of the men who had followed him into battle, for a town none of them even loved, lay to rot in a Kentucky hillside. They had followed Gideon because they'd trusted him, they'd believed that they had a chance at survival if they took his lead.

And they had died for strangers. Strangers who probably saw them as thugs, gangsters, monsters. Gideon hoped that the town's mindset would change. The town wouldn't last much longer if they couldn't ally themselves with the rough bunch of gangsters who offered help.

Gideon rubbed his temples wearily, dark hair falling over his forehead. The battle at Springtown had been fast, bloody, but it'd also been a hoax. The gangster who had led it had been paid to do so. George had let Gideon go and save that town—but for what reason? Springtown hadn't done anything to benefit George or the Civil War.

He'd spent over a week trying to figure out the puzzle. He'd been sure it was a test for him. He knew that the previous mayor of Springtown had been in agreement with Shane, the Union spy who attacked the poor town. Mayor Knight had been letting Springtown sink into famine and hopelessness while his pile of cash grew, until Shane came to finish his intentions. Shane had been killed, Mayor Knight casted out of town, and Gideon still had no further clues as to who sent Shane and why George cared if the town survived.

Between the looming mystery and too many painkillers, Gideon's rage was hard to control. He watched the holographic reports with glazed eyes. Footage of caravans being chased away from the grounds they'd stolen, footage of Union and Confeds shooting each other from various locations across the US, footage of buildings burning and people rioting. The media never showed the luxurious houses of the rich politicians or the gangster leaders, of course. The people with power were causing more hell, not solving problems.

He closed his eyes ever so briefly as the footage showed children being herded out of an orphanage, Union men in dark suits escorting them to buses. *They don't show the footage of the radical Jihadists herding infidel kids into their groups, gang raping them till they die, or strapping bombs onto them to be martrys. They don't show the little kids being sold to the highest bidder at domes. But I see it. I see it all the time.* Gideon turned the tablet off and leaned forward, back aching. He kept up with the news because he had to keep up with the mindset of the divided nation, but he knew most of what was shown was total bull.

The front door creaked open. Alex Thompson, his closest friend and basically his brother, peeked his head in. His blond hair had grown a bit shaggy. "Ah, crikey, you're awake. It's 1 AM! You're supposed to be asleep!" Alex shut the door behind him, locking it tight.

"Couldn't sleep. Dinner's finished." Gideon crossed his arms onto the table, sighing.

Alex hung his coat up onto the wall hook, setting his heavy duffel bag carefully by the door. "Did you burn it this time?"

"Look for yourself."

Alex stepped over with a small frown. "You all right, mate?"

"I think I'll ease off the drugs."

"You're not even resting, Gideon. If you hurt yourself —"

"The stitches are gone now. I can't afford not to get back into the game, Alex." Gideon shook his head slightly. "I'm fine."

"How many times have I heard that before?" Alex rolled his eyes and stirred the stew in the pot.

"I still don't understand," Gideon began tightly. "I need to understand why that battle went down the way it did. I can't find the answer. And I can't figure it out when I'm on painkillers." "Maybe it wasn't a test at all. Maybe it was just how it was and that's it." Alex dipped himself a bowl, jaw tight as he glanced at Gideon pointedly. "Not everything that happens is a test. George can't control everything, you know."

Gideon tilted his head in annoyance. "What if it is a test, I don't have the answer, and I pay for my incompetence?"

"Oh, for pity's sake," Alex groaned, sitting down. The bags under his eyes and scruff on his chin were hard to ignore, but he refused to slow down and rest, though he nagged at Gideon for not doing so. "Shane and the mayor had their gig and it was a bad one, but George letting you interfere and wipe Shane's group out—isn't that enough as it is? George gave you the mark. Just because you don't know why he let you interfere doesn't mean he's gonna break your neck. Just leave it alone." Despite the firmness in his words, Alex's eyes burned with irritation. He knew Gideon wouldn't leave it alone but he tried to warn him, anyway.

"It was more than that, Al. I don't know how to explain it to you, but there's more to what happened." Gideon dug his fingers through his hair, glaring down at the table covered in scratches, dents, and marks. One of the dents had been made by Clint, one of George's finest special operatives. The man had been a wild card but after bunking with Alex and Gideon for a few months, grew close to them. Too close. He'd been killed during an operation. Neither Gideon nor Alex would forget that disaster, but it was one of many.

It was Gideon's job to protect, defend, and kill. Not bury his own. But such was war. The wolves bled out so that the sheep moved on unscathed.

Alex was silent for a long moment, downing some stew before leaning back. "If you think there was more to it, then there probably was."

"But I don't have the answer," Gideon muttered.

"You're human. Humans usually don't have all the answers."

"I need them."

"Let's think it through," Alex smirked. "Been a while since we sat and talked, anyway." It'd been two weeks since the battle at Springtown, and between Alex's jobs for George and Gideon's muddled sleep schedule, they hadn't had much time to talk. They had to focus on surviving. And most of the time, they saw the worst of each other— like the nightmares that woke Alex up screaming so often and the bouts of rage Gideon had when he didn't sleep enough.

Gideon glanced up. "I think someone paid Shane to attack Springtown. There was more going on than his betrayal with the mayor."

"Seems legit. Why do you think so?" Alex ate some more.

"I called George after you told me he'd warned about the attack on Springtown, but he wouldn't tell me that Shane was the rogue attacking the town. Probably just a detail he wanted to play about. I figured it out, it worked out, Shane's dead. He was growing bothersome in George's plans, anyway."

"I'm following." Alex wiped his mouth with the back of his hand. "Who paid Shane? You don't think he came just 'cause the mayor wasn't cooperating?"

"Doubtful. The mayor was a coward, he wasn't causing Shane trouble. As far as I could tell—and I spoke with Mr.

Fisher and Officer O'Malley—the attack was random. Shane's never random. He's calculated."

"You think someone paid him to attack. Who?" Alex rubbed his temples tiredly. "Springtown doesn't make enemies. They're... well, a town full of small town conservative nobodies."

"They're also one of the last remaining republican townships left in the US." Gideon pointed out.

"Which is strange, but—"

"What if that's not a coincidence? What if there's more going on there than a township full of men willing to defend their rights? Something else has gotten them this far. I wasn't sure before, but after Shane's attack, I know there's more." Gideon shook his head. "I don't know who would've paid Shane. You're right—Springtown doesn't have enemies. Which means the attack was for *me*."

"I'm lost, mate," Alex sighed. "How so?"

"Shane was one of the best. He was in my league, even if he wasn't one of George's own."

"You think someone hired Shane to show up, someplace you would know about, to fight you... in some, what, territorial example that you're the best?" Alex scoffed. "Gid, how many painkillers have you taken?"

"How many people knew I was helping protect Rene' Fisher?"

Alex fell quiet, leaning forward. "What?"

"How many people know that I kidnapped Rene' Fisher, Brian Jones' little sister, and fooled Jed? Jed, one of the worst players George has? How many men know that I helped get her home, that I helped defend the supply drops Simon and Nate were arranging?" Gideon swore softly. "George knew, Al, and that attack was a test for me, somehow. Someone paid Shane. George let it happen, he let me go. It's been a week and I've gotten nothing but praise for what I did. He's not furious that I laid to rest thirty of his best guys in Springtown. He's proud of me. *Why?* Why would George care about Springtown?"

Alex took a shaky breath and clasped his scarred hands together, rubbing them nervously. "Wh-what are you getting at? You think George knew you'd go to Springtown and play hero or something?"

"Maybe." Gideon didn't dare voice a yes or no. "If he did, I need to know why."

"Springtown can't really benefit him. I don't understand why he'd care if they survive." Alex's eyebrows furrowed.

"He could wipe them out, sell anyone valuable, but that's a lot of work and he has no reason to nitpick like that. It's gotta be something bigger." Gideon sighed wearily.

"Any idea who might've hired Shane? What if it was just George who sent him?" Alex asked dubiously. "Shane would never have worked for George again." Gideon got up and stretched, back aching. "No, I don't know who made Shane go fight Springtown, but George knew I'd interfere even before I requested permission to do so."

"We *won*, though, Gid. Because of you and our men, that town was spared. Can't you just be grateful for that, just for a moment?" Alex looked up, eyes heavy. "You haven't spoken a word about the men we lost. You haven't —"

"That can wait."

"You can't bottle it up, Gideon! I know you have a job to do, another puzzle to figure out, but you can't just ignore what's happened." Alex stood up and stepped in front of Gideon. "God, I know it hurts, but we can't ignore it forever."

"Talking about it changes nothing," Gideon said calmly. "Compartmentalize, move on. You need to talk, you know I'll listen, you know I'm there when the nightmares rage, but I can't deal with it the same way you do."

"You could never scare me off, Gideon." Alex's eyes burned with fury. He didn't often get angry, and his anger was usually controlled, but he never let Gideon get away with being foolish.

Maybe ignoring the pain inside was stupid, but it was all Gideon could do. If he tried processing all he'd faced, even for a moment, he'd snap. Break into a thousand pieces. Right now, he was officially one of George Johnston's greatest, marked and loaded for action. He couldn't afford to break.

Gideon's shoulders sagged. "I know." He believed his brother—but he still couldn't tell Alex everything. He couldn't explain how he woke with the battle in his mind every morning. The images of the teen who had been brutally shot down beside him. *It's the job. It's my duty to undergo hell to help others. I'll be a monster to honor my father's legacy.*

Alex squeezed his shoulder tightly. "I'm here if you need to talk... And even when you just need to not be alone for a while."

"It's late..."

"I meant what I said."

So did I. "Goodnight, Al."

THE NIGHTMARE ALWAYS SUFFOCATED with clutches of iron, like a prison around Alex's mind. He never could wake up. Never could make his mind override his heart. He was weak, in every sense of the word. Drenched in sweat, weak sobs wracking his thin body, he clutched his head and sucked in deep breaths. *Breathe. In. Out.*

Fire, flashing in the dark and running along his flesh.
In.

Screams, raw and terrified cries lingering in the air, ringing in his head.
Out.

Faces. Oh, God, the faces. So many faces. And he'd failed every single one of them.

Thomas Flannery stared down at him and held the fire to his skin. "Stop running, thief. I'm coming for you. Always have been... always will."

"Alex." Gideon's voice came from right beside him. Always beside him, always strong and steady. Like a good brother ought to be.

Alex sobbed hard and covered his face, a cry rising in his throat. The faces piled up in his mind, countless souls wrapping their hands around his heart and clawing him into a million pieces. His heart hammered.

In.

"Focus on me, Alex. Everything's all right."

Out.

"I can't do it again," Alex choked, voice sharp and jumbled. "I can't fight again. I can't! I can't watch anyone else die. If I have to pull that damned trigger again—"

Gideon wrapped his arm around him and held him tight. He didn't try to talk him down. He just listened until Alex's panic-stricken words ran out. Alex's tears stopped when the screams faded and he slowly came back down.

"I'll get you some water," Gideon sighed, pulling away.

"I-I'm fine." Alex shoved his legs over the edge of his bed, peeling his sweaty t-shirt off weakly. "I'm OK. I'm sorry."

Gideon opened the dresser, tossing him a new shirt. "What I'd say about apologizing?"

Alex stared at the shirt in his hands, sucking in a slow breath. His tiredness grew from deep inside his bones, like a sickness he couldn't fight. *God, forgive me. Sometimes I think I'm weak, that I'm weak to struggle, that I'm weak to face these demons... but... but with You, I'm strong... For everyone I lose, please, God, just let me save another.* He tugged the shirt on, bit his lip.

"Flannery?""Yeah." Thomas Flannery had been Alex's previous boss and puppeteer when Alex had just been a scrawny teen. Alex had been too smart and bold for his own good back then—Thomas had put him in line. Alex had been a good thief, but when he had stolen and outsmarted Flannery, a ganglord feared across the US—if not the world—he'd gone too far. Alex had barely escaped with his life and Gideon had found him in a ditch.

They'd been kids then. Just kids. Stupid kids too deep in the gangs.

And now? They were stupid adults, even deeper in the gang, but with more demons and nightmares haunting them every night. The nightmares had started again after Gideon's mark, but Alex wouldn't say so. Almost losing Gideon had messed with Alex. If he couldn't protect Gideon, maybe he wasn't as strong as he thought.

Maybe Flannery would win in the end.

Maybe the whole world would.

Gideon was quiet before sitting beside him again. "Al... now might be a bad time to say this, but... I haven't had the guts to say it before."

Alex looked at him, the small night light in the corner of the room casting light on their faces, just enough light so that Alex saw the fear in Gideon's dark eyes. "Yeah?"

"When George gave me the mark, um, the drugs messed with me. A lot." Gideon stared at the wall. "I saw a lot of things I shouldn't have. A... a lot of things that weren't real."

"Like what?" Alex asked quietly. He didn't mean to push Gideon too far, but maybe if he talked, it would help. *I've got to help.*

Gideon exhaled for a long moment. "It messed with my head. I saw people I trusted trying to get a dig at me. But the hallucinations weren't just that. There were more than you guys, more than the people I've failed."

Something in his tone made Alex's blood run cold. He grimaced and gently gripped his brother's arm.

"I can't believe I'm saying this," Gideon chuckled mirthlessly. "When I was bleeding out and the drugs had me in la la land, I saw Jesus. I heard that's not something people can do, and that it's not for this world anymore, but I don't doubt what I saw. Not for a second." He clasped his trembling hands together.

Alex gulped hard. "I believe you, Gideon. I've... I've seen Him in a torture chamber, too."

"But I need to understand *why* I saw Him."

"What did you see?" Alex asked softly. He didn't doubt Gideon had seen Jesus, but Gideon was never afraid, and right now, his voice was tight—right on the verge between control and breaking.

"The people were all screaming and talking all at once and they just filled up the room. I know it wasn't real but it *was* real in that moment. The man was naked and covered in blood and had holes in his hands and feet," Gideon tapped his palm a bit too hard, "like I read in the Gospel. I've read the Bible cover to cover, countless times, Al. I know what I saw."

"I said I believe you," Alex whispered.

"It doesn't make sense. He was absolutely silent. No holy words, no words of comfort, He was just there, and He looked..." Gideon's voice broke but he straightened, immediately pulling himself together. "And then He was gone. But I remembered something I read." He took a shaky breath. "I remember the verse about God binding wounds, remember that one?"

"It was one of the first I shared with you, back when we were teens," Alex said, resting his elbows on his knees.

"I passed out after that. But I remember seeing Jesus. I don't understand why."

"Gideon... He's always with you. He was trying to show you that He was there, that He cares." Alex looked up, eyes burning with tears again. "Even when I'm not there to protect you, He is." *The world won't win. God has already won.*

Then why am I so weak?!

Gideon reached over and pulled Alex's shoulder back firmly. "What happened was not on you. I lied to you. Brothers don't lie to each other, but I did. You couldn't protect me from the mark when I chose it," he said sharply.

"I-I knew the test was coming, Gideon. I knew you'd get the mark. But I'm your brother. I was supposed to be there." Alex pulled away, jaw tight. *I was supposed to be there, but I wasn't. I was too busy helping others, while the only family I have was screaming for his bloody life in some torture room.*

"I knew it would hurt you—""It hurt me worse to not be there!" Alex snapped. "You know exactly what it's like

33

to be there while your best friend is in agony, it's no worse than knowing you aren't there when they need you."

"I couldn't have gone through with it if you'd been there." Gideon's voice was weak. "I'm sorry for what I did... but... I couldn't have handled it if you'd been there."

"Every time I'm in the fire, you get me out. But I'm not allowed to help you? How is that fair?" Alex demanded.

"It's not." Gideon met his gaze. "It's not. I know I was wrong."

Alex rubbed his forehead and let his shoulders sag. "Jesus isn't gonna fail you. I do. We all do. But He won't. Sometimes He just wants us to love Him, not just understand His ways. Maybe it'll cost us our lives. Maybe it'll cost us our family. And I know those are things you've been trained to never, ever give up, but..." His chest ached with a strange pain that he couldn't shake. *Could I give up the lives of the ones I love for You, Lord? I would die, I would take my own life, I would undergo anything for my brothers, my friends, my comrades. But could I watch them die and not renounce You?* Over a year ago, and the memory of a small group of Islam extremists breaking into a Baptist church in South Carolina, shooting the family of any father who wouldn't renounce their faith, still stuck in Alex's head. He hadn't been there, it hadn't made the news, but one of the surviving fathers had joined Gideon's group in an effort to kill as many Jihadists as he could. The father had died during a raid but he'd taken out ten extremists alongside him.

On his worst nights, Alex remembered what'd happened. His faith was strong—but could he bury his brothers after looking them in the eye and watching them breathe their last? *I'm not* that *strong.*

Gideon spoke finally, "I know that. Listen, Alex, I'm not getting saved or anything, but I can't deny what I saw. I've tried to reason my way through it and, sure, maybe the drugs showed me a man who happened to resemble Jesus. And as much as my mind wants to chalk it up to that, I *can't.* Something in me won't let me because deciding that is just as foolish."

"Supernatural encounters with God tend to be undeniable." Alex licked his lips, voice falling into a whisper, "but that's not what you're afraid of, is it?"

Gideon raked his hands through his hair. "No."

"He wasn't judging you, was He."

"No." Gideon breathed.

"He loved you. He saw all you'd done, He saw you in a moment that you never wanted anyone to see, and He still loved you."

Gideon wiped a hand over his eyes. "It doesn't change anything. Whether God loves me or hates me, I'm doing what I need to do. I'm going to hell. I'm a monster, in the simplest form of the word, and God had best focus on His saints."

"God loves all of us and that changes *everything*. You aren't a monster. You're a good man. We've done hellish things, we'll keep doing hellish things, Gid, but God loves us. As much as He loves the innocent kids we protect that George doesn't know about." Alex couldn't stand watching Gideon believe such a lie. Gideon was far from a monster, but nothing Alex said or did changed what Gideon believed. Nothing pained him more.

"And if George knows of the secret missions we've taken? If he knows we spare lives?" Gideon rubbed his face angrily.

"He wouldn't have given you the mark if he did."

"He might know *now*."

"We keep doing what we do." Alex shrugged weakly. "And if we can't figure out who tested you, and you don't think it was George... maybe he knows. We... we could ask."

Gideon stared at him like he'd grown three heads. "Ask?"

Alex scoffed. "Yeah. Ask George why he let us protect the town when it drained our numbers. You're supposed to be one of his best—I don't think he'll strike you down for a stupid question."

"Maybe not," Gideon muttered.

"Gideon?"

"Yeah?" "You aren't a monster." Monsters came in different shapes and sizes and types. The silent monsters, who watched the innocent burn without lifting a hand to help. The wicked monsters, who slaughtered women and children in townships. Alex's stomach twisted just thinking of the vile men he'd faced—but Gideon wasn't one of them. A killer, a thief, a man who did terrible things, but his intentions were never selfish or wicked. "The hearts of men are wicked, every single one of us. We're all monsters. You're no different than I am. Our hearts, our sins, they're all black." He squeezed his brother's shoulder tightly. "But God changes that. He loves us. The next time He comes, He'll come to judge, to get rid of the bloody bastards who killed so many, but He still offers salvation to those who repent."

"I can't repent when I'll repeat the same monstrous behavior," Gideon murmured.

"This war will end, Gideon. Whether it ends when we die or it ends with the Union or Confeds declaring victory... no victory is as great as God's, and He's already won." Alex hesitated. "I know you don't believe and I won't force you to, mate, but please... Don't let go of what you saw."

"I won't." Gideon stood up. "I'll be right across the hall, Al."

Alex watched him leave the door open, so light from the hall filled Alex's room. He couldn't stand the dark. Leaning back, Alex pulled the covers tight to ward off the chill. He closed his eyes tightly. *God, help me. Please. I can't lose my brother to the darkness. I can't lose him to his own mind. Soften his heart... whatever I can do to help him find You, please, show me. I can't lose anyone else.*

CHAPTER THREE

September 15th, 2027

RENE' FISHER LOOKED OVER the checklist in her hand and then back at the stockroom full of supplies, her chest heavy with both relief and pain. Ever since Simon and Nate had gone back to work with Nate's father, Kaleb, they hadn't been bringing the supply runs. A few of Gideon's men, under Jack's instruction, brought supplies almost weekly now. Every provision they brought was distributed among the town, or stocked away, but Rene' couldn't shake the emptiness in her heart. She missed Simon, missed his goofy jokes every time they unloaded the vans—but he had a duty, and so did she.

"Rene'?" Bethany Tanford, Rene's childhood best friend, finished stocking a shelf of canned vegetables.

"Hmm?"

"You OK? You've got a... kinda sad look in your eyes." Bethany stepped over, lips pursed. Bethany was a beautiful young woman, as short as Rene' but with brown eyes instead of blue ones, short brown hair instead of long, and overall, Rene' was certain Bethany was at least seventy percent nicer as a person than she.

"Sorry, I'm fine."

"Thinking about Springtown?" Bethany peered at her as they turned to the second row of the shelves.

"When aren't we?" Rene' scoffed. "They finally have a chance but would rather not befriend gangsters to gain survival." She paused. "I'm not making any sense, am I? I was up at 5 AM—"

"No, you make sense. I agree." Bethany knelt and organized a lower shelf. "Most of us with common sense know how important this chance is. Gideon and his guys didn't have to come fight to protect us from Shane, but they did. Simon, Nate, and now Tyler and Jack's guys, they don't have to bring us supplies every week. But they do, and the town needs it."

"But they still see them all as the enemy." Rene' ran a hand over her face. "I keep praying, Beth, but some things don't change." Like the peoples' stupidity. Would they choose starvation over choosing to trust thugs? Which option was riskier? They were all truly doomed if they didn't maintain relationships with the so called enemies. After all, they knew that risk when accepting Simon and Nate's help. Rene' remembered back when they'd started —maybe a year ago now, she couldn't remember exact dates. AJ McCon, her father's close friend, knew the boys and told them to slip their extra supplies to the tiny town in Kentucky. The boys had started begrudgingly but never looked back.

The two teens had been selfless. They'd saved lives. Now, Springtown refused to extend trust, and countless men claimed that the gangsters would stab them in the back.

"Lots of 'em think trusting the guys is stupid, but most remember that we were dead and dying before the supplies, living in fear of caravans or bombs or..." Bethany shuddered, forcing a smile as she stood. "God listens to our prayers, Rene'. I know He does. Even if His answer isn't what we were praying for, He listens. I really think the town will come to terms with the big change."

The United States' division had been brought on by many things. The nation had split up over gun laws, abortion laws, sex trafficking, and various other government control issues. Martial law had stirred the whole nation into the fire. Two sides formed: the Union, based from the government, and the Confederates, who elected their own president and rebelled against any laws they saw immoral. Since martial law, Springtown had changed, just like the rest of the world—but not so much. Springtown remained strong while many towns had burned or been scattered, if they had not surrendered to the Union government.

Rene' missed the old days. She missed the town being normal, with places to go eat, play, and shop. She missed the world as it used to be—united and kind and beautiful.

Now, the world was a bunch of walls, a bunch of caravans and gangs and soldiers. Very few civilians held freedom anymore.

"Let's keep praying the guys don't start leaving to join the Confeds, too," Rene' said softly, scribbling a note on her pad and pulling herself from her mourning reveries. She didn't talk about the troops much, or how the Confed had gained D.C., but it all frightened her. More than it ought to. *What is war without fear? Triumph. And I know You've won this war, God, but still, I'm afraid of what the war might do, what it has done, or if nothing can undo the chaos already done.*

Bethany sighed. "Your dad's mayor now, and he's got lots of good guys behind him. I think they'll declare some rule or something to make sure no one leaves to fight. We need to fight to protect *here*."

"We're in a better place for this winter than we have been in a while." Rene' tried to be optimistic.

Bethany smiled softly and smoothed her shirt. "I'll go up and see if there's anyone else needing anything before we head home." She headed out of the stockroom.

No one was allowed in the stockroom alone. Rene' didn't mind the rule since the room gave her the heebie jeebies. *Jared's in the back, I'll finish up here and head up.*

Rene' stepped away from the shelves. She hated talking about the chaos, but she talked with Bethany about everything under the sun. They'd all asked God for a miracle, for protection and provision for their hometown, and God was giving it to them. Rene' had no right to be sad it wasn't Simon bringing the supplies anymore. *I'll see him again.*

The soft sound of footsteps behind a nearby shelf made her stop. "Jared?" she frowned. "I already accounted that section—"

A tall man stepped around the shelves, wearing dark jeans and a checkered shirt. He grabbed her arm before she could move away. "I need the pills. Where are they?!" He clamped his hand over Rene's mouth before she could call for Jared. "Just tell me where they are!" he hissed. Loden was known for stealing medicine whenever he could, specifically, the meds that he could get high off of.

Nonono! Not again! I can't get hurt again! Panic burning in her chest like fire, she stabbed at his eyes with her fingers. She kicked at his groin but he shoved her back against the wall, swearing darkly. She saw a face hovering inches from her own, but it wasn't the young man in front of her. This face was wrinkled and laughing and cold. She sobbed hard with rage. *Jed's hand wrapped around her neck tighter, tighter, tighter.*

"Hey!" A familiar Irish voice came from the doorway. In a second, the man was off Rene' and flat on his rear end. Officer Sean O'Malley stood over the thief, face red with rage. "You get your hands off her!" he snarled. Sean had a token Irish temper but was one of the kindest men the town had—Rene' had never seen him so fierce before, like a short leprechaun ready to rip the offender's throat out.

Loden—*not Jed, not Jed, not Jed*— sneered and staggered to his feet. Rene's mind was far away, like her body and head were jumbled pieces, and she couldn't feel anything. Numbing fear and shock closed her mind off like a sealed dome dropped over her conscience.

"I don't know how you've got yourself in this state, but you're not going home tonight." Sean grabbed the man forcefully.

The man swung at Sean, spittle flying. "Get offa me!"

Swearing like a sailor, Sean decked the man upside the head. The man dropped like a sack of potatoes, moaning. Sean shouted for another officer. That yell penetrated Rene's numb mind well enough to make her flinch back.

Sean grabbed her shoulders gently. "Are you all right, lassie?"

"I'm fine," she said, much weaker than she'd intended. "H-he didn't hurt me." *But I didn't see him. I saw Jed. Barely anything happened and I lost my head!*

Sean wrapped his arms around her, drawing her against his chest. "I'm sorry, Rene', this shouldn't have happened, he never should've been let in."

"I'm OK," she repeated. "I-I thought Jared was down here. My mistake." Her hands shook but she hugged him tight. Sean was the closest thing to an older brother she had, ever since Brian left home to join the government, long before the war broke out.

"It's OK to not be OK, Rene'." Sean held her close.

Officer Artie dragged Loden out of the room, but Rene' didn't dare watch.

She just wanted to be all right. She just wanted the nightmares to stop. She just wanted to be able to breathe throughout the day without expecting every single shadow to reach out and choke her. "It's fine."

"You can't lie to me. You're shaking like mad." Sean rubbed her arms, though that wasn't easy due to the thick coat she wore.

"Just nerves." She tried pulling away. "Honest, Sean, I —"

"Stand still," he ordered. Almost swallowing her tongue, she dropped her head and obeyed. His tone softened, "Just stand here a minute and breathe, get your bearings. That's all. The world won't stop just because you have to grieve."

"I don't have time to grieve," she murmured.

"What?"

"I don't have time to grieve. I don't have time to process what Jed did to me! I *can't*." Her voice trembled but she pushed on angrily. "I have a family to help and take care of, Sean. I've gotta be strong for them. I've gotta be strong for Simon. I've got to keep going and mourning and being afraid and letting myself break down helps *no one*."

"I know you feel that way, but you can get through this, and you can do so without bottling it all up. Holding back will only make it worse." Sean held her shoulders gently. "I know that you think you've gotta be strong and feel nothing, because it's apocalyptic America and all, but that's not how humans work. It's OK to break down, to be afraid, because you can keep going anyway."

She bit back hot tears, lump tight in her throat making it hard to whisper. "I just want to be OK. I don't want to feel this anymore." There, she'd said it.

"You will be OK," he coaxed. "I've seen a lot during my time in the force, lass, even before this war started. And you know what? You can heal. You're strong enough, with

God and all of us backing you up, to get through this part, and you'll be just fine."

"I don't want to be weak!" she choked. "I could list so many who have it worse than I do, Sean—"

"You don't know how much they break behind closed doors, either," he stopped her firmly. "Pain shouldn't be compared. You're not weak because you feel things deeply."She struggled to calm her breathing, closing her eyes briefly. *He's right. He's right, isn't he? It's OK to feel? It's OK to be broken, as long as I push closer to God to be healed? I'm so tired, Lord, I don't know what to do.* "I... I love you, Sean."

He led her out of the stockroom slowly. Bethany's loud, angry voice came from upstairs—she'd probably just found out what'd happened.

"I love you, too, little sis."

RENE' SCRUBBED AT THE dinner dishes tiredly. Her mother was at Terri's, Rene's oldest sister, home down the dirt road, helping with Terri's newborn boy, Aiden. Mama was often called over so Rene' had grown accustomed to chores alone.

Usually, she had silence. Tonight, her little brother Lee came into the kitchen and cut another slice of bread that Bethany had baked a few days ago. "First meeting of the

Springtown Spec Ops Militia is tomorrow morning," Lee said, a hint of satisfaction in his deep voice. At fifteen years old, Lee refused to sit by and let the grown men defend Springtown alone. He wasn't much of a fan of the Springtown civilians trying to rush off to the Confed troops, either. Lee had started his own militia with his closest friends. Most of the young men and teens joining him had fought at the Springtown battle and were willing to bleed again for their home.

Rene' took a slow breath, glancing up. "Yeah?" She hated her brother fighting in battles where he could get hurt—or worse. After all, his friend, Mo, had gotten his leg injured in the battle, less than two weeks ago.

"Danny's gonna come," Lee said, leaning against the countertop beside her. Danny Dunnham, a teenage boy, had been honed by George Johnston himself, in case George needed a new right hand man if West were to die before he took the Johnston legacy. Or, so Danny had told Rene', while they'd been at AJ McCon's in Alabama. After Rene' had been assaulted by Jed, she'd recovered for a short time at AJ's until her father picked her up. AJ had sheltered Danny and Phil, too, after Phil got shot. The two brothers had narrowly escaped George's scope, and Gideon had helped fake Danny's death so he was free from George's cruel hands.

The brothers hadn't intended to stay in town but they hadn't left. No one was stopping the two gangsters from helping. Rene' didn't trust them—Philip had worked close with Gideon and Danny was a broken soul—but she wanted to give them a chance. Especially if Danny was trying to have Lee's back. It was only fair that she took the risk of trusting them.

"Rene'," Lee frowned. "Aren't you gonna say something?"

She blinked, shaking her head softly. "Sorry. Yeah. That's great."

"You OK?"

"Just tired."

"You can't lie to me," Lee mumbled. "I talked to Sean. He told me what happened at the courthouse today."

Rene' tensed and met the dark gaze of her brother who towered over her. "He promised he wouldn't tell anyone.""I'm not *anyone*. I'm your brother."

"Loden was just... not in his right mind." Rene' fumbled for words.

"Loden's gonna sit in a cell till Dad and the men figure out what to do with him, but why didn't you tell me?" Lee asked tightly.

"It wasn't a problem." Rene' focused on scrubbing a fork. "It wasn't a big deal. He didn't hurt me."

"He never should've touched you!" Lee growled.

"It's not a big deal, Lee, honestly. I got upset but I didn't mean to scare Sean." Regret ached in her chest. Sean had enough to deal with over his job, and the man didn't get enough sleep. He didn't have any family in Springtown besides the Fishers, who had basically adopted him.

Lee grabbed her arm. "Would you *stop* it?"

"What?" she scowled, pulling away.

"Stop acting like it isn't OK for you to be hurt. You were hurt, Rene'. Maybe not the worst as you could've been, but getting cut and drugged and tied up by Jed isn't a small thing. No one expects you to magically move on. You expect that but it won't happen so... so just stop lying to yourself." His dark eyes filled with pain and he slowly wrapped her into a hug. "We love you. We wanna help when you hurt. We all hurt, and you always help us."

Tears burned her eyes, but Rene' refused to break in front of her brother—again. "I-I know. I'm sorry."

Lee sighed, smoothing her long hair. "How about you go get cleaned up, OK? I'll finish the dishes tonight. You deserve a break. You can write or read for a bit before Mom gets home, yeah? I can bring you some tea. Your birthday is in like a week. Call it an early present." She took a deep breath. *God, I want to protect him, but I can't stop him from growing up. I can't change the world he has to face, either.* "I-I'd like that."

He smiled that charming Fisher man smile. "Deal."

"I love you, Lee. And please, don't remind anyone about the birthday thing." She'd be eighteen years old and didn't want to think about how that would look like if the world wasn't so terrible. She didn't want to have anything else to grieve over. Not now.

"I know." He teased and sent her off to her bedroom. She cleaned up, got dressed into warm pajamas, and let her dog, Elvis, curl up on the bed beside her. She got her Bible but struggled to focus on Psalms. She closed her eyes and prayed, instead.

Her phone buzzed, a phone Simon had gifted her that worked pretty much anywhere and couldn't be bugged by the government. She rolled over and read Simon's message, smiling. She texted back quickly, *We're doing fine. The supply drops have been going good. How are you?* "*Tired but in one piece. You ok?*"

She rubbed Elvis' furry ears before texting, "*Long day, that's all.*"

Her phone rang shortly after. Simon spoke quickly but tiredly, "Hey."

"Hey," she chuckled. "You sound beat."

"Rough job."

"You took it with Alex, right?"

"Yep. He's neat to work with but we might've gotten lost on the way home." Simon yawned. "Ran into a caravan of Muslims. I'm never letting him drive again."

Rene's heart lodged into her throat. "Are you—"

"We're fine." He assured her. "You sounded upset by your texts, though. What's going on?"

"What?"

"You sounded—"

She gulped hard, managing, "Sorry. I heard you. Just didn't think you could hear a voice in a text."

"I have a seventh sense."

"Sixth sense."

"My sixth sense is the ability to burn eggs, my seventh sense is to hear if you're sad or happy when you message. Now, spill, my dear," Simon said gently.

"Since when do you call me dear?" Rene' snuggled under a fuzzy throw, watching Elvis doze.

"Um... since now, if that's OK?" he asked nervously.

"It's fine. What do I call you?" she teased, exhaustion slowly being forgotten, just a little.

"Most handsome man in the universe?"

"A bit on the nose."

"Babe?"

"Hm?"

"You could call me—wait, did you think I called you babe?" Simon asked incredulously.

"I like *dear* better," Rene' groaned. "Please."

"Of course, dear. So, what's wrong? You sound like you're gonna pass out."

"Are you relaxing?"

"Well, I'm awake in bed because Graham snores pretty bad, but, I'm listening and alert, if that's what you mean."

Rene' slowly told him about Loden in the stockroom. "H-he didn't do anything, honest, I just... It was like I saw Jed instead of him. Everything just came rushing back and I couldn't move or think or... I don't know." She exhaled, shame filling her heart. "It's not a big deal."

"Is he locked up?" Simon asked sharply.

"Yeah. Sean's got him in a cell."

"Rene', what happened isn't 'no big deal'," he said. "I'm so sorry. That wasn't your fault. Sometimes we see things we shouldn't or don't wanna see, that's... that's just how trauma goes, but you'll be OK."

Rene' clamped her eyes shut. "What if I'm not? I shouldn't have frozen up. I should be able to control myself."

"That's not how PTSD works. Trust me."

"I shouldn't have it!" She bit her lip hard, begging herself not to cry.

Simon spoke gently, "Rene', I know you're afraid, and you're angry, and you're hurting, but you will be OK, even if you don't think so. You're strong and smart and God's gonna take care of you. You can't compare your pain to anyone else's." He hesitated. "I used to. I used to get hurt and have bad nightmares, but tried to shake it off, 'cause

Nate always had worse. But that's not how it goes. Pain is pain. Hell is hell. But everyone can heal with God, right?"

She sucked in a breath. "What if God is punishing me? What if I haven't done enough, or had enough faith, and this is what I get?" As much as she hated to voice those words, they were her greatest fear. "I-it was me who went with you and Nate to save that group of girls being trafficked. It was my fault I got caught and Ed died getting the antidote for me so I wouldn't die. All of this, all of this pain, this PTSD, I *deserve* it." Her voice broke and she covered her eyes with her free hand, a small sob choking her.

"That's not true for a single second, Rene'. You listen to me and you listen good." Simon's voice was dark, making Rene' shudder. "I've told you a thousand times that your faith and your love pulls your family on, day after day. You've given me a reason to fight. You have faith—enough to move mountains. God didn't do this to punish you. Ed was killed because George had to force West to do his bidding. That wasn't on you and no one thinks it was." His words came out quick and sharp, but then he paused, voice softening. "Please... believe me."

"I'm trying," she sobbed. "God, I'm trying." She rubbed her eyes harder till her vision darkened and she saw spots. Why couldn't she try harder? Why couldn't she be healed? Why couldn't she move on? *Why do I weep when*

I think of all the bad things that can happen? I'm not strong. I'm broken. Breaking. Gone. And at the time when my family needs me most.

"Baby, listen to me, please. Please just listen. Close your eyes and focus on my voice. Not the voices in your head. You'll be OK. You'll walk through this—and if you can't walk, I'll help carry you. God's right there with you. He's not gonna strike you down for being broken. He'll help you be whole again—stronger than before," Simon said, voice on fire, as if he couldn't speak fast enough.

Rene' took a shaky, deep breath, wiping at her tears angrily. "I-I know but I don't want to be broken. I don't want to be this weak, Si." *My family, my friends, the world, needs me strong.*

"You won't be broken forever and you aren't as weak as you think you are. You saved Onya, her newborn baby, and the girls in the ring. You gave us all a reason to fight together. You helped Danny get out alive, too, when he wasn't sure if he wanted to even *live* when Phil got him. You've given Graham hope and you've never met him! Just because all you can see is the dark doesn't mean you don't shed light." Simon sucked in a breath. "It's OK to cry and break down. You'll be OK."

She closed her eyes, breathing ragged. "I just want to please God, Simon, but it feels that if I'm broken, I've failed Him, and Him picking me up and healing me is just a sign of my failure."

"Your dad told me something, he said that's... kinda the point, Rene'. We are always broken without God. But choosing His healing doesn't mean we failed Him. It means we glorify Him by letting Him be our Father." Simon's voice was gentle, weak. "I know you'll get through this, and I know it's hard to remember all the things you know—I'm sure you've heard Mr. Fisher say that—so I'll be here... whenever you need me."

The weight of his words took a long minute to roll into Rene's heart and lodge there. *He's right. I'm not weak because God has to heal me. I'm choosing strength—His strength. That isn't weakness.* Why was it so hard to believe? Rene' wiped her eyes and said, with all of her heart, "Thank you, Si."

"I love you, Rene'." His voice lowered ever so slightly.

Rene' froze, heart rising to her throat. *He means it. And I believe him.* "I love you, too."

After a gaping pause, Simon stammered, "You... I... *wow.* I... I'll make it up to you for saying that over the phone for the first time. I promise."

She chuckled and wiped her eyes, fingers shaking like she'd worked out for two hours straight. "I-it's OK, honest, I..."

"Did I just make Rene' Fisher speechless?" Simon asked, a smirk to his voice.

"No!" She cleared her throat.

"I'll have to top that. Soon."

"Soon?"

"I'm taking jobs with Randy and Alex lately but... I'll be trying to come back when I can." Simon's voice was on the verge of being heavy but he wasn't one to wallow in self pity. "What do you want for Christmas? Even if I get it to you a bit late."

"You," Rene' said without a moment's hesitation.

"Awww. All you want for Christmas is me. I'm flattered," Simon laughed. "All I want for Christmas is you, too, so I'll work it out, yeah?"

"You'd better. You pinky promised, remember that?"

"I got to hold your hand for the first time. I won't forget it. Scout's honor."

"You aren't a Scout." Rene' curled up under her blanket.

"Well, *ganglord son's honor* doesn't have the same ring," Simon said dryly. A soft cry came from the background and Simon muffled the phone. Rene' recognized the sound —Graham, the teenage boy that Simon and Nate had basically adopted as their little brother.

She stayed on the line, praying softly for God to ease the boy's nightmare. A minute later, Simon's voice came back,

"Hey, sorry. Graham's OK. Just a nightmare."

"It's OK. I'd better head off to bed, Si, it's late." She yawned, exhausted but not truly wanting to hang up.

"OK. I'll call tomorrow night. I love you."

"I love you, too." She hung up and tried not to scream into her pillow. It was childish, feeling this way, but she didn't care. She and Simon had already been through hell together. Him saying those three words somehow sealed it.

Whatever *it* was.

God, keep him safe, please. Keep all of us safe—the Confederates are so close to winning this war. The media is fighting for control, trying to brainwash the Union citizens, but something's breaking through. Something is shifting in the nations' atmospheres. The states are still divided but Your people are uniting, even if it kills us, and that is doing something. I'm not sure what, and right now, we could all really use Your help and guidance. And mercy. So many lives are being lost, but You have a plan.

She thought of Simon and Nate in the gunfire, her brothers and father battling at Springtown's borders, and all the dangers to come. *I trust You and I will do anything You ask of me, even if it kills me. But... if You could help me find peace about what happened, about me getting hurt and believing I got Ed Brookes killed, I'd really like to have that peace before I die.*

CHAPTER FOUR

September 27th, 2027

"I NEED A TACO," Nate Savage complained, watching Simon pack up a backpack for another job. Nate was the only son of Kaleb Savage, one of the nations' most brutal ganglords and right-hand man of George Johnston himself. George had political power and mafia rule, but Kaleb was one of his best men. Nate didn't go a day of his life without being reminded that he, like West, wouldn't get away from his father's legacy.

But he'd tried. He had the whole thing mapped out in his head like some ironic bullet-point: he and Simon had gone off to make a way for themselves. AJ had given them the job of supply drops for Springtown, which they'd done for a while. By the time the big wigs, aka George and

Kaleb, had found out about the supplies, it'd been too late. Nate and Simon had gone back to work for Kaleb. Nate now lived in misery. The end.

Or, he wished it was the end. This whole play-nice-with-the-other-thugs gig was wearing on him. He used to fight and mess around before they'd left. Now, he had to play a good little soldier. He enjoyed himself when Kaleb gave him jobs—but since the last job he'd taken had gone bad, he was on bedrest. Thus, misery.

"Shut up." Simon zipped his backpack. "I won't be gone long."

"You're going with Alex, Spencer, and Bo. You could end up in Florida without realizing they took a wrong turn." Nate crossed his arms over his chest. He was healing up just fine, but Kaleb wouldn't let him work yet. Nate complained, though being stuck at their apartment in Paradise, Kaleb's HQ base, led to a lot of time spent with Graham. The boy was still recovering emotionally from being sexually assaulted by one of Kaleb's best snipers—a young man that Nate had killed with his bare hands. Nate spent most of his days trying to make the stuttering, curly-headed teen talk and open up about things, but Graham didn't budge.

Graham was as stubborn at Nate when it came to being all right when he truly wasn't. The disaster had gotten to the kid's head but he didn't open up. Nate almost gave him kudos.

"They wouldn't get past the Floridian border." Simon rolled his eyes.

"Bo's a Floridian. It could happen."

"Spencer is a Yank and any Confed could smell it from a mile away and shoot him down." Simon headed to the door, pulling his tattered green coat on. "I'll make sure we get to Ohio."

"I don't like you going all the way up there, Simon." Nate growled in annoyance. It was his job to protect Simon. He couldn't do that locked up in a musty house.

"I'm not alone, so stop nagging like a grandmother and clean the kitchen while I'm gone. There's molded pizza in the fridge growing a new biohazard, so if you could toss it, I'll get you a beer." Simon shoved his backpack on, glancing back at his brother. Simon was just as tall as Nate —right at 6'0—but there was a new look about him. *He's gotten older since we came back. Hardened. Or maybe it's just the beard he refuses to shave.*

"See ya," Nate sighed and turned away.

"See ya." Simon went outside.

Nate watched through the tiny kitchen window over the sink. Simon hopped into Alex's truck—they'd pick up Spencer out of Paradise. Spencer never entered Kaleb's HQ since his little brother, Randy, Nate's nemesis, had practically been adopted by Kaleb. Nate didn't care much either way what Spencer did. *I hate Randy and I hate my father for choosing men who aren't his own blood over me. He chose Randy and Robert, not me. Simple as that. No avoiding them.* Randy usually kept behind the scenes because he was a tech freak and not very good in panic situations.

Robert was in his early thirties and had worked for George and Kaleb for at least a decade, as far as Nate knew. Robert worked many dirty jobs. He'd tried to be nice to Nate over the years but Nate had no interest in his kindness.

Nate started running some hot water into the sink. Kaleb kept his base equipped with a few luxuries, like electricity and heat. Not every civilization in America had those things anymore. Most who did paid the price of their freedom to attain a normal lifestyle that kept them away from the war.

Nate scrubbed at a dish, grumbling to himself. God only knew what Simon faced out there, and while Simon worked well with pretty much anyone, Nate trusted no one to have Simon's back. Sure, Alex Thompson and Spencer Anderson—the Sons, as Nate had started mockingly dubbing them—had done nothing but help Simon and Nate, such relationships would die off eventually. Spencer had helped them save Rene' from Jed —but it didn't mean he'd be loyal forever.

Alex had helped Gideon kidnap Rene', too. Though, it was Gideon and Alex who helped West and Jack kidnap Rene'. Sure, if the guys hadn't taken control and taken the young woman, someone else would have, someone closer to Jed in his cruel ways. By taking her, allowing Jed to have some control, they'd also freed her.

Still, it was their fault.

Nate finished cleaning up the tiny, beaten down kitchen, nearly gagging when he threw the pizza out. He'd seen men shot and mangled and his stomach queased less than seeing the monstrous pie. He started to make some mac and cheese, stomach growling only moments after lurching.

"Hey." Graham's quiet voice came from the doorway. He came over, wearing at least three sweaters so his thin frame looked baggy and hunched. He didn't do cool weather well.

"Hey, kid. Want dinner?"

"I can cook it," he kept his voice low so he wouldn't stutter too much. Nate was used to his mumbling after the years he'd known him. "You should rest."

"I feel fine. All healed up. Wanna see my new scar?" Nate joked.

Graham shook his head, black curls bouncing.

Nate sat down at the creaky table. "You doing OK?" As usual, he didn't expect any answer besides "fine" or "yeah, you?"

Graham dumped the steaming noodles into an old colander. "Um... I've been thinking about Springtown. A lot." He poured in milk and a cheese packet, stirring it all up.

"Oh?" Nate tried not to sound too interested. Occasionally, he scared the teen off when he showed too much enthusiasm.

"Yeah..." Graham dipped two heaping bowls of mac and cheese. "I really want to go, Nate."

Nate got two spoons from the drawer and sat down. *How do I react to that? Someone needs to tell him that he needs to stop dreaming impossible things. Simon was bad enough, going head over heels for a girl he can't obtain, fighting so hard for a town who despises him. I can't lose Graham to the same vain hopes.*

Graham sat beside him, his shaky breath filling the silence. He needed an answer. A right answer.

"Why do you wanna go?" Nate asked quietly.

Graham kept his head down. "Simon says the people are real nice... He said Rene' is the nicest girl he's ever met."

"You want to see the people and town? A taste of what the nation used to be?" Nate shoved some food into his mouth. "I get it."

"No," Graham stammered. "No, I want to have a home."

Nate almost choked on his food as those five words lodged in his chest and stabbed his heart. Quickly regaining his composure, he chuckled. "It *seems* safer than Paradise—"

"I didn't mean it like that! You and Si are my home. Paradise isn't." Graham shook his head again, face twisting. "But... I've... never had a home like Springtown. I just wanna try. Just... just visit."

Nate didn't know every detail of Graham's past, or his present, really. The boy talked to Simon about personal details but never much. Kaleb let it slip once Graham came from the streets, but that was it. "OK." He rubbed the back of his neck. "We'll talk to Simon. Maybe the new mayor, Mr. Fisher, he's—"

"—Rene's dad." Graham smiled. "Simon says he's nice."

"Yeah. The Fisher family is a friendly bunch," Nate said, unable to lie about that. After he had gotten injured back in August, he had spent a week or so recovering at the Fisher farm, but he hadn't gotten too close to any of them. Besides the blonde kid, Rene's niece, who had watched him sleep and brought him some kitten to hug when he was lonely. Lily was her name? Jaycee? He didn't remember.

"Do you think Simon would take me?" Graham hesitated. "I-I know Kaleb doesn't want us going back because the war... the war is breaking out... and the caravans and civilians and all are super dangerous and we might be at risk in a town..."

"Kid, I know Kaleb's excuses as to why we can't go back. He likes control but yeah, he's still got some good points. Going to Springtown would be hard to pull off. I mean, it isn't super well defended, and no one is really trained in war or..." Nate stopped, watching Graham's eyes darken with tears. "Sorry. Yeah. Maybe Simon and I can work something out."

"Soon?"

"There's plenty of time, Graham." Nate offered a big smile. Smiles usually hid lies.

"There isn't," Graham whispered. "I hear that the Union, the government," he choked on the last word, as if unable to fathom it, "are gonna bomb the Confeds. D.C., Philadelphia, all of the camps, j-just wipe 'em off the map." His hands trembled and he pushed his bowl back. "We don't have time!"

Nate grabbed Graham's shoulder firmly. "Stop, Graham, stop. Don't talk like that. We will make it through this. The war has gotta stop."

"What if it kills us?" Graham lifted his eyes, tears streaking his freckled cheeks. "What if we die, Nate?

That's what wars do—kill people, kill good people, kill people who do good things. I want to be a good person. I want to do good things. But I don't wanna die." His voice shook but he worked his jaw. That was Graham—even when he was scared, he put on a brave face.

"You're gonna be fine, kid." Nate wrapped his arm around Graham. "Me and Si, and even Kaleb, will protect you. The war is getting bad but it gets worse before it gets better, right?"

"You don't believe that. You said that was vain hope—"

"I was wrong," Nate lied. He couldn't stand to see Graham cry, making it hard to be around the boy much. Simon was the comforter, the healer—Nate didn't know how to help Graham, even when he tried.

"Really?" Graham blinked.

"Yeah. You having hope that the war will end and we can visit Springtown is good. Real good. You hold onto that." Nate smiled, and it didn't hurt so much to lie this time. Who knew? Maybe having hope would help Graham more than it ever had Nate.

Graham wiped his eyes and sniffed, shaking his head. "OK. I will. But... Nate?"

"Yeah?" "You guys won't leave me again, will you?" His voice fell to a whisper.

"No. Never. Now eat before you turn into a pile of bones." Nate's shoulders sagged as he told the truth. Simon had his stupid heart set on Rene' and her family and town. *But me? I agreed to come back here, be Kaleb's little soldier, his perfect machine. How can I give Graham hope?*

I can't.

Why am I sacrificing that ability? I can't make Kaleb happy anyway. He chooses others to fill the gap of family— Robert, Randy, even Graham, in a sense. Kaleb doesn't love me. But I'm sacrificing everything to make him proud.

What if I don't? I stopped trying and left, but what if I stopped trying?

SIMON LIKED HIS WORK, though any job, big, small, dark, easy, could go wrong. This job had gone well: a quick trade of ammo at the Ohio border with some gang friends, all condoned by George Johnston himself. A lowkey ordeal.

The trip to and from Ohio, Simon remained on high alert, until they got to a small gas station. Simon had briefly fallen asleep but swore when he saw where they were. "Alex, you said we were going straight back to Paradise," he growled and sat up in the back seat.

Spencer glanced back from the passenger's seat. "I'm hungry and he has to visit the little boy's room."

Alex whacked Spencer upside the head and got out of the truck, heading into the station. It was one of many gang-owned service stations, offering supplies and expensive fuel. Simon studied the blue and brown brick building before getting out, stretching his long legs. Bo slept soundly in the backseat and Simon didn't bother waking him. He was a grumpy bear when he woke up.

The nighttime air washed over Simon and he ran his hands over his face briefly. He'd be back at Paradise soon, he'd text Rene', and hit the hay.

"Hey, Bucks, long time no see, kid!" A guffaw came from near the gas tanks. Simon craned his neck, meeting the expectant gaze of Tony Aldatraux. Tony was a run-of-the-mill gangster with little to no skill sets in Kaleb's group, but he tried running with the big wolves often. Judging by his shiner, George's guys didn't like him much, either.

"Tony," Simon said, feigning pleasure. "Great to see you." *I'll punch you in the throat if you step any closer, womanizing punk.*

"Where have you and Nate been?" Tony asked. Spencer got out of the truck and Tony peered past Simon to eye him wearily. "Running with the big guns, eh?"

"Not much of your business," Simon smiled.

"Hey, Tony," Spencer said easily. He stepped beside Simon and crossed his arms across his chest, smirking at Tony. "See ya didn't lose the shiner Bo gave ya yesterday."

Tony's expression grew tight in the light of the street lamp hanging overhead. "Ah, he'll pay for it. You're lucky he ain't with you now."

Spencer raised his eyebrows. "Oh, he will now, will he?"

The few men behind Tony exchanged the slightest of glances that made Simon fight a smile. *So, they've run into Bo's hot temper and skilled fists at least once. As long as Spencer doesn't tell them Bo's here and wake Bo, we'll be fine.*

"No one picks a fight for no reason and gets away with it." Tony shrugged, smirking at his tag team. They nodded but only one looked really threatening—a 6'4 guy with a belly to put Winnie the Pooh to shame. Simon gulped. He really wanted to go home. He didn't want to bash heads tonight. Jordan, his ganglord father who ran secret rescue ops behind George's back, had taught him how to fight when he was young. But Jordan preferred Simon learn to use his head to get out of bad situations. Simon liked it that way. It didn't always work out that way.

"Well, I got news for you, pal..." Spencer beat twice on the side of the truck door. The thuds almost made Simon jump.

The right-side backdoor flung open. "What the—" Bo toppled out, brown hair tousled. Bo wasn't much of a looker, and besides his lean muscles that could kill in a fight, he didn't have much height advantage. That didn't stop him. He flashed a big grin upon seeing Tony, swaggering around the side of the truck. "Tones! Back for another fistful?"

"Bo." Tony's smile vanished. "You working with Bucks' boy now?"

Bo draped an arm around Simon's shoulders. "Sure am. He's the best dadgum eighteen-year-old man I know." In a much lower voice, he whispered into Simon's ear. "You take Cherub Face, I got Tony."

Before the words truly penetrated Simon's mind, Bo lunged at Tony with force only a rowdy country boy could harness. He slugged Tony but the three other men attacked him just as quickly.

Simon jumped at the giant man, not because he wanted to: the guy had drawn a big knife. Bo might not have rules against bringing fists to a knife fight, but Simon wasn't stupid. He drew his gun.

Pop.

Something hard struck his head and blackness dotted his vision. Simon staggered back, boots slipping on the uneven asphalt. Hitting the ground, he gripped his gun tightly—at least his finger hadn't been on the trigger. It hadn't gone off. But that's the last thought he had.

SIMON SAT UP ON the couch groggily. Thanks to the painkillers kicking in and the ice pack on his face, he kind of felt human again. "Hey..." He looked up into the worried face of Alex.

"Sorry, Si." Alex ran a hand over his blond hair sheepishly. "Didn't mean to getcha hurt."

"It was Bo's fault!" Nate retorted sharply, arms crossed as he glared down at Simon. "You shouldn't have gotten in the middle of it!"

"Stop yelling." Simon winced, leaning back, his head still throbbing. He was home, at least, and in one piece.

"Sorry," Nate mumbled. "But—"

"Get out of here, Thompson." Kaleb's voice came hard and sharp. Simon's heart hammered as he lifted his head to see Kaleb standing a few feet away from the three of them. "Simon's fine. You'd best get Bo somewhere he can get some medical attention for that gash he earned himself."

"Yessir," Alex said quietly, grimacing a bit at Simon as if apologizing again before darting out of the house. Simon didn't blame him for skedaddling, just wished he could go with him. Kaleb's anger wasn't like Jordan's—it was fiery and mean.

Simon kept his head down. "I didn't start the fight, sir. I know what you say about stupid brawls. But a guy pulled a knife and I didn't want Bo or Spencer to get gutted." *I've been doing well on the jobs Kaleb's given me, haven't failed a single one since Nate was downed. I've got along with the guys and earned respect. Is he really going to make this flub a huge deal?*

"I know. Next time, don't get hit," Kaleb said flatly.

Simon glanced up, eyes widening. "Huh?" "Next time, shoot first."

"Yessir." Simon rubbed his head, feeling a small bandage over his left eye. *Yeah, right.*

"Don't tear the stitches," Nate snapped. "Lie down."

Simon frowned up at them both, anger flaring. "Kaleb, I need to talk to you." His head begged him to shut up and sleep the pain off, but his heart refused. He needed to know when he could see Rene' and when he could take Graham to Springtown. *The kid needs a glimpse of home. I have to help him.*

"Now?" Kaleb raised one eyebrow.

"I need to go back to Springtown," Simon blurted. Realizing his mistake the moment the words left his tongue, he shut his eyes briefly. "I—"

"No." Kaleb never hesitated. He must've had nights where he sat up and planned how he could make everyone's lives utterly miserable.

"I'm not taking no as an answer, sir." Simon tried sitting straighter. *Shouldn't have done this while my head is about to explode.*

"Whether you take it or not, the answer is no, and failure to comply will result in punishment." Kaleb crossed his arms against his broad chest, looking identical to Nate, but neither noticed the irony.

"Punishment?" Simon laughed. "Gonna string me up from a basement ceiling, let me get hypothermia? Come on, Kaleb. I'm not a kid anymore, I'm not scared of you, and I won't keep letting you rule my life!" He'd planned on calm, firm efficiency, but the words rose into a yell.

Kaleb's piercing gray eyes narrowed and he stepped closer to the couch. Nate stepped in front of him, arms falling to his sides. "Simon is right, Kaleb. The war is getting worse. Men, good and bad men, are dying. You can't protect us, we can't stop it all, but we *can* decide where we stand. If Simon wants to stand elsewhere, you're no one to stop him."

Simon's heart jumped into his throat. *He's standing up for me... and he's standing up to Kaleb? Bad idea.* "N-Nate —" He tried to stand, grimacing.

"No!" Nate didn't turn away from his father but nudged Simon back behind him.

Kaleb held Nate's gaze for a long moment. His jaw tightened, a vein in his neck bulged, but at last, he said, "All right. If you two want to get caught up in a small town's crossfire with the rest of the crumbling nation, go ahead."

"W-we didn't say we wanted to leave." Simon held his aching head. "We just want freedom. Haven't we earned that?!" He had worked hard since he was a boy, even harder since they'd come back, to show himself worthy. Not just to Kaleb, like Nate tried, but to his own father. Jordan Bucks was a ganglord but ran a secret underground operation to save victims of sex and slave rings. Simon wasn't helping him—but he could still make a difference with Nate. But not if he didn't have freedom to live. Why fight to save others if he didn't have love? *I'm not strong enough to fight without Rene'. Not anymore.*

"What is it you want?" Kaleb demanded. "I give you jobs, supplies, I cover you when George finds out you're helping a rebel town, I make sure the town is covered, and what do you do? Refuse to help me back?"

"No," Nate snapped. "We work the jobs, we help your gang, we do what the world needs. But if Simon wants to visit Rene', he visits her. No more hiding. No more cowering." He stood tall in front of his father, fists clenched.

He's standing up to his dad... he's risking everything. For me. Simon rubbed his aching temples.

Kaleb looked between them. "The Confeds stand a chance." The words hung in the air like an omen.

"Huh?" Simon wasn't hearing right, the drugs must've started getting to his head.

"The Confeds stand a chance of winning the war. George asked me to send my own men to help the Union... send them in as fodder... to help the Union this winter. They're attacking soon, boys. And I will not lose my own —you two—to this civil war. Springtown is covered, and if you two refuse to do the smart thing, go ahead. But I cannot stop everything. I cannot save you every time." Kaleb's low, dark voice sent shivers down Simon's spine. Simon didn't understand: the Confederates could win? Simon had been praying such, sure, but to hear Kaleb, one of the few who knew the behind-the-scenes of the grisly war, say so... It didn't seem right. And what did he mean by the town was covered?

Nate spoke first, "We know, sir. We aren't asking for protection. You want me as your right hand man in this gang, and I will be. I want to be. But we aren't kids anymore. We need to be men, not slaves. You understand that."

Simon stared, gaping a little. *He actually said it. He's actually saying all of this! God, does he really believe it? Have You finally softened his heart? Does he love Springtown more than proving Kaleb wrong?*

"I understand completely." Kaleb cocked his head. "You two think you can juggle family and a gang. A stupid choice, but I won't stop you. You do as I say, you work, you earn your keep, you keep your place. If you want to pretend you have freedom in this broken world, fine. Simon, you can see your girl. Nate, you have his back. He'll need it." Kaleb turned on his heels and stormed out of the house. The door rattled shut behind him.

Simon sucked in a breath. "Nate, I... I'm sorry... I didn't mean..." He didn't understand a thing that happened, but he knew two things: *I can see Rene'. And if Dad finds out about this, he'll probably chew my hide.*

"Go to bed, Si. We'll talk in the morning." Nate squeezed his shoulder and tossed a cover across him. "Things have to be clearer in the morning. They gotta be."

CHAPTER FIVE

September 27th, 2027

"HOW DID THE CALLS go? Anything changed lately?" Alex called, tugging off his grimey coat as he walked down the hallway. He reeked of cigarette smoke: the guys he'd taken that job with probably hadn't respected his request of sparing his lungs from tar. Gideon respected Alex's strong self-discipline when it came to most fleshly desires other gangsters fell for. Gideon could hardly stand men who chose the bottle over a sound mind, or a warm bed over freedom.

Gideon finished dipping two plates of rations. "Well... no." He hesitantly sat down and picked up a pad of paper on the table. He'd burn the paper but it helped him focus more than keeping a list on his devices.

Alex came back into sight, pulling a white t-shirt over his scarred torso. "Oh?"

"Over a week and I've barely made a dent. I don't know who sent Shane, who wanted me to be there or who is protecting Springtown." Gideon worked his jaw. His job was to find out information, calculate responses, handle situations. He wasn't accustomed to working hard and not gaining anything.

"So, still at square one. Got it." Alex sat down at the table and picked up his fork, mustering a small smirk. "Gonna ask George what's up now? Honestly, mate, you can't understand anything really without talking to him. Too many questions involve him. Like, how did he know you'd protect the town, why did he give you the test when it was obvious you were involved with the town and Rene'—"

"I get it." Gideon rubbed his aching head.

"Sorry." Alex gave a cheeky grin. "I doubt he kills you for trying to understand! You passed whatever test it was, you took care of the town, he's been bloody happy with you—so just ask. I think whatever is going on is really as important as you say it is. We need to know what we're dealing with before time runs out."

Gideon ate a little, forcing every bite down, lost in thought.

"Well?"

"I'll call him tonight."

"It *is* tonight." Alex cocked his head. "You don't procrastinate. Ever. What's wrong?"

Gideon glanced at the pad in disgust. "I couldn't figure it out myself. Forgive me if I'm a bit miffed."

"No matter what happens, I'll be here." Alex, as if that sentence alone set all chaos straight, kept eating. Once their meal was finished, Alex put the dishes in the sink, muttering, "Ya know something?"

"Probably." Gideon pulled his phone out and stood, preparing himself for his pacing session during the call.

"When this war ends, we're gonna get a dishwasher."

"At least we have plenty of toilet paper in this apocalypse." Gideon smirked. The brief memory of a pandemic in 2020 made Alex burst into laughter. Alex's optimism that the war would end never dulled or vanished, even when circumstances proved his viewpoint that of a fool's.

"Always a silver lining to every hell," Alex agreed softly. "Not every hell has to look the same... But we can get through every single one."

Gideon dialed George and took a few deep breaths to calm himself.

George answered shortly. "What is it?"

"Sir, I have a few questions." He kept his voice steady, a craft he'd perfected over his many years of working with the mafia lord.

"I'm free tomorrow at nine, if you can come to the warehouse outside of Hedgeville, away from any peering eyes. I've had too many men trying to capture my face on camera since D.C. was taken," George sighed. He made the media work for him, and when a few men tried to step out of line and pull their own stories, he often sought them out and handled the issue. He had more important things to do than shoot down paparazzi at the moment.

"Yessir, that works fine." Gideon glanced at Alex, shoulders sagging.

George hung up.

"Well?" Alex put a clean plate on the drying rack nearby, up to his elbows in suds.

"Tomorrow morning outside of Hedgeville."

"I'll make breakfast to go."

"If you feed me vegemite again, I will murder you."

Alex grinned smugly. "You know you like it."

"AS ONE OF MY marked, you may ask me anything, Gideon." George leaned on the top of the bar, his dark hair smoothed back. "Especially if something troubles you."

George was far from trustworthy, and Gideon knew this better than many, but Gideon needed answers and only George could supply them. *I can't waste more time. The war waits for no one.* "Thank you." Gideon met his gaze. Gideon had long ago picked up the nickname Cold Eyes, but he had never intimidated George. *One day, I will see fear in his eyes before I end him.*

"It is about Springtown, George. There is a great deal I do not understand about what truly happened in the shadows."

"Oh?" George raised his eyebrows. "And what is that?"

Gideon didn't hesitate. Hesitation meant weakness, and a lion pounced upon the slightest scent of fear. "You gave me permission to protect Springtown from Shane, after you found out about my part in helping Nathan and Simon protect the town, and after you learned I helped Rene'." George did not know *why* Gideon had saved Rene' from Jed—Gideon had a secret alliance with her older brother, Brian—but he had not pushed it. George chalked it up to the fact she was the daughter of one of Springtown's most respected men. *I can't afford him ever finding out about Brian and me. I'd be a dead man. Or worse.*

"Ah," George sighed. "Don't beat around the bush, Gideon. You're one of my marked now. Speak freely."

"I do not understand *why*, sir. Why has Springtown lasted this long? Why should we have protected them, when you are allies with the Union, and that little town goes against the Union?" Gideon asked calmly, searching George for a reaction, anything to show the man had some emotion besides anger, amusement, or sadistic humor.

George smirked, as usual, and his dark eyes twinkled as if Gideon were missing some obvious point. "Shane was paid off to attack."

"By whom?"

"Probably a Union leader or captain," George said. "Someone wanting to gain some campsites in the south or border states. I do not know for certain, I hardly found it important. When you have a thousand enemies, best focus on eliminating those difficult to fend off. I do not have time, nor interest, in sending my men to annihilate enemies of some shack town when suppliers are more than willing to guard the city." George lifted a finger, eyes piercing Gideon's. "You showed interest in defending them. Since it had to be done, I had no issue with you taking the role when you were capable, even if it wasn't what I initially intended."

Gideon processed his words as quickly as he could. "You said something about suppliers protecting the town. You mean there are men watching over Springtown?" Gideon asked, struggling to maintain a steadiness to his voice. *I was right about Springtown lasting this long without coincidence.*

"Yes, but you've known that all along. Or, I hope so." George chuckled wryly.

"I could not find out who." Gideon took a slow breath. "Forgive me."

"I expect better next time, though I understand." George squeezed Gideon's shoulder with a big hand. "I am glad you came to me. It is an important subject, and I, too, have been a bit too busy to make contact with you."

"Understood, sir." At least George hadn't gutted Gideon for incompetentence. *Yet.*

George continued, "There are certain towns, certain provinces, usually small ones, that are protected by suppliers. The suppliers pay off the government to avoid the towns. This doesn't usually mean defense—you know how poorly Springtown is in terms of offense—but it does mean major troops and terrorist groups are to refrain from entering the areas. Some suppliers are Good Samaritans. Some traffic civilians from the townships. Some of them think that if they protect enough locations, that when the war is over, those places can be building blocks to rebuild the government.

"Occasionally, the pay-offs are ignored and the townships lost anyway, but Springtown has remained safe under control. Shane was paid to come, most likely as a test to you, since you were indeed scrabbling with the town folk." George frowned. "But you handled it. There is little more to worry over, Hochberg."

It was a test to hone me. See if I could handle everything. Was that all? "Who is the supplier of Springtown, sir? Do they know they're being protected like that?" He doubted it. No one had mentioned it before and no one had much hope in anything besides what they held behind their borders. *And their God.*

"That's classified." George smiled wide. "I allow Jack and your men to bring that town supplies simply to pacify my son and show him I am trustworthy. However, none of my men will form any sort of genuine truce with the settlement, as the supplier obviously has it handled, and I've no interest in stirring up more issues."

"Understood. Thank you." Gideon smirked coolly. *Some things are still secret, till I take the Test. The mark makes me trustworthy but not George's friend. There's no way of knowing yet how much of his words are true.* Still, the answer, the whole complex maze, couldn't have been such a simple answer. Something was still wrong. Something was still hanging precariously in the balance—but what?

"You should know Brian's intentions this winter." George leaned back, pulling out a cigar from a box on the bar top. "He will nail the Confeds at D.C. with full force.

He's gone as far as arranging for heavy artillery and bombs, if the media doesn't catch on."

"Civilians will be lost if that is done." Gideon tilted his head. "President Kaden is allowing that risk?"

"He is giving his generals and such that freedom to choose what they think is best. He cares little for civilians who do not have the cash to remove themselves from the surrounding area. But I think it would be a fool's choice to choose heavy artillery—too easy to have the media backfire."

"What do you think Jones ought to do, sir?" *If Brian doesn't heed my words, he will regret it.*

"The Confeds at D.C. must be eliminated. I suggested Kaleb send men to seal our alliance with the UN, and doing so would help Jones keep his more valuable soldiers. The fort can be won again without bombings, it would only take more lives." George smiled. "I think that would be the quietest way to go about doing so. It would show the Union as the winning side without making them into bloodthirsty beasts."

"I see." Gideon set his jaw. More men would die, but so long as the media got the story they wanted, that's all the government cared about.

George puffed cigar smoke, expression taut and the bags under his eyes making Gideon wonder if the man ever stopped planning someone's demise. "Jones has not made it clear what he will do. Kaden is one unhappy president but I do not think he minds too much—the world knows he is in hiding. He will take less blame." He scoffed. "Cowards. All of them."

Gideon nodded. The nation was full of spineless fools and blind men. The war raged on because not enough good men rose above the ruckus. *But I will. I will be smarter than the stupid soldiers shot down for their cause. I have a place to serve in this war. And it's the monster. The spy.* "Well, Jones has proven himself to be one of the best leaders the Union has known. I doubt they fail to regain the city."

"Perhaps. Perhaps not." George rolled the cigar in his big fingers. "But I am excited, Gideon."

"For?" Gideon feigned curiosity.

"For the nation to completely rip apart. We're so close." His eyes shone with a strange, dark glint. "First, the South and North, just like old times, tear up—over what? Human rights, medical exemptions, and the good ol' boys crying over firearms. Now? It's been over three years since this war started lifting its head. We will never be the United States again." George laughed as if at some great feat. "I'll have it all. The Johnston legacy..." His eyes met Gideon's, the glint enough to make Gideon want to punch him. "And you'll be West's right hand man."

"It would be my honor."

GEORGE HAD LOADED UP in his SUV with his guards and driven off. Gideon got into his truck, slamming the door behind himself, glaring at the road. "Al, it's happening."

"What's happening?" Alex rubbed his hands together, turning the truck's heat up more.

"What have we been waiting for all these years?" Gideon frowned. "Start driving, I'll start talking." They never stayed in one place for long, especially not out in the open.

Alex veered the truck onto the two-way road. "What's that mean? The war is getting bad?" "Bad's one way to describe it."

"The rebels have a chance, Gideon, too many people have been praying—"

"No." Gideon cut him off. "They have near no chance at winning this war, Alex. The UN is against them—the U-freaking-N. What chance do they have, even if they were to take over every government city? They can't turn the whole nation rebel or conservative. They'd all be killed until it was over, even if it took decades."

"God is in bloody control and He will not let this nation fall like that. I know He won't!" Alex snapped. "Just tell me what George said!"

"Jones is going for D.C."

"We knew that!" Alex growled, knuckles white on the steering wheel. "What's new?"

Gideon told him everything, nearly verbatim, slowly calming down. "We've been prepared for this—"

"I know that. But the suppliers protecting towns? We didn't know that. How did we miss that?!" Gideon swore. "Alex, you and I have spent years turning this nation inside out, studying every bunny trail, money trail, leader's records and—" he stopped himself short. "I made a mistake and George isn't killing me for missing that information. Why not?"

Alex blinked at him, then glared at the road. "Well, I'm not upset about the last part, blogan. We're all human, and for a human, you've done well—damn good, I'd say, and George knows it. So... we handle it. We keep going."

"I need to identify the supplier for Springtown." Gideon raked a hand through his hair.

"Maybe talk to Mr. Fisher? He's a sensible fellow."

"He's also Jones' step-dad. If I talk to him again, he'd ask about the war, if I knew anything about his kid." Gideon rolled his eyes. "I don't feel like alerting a town that they not only have a supplier protecting them for, seemingly, no reason, but their son is also leading one of the worst assaults in history, targeting rebels. Like them."

Alex grimaced, cheeks going a little green. "Maybe don't tell them that part."

"You think?"

"Shut your hole."

Relaxing ever so slightly, Gideon looked out the window, eyeing the treeline over forty yards away. "Any clue who the supplier might be?"

Alex chuckled but the sound was dry and tired. "Sorry, mate, I don't. Why is it so important we find out? After all, we're kinda taking care of the town, anyway. The pay off gig isn't flawless, so who cares who's doing it? Crikey, could be Brian Jones paying the toll himself, for all we know." He shrugged, his thick coat prohibiting the motion.

Gideon glanced at him out of the corners of his eyes. "You're not funny." When they'd kidnapped Rene' for Jed, Gideon himself had sent Brian footage of his baby sister being tortured. Brian had refused to save her. The incident had proven that Brian truly did not care about the safety of his bloodkin. It had colored Gideon's opinion of his ally, but little had changed since, besides Brian occasionally ignoring him.

Alex cringed. "Sorry. Wasn't thinking."

"I'm gonna start putting out feelers," Gideon said, crossing his arms. "It'll take some time because of all the crap going down, but we need to figure out who the supplier is if we wanna keep that town alive."

"We wanna keep them alive?" Alex smirked pointedly.

"I'm not heartless."

"Aw, 'course not. Who knows? Maybe you and I can find some gals in Springtown who will put up with us."

Gideon rubbed his temples. He had no interest in such things, but when Alex found a wife, Gideon would be the first one to keep both of them safe. No matter what. Alex's happiness was one of the few things Gideon honestly cared about. But he said, "No one will put up with your ugly mug."

CHAPTER SIX

October 10th, 2027

THE DAYS PASSED QUICKLY, but only because West never stopped long enough to think of anything besides his duty in life. West's true motive was to kill his father. To George, his duty was to continue the Johnston legacy.

These two facts ran across his mind every morning when he woke, worked out, and it was the last thing he let himself remember before leaving his room to visit his parents. His days shifted and changed: some days, he did little, some days he went with George, and some days, he went to meetings. He disliked meetings but they were crucial and full of information he needed to share with his brothers.

Jack. Tyler. Spencer.

He sucked in a tired breath, glancing at his phone. He hadn't talked to Jack in three days. He didn't want to— ever since he'd left his brothers to train under George full-time, something had faded out of his head. Hope, maybe. It was hard to be close to someone as you were trying to save them. *No time for mistakes. Ed died because of my mistakes and I will not lose another friend because of my own naivety.*

West straightened his wrinkled t-shirt and picked up the phone. Jack hadn't taken jobs since West left: he worked to help Tyler and some of Gideon's men supply Springtown and he stayed with his girlfriend, Mels. Something was going on that West didn't know about, but whatever it was, it was just a nag in West's gut. He couldn't explain it and couldn't focus on what Jack didn't tell him. He dialed Jack's number.

"Hey?"

"Hey."

"West," Jack sighed in relief. "How are you doing, bro?"

"Fine," he lied. "You?" "Uh... good." The hesitation made West's brow furrow but Jack continued quickly, "Kinda tired, but keeping up with stuff. The news has gone a little quiet. I figure Brian will make his move soon."

"Maybe so. I'm going with George to a meeting with some of the government leaders. I'll keep you posted."

West smoothed his shaggy hair back. George insisted he cut it but West hadn't given into that minor request yet.

"OK. Look, I got a bad feeling, West. Brian needs to be stopped. You know the mole you got in his lines?"

"Uh, yeah, I sure hope I do," West replied sarcastically.

"You call him first thing. Any news you get. We can't keep screwing around."

"You sound worried.""I am worried. I don't wanna watch a city get blown off the map."

"I'll do whatever it takes to help, Jack." West rubbed his neck, concerned by Jack's tone. *Something's going on. What?*

"I-I know you will. Uh, can you call Ty soon? He's in rough shape."

West's heart hammered. That was a definite improvement since the last time West had seen Ty, who was the closest thing he had to a little brother. *Last time I saw him, I was leaving...* "Yeah. I'll call."

THE TINY MEETING HOUSE sat lodged away in a well-secured gated area in Connecticut. George rarely drove anywhere more than a few hours away and the jet they took made the trip almost blissful. They were led into the home and once the security team decided everything was safe, the meeting began in the large, soundproof basement.

President Kade hadn't come out of hiding to meet with a few senators and "shadow men", which were the powers-that-be in the shadows that dictated more than any civilian realized. West knew plenty about the men and women sitting around him at the table but there were few of them. Instead of attending personally, a few important leaders had sent replacements to come listen in for them.

The meeting was a simple, fast debriefing. The leaders were brought up to speed on the Union's intentions, the addition of 500 men from Kaleb Savage, and so forth. The ultimate update was: Jones had led his men into the Confederate's Pennsylvanian camp recently and made some leeway. The Confeds had lost plenty of men and retreated. "The news is calling it another Union victory," one of the men declared. "But the US is still waiting for D.C. to be taken back."

"Any update on that?" One woman asked. "The media is tearing us apart—they want information."

"Should we tell them the date and time? Give them the chance to paint some signs and troop around the campsite?" One man snickered. "Give it up. Jones isn't stupid enough to give any of us *anything*. It is too risky. We need the element of surprise."

"We need to understand what is going on in our nation!" The woman snapped back.

George lifted a hand. West could read it in his eyes— George would have snapped the neck of every rotten person in the room. He hated handling the alliances but it was a must. *Can't wait till it's me.* West bit his lip, watching as the room fell quiet. Everyone present feared George.

"I think the debriefing is over." George announced with a smirk. "You are each politicians, not warriors, and any information not presented before you is nothing you need to worry over." With that, he stood from the table and left the room. West followed silently, relieved to leave the nagging voices behind.

As they got into George's SUV, West finally spoke, "You know when Jones is attacking."

"Better than that." George chuckled. He motioned for Bashir and Winston, two of his finest bodyguards, to get the car rolling. They sped away from the small home and back into the cool day.

"Father?" West's chest tightened. *That tone isn't good. What has he not told me?*

"We have a mole."

"A mole?" The air withdrew from West's lungs like someone had punched him in the gut.

"We have a spy in the Confeds in the D.C. camp. He has helped us decide when Jones can attack." George grinned at his son, raising his thick eyebrows. "Genius, eh?"

"Brian has had a mole in the Confeds all this time? And he hasn't mentioned it?!" West fumed, clenching his fists. *Control. Be in control.*

"Yes, but I cannot blame him entirely. It's too delicate a matter to vocalize. He told me recently and I will keep it tucked close. You'd best do the same," George said. "He attacks in two days."

Two days. In two days, everything would change, for worse. *No, God, this can't be happening. How many more lives will be lost?* He had lost so many already: friends, brothers. He'd watched the innocent lives of women and children be snuffed out. Their screams and pleas haunted him every single night.

And another battle would mean more bodies, more ashes, more screams.

I have to stop this.

"Of course, Father." West nodded. Over the weeks, it had become easy to let the robot in his head speak for him. "The Confeds will never know what hit them." *Only they will.*

WEST TOOK A DRIVE in the family's Dodge Challenger, leaving his father's estate far behind him, going to a small river. The spot was a piece of heaven in the summer and a piece of hell in the winter. Ice, ragged and white, and the area would fill up with snow like nothing he'd ever seen before—he remembered playing in the tiny spot as a child. His mother had taken him sledding up on the big hill, he'd gone home with rosy cheeks for hot cocoa. Moments of his childhood that didn't consist of George's harsh words, the basement, or mental abuse.

West sighed, made sure the tiny forest was secure, and dialed Gideon. Gideon answered shortly.

"Gideon, listen, this is important." He watched the sun begin its descent into the horizon. He told him about the mole in the Confederate team. "I need you to—"

"On it."

"You'll alert someone in the Confed camp?"

"Of course."

"And Brian?" West's voice dripped with hatred.

"Leave it to me." Gideon didn't seem to falter at any of the news, which unnerved West but he didn't address it.

"Thank you, Gideon." "Call Jack, would you? He and Spencer are awfully worried about you." Gideon hung up.

CHAPTER SEVEN

October 10th, 2027

GIDEON MADE A BRIEF, censored contact with his friend in the Confed army. He gave him the two day warning, told him that the Union would move fast and hard, striking D.C., but he had no solid information on that matter itself. The spy was grateful and promised he'd set to work preparing the Confeds.

Alex bit his lip, waiting. When Gideon hung up, Alex met his gaze. "Can he handle it?" *We're helping the opposing team. Isn't the first time. But if George finds out... No. Don't think that way.*

"Yes."

"Brian's next." Alex chewed his lip and glanced down.

Gideon dialed Brian's number. Put it on speaker phone. Alex's heart thumped in his chest and he tried to steady his breathing while the line picked up.

"Knight?"

"Grandmaster here." Gideon gave his codename in response as their usual form of greeting before snapping, "Call the attack off, Brian. Whatever you have to do, stop this *now*."

Alex tapped his fingers against his arm as he watched Gideon's face distort in pure rage. Gideon took many risks, most if not all calculated, and was often the first to shoot and ask questions later. But these attacks were different. The government was using every way it could to snuff out the rebels. They'd slaughtered Christians countless times over the years, but those stories never made the news. The government hired men to shoot up schools and set fires to homes to anyone who caused trouble or didn't follow protocol. The war had existed long before the United States officially declared war among itself.

But the rebels had won D.C., Richmond, Denver, and other large cities. This was their last chance at triumph. Alex hadn't prayed so hard in all his life. *We're asking for a miracle, God. I know it can be done if it is Your will. For the sake of the men in those trenches, those vehicles, those aviators, everyone... the families at home, watching the news or waiting for the doors to their homes to crack open...*

Lord, have mercy, please. If Jones succeeds, we will lose thousands of rebel lives. Good men. Men simply doing what you want.

And the same goes for the Union—they are good men there, too, and countless good men will die. In two days... He closed his eyes and fought the urge to vomit.

Brian finally spoke, "I do not have time for this."

"You know this isn't just another brawl."

"It is absolutely none of your concern," Brian retorted. "The Confederates are tyrannical and must be ended, no matter the cost. If the nation bleeds because of this deed of justice, so be it. It will be for the best."

"Thousands of Union and Confederate men will die. For what? Dominion over the capitols and Army bases? It is a set up, Brian. Think about it. You're playing puppet."

"You have spent too much time in the conspiracy theorist's world." Brian scoffed. "This is war, and war is won by death."

"War is won by the living!" Gideon leaned against the counter with both fists clenched so tightly, Alex expected blood to seep from his palms. Gideon rarely, if ever, lifted his voice or let rage show through when speaking to Brian, but only hate glowed in his dark eyes now. "The UN will grow tired of replenishing your troops and the Confeds will die out. All of them. Springtown will send their men to help fight, Brian. What of your family? One day, you will pull the trigger and the man standing across the line will be your own damn baby brother!" His voice rose into a growling snarl. "Or what of Rene'? You wipe out the rebel scum, you let the Union and the Muslims come and take their bounty, and your little sister becomes some shaman's whore—"

"*Enough*!" Brian shouted. He had never lifted his voice that Alex could remember, and Alex flinched at the sound. What Gideon had said was awful, and as much as it wrenched Alex's gut, those words were not far from being true. Brian might win the war, but at what cost would that victory bring the nation? Or, the *nations*?

Gideon didn't shut up but his voice grew cool again. "No! You are brainwashed by the government but I can see what these attacks will do."

"They will end this war. They will save lives. More lives than the ones we will lose. That is war, Hochberg! It is a shame you never could grasp this but your father could!"

A mirthless laugh scratched Gideon's throat. "It is a shame you fled from *your* father. You are putting him in a grave. You are putting his entire country in a grave. Aren't you proud of the work you've done?" "Whether you believe it or not, Hochberg," Brian spat, "I have saved millions of lives and will continue to do so. You've never been this emotional and you are making a mistake now.

Emotions and blood relations have no place in war. Don't forget that."

"You attack D.C. and you will lose this war." Gideon's voice dropped, cold, emotionless, like a switch went off in his head. "This war is not being controlled or won by the bodies in the trenches. It is being controlled and won by the bodies in the UN, the leadership positions, the money creators. You are powerless. If you do not understand the men sending you into this battle or only doing so for the sake of gaining more votes, you are a fool. They don't care if the war ends. They can end it when they like."

Alex's skin ran cold. *Lord, let Brian change his mind. Soften his heart, change it, make a miracle happen—let him call these attacks off. Everything hangs on his choice. He has the power to do your will—please, let it be so.*

"You are incorrect. Take heed over your job and your position. Leave my duty to me." Brian hung up.

Gideon lifted his bloodshot eyes, jaw clamped shut. "It's over."

"No. No!" Alex shook his head and grabbed Gideon by his shoulder, throat dry. "It isn't over. God is going to take care of us, all of us, we have to pray. We have to have hope."

"Alex..."

"This isn't hopeless. We wouldn't still be fighting if it were hopeless." Alex couldn't describe the comfort he found in God, but it broke him knowing Gideon didn't share that faith. He could hardly manage the days with God. What was it like for Gideon to carry every burden, every sin, every demon, alone? "I know you aren't sure, but God is with us. He is."

Gideon patted him on the back. "Get some sleep. We have a long two days ahead of us."

CHAPTER EIGHT

October 12th, 2027

SIMON PULLED HIS BINOCULARS up, watching the small house amid the Alabama suburb. The little suburb wasn't much but it was Union and protected—thus, no one of them would have the balls to address the fact their guards had just let two of George's gangsters past their gates. Well, *Kaleb's* gangsters, but Simon supposed they truly were all the same. Sort of. *To these pansies, definitely the same.* He chuckled.

"What's so funny?" Randy yawned from the passenger seat. He pulled up his thermos of coffee.

"Nothing."

"*Huh.*" Randy rolled his eyes and chugged his steaming drink. "You're kinda creepy when you do that."

"Do what?"

"That smirk thing and that little head nod and then you don't tell me what happened in your head." Randy mimicked the expression before bursting into a laugh. "Man, you should see your face, you're so easy to—"

"Would you focus on the job?" Simon shoved the binoculars at him. He didn't mind Randy, though Nate hated him, but he wasn't the greatest guy to get hooked on a job with.

Randy caught the binoculars with a sly smile. "He isn't here yet. Why are you so tense?"

"He will be here."

"Simon, Simon, Simon," Randy sighed. "We're asking for payment. What's he gonna do, shoot us? The guards twenty yards away are on our side, too, remember?""You're too optimistic." Simon eyed the gun on his own hip. He didn't consider himself a pessimistic person—less so, since he'd been saved—but he was cynical. Especially on jobs. Being a paranoid man and a man of faith just didn't seem to mix on the job. For the sake of his life, he chose paranoia and cynicism while working. He hadn't reached the level of faith Alex had yet.

"Aw, it'll be fine." Randy gazed at the plain, white and gray suburban house. Every house was identical in size, structure, layout, and the families were all pretty cookie-cutter. Father worked in a big business, oftentimes something politically related, earned enough money to put him in the Union's hands, and had a wife and one or two kids. Living in the secured communities cost money as well as freedom. Simon glanced briefly toward the hundreds of rows of houses.

"Sure." Simon rubbed his sore neck.

"Si?"

"What?"

"How's Nate doing?" "Same as ever." Nate's attitude hadn't gotten much better in regards to Kaleb, especially since their outburst. Nate had even gone so far as acting paranoid, as if him talking back to Kaleb and demanding their right to freedom was somehow enough to grant Kaleb the opportunity to kill the boy in his sleep. Simon didn't blame him. Kaleb had done terrible things to his only child.

"Um, nothing's changed?" Randy licked his lips, eyes dropping from the house across the street a little.

"Not really," he lied. "Why?"

"He hasn't forgiven me yet, huh?" Randy's voice was quiet, almost pathetic sounding, had Simon not known how much the subject meant to the blondie.

"No. But he'll come around." Simon prayed about it, but he really didn't see Nate as the forgiving type, especially when Kaleb had chosen Randy as his son and had only ever used or abused Nate.

"I-I'm sorry. It shouldn't," Randy hesitated, "mean so much, I guess. I'll shut up."

"I don't think you're physically capable of that," Simon chuckled dryly. "Don't give up, Randy. I know it's hard but..." On the very tip of his tongue, he'd almost blurted "but God is faithful."

"But?" Randy eyed him like a curious pup.

Simon scowled. "Nothing."

"Come on, you can't do that twice in ten minutes."

"I was just gonna say that maybe there's a reason things are so hard." Simon didn't like lying. He couldn't just bring up God though, could he? He hadn't been saved for long. Who was he to offer Randy hope? Anyway, Randy's mouth was big enough to fit Pangaea in—he'd tell someone that Simon believed and it'd all be over. Simon couldn't take the chance.

Randy laughed again. "Oh, of course. Hell on earth is to make us love heaven in death all the more, right?"

Prickling at Randy's tone, Simon reminded himself he'd kinda asked for it. "That's not what I meant."

"Nah, it is. The idea that everything happens for a reason and all will work out for the best is one big false hope." All humor faded from Randy's eyes. He watched the house, jaw tight as he spoke, "And it might work for some, but it isn't enough for me. Too vague."

Simon gulped down the lump in his throat. "What do you mean? Like, does that mean you don't think anything will work out or...?" "I think some things can, or will, but blind hope isn't enough to keep a man going."

God, do You want me to tell him about You?

"Here he comes," Randy said eagerly, sitting up a little. A white car pulled past the gate guards and parked in the tiny garage to the house. The garage door sealed soundly behind the car and the driver—their target, James Codde— never appeared to notice the black car across the street. It didn't matter if he had spotted Simon and Randy, since the guards had let them in and they didn't appear to be an immediate threat.

"Go time." Randy flashed a zealous grin and shoved the binoculars into the backpack at his feet. "Can I play good cop?"

Simon rolled his eyes. "There's no good cop, bad cop when we're asking for payment."

"C'mon, Kaleb hasn't let me on many jobs lately. I wanna have some fun." Randy made a face.

"Give me a break." Simon pulled his coat down a bit, ensuring the gun on his hip was covered, and got out of the car. Randy followed, his long strides catching up with Simon's. The cool fall breeze nipped at Simon's cheeks and he inwardly dreaded shaving his "wanna-be" beard, as Nate called it. He hoped Rene' didn't mind it. He might keep it for a bit. If Nate or one of the thugs didn't sneak into his room at night and shave it off for him. After all, it made him look older, and that was useful on a job.

Randy stepped onto the tiny concrete porch to the house. "Please?" he whispered.

Simon rolled his eyes in response, which was enough for Randy. Randy pushed the doorbell and hid a smile. He was good at the good cop gig. Simon doubted he had a mean bone in his ugly body.

The door opened a long moment later, and their target stood with hunched shoulders, his tie half-untied down his white, crisp shirt. "Hello...?" He cast a sharp glance past them and toward the road as if inwardly cursing the guards for allowing anything to bother his downtime.

"Hello, Codde," Randy said, offering a hand. "We're with George." Funny how they didn't even need a name, a gang tattoo, for such simple words to carry so much dark weight.

James glanced between them like a nervous cat. "Ah. I see. Um—"

"Where's the money?" Simon asked calmly.

"I have it." James lifted a defensive hand. "I swear. Just give me a minute."

Simon eyed him, not believing him for a moment. He also didn't want to push the man to act foolishly. He nodded and James ducked out of sight.

Randy quirked one eyebrow at Simon as if to show his surprise. Things didn't usually work this well.

James came back out and thrust a small black bag at Randy's chest. "Here. Take it and go. I'm loyal to the Union, I-I pay my debts to George." He pleaded tightly, a vein in his short neck bulging.

Randy weighed the bag in his hands like a pro, peeked inside. "Seems good." He grinned. "Nice doing business with you."

James started closing the door, but not before Simon heard a young girl's voice call, "Daddy?"

Thud. James slammed the door.

Simon turned on his heels. Skin crawling, he got into the car and cranked it again. *Daddy.* Even the slimeballs on enemy lines had innocent children. He gripped the steering wheel hard, forcing the anger in his chest to dissolve.

Randy hopped in. The moment Randy shut the door, Simon tore the vehicle down the road and the guards let them out of the community. Once the acres of houses lay behind them, Randy whistled. "You OK there, butch?"

"Why would anyone do that?" Simon hissed.

"Huh?"

"Why would a man be a sleazeball when he could do good?" Simon shook his head. "I don't understand it."

"Oh. You mean his kid?" Randy unzipped the bag and started leafing through the wads of hundred dollar bills.

Simon huffed. He couldn't expect Randy to understand. Randy's father had been a slimeball, too, raising both his sons in the shelter of the mafia groups, long before the war started. "Nevermind."

"Some men don't think they have a chance." Randy kept his eyes on the money. "Think about it. Sure, he's a sorry jerk, but his kid and his wife are safe in a broken world."

"You know that's BS."

"Yeah." Randy chuckled. "The gov he works for might give him a big gate and green grass, but... he's just a stock number to them. If you had to choose, though, what would you choose? Despite the risk of trusting the government, he probably just thinks it's keeping his family alive for some time, at least. They'd never make it out of these gates, Si. You know that. The nation is..." he trailed off, a strange expression falling over his face.

"I'd choose freedom, Randy. I could protect a family outside a cage." Simon jutted his chin, voice haught. *Even if that means moving to Springtown... or working with Jordan. Please, God, let me be with Rene'. I don't want to die on some battlefield. I'm not that strong.*

Randy finished counting the cash, shoved it into the bag, and eyed Simon. After a thoughtful pause, he said, "Yeah. You could. And that chick you care about could probably fend for herself to some degree. But not everyone is like you. Most of America happily gave up freedoms for so called safety. Even if the war is won, the issues at the root of the nation remain."

Simon sped the car up. "Didn't know you'd given it so much thought.""I might look stupid, but I'm not." Randy leaned back in his seat. "The government has fooled most of America that they care, that they'll protect and defend the people, if the people surrender rights. But the men following the rules... They're family men, Si, men who don't want their families to hide behind cages and live mindlessly. I know you want a family and all, and you wanna be free, guard Springtown or whatever, but..." he sucked in a sharp breath. "Soon as word gets out about that town..." Randy wasn't even supposed to know, but he'd found out about Rene' and the town earlier that week. He'd "accidentally" overheard Nate and Simon's private conversation one night. He had told Simon later and Simon wouldn't tell Nate—he didn't want to bury Randy. Though he had punched Randy good for eavesdropping and threatened him within an inch of his life if he ever let a single breath slip about it.

"What?" Simon snapped.

"Not every gangster likes the life we have, Simon. You don't think some guys will go break up Springtown?"

"Nothing bad will happen to that town, not if I have any breath in my body." Simon squared his broad shoulders, knowing that with God on his side, he'd be able to do what needed doing. Protecting Springtown was at the top of his list, along with Nate and Graham.

But it wasn't like he'd done a good job at protecting either of his brothers.

"Sure. Kaleb and George both seem dead set on protecting the town—not sure why—but what about the guys showing up, begging to be let in?" Randy insisted.

"They won't be let in." Simon waved him off. He didn't mention Philip and Danny Dunnham, of course, but they'd been doing fine, shacking up with the Fishers. Rene' kept him updated as she slowly learned to trust them.

"Then why would George let Gideon protect them?" Randy grunted. "Something is going on, Simon, and you're too lovesick to notice!"

A stunned rage engulfed Simon's mind like a blaze of fire and he shouted, without realizing what he was saying, "Something is always going on, Randy! *Always*! We're always playing roulette and there's not a single thing I can do to find every single answer. All I can do is protect the ones I care about, and honestly, I'm not even that good at it! So if you wanna start a conspiracy that George has motives when he lets us help Springtown, shoot away, but don't you dare bring Rene' into it!"

Randy slammed his palm down on the dashboard, hard enough Simon expected the airbag to go off. "I am not your enemy! I'm trying to help!"

"Help?! You call reminding me that George is my personal grim reaper *helping*? I'm not free. I can't keep the people I love free. Gated communities or not, I'm just as much a slave as James!" Simon watched the road before him and the trees blur past, refusing to look at Randy.

"If we know what George is up to, we don't have to be slaves." Randy shook his head. "It isn't his MO to let his men—his good men—help a random small town. Haven't you given that any thought?"

"Since the moment George found out, I've been busting my rear end trying to keep everyone afloat and alive. I've hardly had time to second guess his motive. I figured it was something he let us do to make us happy," Simon said sharply, voice dark with sarcasm.

Randy squirmed in his seat, probably enraged and doing all he could to keep himself in check. It took a lot to anger Randy. Simon had pushed his buttons but wasn't sorry about it. Randy had started it. "I think that the reason Springtown is still alive is because of the government, too. Or something like that. It isn't a coincidence, isn't a miracle, there's a reason. And man, if you want your girl, you need to figure out why her town remains so you can better defend it. I... I'm here to help, Si. I wanna help."

How many times had he said that? How many times had Randy shown his big heart? Simon gulped hard, heat flooding his cheeks. "Sorry, Randy. I... know what you want. You're a good friend. But I honestly can only juggle so much. If you're right, God is gonna have to show it, because I can't split myself apart anymore to chase a conspiracy."

Randy squeezed his shoulder. "I know. So I'll help. I can help with this." His voice was fervent, like he *needed* to help with every fiber of his being.

"OK, Randy." Simon turned on the radio, hoping to drop the subject, but a news channel burst to life. Randy swatted his hand off the dial.

"Wait, wait!" He turned the volume up as the report continued.

"Union General Brian Jones led a brutal attack on United States Capitol Washington D.C. but the attack was in vain. Confederate General Drew Beasley retaliated with supreme efficiency. The Union was pushed back..." The reporter's voice flooded the speakers.

Randy lifted his head, eyes wide in horror. Simon couldn't tear his eyes off the road but his heart lodged in his throat. *God, no. No.*

"... the Confederate camp remains in D.C. and as strong as ever. We are not sure how they have survived this long or gained supplies. We... are at a loss. According to the government, over 3,000 Union soldiers were lost in the battle…"

"Oh, my God." Randy choked.

"… and only 1,500 Confederates, from what we gathered."

This is Brian's work. This was his attack. His failure. What was he thinking? Simon grabbed his phone. "Call Kaleb. Now!"

CHAPTER NINE

October 12th, 2027

"THE ATTACK ON THE US capitolfailed drastically."
The newsman's voice shook occasionally as he stared into
the camera. "The bomb was dropped before it hit its
target, the capitol, and has lit aflame a community and part
of the city. Union fire troops are doing all they can to
maintain the fires. The Confederates remain at D.C. but
right now, that's hardly the biggest concern."

Gideon and Alex stood like statues in the living room
of their cabin, the small hologram playing on TV. News
footage of fire troops fighting a large, angry fire lit up the
screen. Videos from survivors played live footage of
women and children screaming and fleeing from the
houses and buildings engulfed with fire. Some victims

were lost, stumbling and falling, going up in flames, but the videos never wavered—the people filming didn't run into the ashes to help a soul.

Half a community had been destroyed and the rest wasn't far behind. Flashes of footage showed the city burning and countless citizens fleeing for their lives in the dusky light.

The newsman continued, "We are devastated by the Union's mishap. An entire Islamic caravan was taken out along with the community. This action was not done with ill intent, it was entirely an accident... We cannot believe the use of heavy artillery here, it was not expected..."

Gideon watched the screen, jaw set. This man was watching people lose their lives on live television, yet all he was concerned over was some radical Islams in the UN taking offence.

"Wait. I've got something..." The reporter held his ear piece and his red cheeks turned green. He swore, not caring if he was on live television being broadcasted to millions of Americans. "I just got word that President Kaden will be speaking shortly. Please stand by."

The live footage zoomed in. A woman in a black suit with a small toddler in her arms. The baby was hard to see but the woman was screaming and crying, running from her burning home.

"Where are the troops?" Alex whispered.

Gideon took a slow breath. The fire troops had enough to deal with. They couldn't save everyone.

The woman staggered on, barefoot, through the ash. Gideon steeled himself. How were they even getting this footage? Why didn't the person recording do something? Couldn't the feed wait—weren't saving lives more important than feeding political agenda?

The woman moved forward and left the camera's view. But Gideon caught movement in the doorway of another burning home to the left. The camera didn't budge. A short man with two children in his arms staggered outside, cloth over his mouth and over his childrens'.

"Oh, Jesus." Alex dropped to his knees beside the couch. "Jesus, no, no, no—"

The small white house crumbled within seconds, the fire raging onward as it snuffed the lives that had tried so desperately to flee.

Alex dropped his forehead to the floor and wept. Through every sob, he prayed. He prayed like God could hear him, could feel the agony of His people, and could change a single thing.

Gideon stood still, unable to comfort his brother and unable to continue watching the footage. He slammed the hologram off. But in countless US homes, people would watch the news. Families with children and nice jobs and fancy cars and 401ks. Families who trusted the government to care for them if they believed every lie and gave up everything that mattered.

They would watch it like any other news broadcast, forgetting that the war going on was far more real than they knew.

I need to call Brian. No, I need to meet with Brian. I need... Alex's choked prayers pounded through his head. He forced a breath, knelt beside him. *I need to pray. How do I do that? Don't you have to be saved for your prayers to matter?* Well, he'd still be there for Alex. He could afford a few minutes without ripping someone's head off.

Make these people pay, God. If You're a just God, help me end this war. Let them *burn.*

CHAPTER TEN

October 14th, 2027

"THE MEXICAN'S ARE RESTLESS. They're afraid we will limit trade with them since the attack immobilized so much." George sighed, pouring himself a glass of bourbon. The previous couple days had been hellish, to say the least. The news hadn't shut up about the failed attack, the loss of civilian lives, and the change in the UN atmosphere. West dissected every piece of information he got. He had to remember it all, piece the puzzle together.

As usual, nothing was going according to plan.

"Is there anything I can do?" West offered calmly, though he hoped George said no. He didn't want to get sidetracked. He needed to stay close to George, get the

Test, and, eventually, kill him. He couldn't very well keep to his scattered plan if he was elsewhere.

"Yes," George smiled. "I need you at the Mexican border."

West fought a frown. "Mexico?"

"You will be in charge of the smuggling, make sure that the trade continues while the war rages on. We cannot lose this alliance and President Kade forgets how vital the Mexican president is to us. We need to remain in control over the border. You can handle that." George grabbed his son's shoulder, raising his eyebrows slightly. "Right?"

"Of course. Looking forward to it." There was never a small request with George. This was a huge task. *God, let it be the final trial before the real deal. I just need the Test. Then I'm in. I can kill him. I can take over.*

"Can you leave tomorrow?"

"Of course. I'll go pack."

"I'll brief you before you head out."

GIDEON HAD SPENT EVERY day trying to track the money trails, but it wasn't giving him answers. He'd put Reese Burns, a top-notch fighter in the domes, on high alert. Reese was a useful man to have on your side, even if he wasn't out and about in the political world, he was deep and low in the slums. Gideon told Nabeel Shahin, a close friend of Spencer and Bo, but instead of blurting out every thought like those two, Nabeel barely spoke. Gideon asked Nabeel to keep him updated if anything, anywhere, changed, or if he found any suspicious behaviour on his jobs. At this point, Gideon didn't want to take chances on missing anything. Someone was paying to guard Springtown, and he needed help finding out who that was. George didn't want him to find out. It was vital he did so.

One man in the CIA had tried contacting Gideon with information but never came through. The next morning, it was shown on a news report the man had been murdered. *Because someone found out he was trying to help me. No one knows it, but that was my fault.* Gideon turned off the news and took a slow breath, eyeing his untouched breakfast. This wasn't going well, but what else could he do but chase trails? He definitely couldn't let the matter drop. If he didn't find out who was guarding Springtown, anything else done to benefit the town would be in vain, because it could all fade with a snap. Lives were at stake and Gideon's job was to protect the innocent.

He got up and went to the hallway, tapping on Alex's bedroom door. Alex always kept the door open but Gideon knocked anyway. "Hey. Got a minute?"

Alex paused his worship music, closed his Bible, and leaned back onto his bed. "Whatcha got? Your mind's spinning a thousand miles per hour, I can see it in your eyes."

Gideon rolled his eyes. He told him about the CIA agent who'd been killed in his apartment.

"That... that was us...?" Alex's eyes widened and his jaw dropped in horror.

"Yeah. That was us." Gideon crossed his arms. "We are no closer to uncovering the supplier."

"M-maybe it's time to step back a bit, Gideon. We can keep the threads open but not push so bloody hard," Alex breathed.

"I can manage both simultaneously." Gideon didn't doubt his ability to pull off both, but he also knew he'd misjudged how touchy the mission would be. "Whatever is going on mattered enough to someone to kill for."

"Maybe it's a coincidence," Alex said tightly. "He's a CIA guy, they get killed a lot, it might not have been connected to us." Alex was nothing if not a hopeful optimist. Gideon usually admired the trait. But not when he was exhausted.

"Alex, come on."

"You don't know for sure." Alex set his jaw.

"We need to proceed with the jobs, together. I'm healthy enough to get back to it." Gideon hid the anger from his voice. "I'll put this on the back burner a little."

"*A little* means bloody nothing!" Alex snapped. "Gideon, please, tell Mr. Fisher. Tell someone else who can help."

Gideon licked his lips, giving the thought consideration. He'd mulled it over since Alex first mentioned it but had refused it. "I'll give it another week."

"You said we were low on time."

"We are but if the town finds this out, they'll implode. Tyler says they already had guys slip out of town this week to join the Confeds." Gideon rubbed his temples. The men who'd fled the town for the "greater good" were utter fools.

Alex exhaled, as if taking the situation in fully, and by the heaviness in his eyes, he didn't want to. "This is just as bad as you thought it'd be. Whatever is going on..."

"We can handle it," Gideon said firmly. "We can handle it on the side and push on carefully. Just like always." Losing a contact was bad news, though hardly coincidental, but they could warn the others to be more subtle in their notes and searching.

Alex stood up. "We tell Mr. Fisher."

"Agreed."

CHAPTER ELEVEN

October 17th, 2027

"HOW ARE THE MEN?" Guns plucked a full bottle of vodka from the shelves of the tiny bar in George's favorite warehouse. They were alone, as usual, and George smiled in delight as he sipped his whiskey.

"They're getting the hang of the ropes. You'd be proud."

"Hmm."

"West has already maintained absolute control at the border. Gideon is trying to track Springtown's supplier, no doubt," George gave him a wry smile, "and President Kaden is very close to handing his power over."

"Over to you or his vice president?" Guns sat down at the bar.

"His vice president sucks up to me more than he does. Either choice he chooses, I can kill the vice and take it myself." A burning satisfaction lingered in George's chest. How long had he fought for this power? And it was finally coming together.

"I doubt the UN would take kindly to such actions." Guns reminded him for the hundredth time. As chums, only Guns was allowed to doubt or pick at George's plans. His insight was usually valuable.

Usually.

"Guns, please, spare me," George said. "The UN will do whatever I want them to do. I have just as much, if not more, power than any of them."

"Aye." Guns sipped his drink. "But I still think, after all these years, you're a fool for wanting that kind of position."

"Once it is mine, I can remove it and begin my empire." George patted his friend on his back. "Age might be dulling your senses but not my own," he teased.

Guns rolled his piercing eyes. "Couldn't change your mind before, not trying now. But you ought to be proud of your boys. You could do with being more humble."

"Hm. Most of them. Philip Dunnham is still gone. I figure he must be dead like Danny." George drank some more.

"A pity," Guns murmured wryly.

George hated speaking of the two, so he switched the subject quickly. "I would keep an eye out for that town, Guns. Gideon is taking this quite seriously." George tapped the bar top. "Think you can handle him?"

Guns laughed out loud. "He won't get the answer he's looking for, brother. You worry about the upcoming election."

"Oh, it's a shoe-in." George waved his hand. "If they even allow it, which I sincerely doubt. I think President Kade will remain president till death. Now, any updates on Jones?"

"He's licking his wounds while leading his troops away from D.C. For the time being, they're just as low in supplies as the Confeds, if not more so. They need to revamp and rest before they make another mistake. I doubt Iran offers more bombs, however."

George chuckled, not surprised that the Iranians would be furious that a few civilians blamed the bombings on their suppliers instead of the Union men wielding them. "And the Union's experiments?" he asked curiously.

"The genetics?"

"No, the werewolves." He smirked sarcastically.

Guns laughed and finished his glass off. "It's moving along slowly and quietly. I don't think those men know what they're uncovering."

"Ah, they probably think what they're creating is controllable." George's smirk faded. "The DNA altering will bite them in the backside eventually. Even I'm not crazy enough to think it can all work out."

"Experiments like this have gone on for decades. If they breathe a word of their progress, I can ensure they're shut down." Guns gave a two-fingered salute. "We can handle it if it comes."

"Disgusting little fools." George downed the rest of his drink and leaned back. "They're taking victims from the fight rings and the sex rings. The numbers are growing higher. You'd best be watchful."

"Nothing will come of it."

"I trust you."

"Poor decision." Guns sighed. "How did Kaleb react to losing all the men he sent to Jones?"

"Poorly, of course, but he has yet to act about it." George had expected a fit of sorts, or at least Kaleb showing up at his house with a knife in his hand. Kaleb followed orders but he still had a temper that George watched out for. Still, after losing hundreds of men, Kaleb hadn't seemed to take his rage out on George himself. "One of his men called me, saying Kaleb was rampaging, but he has yet to address me."

Guns' eyebrows furrowed as he studied George. "Strange of him."

"He is probably busy ensuring the families of the dead don't leave him, also." George didn't care that much. What had needed to be done had been done, and in war, that was all that mattered.

"Probably. Has Hunter shown his face again?"

"Not since our run in. I figure he's still playing vigilante over his boys and dreading having to admit he's alive." George smirked softly. "Keep an ear out, he may reach out to you first." He sipped his drink before continuing, "Hochberg asked me about the town suppliers."

"As you mentioned... What did you tell him?"

"I told him that it wasn't his field. I don't need him forming an alliance with Springtown. But I've given it thought, and I think allowing Kaleb allegiance with the settlement would be a good investment."

"That," Guns said dryly, eyebrows raising, "Was my idea over twelve months ago."

"Well, I accept it, now."

"What changed your mind?" he growled.

"With the war dwindling, we need allies on both sides, yes. Union and Confed. And that town might be lost... say the supplier dies, or a gang gets too greedy..."

"What would Kaleb's alliance do?"

"I can be in control. I wouldn't push anything—Mr. Fisher is a wise man and could smell a trap. He probably will trust Kaleb, and if I can have that alliance, I don't need to act on it. It is safe to simply have control, another ace in the game."

Guns mumbled before standing. "You take my ideas and make your own, you old cuss. If you can make Mr. Fisher agree to that, by all means, good luck."

"I will alert Kaleb and allow him to handle the situation from here on out in a manner and time he thinks best." George didn't bother hiding his invigoration over the turn in events. While he had pondered the plan for over a year, thanks to Guns' initial idea, finally allowing the idea to take action was near brilliant. While he never counted his money before he left the table, things were utterly in his control. West would soon be ready for testing, and the things George had done to earn his trust—allowing Springtown to thrive, allowing Jack his family, and more —were paying off.

While Gideon digging into the suppliers wasn't exactly what George wanted, it wouldn't hurt. Gideon would be ready to do as George needed. He'd proven himself worthy with Shane and had handled that test well. *I'd rather him not form an alliance with Springtown, but I suppose I shall see what works best for my empire's benefit in time. Him thinking he has control over something vital may help his bond with me.*

Guns spoke up, "Kaleb as their ally would be beneficial, so long as they agree, which I doubt. As for Hochberg, no matter what knowledge he finds, he is loyal to you. Perhaps giving him some leash might benefit you, as well. As I've said... you torture your boys too much." A thin smile on his lips, Guns said, "I'd best get back to work. Keep me updated, prude."

"Same to you." George went out to Bashir and Winston, getting into his car, calling his wife. She would want to hear the updates and was one of the few people George kept nothing from.

CHAPTER TWELVE

October 18th, 2027

A HEAVY ATMOSPHERE LAY over Springtown, or maybe it was the gray sky that lingered, leaving a strange ache in Rene's chest. Something wasn't right. She nudged her mare, Sugar, to move a bit faster toward mainstreet. Bethany rode a Fisher family gelding beside her.

"Hey, Onya?" Rene' spoke into her phone, trying to focus on the conversation again. "I have to go. I'll call you back tonight, OK?" Since helping Onya and other girls escape a trafficking ring, Rene' had kept contact with the teenage girl. Onya had named the baby Rene' helped deliver after her, and both were doing just fine. Onya loved talking to Rene' and Rene' had even tried learning some Spanish, just to make Onya laugh at her horrible accent.

"Yes, please do," Onya said eagerly. "I love you."

Heart melting a little, Rene' smiled. "Love you too, Onya." She hung up and turned to Bethany. "Town is awfully busy." Bethany watched as a couple hurried down the sidewalk toward the courthouse. "Hey!" She called out. "What's—"

"Survivors came from outside the city!" the man shouted.

Rene' and Bethany broke their horses into a trot. Crowds of people surrounded the courthouse and an unfamiliar black bus sat outside the doors. Rene' hadn't seen such an uproar since a group of men had snuck out of town to join the Confeds. Bile rising in her throat, she glanced at Bethany while they hitched their horses to the posts. "What's going on, ya think? My dad's inside—let's find him."

Bethany led her through the crowds of civilians. They slipped inside, struggling to get through the foyer, searching for Mr. Fisher. The chatter of voices, some panicked, some almost joyous, drowned Rene's thoughts.

"Aye, lassies, you shouldn't be here." Sean's voice, his Irish accent heavy, came from behind them and he grabbed Rene' by her shoulder gently. Scooting them out of the crowds, he said, "Mr. Fisher is downstairs, best not go down just yet."

"What's going on?" Bethany insisted.

"A van of civilians came home," he said softly. "People who had moved away before the war started, people we thought were dead..." he trailed off, eyes moist.

"Who? How many?" Bethany and Rene' asked in anxious unison.

Sean listed fifteen names but Rene's heart jumped into her throat when he mentioned Chloe Downfield. Chloe, the girl that Bethany and Rene' used to know, over six years ago now. They'd spent days at the library programs, chatted at rodeos. Chloe had never made friends but she'd liked Bethany and Rene', even if she was a few years older than they were. She'd gone to college to become an archaeologist before the war started. Her parents had nearly gone mad with grief after they'd lost contact with her. They'd been hermits before but went off the deep end when she vanished.

"Chloe?" Bethany paled. "She's here?!"

Sean held up his hands. "I know ya wanna see her, but give it till morning. Her parents are here, she's safe, just exhausted."

Rene' bit back a flood of questions, managing, "What's going on?"

"Your father and some other men are discussing the news the group brought back, lots of information. Updates about the war and things. We knew most of it thanks to Jack's guys, but, still. We're just all talking and such. The group is getting medical attention, food, some rest. Mr. Fisher told me to tell you," he smirked at Rene', "to head on home if you showed up."

Rene' huffed. "I'm staying."

"You two deserve some rest."

"You don't rest," Bethany pointed out. "We'll hang around in case anyone needs our help."

Sean tossed his hands up, red curls bouncing. "I'm the one with a badge, y'know! Ya have to listen to me!"

Bethany smiled and Rene' patted his arm, saying, "See ya around, big bro."

He muttered under his breath and hurried off to get back to work. Bethany turned to Rene', eyes wide. "She's home. She's alive!" Tears swelled in her eyes.

"Thank God." Rene' wrapped her arms around her best friend and hugged her with all her might. "We'll see her in the morning."

"A SHIPMENT IS HERE!" Bethany jumped up from the bench she and Rene' had been dozing off in the courtroom basement. She put her phone away, grinning. "Ty just texted me—he's here!" Without waiting for Rene' to catch up, she headed up the stone stairs.

Rene' hid a smile and followed. She couldn't shake the guilt she bore from having a part in Ed's death—she could barely force herself not to think it was still her fault, but she was trying hard—but Ty never treated her differently, though he mourned his older brother's passing. If anything, he loved her, with a heart like Bethany's. Jesus dwelled in both of them, and Ty didn't seem to hold ill will toward Rene'. *And he's crushing on my bestie.*

Most of the civilians had dispersed for the night. Sean was guarding the courthouse, and led the girls out to the supply truck.

"Wonder why they're here so late. Just gave us a shipment three days ago." Sean frowned, watching the truck stop in front of the courthouse. A man came over and set up a large light so they could see in the dark.

"Nice to see you, too," Ty called, hopping out of the passenger side. He came over and grinned at Bethany, a childish glint in his eyes.

Bethany beamed in relief. "Hey, Ty. What's going on? Everything OK?"

"Everything's dandy!" Ty patted the back of the truck. "We got extra supplies from a job so we figured we'd bring it on over. Wasn't too far from here, anyway."

"We appreciate it," Sean said earnestly.

Ty bowed. "Our pleasure."

Rolling his eyes, Sean went to help the men unload the supplies. Jack opened the back of the truck, talking to the men about what they had been up to.

Bethany grabbed Ty's arm. Seeing her cue to make herself scarce, Rene' stepped over, grabbing a box from Jack. She didn't meet his gaze, holding her breath. He didn't talk to her and she hurried inside. *Why can't I look at him? Why can't I smile around Ty? They know who I am—the girl Ed died for. The fool they lost their brother for.* She blinked back tears and focused on her work. *God, help me heal. Or forget. Or move on. Something. Anything.*

CHAPTER THIRTEEN

October 18th, 2027

"WE'RE GETTING TOO CLOSE to that Confed camp." Alex spoke up sharply. "You passed the right turn!"

Simon didn't like the shouting but he was having too much trouble holding on in the backseat to interject. His head slammed against the door. "Ow!"

"I'm driving the best I can! You try driving in the dark with a Jeep at the speed of the Flash!" Spencer snapped, grip tight on the steering wheel. In the dark, going eighty miles per hour, he wasn't having a good time maintaining control of the vehicle. Simon had been out cold during the getaway. He didn't remember much of the job going bad. He remembered thinking "thank God Nate is starting back next week" but little else as the thug had struck him down.

At least the job is done. We got the cash from the gangsters. My luck is running out—how can I be messing up so badly lately on small jobs?! Dad taught me so much. He tells me how proud he is. I do so much, for what? I keep messing up!

"I'm telling you, this is the wrong road!" Alex showed Spencer the GPS in his scarred hands. "Move!"

"I *am*!" Spencer growled, sweat dripping from his short brown hair. "I can't turn around!"

"Crikey! Turn around *now*. We can face thugs, we can't face soldiers." Alex was on the edge of the passenger seat, face ashen.

Simon groaned and sat up, rubbing his bruised head. "What's going on?" No need to wallow in despair when they were about to be killed.

"He's driving us into rebel terf!"

"I'm trying to get us out but if we go backwards, those thugs will be on us, too." Spencer growled. "Just guide me outta here. Use your fancy little map."

"*GPS*!" Alex glared at the screen and shook his head. "They're right—"

Thwap! A multitude of bullets slammed against the right side of the Jeep. Simon swore and ducked, shimmying away from the door. "Down!"

Alex dropped a little. "Spencer, turn around!""Spence!" Simon snarled.

Spencer wrestled for control over the fast moving vehicle, trying to turn it on the small road. The Confeds hiding in the treelines continued fire. Simon braced himself for impact—if they shot the tires, or worse, if they shot Spencer, they'd be dead meat. Simon really didn't want another bullet scar. Or death.

Bullets smashed Alex's window as the Jeep whirled around. The vehicle nearly tipped over but miraculously staying upright. Alex groaned and dropped even lower, GPS in hand, blood gushing from a gash on his head.

Spencer pushed the Jeep as fast as it would go, back the way they'd come, bullets pelting the bullet-proof Jeep. Or, supposedly it was bullet-proof, minus the windows, apparently.

RENE' HUGGED HER PARENTS goodnight, holding tight just a moment too long. It'd been a long night. Her father had taken her home at almost 12 AM and he'd gone straight to bed, exhausted from the night of survivor's telling stories and a supply load. Rene' updated her family —so many watchful, big eyes—on what was going on. After they'd asked questions and she'd answered the best she could, she went to her room, locking the door behind her. *Breathe. Deep. The day is over. God's in control. Cry if you must, but you gotta be OK.* Her shoulders sagged and she kicked her boots off, rubbing Elvis' chin as he jumped onto the bed. "It's hard to relax, bud. Everything happens so fast."

Elvis licked her hand, puppy eyes comforting. She tugged a sweatshirt on over her pajamas and crawled into bed in the darkness. Her mind wandered like it always did. She used to love the dark but now it reminded her of that cell, the cold table beneath her, and Jed's hands on her body. *It ended fine. I wasn't too hurt. Simon and the guys got me out. Jordan helped the kids I saved. Everything worked fine.*

Besides Ed dying.

Fumbling for her phone, she checked messages.

Nothing.

A pang of concern nagged at her gut. Simon wasn't usually this late. *He didn't mention any jobs he was taking today or tonight.*

She texted him. "*Si?*" Months ago, she might've thought twice at messaging him first, out of worry she'd sound clingy or childish. Now, she never thought like that. She cared too much to doubt what they had.

She watched the minutes pass on the screen. Five whole minutes and no response. Even if he were asleep, he always texted her before passing out. He knew she worried about him.

She took a slow breath and texted again, "*You OK?*"

Ten minutes passed without any response. *I asked Dad earlier if he'd talked to Si, and he hadn't, so it's been no contact since this morning when he texted me.* Rene' dialed the number. She hated the thought of waking him but she needed to make sure he was all right.

The line rang a few times before a groggy voice came through. "Hey?"

"Si? What's wrong?" Rene' sat up.

A pause. "Hey. Hey. I'm fine. Honest. What time is it?"

Her heart lodged in her chest. "Si, what happened?" she whispered. "You sound terrible."

"Naw, just, uh, tired. Um—"

"Are you on a job?"

"N-no, just got back from one."

"You didn't tell me—"

"Kinda last minute. It went fine but on the way home, Spence drove too close to rebel lines. I kinda crashed when I got to Paradise." Grogginess laced his quiet words.

"Is everyone OK?" Rene' closed her eyes.

"Yeah. Spencer got grazed but overall, God got us out." There was probably more he wasn't saying, but he didn't often go into detail of how the jobs or dangers worked themselves out. Gruesome details weren't something Simon dwelt on.

"I'm so sorry. You sleep, OK? I'm so sorry I woke you —"

"Nah, it's nice to hear your voice. I was having a bad dream anyway," he chuckled. "You OK?"

"Just fine." She'd update him on all the chaos tomorrow. "You sleep, right now. I love you."

"Love you, too."

She hung up and sucked in a deep breath, tears running down her face. He could have been killed. And she hadn't even known. *God, You're merciful... no matter what happens or how terrible things are... You're there. Thank you for protecting my family when I can't. It feels like I'm constantly helpless, but in my weakness, You are strong.*

She repeated those truths and slowly, like a small storm drifting into soft rain, her heart eased. She curled up beside her Aussie and closed her eyes. Tomorrow, she'd call Simon. One day, she'd see him again.

One day, America would be bonded and united again, and who knew? Maybe they could help rebuild it. Her, her family, Simon, everyone. Alive and strong. *Please, God.*

CHAPTER FOURTEEN

October 19th, 2027

NATE WATCHED JACK PARK his worn-out, 90's truck out front of the apartment. Jack didn't come to Paradise much—if ever—and Nate didn't have a clue where he'd gotten the new hunk of junk ride. He sat his mug of steaming coffee down onto the counter, growling.

"Who is it?" Graham came into the kitchen, a thick hardback book in his hands. "Jack and Spencer, by the looks." Nate glanced over. "Joy."

Graham pushed his glasses up onto his nose, frowning. "I still don't understand why you hate your cousin. I'd do anything for my family to love me." His voice was so quiet, Nate barely heard it. He sat down at the table and opened his book.

Nate opened his mouth to ask what he meant, but the front door opened and loud voices filled the room, the sound more grating than gunshots.

"Hey!" Spencer called. "The hot men are here!"

Simon led Spencer, Jack, and Bo into the kitchen. Simon's dark hair stuck out in all directions, the bags under his eyes proved he'd barely slept all night, and the scowl on his face made Nate pour another cup of coffee.

Graham didn't look up as the men came into the kitchen and started grabbing mugs for coffee. Spencer ruffled Graham's curls, saying, "Hey, champ. How's it going?"

"Reading." Graham mumbled.

"Keep quiet, bigmouth," Jack piped up. "Kid's got more important things to do than listen to you."

Nate eyed his cousin and handed Simon his coffee. "What are you three doing here?"

"Lovely to see you, too, ace." Bo smirked, southern accent slow and easy. Nate didn't mind Bo, besides everything about him. Loud, punchy, obsessed with girls. A real thorn in the side of the gang.

"They're here to kinda talk about everything that's happened." Simon sat down beside Graham, downing a few long gulps of hot coffee. Nate eyed Jack and Spencer. It wasn't like they weren't in the loop—they'd been in the mess since it had pretty much started.

"Oh?"

"Some stuff has changed," Jack said. He glanced at Graham uneasily.

"Hey, G man, wanna go play ball?" Bo leaned on the table and beamed at Graham. "I got a baseball and a bat in the truck."

Graham closed his book with a sigh. "OK. But only because you guys think I'm too young to keep my mouth shut." He headed outside before anyone could say otherwise. Bo followed, grimacing. When the door was closed, Jack sat down.

"Who goes first?" Simon finished his coffee and Nate poured him some more.

Jack leaned against the wooden table. "West is in Mexico."

"So?" Nate challenged.

"George put him in charge of the border that the gang runs, so the trades and deals keep going, even though the Union government is in a frenzy. It isn't an easy job. I think it's the final piece of the puzzle before George tests him." Jack ignored Nate's tone.

"The *test* Test?" Simon's face scrunched up in dismay. The Test had taken Jack's father—Uncle Hunter had been one of the best men Nate had ever loved, and he'd been killed at George's hands. George called him weak, but

Nate knew he had always been stronger. *But he's dead. Doesn't matter now.*

"Yes," Jack said simply. "This is a big order and West is already off to a great start. I think George is gonna give him the Test soon. And I... well, I promised I'd be there."

"*But.*" Spencer prodded.

Jack shot him a look that could have killed a puppy. "But," he glanced back down at his hands. "I might not be able to."

Nate frowned. "What is that supposed to mean?" "Nate, Si, there's something I haven't told you." Jack clenched his coffee mug so tight it might break into pieces. "I'm engaged. Have been for months now. And I'm going to be a dad."

All the air left Nate's head and he stared at Jack like he'd summoned a demon in Latin. "You what?"

"Whoa." Simon ran a hand over his face. "*Whoa.*"

"Whoa?" Nate snapped, gaining control of his thoughts and erupting. All these years of Jack treating Nate like he was the idiot, and Jack had gone and screwed up everything. Every time. Anger rose higher in his chest till he could barely see straight. "You *idiot!*" he hissed. "You're close to George yet you decided to up and go have a family?! Have you lost your—"

"Nate," Simon cut in, voice shaky. "Stop. Please."

"No!" Nate didn't care if Jack dropped his head like a beaten dog. He deserved everything he got. "What the hell were you thinking?"

Spencer lifted a hand. "I know this is bad but there's more going on than Jack's personal life."

"Stay out of this!" Nate slammed a hand down onto the table, causing the coffee mugs to splash with coffee.

Jack lifted his head wearily. "It's fine, Spencer. He's right. I—"

"Don't give me that bull!" Nate snapped. "You knew better. You knew choosing a family was freaking stupid. They're gonna get killed. You couldn't keep it in your pants, and now, West is gonna suffer for it. *Everyone* suffers because of your mistakes!" He couldn't shut up. Didn't want to. Years of rage and hate and pain struck at the walls he'd built around his heart. He hadn't known Jack had a girl or was gonna be a father and who knew who else. *He doesn't care about me. Never has.*

"West isn't gonna suffer," Spencer said sharply. "If Jack can't stop the Test, I will. I've got Bo and Nabeel, we're some of George's best, we can interfere."

Nate laughed out loud. "You three are gonna go against George? At least Jack had the advantage of being near bloodkin—you guys can be replaced!"

"Hey!" Spencer stepped closer, facing Nate head on. "At least we're doing something, Nathan. You come running back to daddy to play him like a fiddle—who are you to bite Jack's head off for trying to have a family?"

"He cares more about his selfish gain than the innocent lives already at stake. I might be a freak but at least I'm not stupid enough to make a family. I have enough to care for and I won't fail my brothers," Nate spat, eyes on Jack as he spoke words of venom. Spencer stayed between them but Jack dropped his head as if every word stabbed through his heart. *Good. Let him feel what I've felt for years.*

"Nathan, shut up!" Simon stood up sharply. "We can handle this later. What else is there, Spencer?" He seemed sure there was something else important to be said, but this didn't calm Nate down any.

Spencer sighed. "Gideon found out something about Springtown." Simon paled a shade. "What?"

"We found out certain towns and civilizations in North America can be "paid off". There are people, suppliers of sorts, who pay the government, gangsters, and powers that be, in order to protect the towns. The towns are pretty much left alone." Spencer explained carefully, rubbing his temples. "We figure Springtown is being protected by a supplier."

"Who? Why?" Simon pressed.

"I don't know." Spencer shook his head. "No answers, big guy. We don't know who is protecting Springtown, why they are, nada. Gideon's on the case, though."

"Lots of help he'll be," Nate scoffed bitterly.

"He lost his own men guarding the town." Spencer cut his eyes at him, voice cold. "He might do bad things for good means, but don't act like any of us could do better, kid."

"When did we find this out?" Simon insisted. "Does Mr. Fisher know? Does George know?"

"George knows, yeah, but he wouldn't tell us who supplied Springtown's protection. He kinda told Gideon to drop it."

"He talked to Gideon about it?" Simon sucked in a breath.

"Yeah." Spencer hesitated. "Kinda ties in, doesn't it? He knew Springtown was being protected even before he knew you two were giving supplies. Maybe that's why he wasn't so mad. Who knows."

Nate bit his lip. Spencer was playing mediator, trying to focus Simon's attention on the town, but Nate wasn't easily swayed. He watched Jack but Jack didn't make a sound.

"We'll save West." Spencer jutted his chin. "Like it or not, Nate, we're all we have. We need each other. Mistakes or no mistakes, we're in this hell together."

Simon nodded but his tense jaw and bulging neck vein ruined his brave act. "Yeah."

"Anyway, Mr. Fisher hasn't been told yet. Gideon wanted to talk to you first, Simon." Spencer picked up his coffee. "That's about all we got. You guys know the UN has ruffled feathers and the nations are mad about the Union and Confeds, but the rebels still have the high ground. We can't be blind sided. If West and Springtown mean anything to us, we need to handle all of this at once."

"We can do it," Simon said quietly. He held so much resolve and strength.

All I hold is hate. Nate bit his lip even harder.

"Do not push your noses into this," Spencer continued. "Gideon doesn't want help—he can handle this job in secrecy and we can't—but he just wanted you in the loop."

"He couldn't be here to tell us himself?" Nate smirked tightly. He was seconds away from erupting, going all out, but after years of Kaleb's training, he remained silent. Collected. Deep inside, he had control, and letting sharp comments slip would let the others think he had already blown his top.

"Cut the crap." Spencer raised his eyebrows. "Jack's been beating himself for months now. No need to add to that."

"Drop it." Simon butted in calmly. He didn't want Nate to explode. Nate wouldn't, but only because he didn't want Kaleb to think he was losing his "good behavior."

Spencer sighed and turned away. Jack hadn't moved an inch from where he sat, shoulders hunched. *He should have used his head. He should be out here suffering with the rest of us, but he's been off hiding like a coward.*

"I'm sorry, Nathan." Jack didn't lift his head. "You're right. About all of it."

Nate opened his mouth to retort but the last two phrases rang in his head. *I'm not falling for that tactic.* "Anything else we should know?" he asked Spencer.

Spencer rinsed his coffee mug out. "I think those things are pretty much it for now. If something changes, we'll let you know."

THE LAST TIME SIMON recalled seeing Jack and Spencer look so defeated, Ed had been killed, and Ty and Rene' lay dying in AJ's house. The two men didn't show a lot of negative emotions. It was vital for them to always have it together. Yet, here they were, vulnerable, openly unsure as to where could possibly be done beside the human nature survivalist mindset of "it has to be done, even if I don't know how yet".

And it made Simon's chest ache.

Humans were made for more than survival. Jack had a right to family, didn't he? Sitting at the table with an ashen face, at least fifteen pounds thinner than the last time

Simon had seen him, Jack looked far from OK. *Is he happy about his girl and the baby? Or is something bad going on? Nate's so quick to shut him down—he could need us. But how am I supposed to help him?*

How am I supposed to help anyone?

The front door burst open and heavy footsteps filled Simon's ears. Graham stepped in, clutching his bleeding nose, Bo leading him by the shoulders.

Simon jumped up and stepped over. "What happened?!"

"I-I might've hit him in the face with a baseball." Bo admitted sheepishly.

Nate wetted a rag, ordering Graham to sit. Graham did but a strange choking sound escaped him. A laugh. He laughed and laughed as Nate held the rag to his nose.

"Stop laughing," Nate said. "You'll suffocate."

"What's wrong with you, Bo?" Simon turned back to Bo, fists clenching.

"I'm sorry!" Bo lifted his hands in surrender. "Honest!"

"Not his fault," Graham stuttered. "Too slow. Didn't catch it." He spoke awkwardly, trying to breathe and stop laughing all at once. Nate held his shoulder gently.

"Well, that's one way to learn the game." Spencer smirked. "You OK, G?""Yeah." Graham sat still, holding the rag to his nose.

"Where are his glasses?" Simon frowned, worrying like a mother hen but someone had to do it. Graham was too fragile to be treated like a baseball player. Simon liked baseball but it wasn't fit for the curly-haired teen.

"Outside on the porch. I told him to take them off." Bo hurried off to grab them.

"You're not getting a medal for it!" Simon called after him.

"Easy," Graham mumbled. "He's nice. Just trying to help."

Simon groaned, running a hand through his hair. Everything in his life had just been shattered into jigsaw pieces. He shouldn't take it out on Bo. "Sorry." He didn't know what to do with himself but he just had to keep it together till the guys left.

Bo came back in and set the wide-brimmed glasses onto the table. "I'm really sorry, Graham."

"No problem." Graham smiled a little. The blood flow ceased and he dropped his eyes, embarrassed by the attention.

"Uh, well..." Spencer noticed his unease and straightened. Spencer was good at that sort of thing. Usually. "We'll head out. Bo and Nabeel have a job I'm tagging along for."

"Shut up." Bo rolled his eyes. He patted Graham on the back lightly. "You good?"

Graham gave a thumbs up. "Are you... coming back for another lesson?"

"It's a coaching session, and sure." Bo grinned and headed outside with Spencer. Simon left Graham with Nate, following Jack outside into the crisp winter air.

"Jack... Is everything OK?" Dumb question. Nothing was OK.

"No." Jack didn't expound his answer.

"I mean, are you... happy?" Another dumb term.

"What?""You don't seem thrilled about the whole husband and dad gig." Simon regretted saying such a thing but it was too late to take his words back.

Jack gulped hard, Adam's apple bobbing. "No, I am. But Nate is right. I've failed West when he needs me the most. I didn't keep my head in the game and now, others are suffering for it. Mels and the baby will suffer, too. I'm a thug. The world knows it and I can't change it."

Simon scoffed and stepped closer, inches from his friend. For a moment, he understood Jack. The nagging voice in his gut, the one that insisted he was powerless to protect his loved ones, lifted it's head. But this time, Simon wouldn't let it stay. "Don't give me that," he said quietly. "You've got two families now. You can handle it. You aren't the first one to. No matter what happens, we can do whatever we can to win."

Jack blinked, looking toward the truck where Bo and Spencer waited. "And if I fail?"

"You won't. We won't fail. God's with us. He's gotta be. He'll provide when we can't. But we gotta do it for ourselves, man. We gotta push on no matter what mistakes we make." Simon smirked a little. Something burnt inside his spirit. Something bold. Something unquenchable. Something not of his own.

Jack took a slow breath and squared his shoulders. His weary eyes flickered with life. "You're right."

"More than Nate is."

"As usual." Jack tried cracking a smile.

Simon patted his arm. "We've got West's back. We can figure out the deal with Springtown. You focus on your family." As firm and faithful as he sounded, the words tasted almost bitter on his tongue. It wasn't right for him to be jealous, he'd read it plenty of times in the Bible, but it didn't seem... fair. *Life isn't fair. But if I work hard, and God's merciful, maybe I can have a family one day, too. Maybe I can stop being a slave.*

No. I'm not a slave. God's with me—I'm doing His will. Aren't I?

He didn't let such a question linger.

"Bye, Simon." Jack headed to the truck and pulled out his keys.

"See you guys." Simon went inside, locked the door, and forced himself to stop. He tried to process all the news but Nate's sharp voice from the kitchen cut him short.

"What did you say to him?"

"I told him we could handle this." Simon came in and started making something to eat for them. Graham sat quietly, nose cleaned up and now in his book again.

"Yeah. *We*. Lotta help Mr. Jack *Noble* is." Nate opened the fridge, looking for a beer, judging by the look on his face. Simon had kept it out of the house. Nate slammed the fridge door shut.

"Nate—"

"Don't *Nate* me. Even you have had the chance to screw around and you haven't. He has *no* excuse."

"I'm not saying he does," Simon said. He wished Nate would shut up. He wished he could think of everything in silence instead of clashing heads all the time. "What's done is done. Whether we like it or not, we gotta deal with it."

Nate swore under his breath. "What do we do?"

"I'm gonna talk to Kaleb." A terrible idea, probably, but Simon needed more answers, and Kaleb was the best shot he had.

NATE WENT FOR A walk to clear his head. His cellphone rang, interrupting his luxurious silence—Ben

Bordalli, AJ's best friend and one of the most annoying old timer's Nate knew. Ben was the biker gang's farmer, who both teased Nate mercilessly and had his back when other bikers got too rough with him. AJ was Nate's rock. Ben had slowly morphed into a weird uncle who was either ribbing Nate over how he styled his hair or trying to teach him more about the Bible.

Right now, Nate didn't want to talk to him. He ignored Ben most of the time, anyway. But he answered with a growl, "What?"

"Lovely to hear your voice," Ben chuckled. "I had a feeling I oughtta call.""One of your God feelings?" Nate snapped.

"Yep, one of those. You all right? Sound rough."

Nate couldn't tell him the details of what he'd just been informed about, but he mumbled, "Just family issues."

"Jack?""Yeah. How'd you—""Y'know, you don't talk much about Jack." Ben's voice was gentle. "I had a brother like that."

"Like what?" Nate walked down the sidewalk, focusing on his steps and his surroundings, but no one messed with him.

"The big hero who left the person he should've protected behind."

Simple words that cut Nate deep. Too deep. "I'm fine —"

"Sure you are. Just like I was. But life goes on, Nathan, and you can't protect yourself with hatred forever. My brother was killed. I never got the chance to apologize to him, and maybe, he never got to apologize to me, either. I don't want to see you become the same person I am," Ben said softly.

"You don't seem that bad." Nate bit his lip. He'd never guessed Ben had had a temper at some point in his life.

"I think that's the closest you've ever come to complimenting me." The old timer laughed. "Thanks. But the point still stands. Do better than me, Nathan. Whatever has happened, whatever you have to do, do better than what you think you can."

Nate clenched his jaw. He almost told Ben off—he wasn't his boss, he barely knew him, but Nate stopped. Ben had helped AJ save his life, and Rene's life. He gulped down his pride, forcing, "Thanks for the call, Ben."

"I'm praying for you, boy. If you ever need to reach out, God's there to help."

"Yeah, so Si tells me." *I don't need God. Not yet. He wants too much.*

CHAPTER FIFTEEN

October 21st, 2027

MEXICO HAD BEEN A beautiful place before the gang activity and raging war. West remembered the few trips his parents had taken him on to the Mexican towns and beaches—he'd adored the trips as a kid. They rarely did normal, relaxing things as a family. He figured Cindy had fought hard to make her husband give West even a few days a year of bliss instead of punishment or tests.

Mexico wasn't like it used to be, just like America wasn't the same.

The border wall, which originally had been made strong only years before, now had weak points and annihilated sections that people passed through. The largest passageway was guarded by George's men at all times. A small militia base had been built on either side to protect it. Only traders and people who could pay well were allowed in or out. Because of this, only gangsters bothered using it when they had goods or slaves to move. Most civilians were sent away or shot down.

West took a deep breath as he looked the base over. *It's my job to maintain the peace and keep things working smoothly.* After a few days, such a feat proved to be more difficult than he thought. The base was full of Americans, most of which were blatantly Union, and Mexicans. Some were gangsters and some were just civilians. Most of the men obeyed orders, but many tested West, challenged his leadership. While he didn't blame them, he had almost expected them to roll over for him—he was a Johnston, after all. But he'd been foolish to let that expectation linger.

The Alamo, which was the ironic name chosen before West arrived, wasn't a large base but it had enough men to man, ship, and handle the transactions. West didn't trust any of the men but tried to learn what made them tick. Juan, one of the higher ranks, was a brutal man but worked at the border only to feed his family. Ricardo was one of the top ranks, as well, a younger man with enough intimidation to make a rhino cower. West noticed the others, of course, but Juan and Ricardo were vital leads. Juan led most of the men in allegiance and worked hard to help West and do as he said. Ricardo stirred the men and pushed them for trouble: he didn't think West was to be trusted.

West spent day after day working his rear end off. The security systems had to be checked and protected and he made sure that was done daily. Sentries stationed along the border had to call frequently to ensure their position was maintained and without breach. He was kept busy with ensuring everyone did their jobs right—the base needed more supplies and countless repairs.

Gazing at the shack-like tents the men lived in, West turned away and went back into the main building. Juan had offered him the office in the building, and though West disliked giving himself better treatment than his own group, he had things he had to do in private. They couldn't overhear his plans with Gideon.

"We have word from tomorrow's shipment," Ricardo approached him at the door, his broad arms crossed against his chest. As usual, he wore tan pants, a green t-shirt, and a gun and a knife on his belt. He stuck out from the others by his utter refusal to ever smile unless he was laughing at someone less fortunate.

"Did they cancel?"

"No." Ricardo quickly walked beside him, refusing to follow in any shape or fashion. "Seven AM sharp. They've got ten girls and five boys."

West worked his jaw. "We'll send them to Jed in Arizona?"

"We could send them to the moon, if you think they'd like that trip better." Ricardo bit icily.

West chuckled at the jab. "Any trip is better than the one they're about to go on." *They've probably already faced hell. I can't save them. I can't save everyone. I'm leading slaves into another world of hell—and I can't do anything about it.* He shut the emotions off as soon as they pricked his conscience.

"They have it no worse than anyone else." Ricardo cut his black eyes at him.

West held his tongue. No sense arguing morals with the man. "I'll get the men ready for tomorrow. Good work."

"I can get them ready." Ricardo tossed his hair. He mumbled something else in Spanish and West had half the mind to swear back at him in Spanish to prove his point. "You aren't needed here, Johnston. Don't you have bigger fish to fry?"

West smirked. "I do. But George placed me here."

"That's the problem with you rich Americans—you never question orders." Ricardo muttered. "You're a—" They rounded the hallway corner and Ricardo nearly bumped into Juan.

The older man smiled at them both. "Good news! The west side is restored—no sleeping out in the elements tonight for group D." He clasped West on the shoulder. "Thank you for your help, *señor*."

Uneasy at both the praise and being called sir by a man near George's age, West smiled. "You have all worked to earn that much." It wasn't much, compared to the things he wanted to do: sneak Juan a few extra hundred dollars to really help his wife and three kids. Relieve the fourteen and sixteen year old boys working in group C. But he couldn't do that, yet.

Ricardo scoffed. "He can build shacks but let's see how well he handles this shipment. Some of the roughest guys we trade with will be here at seven. If we touch a hair on any of the slaves' heads, Jed will have ours." There was a snicker to his words though he had never been one to mess around on the job.

Juan's smile diminished and his broad jowls stiffened. "We best prepare."

***

SEVEN AM SHARP, A large white truck skittered across the Mexican sand. At the wall, every man stood ready and in position, some behind the lines and some stationed at the top of the border. West maintained a fluid order of things, and most of the men kept good time. He wasn't a Green Beret, for sure, but he wasn't a limp noodle.

The truck stopped before the border. The guards kept a few guns aimed at the vehicle in case anything got out of hand. This group of workers weren't known for civility. West left his spot at the gate shack and approached the truck, head held high, gun on his side. The driver's window rolled down and a tall, broad Mexican eyed West with derision. "You Johnston's boy?"

"I'm West." West glanced at the back of the truck. "Let's keep it simple. Open up."

The man slipped out of the truck and walked to the back, popping the lock. Once the doors swung open, a couple unwelcomed stenches jumped at West's nostrils and he set his jaw. As the deal stated, ten females and five males sat crowded in the back, most bloodied, bruised. He ignored the wide-eyed and dead-eyed stares of the victims and turned back to the man. "All right. Let me see the papers."

The man nodded to another guy who'd gotten out of the passenger side. The mustached guy thrust a small stack of papers at West.

West checked the papers over carefully: they were proof that the kids had been cleared. Cleared meaning they had completely disappeared off the face of the planet and couldn't easily be found by the government. He pictured the innocent kids behind him in the van and steeled himself.

"OK," he said, handing the papers over. "That passes. We'll sweep the truck."

The men exchanged glares and stood by. West waved a few men over. They searched every nook and cranny of the truck, inside and out, ensuring there were no unreported drugs, bombs, or artillery. Once it was cleared, West gave the men the go-ahead. They got into their truck, mumbling in Spanish. West gave the order that they be allowed through.

Ricardo stepped over beside West, his dark hair dripping with sweat—Mexico didn't care it was fall. "I don't like the looks of them," he muttered.

The truck passed through and sped onto the beaten-up road that'd lead them into the US. West eyed Ricardo. "They're thugs. That's the idea."

"They'll come back to bite us. Just wait."

"If they come back and cause trouble, we'll handle them." West smirked. "Unless you're afraid of a little gunfire, *amigo*?""I do not understand why my president would ever agree to allowing you here." Ricardo headed to the mess hall. West pondered the man's words. He did need to stay alert—they might have entered America relatively harmless, but they could exit it in a fury of fire. It wasn't unheard of. *I have to keep ready. I have to strengthen this border.* First, he'd contact Jordan, letting Simon's father know that he needed to go rescue fifteen kids. Then, he'd call Tyler, apologize for being so blasted late, and try to get his little brother to open with him.

CHAPTER SIXTEEN

October 22nd, 2027

"THE WAR IS HELL and we're all gonna die." A man's laughing voice came from the bar to Simon's left. As fast as Simon tried to walk down the sidewalk, he couldn't ignore the voices. The men weren't flat out drunk, since Kaleb didn't allow such behaviour in Paradise. Nate killing Brock for throwing a party and assaulting Graham a few months or so ago had only strengthened the base's healthy fear of the rule. But these men were getting close to the edge, Simon heard it in their laughs.

"I'd rather die as I am than join a side," another voice sneered. "Union, rebels, they're all idiots."

Simon bit his lip and avoided a hole in the sidewalk, hands in his pockets. The cold air washed over him, chapping his lips. He gave the men a brief smile of acknowledgement—maybe they'd remember to lay off the liquor if they saw the man who helped end Brock's teenage life.

They eyed him, all right, but one shouted, "What do you think, Si? Is Kaleb gonna send us off to war like lil' soldier boys, too?" Simon slowed his steps. *Don't stop. Keep moving.* But he couldn't hide his rage anymore. "Kaleb sent *willing* men. He made sure of it. You don't wanna fight? Don't worry about it. Kaleb won't make you put your purses down." *Crap. Should've left that last part out.* He started walking again, fully expecting the men to chase after him. They didn't. They bickered and swore behind his back.

Simon honestly disliked confrontation. Especially since becoming a Christian—his mind was often at war with his heart. His heart wanted to jump in, head first, and follow God. But that meant learning about God and His Word. That wasn't easy, even though Rene' and her father, Mr. Fisher, were pretty good at sharing the Bible. Despite working hard for almost a year now, Simon often felt just as stuck as the other gangsters who didn't know Jesus. How could he help them if he didn't have all the answers?

How can I help them when I can't help Nate choose God? I can't help Graham's nightmares stop? I can't end this stupid war? It was all too much to carry. Simon knew he needed to hand it over to God. Usually, he did. Some moods were harder to let go than others.

Simon hurried the last stretch and practically ran into Kaleb's house. Kaleb glanced up from the kitchen table, eyebrows furrowed, blond hair disheveled. "Boy, what is your problem?"

"Cold." Simon lied, locking the door behind himself. "You wanted to talk?" He'd dreaded the conversation all day and was five minutes early, but considering he'd wanted to swing by two hours earlier, he was doing good. The busier he kept himself, the less time he had to doubt himself.

Kaleb scoffed and leaned back. "You're early."

"Yeah, well, Nate was driving me crazy over the job you gave us. He's got cabin fever and the job has got his gears all grinding." Simon pulled out a chair, straddling it.

"Well, you both wanted to work." Kaleb chuckled.

"What's this about?"

"Always do jump the gun, don't you, son? Just like your dad."

Simon held his tongue. He had considered calling his father and asking him to step in and give Kaleb a talking to, but decided against it. No use in acting like a baby, even if Kaleb was.

"This is about you and Nate's little speech the other day. Remember that?" Kaleb quirked one eyebrow, gesturing at the scarring gash on Simon's head. "You being banged up and all, not sure if you do."

"I remember." Simon smirked dryly.

"I've been thinking about what you two said…" Kaleb rubbed his temples. The words probably tasted like vinegar on his tongue—he'd never been one to admit to considering anyone else's ideas. Especially not Nate's.

"Yeah?""Yeah. You two have worked hard, but I know it's been nothing but a sham to gain knowledge so you can run again," he paused to watch Simon's reaction.

Simon's eyes widened and his throat dried up. "What makes you say that?" *He knew all this time?!*

"I'm not stupid, despite what you teenagers may think." Kaleb stood and grabbed a beer from the fridge, popping the cap off. "You two only came back from your little adventure of playing rogues because you needed protection, more supplies, and experience."

Simon's heart hammered. *Lie. He can't know the truth —lie! We've worked too hard to get where we are and gain his trust.* "Kaleb, that's not true." *Try again.* "We decided to come back because—"

"Don't bother, boy." Kaleb lifted a large, calloused hand. "I knew your motives before Nate came into that bar to tell me he was game."

Simon worked his jaw for a long moment. "And?"

"And... I gotta admire it." Kaleb's lips twitched in a smirk. "You're both pretty stupid for thinking you could pull one over me, but, still, you're back. You can do more with me than you could alone."

"We know."

"Obviously." Kaleb sat down into the creaky wooden chair. "Now, you two want more freedom. I don't think you grasp just how dire the war is right now."

"The war is a fight for freedom. If I can't exercise some freedom, what's the point?" Simon frowned.

"Don't get smart with me."

"Well, you're talking slow. What's this meeting about?" *I'm asking to get punched. Shouldn't talk this way to him but... I'm tired of kneeling. Isn't doing us much good to bow down to him, anyway.*

"I will be extending freedom to you and Nate, but with conditions." Kaleb took another swig of beer.

"Like what?" Simon held his temper in check. *Can gang leaders not talk like normal people? Do they sign some creed of "I must talk ominously at all times?"*

"You can't just run off when you please." Kaleb smirked. "You guys can visit Springtown, so long as they don't change their minds and try to kill you."

Simon hesitated. *Does he know that Springtown is protected? Has he known this whole time? Probably. But I can't test it or show that I know.* "Sounds like freedom," he said wryly.

Kaleb leaned forward, elbows on the table. "Sounds like you don't want it."

"No, I just... I wish you'd come out with it, sir."

"Pushy like your dad, too." Kaleb rolled his eyes. "As I was saying, you two can visit, but you tell me when you go and you don't stay gone for long. It's dangerous out there, Simon. You two might be seasoned fighters and have plenty of street smarts, but we're in a warzone. There is no point in taking unnecessary risks by gallivanting around alone all the time.""Why let us go if you think it's stupid?"

"You deserve—"

"No. If you're so worried about our safety, and us getting dragged into the grand old Second Civil War, you don't have to pull the "you guys deserve happiness" card. That's not what this is about, is it?" Simon asked, calm and collected, though his stomach flipped. *Bad idea, bad idea, why can't I keep my mouth shut?*

Kaleb sipped his beer for a long moment. "Kentucky is a border state, but it leans more Union, right?""I know."

"And Springtown is a conservative town in no man's land, right?"

Simon frowned. "Yeah?" *He knows, too...*

"And you, after what, a year of helping drop supplies, haven't stopped and wondered why they made it this far and haven't been wiped off the map?"

"I have."

"Got any answer?" "They're well armed, got some able-bodied, but no, I never did figure out the logical explanation of why no gang or caravan ever took over." Simon admitted, waiting for Kaleb to spring the news on him, news Simon already knew now. *Would've been nice if he'd let us know sooner.*

Kaleb sat his empty bottle down. "Because as far as you know, there is no coincidence, so it must be impossible. They probably chalk it up to some grand miracle of God," his smirk grew taut. "But it isn't."

"Then what is it?" Simon's chest grew uneasy with concern. Why was Kaleb pointing all of this out now? What did he have planned?

"I'm going to tell you something and you must swear to keep it a secret, besides telling Nate, no matter the consequences."

Simon licked his lips. "OK."

"Springtown has been protected since the war began by a supplier—a man who pays off incorpoprations and gangs to ensure the town stands alone. I do not know the supplier's identity—no one does besides George—but it's time you two understood it."

"Why?" *Wait, I should look surprised. Look surprised, Simon.*

"Because the war is going to end soon and it is going to end in a bloodbath and chaotic disaster." A vein in Kaleb's neck bulged. "I do not want to lose you two to the chaos, Simon. Anything could happen if you aren't close to me. The Union or Confeds could grab you, politicians could have you kidnapped and tortured to get to me or Jordan, anything." He took a slow, deep breath. Simon hadn't seen him so worried looking before, at least, not when someone wasn't injured or dying.

"OK, but...?"

"You two have also proven yourself capable, and while I want to protect you, I know you'll leave again. I can't afford that. I'm going to work with you two, give you the freedom to see the town, so long as you take a few jobs, maintain your rep in the gang, and help me with intel." Kaleb tapped his empty beer bottle, watching Simon's reaction like a hawk.

"Intel?" The hair on the back of Simon's neck stood up. "What sorta intel? You said you didn't know the supplier?" "I don't, but Springtown will most likely play a vital part in the future of this nation—if it is to unite once again, in any form or fashion. To lose the town to destruction would be a pity the nation cannot afford, period." Kaleb's eyes narrowed. "Do you follow?"

"I don't understand. I think Springtown should be protected, and if some phantom is doing that, so be it. What could Springtown possibly do for the nation? You honestly think the war is gonna end and everything goes back to normal?" Simon could hardly control his surprise —and slight, naive hope.

"The war will end, as wars do, but nothing ever returns to normal. Wars leave scars on the DNA of humanity and once DNA is altered, there is little to do to fix the blemish." Kaleb shuddered. Simon blinked at the motion but Kaleb quickly continued on as if nothing had happened, "Springtown is a stable town with good men and a solid justice system. When the war ends, the nation will need men like those civilians, it will need them as a beacon of hope."

"OK..." Simon exhaled. "I think I follow. Springtown's got someone paying off bad guys, but instead of figuring out who it is, you want Nate and I to join up again to make sure the town stays safe... because the town is gonna be important to the nation." His blood boiled just thinking about Kaleb's mindset. Springtown deserved protection because it held lives, innocent lives, good lives. How many other towns had been demolished because they had been unimportant? How many innocents had died already?

"More or less. I don't want you two handling supplies —too risky, leave that to Jack and Tyler." Kaleb nodded.

"What do we do, then? Intel? You said you didn't want answers?"

"The supplier doesn't matter. I need you two to play mediator between that town and the nation."

"What?" Simon blanched.

Kaleb laughed. "In a sense, anyway. You'll be reporting back to me the moods of the men, their plans—"

"You want me to be a spy?" Simon shot out of his chair like he'd been stung by a mad hornet.

Kaleb cocked his head up at him. "I want you to help me help Springtown. Our alliance with Mr. Fisher would very much be a private matter, at first, to be on the safe side."

Alliance? The word slowly sank into Simon's head and his jaw dropped. "You...?"

"I am going to offer Springtown an alliance with my men and myself, under George's goodwill."

A knock on the front door rang in Simon's ears and he moved toward it, hand falling to the gun at his side.

"It's just Rob." Kaleb sighed. "Let him in."

Simon obeyed, unlocking the door to let Robert ease in. Robert was one of Kaleb's best special ops and specialized in assassinations. Simon didn't know many names of the men Robert had killed, and he didn't want to know. As far as Simon knew him, he'd been the guy hanging on the outskirts of his whole life. Robert used to help Jordan, Simon's Dad, set up birthday gifts for Simon and Nate back in the day. Robert had refurbished Simon's first car for Simon's 16th birthday. Nate never let Robert get close, but Simon knew that the assassin meant a great deal to both of them.

Right now, Simon wasn't happy to see him. "I'm trying to talk to Kaleb. What do you need?" he growled.

Robert smiled, amused by Simon's annoyance. "Must've interrupted something, huh?" "Kinda." Simon stepped back. Robert shut the door behind him.

Kaleb studied Robert closely and poured himself another glass of alcohol. "We'll chat later, Si." His tone left no room for argument.

"But—" Simon was known for ignoring blatant requests.

"This is important, too, Simon." Kaleb eyed him. "Goodnight."

Simon looked between them before storming outside.

Maybe Robert had killed someone. Maybe they had some big plan in the works. That's all the gangs were, anyway. A bunch of lethal plans and webs. Simon was getting tired of it. *Maybe I should work with Jordan. I could help him save kids. Heck, maybe Rene' would want to help us help kids and victims in the sex trafficking.*

But I don't want Rene' in danger and I don't want to leave her.

He was stuck where he was, in the balance of a normalish life with Rene' and the reality that he was a ganglord's son and lived in a gang. And that meant death.

God... If You're listening... I could use some help right now. I'm sorry I doubt myself—I doubt You—so much. I try to sound like I have it together with Nate. I guess I do, usually. But it's all getting to my head. I need Your help. We all do. Simon headed down the sidewalk but the thugs outside of the bar watched him silently when he passed this time.

Simon hesitated, then called out, "We're all gonna die, whether it's on the battlefield or in an alley. Only choice we've got is where we're going."

The drunk men didn't respond. But maybe, one day, they would. Maybe Simon was in Paradise for a reason. Maybe he could minister to the drunks if his own brother didn't listen.

CHAPTER SEVENTEEN

October 25th, 2027

RENE' FINISHED DUMPING FEED for the horses in the pasture, rubbing Sugar's furry rump before heading to the barn. Dax was out riding with a friend of his, and once he got home, she'd be helping him with chores. Terri had her kiddos at home and Mrs. Fisher was helping her clean up for the day. Lee had gone to a friend's house, probably to discuss his militia movement some more. Rene' and Dax had the house to themselves for a while. A rare treat.

She put the bucket up in the tack room, leaned against the wall. She wasn't quite as tired anymore—not the deep exhaustion that settled in your bones and made every breath a weary process. Everyone was tired, but their spirits had slowly revived the past couple weeks. Her father had organized more church time among the community. What had most often simply been the Fisher family and a few friends coming to the farm to pray, read the Word, and sing, had grown into joining the churches and holding services together as a town.

Many families attended the Sunday services, more than Rene' had expected. A few pastors stepped up to the plate and worked together to ensure no one was run too thin—though, in post-apocalyptic America, fellowship was more important than ever. Or, Rene' thought so.

Lord, help the town. We're afraid of the war, we're afraid for the men who ran away to fight, and we've still got winter to hold out to. But You're blessing us. We'll trust You.

Rene' leaned against the wall a moment longer, absently running her fingers over a few carved initials in the wood. Her family had built the barn and carved their initials the day it was finished. T.F. for Terri Fisher, back before Terri got married. R.F. for Rene'. Beneath her tiny carvings, L.F for Lee, back before he could carve well. Under his own, in larger carving, K.F.

"Rene'!" A loud, urgent voice shouted from outside. Rene' started and ran outside of the barn. The farmyard was empty besides a few chickens who had escaped their pen. A pounding sound came from behind the barn and she hurried after it.

"What?" she called.

"*Rene*!" A teenage boy on horseback tore into the farmyard, a sopping wet body draped in front of him. "It's Dax! Help me!" The young boy cried.

Dax. That's Dax's body.

Something flipped in Rene'. She ran over and grabbed Dax. "Hold the horse steady. Be still." She ordered, carefully lifting Dax's body off the mount. If the boy's horse had been any taller, or Dax any larger, she wouldn't have been able to do such a thing.

"Something spooked his horse and he fell into the creek and hit his head," the boy sobbed.

Rene' pulled Dax against herself, supporting his head, and lowered him to the ground. The left side of his head poured blood. "Ride to Terri's. Get Henry. *Go!*"

The boy kicked his horse into action and tore off onto the dirt road.

Rene' took off her coat, using the inside of it in hopes it was clean, and gently pressed it against Dax's head wound. *I can't get him into the house without risking hurting his head more.* She couldn't tell how deep or how bad the gash in her nephew's head was. The sight of blood turned her stomach.

"Dax?" She choked. *Calm. Be calm.* "Dax, baby?" He didn't wake up, but she found his pulse, watched his chest rise and fall slowly. "Jesus, save him. *Please*." She held the wound and begged God to make the blood stop flowing.

An eternity later—or was it less than two minutes—Henry's truck roared into the driveway. He jumped out, ran over, Terri on his heels, and scooped up his eldest son carefully. Terri helped get them into the car and then crawled in, keeping pressure applied to Dax's head. Rene' shut the door behind her and watched Henry drive down the road.

Rene' hurried to Terri's, staying with the kids while her parents went to the hospital to wait. She busied herself with cleaning, helping the kids with some school, and trying not to break. Lee got word of the accident hours afterward and rushed over. Rene' watched him and Danny hitch their horses outside before bursting into Terri's home.

"What happened?" Lee demanded, breathless. Danny had followed him inside but stood tentatively, face pale with fear. He'd hardly known Dax but looked awfully afraid.

"Dax and Andy had an accident while riding. Dax fell into the creek and hit his head. I haven't gotten any updates yet." Rene' forced her voice to be steady. The kids were in the living room doing school, all quiet with fear for their brother. She didn't want them to hear Lee's panic.

Lee swore. "Where—"

"Everyone's at the hospital." Rene' stopped him.

"I'm gonna ride to town to check them, I'll radio." He tore back out of the house. Danny followed, casting Rene' a weak, almost apologetic glance before the door slammed shut behind him. Rene' clamped her eyes shut briefly before heading into the living room. She sat with the kids, comforted them, and prayed.

RENE' SLIPPED INTO THE Springtown courthouse after dinnertime, her mind numb, her heart tugged in a thousand different directions. Dax had a concussion and blood loss, but the doctor assured them nothing of lasting consequence. He'd be just fine and would heal quickly, so that morning, a day after his accident, they'd taken him home. His siblings had barely been convinced to leave his room so he could rest. Rene' had worked hard feeding everyone, cleaning, offering her family comfort, and trying to keep it together.

Keep it together.

She'd gotten a call from Bethany, who'd offered to bring her over some ginger root tea, which Rene' disliked but was in high supply. Rene' suggested they go to work instead. Tyler and Jack were bringing a small shipment. Bethany was willing to miss the chance to see Tyler just to give Rene' some rest, but Rene' wouldn't let such a thing happen. Bethany and Tyler deserved to see each other.

The courthouse was strangely quiet at that hour. No one had been told about the shipment, probably, so it could be quiet and simple. *I'm fifteen minutes late. The truck's still outside, maybe I didn't miss seeing them. God, please, let Jack have some updates about Si and Nate. Simon glosses over things too much, I need to know he's really OK.*

Mr. Fisher was at the courthouse, in the office with the door shut but she could hear him. And another voice came quietly. Jack. She bit her lip and headed downstairs. She wanted to check in, but she simply couldn't handle seeing her father's exhaustion in his weary eyes. If she were honest with herself, she'd cry if she had to force another smile for him. Dax's accident had shaken them all, and Rene' hadn't had the strength to plaster on a whole lot of hopeful smiles or encouraging words.

Rene' headed down the stairs. She turned the corner, running straight into a man and jumping. Temper flaring, she grabbed the railing. "Hey!"

"Hey yourself," Quinn snapped. Quinn, one of the troublemaking bullies that was only one year older than she was. "What are you doing?"

"Going to help stock shelves." She jutted her chin. "What are you doing?"

"No one's stocking anything." He didn't back up, one stair step below her but still taller than she was. She refused to budge back or move sideways. "You still cryin' over Dax?"

"Are you still beggin' for painkillers?"

He smirked. "You know something, Rene'? It's a big world out there. You can't play hero forever. I hear folks whisper how strong you are—but most of 'em? They think you're weak. You should do yourself a favor and stay home." He said the last words in a sharp snap.

Rene' clenched her fists. Her heart ached like a knife hung there. *It's not true. I know it isn't.* "It is a big world, and I'll do what it takes to make sure this town stays in it." She tried stepping past him.

He grabbed her arm. "I'm warning you."

She slapped him hard, realizing too late what she'd done. Time froze—but Quinn didn't hit her. Didn't push her down the stairs. He let go and laughed bitterly, "It's hopeless. You people are gonna get yourselves killed."

Rene' turned and hurried down the stairs, blinded by rage. Her heart raced and blood throbbed through her veins. *What did he mean? He never talks to me. How dare he say that kind of thing? What does he know?! We're going to be fine. It's men like him—lazy bullies— who tear the town down. Men like him who lost our nation to start with!*

Thud.

"Oof—sorry! I wasn't paying attention, Beth text—" Tyler steadied her, his smile disappearing. "Hey... you OK?" He slipped his phone into his jeans pocket.

Rene' blinked hard. "I'm sorry, I didn't even notice you. I'm fine." *Liar! You're not fine!*

Tyler tilted his head, brown curls falling over his forehead. "You don't look fine. What's wrong?"

I can't stop hurting. I can't find the same hope as I used to. I'm failing God. And now, Quinn is on my back. "Nothing. Where's Beth?"

"She had to bring some medicine for her brother. She'll be right back." He frowned down at her. "I heard about Dax. I'm really sorry."

The tears burning her eyes threatened to spill. She smiled despite the lump in her throat, refusing to be weak.

Tyler glanced at the office where her father and Jack spoke behind closed doors. "Hey, how about we go get some coffee? I brought some extra stuff, pretty expensive, all the way from South America. Figured you and Beth deserved first taste. It might help ease your head, yeah? Beth won't mind if we get it ready."

She nodded weakly and followed him toward the break room. As they walked, he gestured to a large plaque of papers in the main hall. "I saw a guy changing names on the "Deceased" wall, since those survivors got back." He hesitated. "Um, I saw another name. Kelsey Fisher. Is she your family?"

Rene's chest tightened. "Yeah. My sister."

Tyler's blue eyes widened. "Oh. Wow. I'm so—"

"She got married and left before the war broke out. Lived in Tampa, so we figured she didn't make it through the bombing last year." She didn't often allow herself to think of her sister. With the survivors coming, was it possible more might, too?

"That must be hard..." Tyler spoke softly. "Were you close?" Then he groaned. "I'm sorry, I shouldn't—"

"It's fine," Rene' assured him. They stepped into the empty breakroom, the coolness of the room making her shiver. "Yeah. We were. I mean, she was always pretty selfish, but we loved her. You know how family is." She cringed, blood rushing from her face. "Oh, I'm sorry—"

He chuckled and lifted a hand. "No, it's true. I do know how family is."

But you never had parents. You lived in some orphanage, then the streets, and then your only bloodkin died because of me. She bit her lip.

"Maybe not a lot of bloodkin," he mused, pulling a small tin of coffee from his big green coat. "But lots of family. Lots of them stabbed me in the back."

"I'm sorry. You never deserved that." She grabbed three white mugs from the shelves.

"I'm sure you guys didn't deserve Kelsey ditching you. You don't deserve to think she's dead without knowing for certain. That kind of thing..." Tyler voice trailed off. He cleared his throat, starting up the coffee pot and adding the exotic coffee grains. "That kind of thing isn't easy. But we'll get through."

Rebe' rubbed absently at a stain on the old counter. The coffee pot groaned in protest as Tyler started it up. They waited a long moment, Tyler leaning against the counter, arms crossed and thumbs stuck up. He studied her. "You wanna tell me what's wrong? Beth says I'm a really good listener."

Rene' took a deep breath. "Dax getting hurt kinda threw me off. I wasn't there to protect him. Maybe I should've gone with him and Andy. If—"

"Wait." He cut in. "They're kids. You can't stop them from getting hurt. You can't think in what ifs."

"I know. I know a lot of things. But ever since..." She stopped herself, tears threatening once again. *He doesn't need to know any of this. He doesn't care. Be stronger than this.*

Tyler dropped his head. "Ever since Jed, things have been harder, right?"

She could only nod and hope he left it at that.

But people rarely dropped things when they ought to.

"Rene'... What happened... what happened to Ed... it wasn't your fault," his voice was small but firm. "I know that you feel guilty, but Ed never would've wanted you to be hurting over what he did, and it just... It wasn't on you."

Hot tears escaped Rene's eyes and ran down her cheeks. She choked out, "No, Ty. I'm sorry. I'm so sorry. I never meant—"

"No. It's true. Beth told me what you felt. I can't stand it!" Tyler worked his square jaw. His eyes held a grief Rene' couldn't quite grasp, but they held something else, too, something a little stronger. Hope, was it? Compassion?

"I'm sorry..." She mustered.

"God doesn't want you carrying that weight. I should know. I'm carrying the same one," his hoarse voice cracked. Tyler dropped his head and his slouching shoulders trembled softly. Just as soon as he broke, he lifted his head back up, shook it hard. "No. We can't blame ourselves. Ed didn't want that. George got him killed and George will get what is coming to him. God'll make sure of it." His voice grew cold, a coldness unlike any Rene' had ever heard.

Rene' bit back sobs, hugging herself. *How does he have so much hope? So much faith? He's seen worse than I have.*

Yet, he has just as much love for everyone he meets. Even after being hurt countless times.

"Ed warned me this would happen, it could happen, that it'd be an honor to die to help someone else. I've always been scared to die like that, Rene'. But then I met you. And I realized why Ed did what he did. And I met Beth... a-and... I'm not so scared anymore. Ed loved you, and the love I have for Beth is different, but it's love." He wiped his eyes roughly, his pale face wet with silent tears. "Love is worth the pain."

Love was worth dying for. But Rene' couldn't talk past the lump lodged in her throat.

"Ed's all right now, Rene'. We gotta keep fighting." He stared at the steaming coffee, blinking back more tears as he sniffed.

Rene' pulled herself together. She felt... all right. Not good. Not perfect. Not healed. But all right. Like Tyler had taken a weight off her shoulders, and God had put His hands on the scars they'd left. *Please, God, help Tyler lose his burdens, too.* "Thanks, Ty."

He smiled at her, but it was a genuine one, like his peace couldn't be contained. "Thank you, Rene'."

By the time Bethany came in, both of their tears were subsided, but she noticed anyway. "Have y'all been crying?" Bethany paled. "What did I miss?"

"Just talking." Tyler rested a hand on Bethany's arm and squeezed.

Bethany hugged Rene', sitting beside her and pulling her mug of coffee close. "Fill me in. You two are my best friends. I'd rather not be clueless as to what's up."

Ty explained quietly, tone calm and steady this time. Bethany took his hand in her own while she listened. Once Rene' and Tyler had finished explaining, Bethany gently apologized for both. As a best friend, she overlooked nothing, and after a moment, turned to Rene'.

"What else happened?" she prodded.

"Huh?" Rene' took another sip of the delicious sweetened coffee.

"Did something else happen when you came here?"

"Well, I, uh, asked about Kelsey. That probably didn't make her feel better. I'm sorry." Tyler piped up tiredly.

Rene' shook her head. "Nah, it's fine, honestly. I hardly think of Kelsey."

"So what was it?" Bethany frowned.

Sometimes I hate when she has her gut feelings. "Um, I ran into Quinn. He was acting awfully strange." Rene' shrugged it off.

"He is kinda weird." Bethany made a face. "What did he say?" She finished her coffee and pulled her pale blue jacket tighter.

"Just some stuff about the town making a mistake by fighting."

"What kind of stuff?"

"He thinks we're doomed," Rene' muttered.

Bethany's eyes flashed. "That jerk!"

"Jerk's one way to put it." Tyler grimaced. "He shouldn't be coming at you, Rene'." "No! He shouldn't!" Bethany agreed, vehement. Rene' cringed at their reactions —the exact thing she hadn't wanted to happen was them getting upset.

"It's fine," she said. "I'll let Dad know he'll keep causing trouble. We'll just stay alert, as always."

Tyler glanced at Bethany, puppy eyes concerned. "Do you guys need my help? I mean, I could…"

"We can handle him," Bethany smirked. "Don't you worry."

CHAPTER EIGHTEEN

October 26th, 2027

"THANK YOU FOR COMING on such short notice," George Johnston said easily, pouring two glasses of bourbon. At the late hour, he knew Kaleb Savage and Robert Hyde wouldn't be expecting anything besides another job request. With Kaleb's experience and Robert's submissive attitude, they were quite the pair. For years, they'd done nothing but please George when he assigned them dirty jobs.

Tonight, however, George would be addressing something unfortunate. Robert had pulled against his chain for too long.

"What's this all about, George?" Kaleb demanded, not taking the glass of bourbon. He shifted on his feet, not out of nervousness, but out of frustration. The cabin floors creaked beneath his weight. George didn't care much for the shabby shack meeting place but it had been close to Paradise.

"I have much to tend to, but there's one matter I needed your input on," George said, nodding at them.

Robert, who'd been silent the whole time, took the second glass.

"Shoot," Kaleb snapped. "Ain't getting any younger.""Kaleb, you are one of my right hands," George began, leaning against the counter, "and I trust you."

Kaleb raised one eyebrow. "What do you need?"

"That's the thing..." George smiled and sipped his drink. "You're one of the best workers I have. You have plenty of well-trained men. Plenty of smarts. You follow orders—usually."

"Am I getting a promotion? A corner office has always been a dream of mine," Kaleb smirked.

"As of late, you have taken leniency, Kaleb." George shook his head. "You have a weakness in your own ranks and have not dealt with the matter."

"Weakness?" Kaleb straightened like a tiger ready to pounce. "Don't make quick assumptions just because you're getting trigger-happy, George. I've always been able to handle my own and you know it."

George sighed softly. Kaleb was a smart man with a big temper, but he was still fun to play games with. "I do not deny your abilities as a warrior." George wasn't one to get his hands dirty unless the matter was personal. And tonight, the matter was quite personal.

"Nathan and Simon are both fine, they've got their act together. The rest of your boys are managing fine. Things are smooth, George, we're all preparing for the end of this battle. I know your plan." Kaleb crossed his arms, eyes growing cold. "Now, wipe that smirk off your mug and explain why you're playing with me."

"I would, if you had patience." George held up a finger and smiled like a benevolent father. "As I said, there is a weakness, and this weakness must be eliminated."

"What weakness?"

"Robert Hyde."

Robert held the glass in his hand for a moment before setting it onto the table top with a soft thud. "Excuse me, sir?" he asked calmly, not a bit of emotion on his chiseled face.

George savored the look of rage on Kaleb's face. *He knew the truth and lied to me. He must learn his lesson. No one lies to George Johnston and remains unscathed.* "Yes, Robert, I'm afraid you've been a weakness in our ranks for some time now."

"I don't see how—"

"You're aware, the government is creating hybrids as we speak. They have for some time. You've heard the conspiracies since the late 1900s... Big, bad science experiments gone wrong, monstrosities of ancient times, and men of war with enhanced capabilities... Well, you were right, Robert." George grinned at the man who Kaleb had mistakenly let himself love. Love was a weakness. George could not only punish Robert for stepping out of line, he could also remind Kaleb who was in charge. Even George's trusted men had to have their hearts broken to keep them in a malleable state.

Kaleb stepped forward, fists clenched. "Don't you dare assume—"

"And whatever the Union is creating," George held up a hand, "must be terribly dangerous, to women and children, especially. What better way to make a man surrender than use his family?"

Robert's expression grew blank. He touched Kaleb's arm.

"Robert doesn't know any of this—" Kaleb insisted.

George showed him a small holographic device. "The UN servers used to exchange information about the Union labs were hacked... Robert is a good hacker, I know, but he slipped up. Even the slightest slip up has dire circumstances."

Kaleb snarled. "Robert is one of my best men. You will not punish him for some damn email glitch!"

George grinned at Robert's expressionless face. The man was mentally going through every step of what he had done—and he had found no problem. Robert hadn't failed his work, he had hacked into the server and left without a trace. George leaned in. "Your mistake was in redirecting that van from Lousinia, Robert. Remember? Three months ago, you went and you stopped a load of children from being smuggled to the Union. You knew that van was going to the labs. The only way you could have known that is if you'd read the emails."

"I saw a van of children in need—" Robert spoke tightly but George cut him off.

"I do not believe in bleeding hearts or coincidence." George shook his head. "You risked your job to save twelve children once. It is time to hold you accountable for your wrong doings."

"He has done nothing wrong, George. That is one hunch. You cannot possibly punish him for one coincidence." Kaleb shouted, slamming a fist onto the table. "*I'm* his boss! Not you!"

"I am *your* boss," George said. He rested a hand on Robert's shoulder. "I do not have time for men I cannot trust. I do not have time for men who believe that a few children being saved is more important than my empire. You know this."

"Yessir," Robert said, tense under his grip.

George leaned into his ear, whispering, "Your life for Abi and the baby's, Robert. Better to die for them than that they die by an unexpected infiltration. What would your child look like if it entered the Union's hands?"

Robert's eyes clamped shut. He was reacting just as George knew he would—submission. Robert would choose death if it meant George showed his family mercy.

Once the words left George's mouth, Kaleb lunged. He wrapped his hands around George's throat like a wolf going in for the kill. "No!" he shouted. "You will not kill him! This is outrageous!"

Robert grabbed Kaleb by his arms and wrestled him back. "Stop it, Kaleb!"

George laughed, rubbing his thick neck to ease the pain. He stepped back and straightened his suit tie. "I'm being merciful, Kaleb." They both knew he was showing them immense grace. "Robert disobeyed my orders. He snuck around and tried to learn intel about the DNA experiments—I can only assume so he could aid the Confederacy and, ultimately, betray his team. Traitors deserve death. Plain and simple."Robert's grip on Kaleb's arms shook. He let go but never spoke a word.

"No," Kaleb seethed. "He's one of our best assassins, George. We would be lost without him and you know it. You've already lost Philip—"

"I have never shown a traitor mercy and shall not begin now." George downed the rest of his drink. "Robert, if you choose to take your execution like a soldier, I will allow your family life. If you do not, I will punish your endeavors by dumping your family in a lab for genetic testing." He wasn't bluffing. They knew he never let traitors live. They had made a mistake in playing a dangerous game bigger than they could imagine. Their fatal mistake had been shedding mercy on the children and disobeying George. Robert deserved death and Kaleb deserved the punishment of losing a son.

George would regret losing another assassin but the justifications outweighed the loss.

Robert's chest rose and fell with one long breath. Kaleb raged at George but George ignored his childish tantrum —Kaleb would fight for Robert, but it wouldn't be enough. Not even a father could intervene when a son had to die for his family.

"I choose the execution." Robert's voice was strong and it silenced Kaleb like a gunshot had gone off in the tiny cabin room.

"No," Kaleb said sharply. "*No.* This is—""This is how it ends," Robert said, shaking his head. "I knew it was a gamble. I'm lucky he's only killing me and not my family. I will take this, Kaleb. I deserve it." He looked his boss in the eyes, giving one nod.

George didn't notice Kaleb's reaction, laughing. "Yes, you are lucky. But Kaleb is not so lucky."

Kaleb glanced at George, his red face growing taut as he reined his outburst in.

George pulled a Glock from a shelf under the table, sliding it toward Kaleb. "As you say, you are his boss. It is your execution."

"You son of a bitch," Kaleb breathed.

"You know I don't like dirty work unless it's a Test." George smiled, something in his spirit growing hungry. Hungry for blood. Hungry to see a life end before his eyes and for a man to lose a part of his soul to the darkness. All of the yearning filled his chest like a lust he couldn't, nor did he want to, shake.

Robert stepped closer to Kaleb. "Pick the gun up, sir."

Kaleb didn't move. His white fists shook and he watched George as if assessing how he could possibly kill him and get out of the cabin before one of the guards outside took him out.

"There isn't a way out of this, Kaleb," Robert said quietly. "We both know it. There's more at stake in this world than me. You're the one who needs to walk out of this place alive for the sake of the freaking world. Pick up the gun."

Kaleb picked up the Glock 19. Made sure it was hot.

George bit back a grin. It was even more beautiful than he'd hoped.

Robert took a soft breath and stood head on in front of Kaleb. Kaleb didn't lift the gun, his jaw tight, vein in his forehead bulging. No emotion shown on either man's face. In their line of work, maintaining a cool exterior kept them alive.

"Take care of Abi and the baby." Robert told Kaleb in a soft, hushed voice. "And please, don't let the kid root for the Redskins." A smile cracked his lips.

Kaleb lifted the gun, leveling it to Robert's head. Robert stood still in the pale light of the cabin's kitchen.

"Pull the trigger, Dad. It's OK. It's over." Robert closed his eyes.

Kaleb pulled the trigger. The gunshot rang in the cabin and George watched the body drop with a burning satisfaction in his chest. No one betrayed him and didn't taste death. No one.

TWO AMS IN PARADISE were usually quiet, since most of the men were all asleep or out on jobs, and the men on guard never made a sound. Nate sat up in alarm when he heard a car zooming somewhere down the street. Kaleb's car. What was he doing back already? The job he'd taken with Robert had been a last-minute one, but they hadn't supposed to return till at least two days. Nate cursed, snatching up his t-shirt and tugging it on.

Flipping his bedroom light, Nate snatched his boots on, grabbed his phone and flashlight. He ran out of the house. Maybe Robert was hurt, Kaleb was rushing him to the med house, something normal.

Nate jogged to Kaleb's house. No one was out, most of the apartment and house lights were dark as the night. He used to run at night, not only to stay in shape, but he enjoyed the time alone with the dark, his thoughts, and the endless dream of running far away from his father.

Kaleb's car sat outside his house, the front end parked over his lawn. Nate frowned and went to the front door. Had Kaleb already dropped Robert off at the medic house?

Crash.

Nate's blood ran cold. *Oh, no.* He pulled out a lock pick, forced the sturdy door open. "Kaleb?" His head screamed against his decision to enter the house, but he ignored it. As usual.

A curse, followed by the thud of a table being upturned.

Nate slipped into the house, shutting the door behind him. Kaleb didn't notice him, or if he did, he was too much in a rage to show it. Kaleb smashed a table chair against the wall, fuming. He'd broken countless beer bottles, most of them empty, glass covering the kitchen floor.

Blood stained Kaleb's arms, hands, face, the dark crimson soaked through his t-shirt and his SOG pants. He lifted his head, the broken chair at his feet, but his eyes were all wrong. The whites showed and the light behind them was gone.

Just like the night he stabbed me.

"Kaleb... What happened?" Nate should've left. Should've saved his questions for later. But he couldn't bring himself to move, as if his feet were screwed to the wooden floor.

Kaleb stared at him. His hands were dark with brand-new bruises and his wall littered with holes. Nate didn't move closer, but hoped the blood all over Kaleb wasn't his own.

Who's is it?

Robert... Oh, God.

"My son is dead." Kaleb's voice sounded distant, like he wasn't the one speaking. For a moment, he met Nate's gaze, as if he saw him, but then, he whirled and slammed his right fist into the wall. There was no sickening crunch of bones breaking. Yet.

Nate moved closer. "Kaleb, stop. You're going to—"

"*Shut up!*" Kaleb shouted, voice so loud the roof seemed to rattle. "Don't you pretend to give a damn. Get *out*."

"You're going to hurt yourself. You have to stop." Nate had no clue how to talk Kaleb down from a raging fit. He'd never done it before: he was always on the receiving end of those fits, getting beaten, tossed around, and once, stabbed.

Kaleb stepped over the debris and grabbed Nate by his shirt front. "I said get out!"

"No!" Nate blurted. "He was my friend, too! He wouldn't want you breaking down!" His voice was strong considering he couldn't feel his legs. "What happened?"

"Don't ask me that!" Kaleb screamed. "Don't ask me what happened! It's none of your business!"

"What was the freaking job!" Nate yelled back. "Who killed him?! Where is he?!"

Kaleb's bloody hand raised and swung at Nate's face but Nate blocked the heavy blow. Kaleb sneered, spittle flying. "Don't pretend to care about him. You never cared about him. He was more of a son than you've *ever* been!"

His words rang in Nate's ears but instead of cowering, Nate shoved him off. Hard. Kaleb stumbled back, chest heaving.

"No!" Nate yelled. "I did care about him! Maybe he was a better son than me. Maybe Randy is, too, and Graham. But if you hate me so badly, why keep me? Why protect me? Why give Si and me the alliance gig with Springtown?!"

Kaleb's expression darkened but he didn't move again. "Why do you think?" he hissed.

"I don't know!" Nate snapped. "So we can be your little puppets again? So if we ever disobey an order, you can accuse us of ditching again and punish us?" He'd gone over all of his doubts with Simon. Simon believed Kaleb was changing, that the alliance was good without strings attached. Nate didn't think Kaleb was capable of any sort of good deed. Especially if George was conducting it. Simon admitted George being in on the deal was fishy— but what could they do?

I can get answers.

"Robert is gone, and all you can think about is saving yourself?" Kaleb's voice dropped. His body shook ever so slightly, from rage or pain, maybe both.

"Robert told me to protect what I loved with everything in me. That's what I'm gonna do." *Push through.* Voice hard, Nate lifted his chin slightly. "We make him proud."

Four simple words.

Kaleb closed his eyes and dropped his head, his demeanor shifting. His rage disappeared as if he'd crammed it behind bars deep within himself. "Robert was the one who pushed me to give you and Simon the chance at the alliance with Springtown. But nothing is safe. *Nothing.* You two could get killed on that mission. But you want it. And I can't... I can't imprison you from the world. I can only protect you and hope to God I made you into a man who can survive."

He'd never, ever spoken such things. Ever. Nate blinked hard, not sure he'd understood.

Kaleb sucked in a breath, vein in his forehead throbbing. "The alliance must be made with the town, George insists. If there are strings attached, ulterior, bad motives—it isn't on me, that's on George, and I'll be a middle man to handle him accordingly." Pure hatred dripped from his words.

Focus on the job. No time for grieving. Find a course of action and move on. "OK. That's what I wanted to know."

Kaleb stepped past him, heading into the hall. "I need to get cleaned up and go to Abi."

Nate flinched but didn't move away. He stared at the mess in the kitchen, the drops of blood on the floor. *Why? Why Robert? What happened? Why didn't Kaleb protect him?* He pushed his racing thoughts aside and started picking up the disaster.

Kaleb washed up, leaving the house, started up his car. Robert lived across the base and Abi was usually home. Nate hoped she hadn't found out about Robert's death already. Kaleb must've dropped the body off at the med house for it to be dealt with.

Nate tossed the pieces of glass and wood into a trash bag. *Why didn't Kaleb tell me what happened? He takes lots of secret jobs, and Robert was ex-military, so the job could have been any sort of horrendous.*

He doubted he would ever find the answer.

I can focus on Springtown with Simon. I can do that mission till my dying breath, or till the war ends. Whichever comes first.

CHAPTER NINETEEN

October 28th, 2027

THE NEWSCAST PLAYED LIVE on West's hologram laptop. Most truth came directly from George, but West watched a few broadcasts to see what the people were being fed. Today's misfortune was two Union politicians being murdered in their well-secured homes, which was "impossible and being thoroughly investigated," according to the report. West chuckled. *Sure it is. The UN had these guys killed. Doesn't take a genius to realize it.* The citizens would think the killer was a terrorist or rebel spy, and the report would change to whatever lie best protected the UN's secrecy.

West turned the laptop off and leaned back in his crummy office chair. *That's four Union politicians dead in two weeks. That can't be a coincidence. Only one Confederate general was killed, and that was during an attack three days ago.* He sipped his black coffee. *George hasn't given any insight on the deaths. Why not?*

West poured over his plans for the day. It was five AM and his men would be rousing to start their routine soon enough. He didn't have much time to breathe, and even his breathing time was used to plot.

His cell phone buzzed, the grating sound making him groan. He checked the number and immediately answered. "Joker?"

"Grasshopper," Gideon's dry voice answered. "You're up early."

"Never sleep," he joked. "What's up?""It's about Springtown."

"Did you find the end of the rabbit hole?"

"No. I found another hole."

"What?" West leaned against his desk.

"You were right, Johnston. There are bigger things going on than what's shown. Springtown is being targeted by the Falcons. I got an anon alert—no clue who told me off, I couldn't identify it for the life of me. It could be a trap, but they said they'd be attacking in two days. My gut says we should heed this warning." Gideon's voice was rigid with unbridled rage.

West's heart lodged in his throat. "Falcons? Thomas Flannery's Falcons?" The image of a tall, broad ganglord filled his mind—Thomas, leader of the Falcons, lover of torture, money, and leather. West hadn't met him in person. *Alex used to work for him. If Alex gets anywhere near him, he's dead.*

"What do you think?" Gideon snapped. "Someone paid him, someone paid him big, and he's going to take that town off the map."

"Why?" West hissed. "It won't do any good!"

"You think?"

"What do you know?" West drew in a sharp breath. "Just start from the top."

"I've tried to keep quiet and track the Springtown supplier, but then I got this info from this anonymous guy. He—I assume it's a he—let me know Thomas' plans. He didn't know a lot but from what I gather, someone is catching on the supplier detail, West. Either that supplier has been killed or someone is paying Thomas more to attack than the supplier was paying to defend the town."

"We need to protect Springtown. Answers can wait, but right now, that town hardly stands a chance against Flannery."

"George let me defend the town once. If he changes his mind..." Gideon swore under his breath. "He knows

Alex's history with Flannery. He might consider it a risk if we get involved again."

"I'll talk it over with him."

"You're in Mexico!"

"I can help."

"He might think—"

"He knows I was helping before!" West snapped. "Ed died because of it, remember?" "What about Mr. Fisher? He's the mayor now. He might not agree with us helping in the way we need to." Gideon ignored West's outburst, tone cold.

"He doesn't have a choice. I'll take Fisher, you take George." West had immense respect for Mr. Fisher, the only man he'd ever known to shew compassion and grace toward him, even when West had helped kidnap his daughter. West hadn't taken his kindness lightly. *I have to save them. All of them. Somehow.*

"I'll handle Mr—"

"No, let me talk to him," West said. "I can make them listen. They trust you less."

A long pause followed, then, "West?"

"Yeah?"

"The South has gotten far more aid than the news coverage is sharing. I saw that much. There's more suppliers than the UN is letting on."

West rubbed his temples, mind racing. "Yeah, I figured. It changes the playing field a little. It'd be best if we could push this war to a close before those aids get taken out."

"We're going to kill Flannery." The rage in his clipped tone made West shudder. How long had Flannery been on Gideon's kill list? Ever since he'd realized the things Flannery had done to Alex, most likely.

"Of course." West hid his doubt. Thomas Flannery was one the cruelest men out there. He'd run with Kaleb and Jordan for a few years, but they never breathed a word of him, as if his betrayal never happened. "All right. I've gotta get out there," he said calmly, "but we made some progress on the suppliers and hopefully, Springtown's aid isn't dead. I'll call Mr. Fisher right now. You call George." They had no time to waste if Springtown was going to survive.

"Roger that."

"Don't lose your head, Gideon."

"He tortured my brother. I have no intentions of allowing emotions to rule this mission. I will not fail." Gideon hung up.

West sucked in a breath, beginning to dial Mr. Fisher's number, but his hologram beeped. Muttering a curse, he read his mother's name on the call-up screen. *She never calls me...* He answered and watched his mother's face appear over his laptop, the 3D image a crystal clear, colored version of his dear flesh and blood.

"Hello?" he frowned.

"West." Cindy's lipstick stained lips were pursed. "The game is over."

"What?" He gaped at her in dismay.

"We need to talk. Soon, it can't wait any longer." She gave a list of coordinates—numbers that meant something to West, but he couldn't believe what she was saying.

"Mom, what is this?" his voice was barely a whisper. "It's time you learned the family secret." She closed her eyes briefly. "*Alea iacta est.*" The hologram disconnected.

Alea iacta est. The code phrase she had taught West as a boy, if ever a time came when the world as they knew it would be changed forever. *If ever a time came when she needed me.*

His mother would have to wait. He had a mini army of men outside, waiting for him to take the lead. He couldn't leave them. Any sign of suspicious activity and Ricardo would pin him down like a fish. No, he needed not only the men's trust, but he needed to prove to George he could handle this mission.

Is that what Cindy meant? This is truly the last gig before the Test. The last dance before the truce. Better make it a good one. He dialed Mr. Fisher and prayed.

CHAPTER TWENTY

October 29th, 2027

WEST HAD CALLED SPRINGTOWN in the early hours yesterday, warning them of an oncoming attack from a gang called the Falcons. Shortly after, a large armada of Gideon's men had arrived, and despite Springtown's uncertainty and many questions—what if it's a trap? What if Gideon and the other "good guy" gangsters are in on it? Countless others agreed to the assistance. But it hadn't stopped there. Not only was George allowing Gideon and Alex to help, but Simon and Nate offered an alliance with Kaleb, too.

Standing in the courthouse with dozens of people, hunkered close to Simon, Nate, Sean, and her parents, Rene' could hardly believe her ears.

"Let me get this straight," Mr. Fisher said, lifting a large, rough hand. "Kaleb Savage is offering this town direct alliance, a pledge of loyalty?"

Simon's face grew heavy with urgency. "Yessir. I know it sounds out there, but he isn't bluffing, he wants to help." He glanced at Gideon and Alex, who stood solemnly nearby.

Voices erupted but a sharp bark of silence from Mr. Fisher made the civilians pipe down. He glanced back at Simon. "And his motive? I doubt he cares about us."

"According to him, sir, this town needs to survive the end of the war—you guys are one of the last such townships. The nation will need you when this is over. It will need a beacon. Without places like yours, this nation will resort back to madness, because the people will think everything hopeless—" Simon struggled to explain, but a part of Rene' wondered if he was hiding something. Or, maybe Kaleb was hiding something, and Simon could only explain what he knew.

"What's in it for him? What does he want from us if we agree?" Sean asked quietly, his fiery hair tangled and his pale face taut.

"He asked that while his men are ready to defend you, in return, you keep quiet, keep together, and prepare for the war to end. He didn't say anyone would have to fight or go out into danger." Nate crossed his arms. "I know it sounds too good to be true, sir, but we're wasting time."

Rene' caught a glance of Gideon nodding his head. She bit her lip and stepped a bit closer to her mother, who hadn't spoken a word.

Mr. Fisher glanced at his wife, eyes narrow. He whispered something to her and she gave a small nod.

"All right," Mr. Fisher said. "We agree—for now, until this mess is over. Then I talk to him in person."

Nate blinked. "Yessir."

Simon spoke up quickly, "I won't let this go bad, sir. Whatever is going on, we can handle it." He kept his tone down so only Mr. Fisher, Mrs. Fisher, and Rene' heard. Mr. Fisher patted his shoulder before turning to the men and ordering action. They had a great deal of preparations to follow through on.

Did You tell Mom and Dad to do this, God? They never make decisions without Your say-so, right? Rene' followed Lee, Simon, and Nate outside. Lee glanced at his older sister silently, but she saw the zeal in his eyes. He went to gather his militia.

Rene' turned to Simon, grabbing his arm. "Si?"

"I don't know anything else. I told you guys all Kaleb said, about the alliance and the supplier—"

Rene' hugged him with all her might, taking a deep breath. He smelled like sweat and coffee. "I know."

"God's gonna get us through, He has to." Simon held her close, rubbing her back.

"The Falcons are worse than Shane. You really think we all stand a chance?" she whispered.

"Yeah, Rene', I do. God's got something going on, but we'll win." Simon pulled away, cupped her chin. His smirk was tired but encouraging. "Believe?"

"Believe." Rene' pushed him away softly. "Let's get to work."

———

SPRINGTOWN SPENT THE DAY preparing for the attack. Stocking up on guns and ammo, distributing weapons and grenades, and assigning positions for every able-bodied man and woman ready to fight. The entire border would be surrounded with fighters. The roads leading to the heart of the town would be defended, too. The farmers, ranchers, and poor folks living in the ditches and outskirts of town were urged to go into the city to hide where it was more safe. Most obliged but a few families remained.

The Fisher family headed to the courthouse and various other large buildings open for shelter, but only at Mr. Fisher's orders. Rene' didn't help get the kids to the building, but Terri called her once they finished.

"Hey, sis, we're all OK. Most of the town is here. Henry's gonna find Dad to help. You OK?" Terri asked, voice heavy with exhaustion and worry.

"Yeah, we're fine, about finishing setting up defenses. All the roads should be blocked off. I'm still with Simon at the border on Buffalo." Rene' watched Simon jump into the truck, forehead dripping with sweat from exertion. He offered a grim smirk and a thumbs up, shoving the truck into drive. They rode down the dirt road, away from the small clearing beside an outskirt house they'd just prepared for sentries.

"Thank God. You really OK, sis?"

This isn't the time to talk about feelings. "Sure, keep praying."

"Mom really doesn't want you shooting. Neither do—"

"I know and I haven't decided." A lie, because she intended to fight, even if it meant somewhere midway and not out on the border. She'd been too injured to defend her town in August, but not this time. *Even if I am terrified of getting killed.*

"OK..." Terri sighed. "Are you coming back?"

"Yeah, we won't be too long." Rene' assured her. Simon's phone rang and she dropped her tone, "Si's got a call, see you soon. Love ya." She hung up and listened in as Simon answered.

Simon's face blanched. "You're... here? OK... Yessir. I'm on my way to the courthouse now. Got it." He hung up, blurting, "Kaleb is on his way to Springtown with his own troops. Holy freaking hell!"

Rene' stared at him, throat dry. "Isn't that a good thing?" *Hopefully. Unless he wants something from us we can't give.*

"Yeah. I mean, I think. His guys are some of the best out there, for sure, but apart from what I already explained, he barely explained why he was doing this. It just hardly seems like I'm missing something."

"Maybe he cares," she mumbled bitterly. "If he's coming, he can talk to Dad face to face. That ought to help a little." The thought threw her for a loop. *It's most likely they just clash heads. They're both stubborn and dangerous and... they both have people to defend. How can this alliance ever work, God? Is it a trick?*

"Yeah. Who knows with him." Simon's eyes narrowed slightly, a distance to his voice.

"Si?"

"Hm?"

"You OK? You've been oddly quiet." Rene' almost asked if she'd done something wrong but decided against it.

Simon sighed and adjusted his grip on the steering wheel. "Robert died."

Rene's heart fell as she remembered who Robert was—one of Kaleb's finest, the man whom Nate had both loathed and idolized. Nate hadn't spoken much of him but Simon had, during the week they had stayed on the ranch. "Oh... I'm so sorry..." she whispered.

"It's been hard on Nate and Kaleb. Kaleb kinda, well, snapped. He kept his word about the alliance and he's moving on, they both are. I figure it'll catch up with them if they can't figure out how to grieve without..." he trailed off. "Who am I kidding? Everyone dies. We can't always grieve how God wants us to. Keeping on fighting is all we got."

She reached over and squeezed his arm tightly. "I'm sorry. God'll help them, Si, you can't carry everyone's burdens... I should know... remember what you told me?" her voice was small.

Simon's shoulders slacked. "Yeah. I do. You got me there."

"And Robert's wife..?" Rene' mustered. "Is there anything I can do to help?"

He hesitated, forcing, "She's pregnant. Kaleb told me a couple days ago. He... he was hoping your sister or something could help. Abi's really scared. I know you guys have done enough, and you were freaked out with Onya, and maybe you guys are tired of helping with babies—"

"We'll help." Rene' cut him off simply. "She's in a base full of thugs. She deserves our help. Even if things don't work out well with Dad and Kaleb and the town... maybe I can still help her." *Mom will not let it go, for sure. She's too kind to let egos get in the way of a baby's wellbeing.*

Simon nodded and was silent the rest of the drive to the courthouse. The town was bustling with heated activity but a strange silence enveloped the town like a heavy cloud. Rene' prayed hard as they went into the courthouse to find Mr. Fisher, who had just gotten back from helping with grunt work. He was helping gather more ammo from the safes.

"Dad," Rene' called, hurrying through the men. "Dad!"

Simon followed on her heels. Some men cast him distrustful glares, but most of the men trusted him, and even a few were glad to have him and Nate back in the game.

Mr. Fisher glanced over, frown deep. "What is it?"

"Kaleb's coming," Rene' whispered.

"He'll be here any minute. We need to get to the border and make sure no one shoots him." Simon added. "Nate doesn't know yet, I gotta call him, probably shouldn't let him join the meeting."

Mr. Fisher eyed them both and glanced to the crowd of men. "Kaleb Savage is coming here?"

"Yessir," Simon said. "Is that OK?"

"At least he's facing me and not sending his boys to do the dirty work alone." Mr. Fisher clasped Simon's shoulder briefly and kissed Rene's forehead. The gestures were not unusual—her father was a kind man—but something about them now, only a day before all hell would break loose, made Rene's chest burn. She couldn't lose him. Ever.

"You two help outside. I'll meet him at the border," her father said.

CHAPTER TWENTY-ONE

October 29th, 2027

NATE HEARD THE NEWS erupt from Alex's mouth: "Bloody hell, Kaleb's here!"

Nate ducked his head around the car. "What?" He gripped his rifle tighter, handing it off to a young teenage boy of Gideon's.

"*Al*!" Gideon cast Alex a glare and finished setting a box of ammo into a small cabin that was abandoned and would be used as a small med house.

"Sorry," Alex groaned. "I just got word that Kaleb's at the courthouse. Didn't know it was a secret!"

Nate didn't wait for further explanation. He ran over to a truck, hopping in and tearing down the tiny asphalt road. *I can't believe this! He can't even trust us with a job!*

He drove toward town but realized something was off —vehicles, some heavy artillery Army-grade vehicles— coasted down the streets. *Kaleb's men.* Once Nate reached the courthouse, he'd passed at least three of the Army grade machines and a few other gang cars he recognized. He jumped out of his car and ran inside, not stopping till he found Mr. Fisher, Kaleb, and a few others inside the office.

Simon and Rene' both cast him a guilty glance. He moved beside them but kept his eyes on Kaleb, who didn't notice him and spoke with the leaders. Kaleb told them the same things that Simon had, that the alliance was not held with ill-will, and that while he did not know their supplier, he was more than willing to help them survive.

"And George?" Mr. Fisher asked coldly. "This is his idea. We will not form an alliance with George Johnston. That is walking into a baited hunting ground."

Kaleb nodded slightly. "It looks like it but you don't have much choice. We will help either way—my honor, sir."

Nate had never heard Kaleb Savage say *sir* and gaped, then slammed his mouth shut.

"Your honor?" Mr. Fisher's voice dripped with sarcasm. "Savage, I have no reason to believe you."

"I understand that, Mr. Fisher, but at this point, you need all the help you can get when you face Thomas

Flannery. You've heard rumors about him and most of those rumors are true. If you do not want the alliance once this is over, we will not force it, and George will not take out the town," Kaleb said firmly. "I'm a saint compared to Flannery. You know that's true."

The leaders were quiet for a long moment. Mr. Fisher looked toward Mrs. Fisher once again from where she stood nearby. Nate wondered if they'd take the chance. He didn't trust Kaleb, but did they truly have a choice? *What would I do in Mr. Fisher's place?* He didn't know.

Mr. Fisher took a slow breath. "We'll discuss this for a short time before we come to any agreement. Art, go out and make sure all work continues." He led his wife and the leaders into an office. Officer Art ran out to follow orders.

Kaleb waited calmly and didn't look at anyone else. Nate glared at him before nudging Simon hard. "Why didn't you—"

"Shh," Simon whispered back. "We didn't want you throwing a fit. How's Gideon and Alex doing?"

"Fine. How—"

Simon led Rene' outside, ignoring Nate. Nate's temper flared and he followed without looking back at Kaleb. Once they were outside, Simon answered, "Sorry. We didn't think you two being in the same room would be a good idea."

Nate thought of Kaleb breaking over Robert. They hadn't spoken since. "You were probably right. I don't believe him right now. The town doesn't have to hear that."

Rene' gulped hard and looked down at her boots. "What do you guys think? Is a joke from George?"

"I honestly don't think so." Simon shook his head.

"It might be. We don't know." Nate insisted.

"We have no proof either way. I mean, George did let Gideon assist before with Shane, but twice in a row...? Something's up." Simon agreed, but with a hint of caution in his voice. Anger lay in his eyes though he played it off. Probably trying to make Rene' feel like the town had a chance, but in truth, no one could possibly know what George was up to.

Unless... Nate paused. "I'm gonna go back to Hochberg. You guys call me when you get updates." *I really don't wanna see Kaleb again. I have a job to do. Jack's not here to help. This is my chance to show Kaleb I can do more than retrieval jobs when everyone else is unavailable.*

Nate forced his heart to harden. No use in thinking of the Fisher family, the fact Simon and Rene' deserved happiness. He'd fight out of rage and to prove himself. That was safe.

"OK." Simon frowned, cocking his head. Nate didn't let his brother look through his disguise—he turned and went to his truck.

GIDEON HEARD NATE'S FOOTSTEPS on the crunchy gravel and focused on speaking to Percy and Preston, Percy's younger brother. "Take the group and scout out the woods behind the mobile home—it's less than a mile from the border and if they try to go through, we'll need to have a rough idea of this last section."

They nodded and ran off into the woods with another guy.

"Gideon," Nate piped up sharply. "We need to talk."

"Talk and work." Gideon headed to his truck. Alex stood on the porch of the cabin with a few civilians, showing them how to properly use some of the medical supplies—he stressed the use of the sponge injector used for bullet wounds.

"What do you know about George and the town's supplier?" Nate demanded.

Gideon turned, meeting his gaze. "Get to work, Nate. There's plenty to do."

"I know you're hiding things from us, as usual."

"I don't know who the supplier is." Gideon shrugged. "The fact Kaleb found out doesn't surprise me." He wasn't about to go into detail with the boy.

"George knew?""Yes, he probably told Kaleb. I couldn't tell you if it's a new slumber-party exchange or if Kaleb knew all along," Gideon said dryly.

"Are you investigating?""What would it matter?" *He'll figure the truth out sooner or later.*

"Does George want this alliance with Kaleb?"

"All I know is he thinks Springtown could be valuable. He's shown no signs of wanting to cause trouble. I've watched for those signs from the start." His tone grew icy. *I got my mark shortly after kidnapping Rene' and protecting Springtown from the traitor Shane. I'm far ahead of Nate in that regard.* "It's Mr. Fisher's decision. West spoke with him, hoping to help him make the best decision, but Mr. Fisher will do as he wants. I think he'll make the wise choice."

"What would the wise choice be?" Nate spat.

Gideon smirked. "How should I know?"

"Mr. Fisher thinks it's an alliance with George. He'll never agree to work with a monster." Nate clenched his fists tightly.

"Maybe not," Gideon said. "There's more going on and he must understand that. Lives are at stake."

"What if George pulls one over on them? Comes back to kill them all or worse?" Nate stepped closer, pointing a finger at Gideon's chest. "They don't deserve George's games!"

"No one does." Gideon cocked his head. "I will handle this, no matter which direction it takes. You want to help, we work together, but I will not work with you at my throat."

Nate fumed but stepped back. "You don't think George is bluffing?"

"I don't think so, but I could be wrong, so we stay alert, survive, and I pursue the answers." Gideon glanced over at Alex on the porch, hesitating.

Nate's eyebrows furrowed. "You worried about Alex and Thomas?"

Gideon cut his eyes at Nate. "Just focus on work."

"Sure." Nate turned away. "Keep me updated. I'll finish up the east side."

CHAPTER TWENTY-TWO

October 30th, 2027

ALEX COULDN'T SLEEP. HIS military grade watch read 12:11 AM, October 30th, 2027, and he mentally added the words, "Date of the attack of the Falcons on Springtown, Kentucky", but that just made his stomach twist. He closed his eyes, but no matter how much he begged God to give him peace—the sort of peace Peter had had the night before his execution in the Bible, even though the angel had helped him escape in the nick of time —peace was out of reach. And no angel came to save them.

Alex tried but couldn't surrender to God. *Lord, forgive me, I can't make the fear stop.* He sat up, eyes burning with shame. What kind of coward was he? What kind of Believer couldn't find faith before probable death?

Alex got up, sneaking over the bodies of his sleeping comrades. Most of Gideon's men slept outside in tents, but a few had been given shelter in a home that a family offered—the Downfield family. He had spoken briefly to Mr. Downfield and the men were careful not to damage the home, setting up sleeping bags in any floor space available. Alex slipped outside into the starry night.

Gideon sat on the porch step, his coat collar up around his ears. He stared off into the distance. "You all right?"

"No." No need to lie, Gideon could see through those. Alex sat beside him, rubbing his gloved hands together. He really didn't want to be reminded of the scars on his hands and arms right now.

"You can stay at the courthouse tomorrow."

"With the elderly, women, and babies?" Accent heavy, Alex shook his head, seething with rage at his own self. "I have to fight with our men, Gid. Isn't fair or right for me to hide like a—"

"All right, don't get yourself worked up about it." Gideon stopped him. "I tried to convince Philip and Danny to stay behind to guard, by the way. They say they don't care if they get recognized. I suppose they would rather fight for the town than hide and keep the life they've worked so hard for."

Alex knew that the brothers weren't afraid of George finding out they were alive. They were more afraid of being cast out of Springtown than going back to the life they'd escaped. Alex understood. He wasn't about to back down, either.

Alex sucked in a breath, focusing on the cool air that entered his lungs. *In, out. In,* "I'm scared, Gideon," *out.* "I shouldn't be. I know that. God has taken care of me always and this time won't be different, even if the worst happens—"

"Nothing will happen. I've got your six." Gideon didn't look away from the forest line.

A dog that'd been left behind to guard the house howled from the woods. The sound sent shivers up Alex's spine. *Never alone. No matter where I go, I'm never alone, not even now.* He bit his lip hard and focused on the howls, as if the raw, lonely sound spoke a million things he couldn't voice himself.

Gideon sighed softly. "You should try to sleep."

"You aren't."

"Let's both try." Gideon stood up and offered Alex a hand, his black clothes still covered with grime, dust, and dirt. He tugged Alex to his feet and led him inside. Alex crawled into his sleeping bag, shut his eyes, listened to the men snoring around him.

He couldn't help but remember. Remembering was a horrid thing to do. It was one of man's greatest weaknesses.

Thomas stood over him, his bearded face lit up in a wicked grin. He held the small torch closer to Alex's left arm, eyes drinking in Alex's terror. Alex screamed and lurched but the ropes bound him tightly to the metal chair. The heat singed his skin, and between the pain and the smell, Alex wretched.

"A thief is a thief." Thomas grabbed Alex's throat. "You're lucky I don't chop your hand off. Want me to take a finger?" Alex begged Thomas to let him go, vision blurred with agony. "Let me pay you back!" he sobbed.

"You could never pay that debt." Thomas lifted the torch close to Alex's neck. "You're out of the Falcons. Good luck out there, kid. No one wants a thief. You'll die in the ditch I'll toss you in."

Thomas' words played over and over in Alex's mind. *They aren't true. God saved me—Gideon saved me. I'm not a bad man. Sometimes good men have to do bad things.* He sucked in a weak breath, willing himself to sleep as he asked God to protect them. He hadn't begged a man since Thomas, but he felt like begging when he prayed.

GIDEON DIDN'T RECEIVE ANY further word from the anon mole, but Springtown was ready by six AM the day of the attack. Men had been on guard all night in case the attack happened in the dark, but it didn't. Gideon found this fact a little strange—Thomas was known for night ambushes. Why hadn't he snuck to the border at three AM or something insane?

He kept his thoughts to himself and stood ready at the border with countless other men and women. Mr. Fisher was calm and composed. Kaleb told the town what kind of defense techniques they'd best use. The weight of what was to come hung over everyone, making the militia of gangmen and civilians rather silent. Gideon could hardly believe his eyes. His own men, Kaleb's men, and men from the town—fighting together. Some would die. Some would be injured. The majority present had no love for Springtown and if they died, they'd die as thugs.

Not this time. Not again. Gideon bit his tongue, glancing to Alex at his side.

Remember that deal we struck, God? Think we could keep it going, for Al's sake? I think I'm asking for a miracle. More than anything else, Gideon needed God to help him protect his brother.

An hour dragged by. Men tried to eat, some drank coffee, but barely anyone spoke. Lee had his militia—over fifteen civilian boys, Danny, Phil, Simon, Rene', and Nate —near another road at the border. All of the radios were cleared and they'd alert the other groups if they caught sight of Thomas' group.

Gideon watched the horizon with his binoculars. Vehicles and bikes approached the border, growing closer at a steady pace. *Game time. Finally.* The alerts were given, men readied their guns, and the radio warnings were sent to the other groups.

"Stand by," Kaleb said firmly. The vehicles sped closer, closer, closer, and every hundred feet, Gideon practically felt Alex stiffen just a bit more beside him.

A strange sensation flickered in his chest. He looked over at Mr. Fisher and Kaleb, opening his mouth to speak. *They aren't gonna stop.*

"Take cover!" Kaleb shouted.

Thomas didn't reach the border before his men in the heavy artillery vehicles hailed gunfire at the border.

CHAPTER TWENTY-THREE

October 30th, 2027

THERE WAS NO GREATER hell on earth than in a battlefield. Nate covered Simon and Lee. Simon and Phil stayed close to Rene'. Lee's militia was surprisingly collected, all things considered. The gunfire didn't stop, blasting away from both sides. Most of Flannery's vehicles had stopped just before the border but a few had ripped into the line of defense, smashing the upturned cars. Nate hoped the civilians had all gotten out of the way but had no time to go check. A few motorcycles raced toward the woods and those were the first ones Philip sniped in quick precision.

The bomb launcher wasn't so easy to defend against.

The first one shot far past the border. From where Nate was, he couldn't be sure where, but it exploded quickly after. *Nowhere close to us. Yet.* "Split!" Philip shouted. "Move!"

Nate grabbed Lee, pushing him backwards. "New position!"

Lee's guys followed after them as they moved deeper into the woods. "Where's Kaleb's freaking artillery?!" Lee snarled.

"It'll be here." Simon spoke up, running with Rene' through the bushes.

Boom.

The bomb went off somewhere behind them. That was all Nate could tell before he crashed hard, ears ringing hard enough he figured he was a dead man.

By the time he came to, Philip was desperately pulling him to his feet. His mouth was moving but all Nate heard was ringing.

Rrrrr. Rrrrr. Rrrr.

Nate looked about, smoke and flames engulfing a few trees to his right. *Fire's bad. Fire's...* Simon dragged a body away from the fire. *A body?*

"Simon!" Nate tried shouting. He didn't notice anyone else but as he darted for Simon, he tripped over something soft and big. Tumbling, pain erupting in his left leg, Nate scrambled to his hands and knees in the dirt.

A teenager, about Nate's age, the left side of his gashed body soaked with blood. His face was mostly torn up from pieces of tree debris. He grabbed at Nate's arm.

I know him. Nate leaned over, taking the teen's hand. *He was at the party. He's one of the guys who hurt Graham.*

The teenager mouthed something. Nate couldn't hear him, but he could scarcely read his lips.

"I'm sorry."

Nate set his jaw and squeezed the boy's hand tight. He couldn't look at the boy's mangled body or the absolute terror in his eyes without his stomach flipping. But he sucked it up, stored it low, and nodded.

Once the boy stopped seizing and Nate was sure he was dead, Nate jumped up. Running to Simon, he picked up the body by its legs and helped Simon carry him. Nate didn't let himself look to see who it was.

They reached the medic cabin and carried the body inside. Philip was carrying a teenager of Lee's—dead, probably, telling by the brief glance Nate got—and Lee helped another injured boy stagger along.

Once inside, most of them collapsed, but a few men ran back outside to fight. Rene' had first aid supplies and went to work tending the men. Somewhere in Nate's mind, he wondered if she still got sick at the sight of blood, but maybe the heat of the moment would get her through.

A doctor from Kaleb's group was waiting and he helped Simon and Nate situate the body onto a cot. Nate stepped back, allowing himself to identify the limp, bloody body. It was Tyler.

Nate turned and followed Simon out of the cabin and back into the fire.

GIDEON JUMPED BACK DOWN behind a vehicle, sweat dripping down his forehead despite the cool autumn weather. Kaleb's tanks rolled out but the gunfire and artillery had gotten unbearable. Kaleb and Mr. Fisher had pulled all of their men backward, away from the chaos of the border. Everything moved quickly, time ceased to exist, and Gideon could focus only on killing the men and bikers slipping past the brute force and gunfire. For now, Kaleb was in his element—bombs, grenades, launchers, and guns.

Gideon ran over to Alex and Percy behind one of the vehicles. "Any sights on Flannery?"

"Total phantom." Percy reloaded his AR-15 quickly.

"I'm going closer." Gideon readied his gun and glanced at them both, ignoring the fear in Alex's eyes. "Cover me." Without waiting for confirmation or rebuttal, Gideon ran toward Kaleb's bomb-proof infrastructure that Kaleb's group had brought in. About three of the iron-looking boxes sat in various positions along the border. Bullets went off around him but Gideon didn't get hit so he paid no heed.

The bunker door opened just long enough for Gideon to enter. "Kaleb—"

Kaleb glanced up, covered in grime. He'd been out in the heat of it at first, till heavy artillery entered. "We're ending it." He snapped, giving orders through his radio.

Gideon didn't argue. He ran back outside to the battle and started the retreat.

RENE' FINISHED WRAPPING XANDER'S right arm before moving to the next wounded man who yelled for help. Hands shaky, she gave him a shot of morphine. A bullet hole in his leg had been filled with sponges and the blood had stopped flowing, a makeshift fix that'd last about six hours until further help could be given. She moved to the next victim, helping the doctor with a woman screaming from pain. A big chunk of debris lodged in her stomach had to be removed and so long as Rene' didn't look, she could hold the woman down long enough for the doctor to work.

The gunfire ceased just long enough that one of the wounded men tried to shimmy toward the door. "What's going on out there?" he groaned. "Anyone else hear that?"Screams. Shouts. Far into the woods and barely audible over the chaos.

The doctor finished the woman and Rene' ran to the cabin door, heart pumping. At least ten men tore out of the woods, one waving his arms, another shouting, "Evacuate! Load them into the truck, let's go!"

Rene' helped the wounded outside. The men carried the living, dragging the dead out last, until everyone was in the large truck bed. As she worked, Rene' overheard the panicked voices: "The fire is spreading. They dropped some aerial bomb or something—lit the west border up like the fourth of July. Barely had any men over there— probably a distraction."

Panic stricken, Rene' prayed. She couldn't contact her dad, Lee, or Simon, and God only knew where they all were. She focused on the injured woman, trying to convince herself she didn't need to be out there. *But I do. I should be with them. God Almighty, save us all. Don't let it end in fire.* They reached the edge of main street and took the injured into a med tent.

Rene' helped with whatever she could. At one point, she was vaguely aware of Terri working beside her, but she couldn't bring herself to speak or tell her sister what had happened.

Instead, Terri quickly brought her up to speed. "The west is in flames. They retreated and the Falcons left. I heard it all happened in less than ten minutes. Men are putting out the fires. It all happened fast. So fast."

"Where's—" Rene's breath caught.

"Henry got shot. He told me everything, he's all right. I don't know about anyone else." Voice on the edge of breaking, Terri turned and went to another wounded middle-aged man and started tending his wounds. She'd always been better with helping the wounded. Rene' looked briefly at the blood on her hands.

"God, let them be OK." *Ten minutes. It'd taken a little more than that for the evac to occur. So, what, it's been twenty minutes since they retreated? Shouldn't the men be coming back? How hard is it to quench a forest fire? No, be sensible. Be calm. Don't panic. Fire is hard to handle.* The fires back in 2019, 2020, and 2023 reminded her of that. Rene' sucked in a breath and went back to gathering plastic containers of bandages as fast as her shaking body could move.

CHAPTER TWENTY-FOUR

October 30th, 2027

IT TOOK ONE SMALL helicopter to rage hell onto the west road at the border. Two men in protective gear used fire-launchers to set the forest up in flames. Nate saw the helicopter from the bunker he hid in and something in him snapped. They disappeared as fast as they came, leaving destruction in their wake.

Over the radio, Kaleb's voice came. "Boys, it's a distraction. Get away from the fires. All hell is gonna—" the radio cut out.

"Retreat." Nate looked back at Lee and Danny. "We gotta move!"

"Get the trucks!" Simon snapped, racing outside to do just that, not waiting for anyone to cover him. Nate followed him. The militia, along with various other gangmen and civilians, fled the border.

The bunker was near surrounded by burning trees, bushes, and grass. The men had each other's backs but no time was wasted in running from the danger and making it to the vehicles.

No gunfire. No grenades. No one is attacking.

Nate didn't know what Kaleb's intentions were—should they stay, protect the weakest point of the border, or flee the lethal fires?

The fires burned steadily. Maybe they weren't so lethal. Maybe they *were* just a distraction. *We're falling for it. But what else do we do?*

They reached the vehicles and Nate jumped in, starting one truck up as the men piled in.

"Wait!" Simon froze mid-swing over the truck bed. "Where's Danny and Lee?!" He looked around, dark eyes reflecting the raging fires to their left. The bunker was engulfed now, the flames rising. Nate didn't think the Kentucky winter forest ought to be so flammable.

Simon jumped off and ran toward the bunker.

Nate screamed for him. "Simon!" He got out, yelling for the others to roll out and leave them one truck. A pitiful request and he almost didn't expect anyone to heed it.

Simon didn't reach the bunker. About halfway, he tripped and fell into a foxhole. The gang members and civilians had spent hours before digging various holes.

Nate stumbled to a sharp stop, swearing. "Si—"

Danny lay in the dirt, his jeans singed and dark with soot. Lee wrestled to drag him out of the hole but his lean frame was shaking and jerking—out of shock or pure exhaustion, Nate couldn't tell. Nate grabbed Lee off of Danny, racing him to the car over thirty yards away, struggling for breath. He wished Philip were there but the man had gone to find Gideon and the men he was used to working with.

When Nate turned back, Danny was crawling over the forest floor and Simon was nowhere in sight.

Nate dropped Lee into a farmer's arms and ran back to the fires. "Simon!" The name erupted deep from within his lungs, right from his broken soul. "Simon!" He ran over the forest floor, stopping beside Danny and scooping him up. "Where is Simon?!" he panted.

"S-someone was there, someone took him!" Danny's eyes were wide and he moaned, right before passing out.

A large man reached them and tossed Danny over his shoulders firefighter style. "Move out!" he snarled. "Let's go!"

"But Simon—"

"You heard the boy! He's been taken!"

In a blind stupor, Nate ran back over with the man. He drove the truck back to Springtown's medic tent but he didn't help unload the wounded. The town buzzed with utter pandemonium around him—wounded cries, weeping women, orders from men trying to maintain control. Body screaming in pain, Natee radioed Kaleb.

He ignored it all and when Kaleb answered, Nate said, "Flannery took Simon. We have to move."

———

"GIDEON!" ALEX YELLED INTO the crowd of men withdrawing from the attack. The boxing technique hadn't quite worked out—no war had really broken out for any technique to be carried out. *Thomas didn't break through the defenses for a reason. Why not?*

If Flannery had come only to harm the town, he'd done a good job. The fires roared as the trees burned, the flames reaching for the clear blue sky. Alex's breaths were short and shallow, his hands sweating into his gloves. A part of him screamed for him to run, follow the others to safety, get away from the flames.

But Gideon was out there. He'd run into the heat of it all to snipe out the runaway thugs. His words rang in Alex's ears, "Get to shelter."

I can't leave him behind, no matter what he told me to do. Alex summoned up every ounce of strength he had left and ran toward the line of burning trees.

No enemies were left. Flannery's retreat had been as fast as his arrival.

Gideon had hopefully passed through to the other side, but there was no other fast way to reach the road. Alex couldn't think straight—would anyone have his back? He didn't know where Kaleb was. He didn't know anything besides he was going too close to the fire.

The heat surged and hit his skin as he tried to find a way through the fire. Why was it burning everything? He struggled for breath. *Breathe. Gideon needs you. You have to have his back. Now* move.

He snarled past his sobs and jumped over a smaller patch of fire, stumbling to the other side, a strip of clearing that ran down the side of the road. The smoke and flames made it hard to see. He'd no clue if anyone from the border could see him. *They'll probably think I'm the enemy and shoot me.* He kept running.

"Gideon!" he shouted, but his voice was hardly a groan. He tried again, louder.

A few vehicles, bikes, and one heavy artillery vehicle lay strewn across the road. One vehicle was still fired up and Gideon poked his head out. "Get in!" he shouted.

Alex ran over and jumped into the passenger side. "What the bloody—"

"We're hunting the escapees down." Gideon thrust the truck into motion, tearing it down the road, away from Springtown.

Alex braced himself. Grabbing the radio on his hip, he tried contacting Kaleb. The truck bumped over the road but Gideon, reeking of smoke and his arms and face streaked with fresh blood, kept his piercing eyes on the road.

"Gideon, it isn't your job to take him out." Alex waited for Kaleb to respond, voice hoarse.

"The hell it isn't."

Kaleb's voice came through: "Where are you, Thompson?!"

"Gideon and I are hunting the runaways." No sooner did he get the words out of his mouth did he see something coming at them from ahead. "Gideon, bomb!"

Gideon lurched the truck sideways, trying to avoid collision with the small shuttle, but was too late. Blackness engulfed the world and Alex couldn't get away from the fire.

When he came to, a dull pain throbbed through his legs. He opened his eyes, moaning, "Gideon?" He tried lifting his head, but a sharp, sudden pain erupted in his neck. Alex grabbed at his neck and hit a small dart, jerking it out with a curse. He looked about, lopsided, like the truck lay on its side. Gideon was sunken in the driver's seat, the side of his head busted, shattered glass covering his black coat and pants.

"Gideon!" Alex reached for him but his vision swam. He couldn't move his arm. *Drug. The sleeping dart.*

The fire was for me.

Terror seized his heart and he screamed, reaching, reaching, but he couldn't reach Gideon.

God, don't let him be dead.

He screamed again, everything in him breaking till there was nothing left. "Gideon! Jesus, no, no, no—"

The attack was all for me.

His vision blurred and he crashed back. A loud thud filled his ears. The passenger door was torn open. A big hand reached down, gripped Alex's face.

"Long time no see, boy. You've grown since the last time I seen ya." Thomas Flannery flashed a wide grin, his green eyes shining with hunger. He glanced at Gideon. "Did I kill the rat? That'd be a shame, him being the only man alive who has proven me wrong and all."

Thomas heaved Alex up out of the wreckage with both hands, dragging him into the dirt. A large man with short, bleached hair beat at the opening, trying to haul Gideon's body out. "He's stuck, sir."

"Unstick him, Grant." Thomas snapped. "Let's move, backup's coming."

Alex fought against Thomas with all his might. "No! Leave him!" He hadn't begged since Thomas tortured him. He'd sworn himself he never would again. But this time, he begged for the life of his brother. "Just take me! I'll do whatever you want!" The words burned like acid in his throat.

Thomas tossed Alex's limp body into the back of the truck that'd launched the little bomb. "Save the begging, Alex."

Ping!

A bullet hit the side of the truck. A second lodged into the bleach-haired man, dropping him dead where he stood. Thomas didn't flinch but slammed the door behind Alex, jumping in and tearing off down the road. The truck jostled Alex around like a bag of potatoes.

As gunfire trailed after them, Thomas whistled to himself. The same tune he'd whistled when he'd tortured Alex, all those years ago.

Tears ran down Alex's face. *God, I don't want to die.*

CHAPTER TWENTY-FIVE

October 30th, 2027

"FLANNERY TOOK SIMON." Her father's remorseful words played again and again through Rene's mind. She watched Kaleb load up men at the border as they prepared a rescue mission. There was no time to waste. The fact that Kaleb stressed this, even when his men were exhausted and many injured, terrified Rene'.

She hugged herself and eased closer. "Dad," her voice was small, but she looked up at him. Mr. Fisher had escaped the fighting uninjured, his shoulders sagging as he helped the men gather rifles and grenades.

"Rene', you're not going." Mr. Fisher snapped.

Rene' flinched back, tears running down her face. She glanced over at Gideon. He was injured, blood covering his body, barely received treatment, and was packing up to leave. He'd hardly spoken to anyone, except to tell Kaleb he was going and they needed to leave soon. Rene' had met his gaze once—the burning fire in his eyes held nothing but hatred.

Mr. Fisher grabbed her arm. "Stop it. I would go, too, but we can't. We have to stay here. Go to the courthouse, Rene'. *Now*."

She turned away and nearly ran into Nate. He rested a hand on her shoulder, voice low, "I'll get him back, Rene'." He went to the others.

Rene' didn't let herself look back. *Philip found that teenage thug—maybe he'll know where Flannery took them.* She fought the tears and took a truck to town. It took a few minutes to get an answer amidst the pandemonium, but she found that the prisoner was in the police station. Rene' parked out front, ran inside, and looked for someone who'd talk to her.

"Rene'!" Sean's voice. "What are you doing here, lass?" He was bloody and haggard, a radio in one hand as he slipped into the hall.

"Do we know where they were taken?" Rene' panted hard.

He put a hand on her arm. "Just finished talking to the boy—he spilled everything. I'm radioing everyone the info now." He headed outside.

Rene' hesitated. Should she go to her family? Glancing down the hall, she bit her lip and started walking. A few doors down the hall, the door was shut but she heard weeping. Loud sobs that made her gut twist. She stopped at the door, listening closely.

Philip's sharp voice came, "Shut up. You're lucky I didn't pull the trigger, kid."

Rene's blood grew cold. She'd never seen Philip working a job. *The sobs... they sound genuine.* She opened the door. A scrawny teenage boy sat tied to a wooden chair in the tiny room. He had black curls and was covered in blood and bruises, head down as he wept.

Rene' froze in her tracks. "Phil..."

Philip stepped in front of her, face flashing with anger. "Go to your family. I've got this under control."

"Who is he?" Rene' asked quietly.

"Says his name is Noah Gyles. Cracked like an egg, told us everything we needed to know." Philip shrugged.

Noah didn't lift his head, his sobs grew silent.

"Why are you yelling at him? He's scared!" Rene' stepped closer. Noah kept his head low, flinching when she came too close.

"He works with Flannery, Rene'. The man who just kidnapped Simon." Philip grabbed her arm tightly.

Tears threatened to spill but Rene' lifted her voice. "I know that! But I also know this kid can't be older than

Lee and if he hadn't told us their location, Simon would be *dead*!"

Philip set his jaw, eyes heavy with pain as he looked down. Rene' turned back to Noah, lump in her throat. *God, help me. I'm gonna break. If I can just focus on this...* "Noah..? I'm Rene'. We won't hurt you."

Noah trembled hard. His clothes were nothing but rags. Old bruises mingled with new ones on his skin—he wore short-sleeves despite the season. Rene' hesitantly removed her coat, stained with grime and blood, wrapping it around his thin shoulders. "Flannery hurt you, too, didn't he?"Noah cried softly, tears running off his face and nose, dropping onto his jeans. "Please, don't hurt me. I'm sorry. I'm sorry for what he did—"

"Philip, can we untie him?" Rene' cut the boy's hysterical apology short.

"No!" Philip grunted. "I got orders not to."

"By who?""Everyone!"

Rene' set her jaw and pulled a knife from her pocket. "I'm untying him." Even if he were to fight, she could take him, and Philip surely could. She cut the rope carefully, bracing herself for Noah to strike her. He didn't move besides wrapping his arms around himself, breath hitching.

"Are you hurt?" she asked.

He shook his head.

"I'll take that as a yes. Phil—"

"You go get a kit," Philip growled. "I'll stay with him."

As Rene' hurried down the halls, she prayed for God to protect Simon and Alex, and every soul going to rescue them.

CHAPTER TWENTY-SIX

November 1st, 2027

THUMP. THUD. The steady droning of his heart in his ribcage brought Alex to his senses. He forced his heavy eyelids open. The throbbing in his head drug-induced, he was certain. Thomas Flannery liked drugs—they could stir up great fun, like hallucinations and paranoia—but he often preferred old-fashioned techniques. Like torture, with knives, electric prods, and fire.

The images of the border forests going up in flames gave Alex a small surge of fear. Lifting his head, he realized that he hung from chains in the ceiling. The only source of light in the small, dank room, was a spare light bulb above him.

Not again. God, not again, please!

He strained his eyes until he made out the form to his left—another man, dangling from the ceiling, same as Alex. Simon. He was naked and bruised, just like Alex. Thomas always stripped his victims, beat them, a the good measures ensuring the victims had a basic lesson in humility.

Alex forced his breathing to remain steady. Like Gideon had taught him, way back when Gideon hadn't trusted him, back when they'd been two teens with absolutely no idea what they were getting themselves into. *Back when I was a terrified thief with new burn marks. Even all those years ago, I trusted Gideon. He pulled me out of a ditch and helped me. Even after I unloaded all my demons on him, he stayed.*

And now? God, if Gideon comes, he'll snap. He'll kill anyone who gets in his way. He's wanted this chance for years to end Thomas. I never thought it'd end like this.

The door in front of him creaked open. A soft light flooded the room.

Will I ever see the sun again, God? Am I going to die in this basement?

"Wakey wakey, kangaroo Jack." Thomas' rough, sing-song voice penetrated the musty air. "I left a light on for you, see?" A gesture toward the light bulb. "I know you're scared of the dark. Or did you outgrow that fear?"

Alex licked his busted lips. As a teenager, he'd had a smart mouth. But the torture sessions had instilled something he was downright ashamed of—fear. He met Thomas' gaze, but that was all the courage he could muster.

Some man I am, God. Look at me. I'm terrified.

Memories of knives and cold blades and pouring blood and cries flooded his mind. Tight chains and dark rooms and fire, close to his skin, burning him—

"Aw, did the beating rattle your brains too much? Don't tell me you're deaf now." Thomas stepped over the floor, slapping Alex on his aching cheek. Alex resisted the urge to flinch and didn't look away from Thomas' pitless eyes.

"There's some recognition! Dare I say a little fear, too?" Thomas smiled. "Mercy, you've grown, boy! Even got some muscles on those bones. What's Gideon been feeding you?" He grabbed Alex's arm tight, fingers digging deep, pushing through muscle painfully. Alex bit his lip to keep from grimacing.

"I was gonna take Gid, but things will work with you two. I hear he puts up a big fight—would've been interesting to see you react. Wonder if he would've begged me to chop him up instead of you. Your last friend didn't, remember him?" Thomas drilled on, a smirk growing on his face.

Alex forced his breaths in and out. He didn't answer. He had forgiven the kid who'd betrayed him. Alex couldn't count all the times he'd run, too. Alex probably would've ditched his old friend, too, once the torture had begun.

"I asked you a question, boy," Thomas said smoothly. The glint in his eyes grew darker.

Alex gulped hard. "We were just kids," was all he could muster.Thomas laughed, a loud, gravelly sound that made Alex almost look away. "Kids? What did I do, stick pacies in your mouths? I made men outta you. All of you. You never would've survived this world if it hadn't been for me, orphan Annie."

Alex's ears rang. *What would Gideon say? He'd probably keep quiet. If he did talk, it'd be something sarcastic or tough.* He kept eye contact with Thomas but anything tough or sarcastic died on his lips when Thomas pulled a knife from his side.

"You still have that puppy look whenever you see something that can hurt you." Thomas raised his eyebrows. "I must've failed somewhere—you never reacted right, you know. Never toughened. But I liked the screams."

He's just trying to get in my head. Shut off. Shut it all off. Work the job. He clamped his jaw shut. *It's just another job. Thomas can't do anything worse than what he's already done to you.* He didn't believe that last part.

"We have about one hour, maybe one and a half, before your armada arrives. You tell me everything you know about George Johnston, where he is, what plans he has in the works, *everything.*" Thomas stepped closer to Simon, who hadn't woken up. Blood dripped slowly from Simon's mouth and onto the floor. "If you don't, I start cutting off Simon's fingers."

Fear rose in Alex's chest and bile burned in his throat. He had to tell the truth. But what truth? It wasn't like he knew everything George did. "I don't know everything, but I'll tell you what I know," he spoke quickly, like if he slipped up on one syllable, Thomas might take off Simon's thumbs.

Thomas smiled. "Go ahead."

He wasn't gonna question me. He was gonna question Gid and rip into me if Gideon didn't talk. Why bring Simon? He'll have a whole armada on his back soon—stop thinking. Talk. Alex moved a little, arms aching against the chains. "Look, I don't know where George is. He's always moving around. You know about his mansion—he's still got it."

A brief realization hit Alex that if George ever found out Alex had opened his mouth about this, he would kill him. His stomach twisted. *Either way, I'm dead or Simon is.* "Right now, he's focusing on the UN, the alliances, anything he can to make the nation crack open for good."

"You say that, yet, he sends you boys to that blasted town as heroes. Doesn't seem like he wants the nations completely pitted." Thomas flipped the knife in his hands a few times. "Wouldn't you think?"

"I don't understand it all myself," Alex said. "He let us go but didn't particularly care if Springtown ever gets destroyed—far as I know or understand, anyway."

"He tell you about the supplier?" Thomas smirked.

Crikey, were we truly the last to know? Some genius spies we are. "Yessir."

"And?" Thomas gestured with his knife at Simon. "Talk, boy, or I make Simon scream."

"We came to protect the town—"

"Why was Kaleb's group there?" Thomas smirked softly. "He playing crusader now?"

Alex hesiated briefly. Ought he tell about the alliance? Maybe it didn't matter. *Bloody hell, he probably already knows.* "Not sure. I think he had something to discuss with the mayor. And, I mean, if he got word you were the enemy, that could've been enough for him to get involved." George and Kaleb both hated Thomas. It wasn't stretching the truth too much.

"Kinda reaching, kid." Thomas tapped the knife against his chin. "You're awfully bold, assuming I've got a mole who sold me out."Alex breathed deep, trying to keep the blood in his head. "I'm not assuming that. A caravan or someone along the way could've spotted you."

"You think we don't move in the shadows?" Thomas' lips turned upward again. Cat and mouse, that's all this was to him. Making Alex squirm. Thomas had always done this sort of thing, whether he was conditioning his boys or preying on young girls.

"I'm not saying that, either, but you wanted me to talk, and I don't know why Kaleb came for sure. I'm a thug, remember? The town doesn't trust me. Kaleb isn't my direct commander, Gideon is, but there's still only so much George tells us." He didn't want his voice breaking but he could almost feel a blow across his cheek—but none came.

Thomas studied him for a moment. "Gideon got the mark?"

Alex nodded.

"Were you there?"

A breath. "No."

"Why not?"

"He... tricked me into being gone. Helping some victims. I... I wasn't there." Alex didn't look away but shame tugged at him.

Thomas' eyes grew hard. "You should have been. I taught you about loyalty, remember? Only thing a man needs after a thing like that is his brother."

Alex licked his lips, the coppery taste of blood flooding his senses. "I failed."

A moment of silence passed and Thomas lifted the knife again, pointing it at Simon. "Your group came to aid Springtown with no strings attached. Kaleb is no doubt doing George's dirty work. And you," he dropped his voice, "you're lying to me. Lying to your own father."

Rage exploded within Alex's chest and he jerked involuntarily against the chains. A scream rose in his throat but he didn't open his mouth. *You aren't my father. You are nothing like my father!* He kept silent. If he spoke, Simon would get killed.

"Why was Kaleb there?" Thomas demanded. "It's no coincidence that you know about the supplier."

What is the big bloody deal about the suppliers? Why is it all playing a part all the sudden? Because it's a crucial detail, however minute, almost lost to the ending war? "He wanted to talk to the mayor. Maybe about a trade or —"

Thomas moved the blade against Simon's throat.

"Or something! Alliance, deal, something, anything." Alex's insides sank like a pool of acid enveloped him. *No. God, I don't wanna die, I don't want George to kill me for talking. But... Simon... He deserves to live more than I do.*

"Alliance," Thomas spoke quietly. "Hm. You think Kaleb would strike an alliance with that town?" Instead of waiting for an answer, he rubbed his beard, eyeing Simon. A smirk lifted his lips again. "You think the mayor will agree? I hear he's more noble than Knight was. Rest his merry little traitor soul."

Alex gulped hard. *Thomas killed Springtown's previous mayor? When?* "Uh, I doubt it. He has no reason to trust Kaleb."

"War makes men do desperate, stupid things."

Not Mr. Fisher, Alex held the words back. "Guess so. I don't know."

"Where's George going next?" Thomas flipped the entire conversation like the previous topic meant nothing. A tactic to make Alex lose his guard.

"I don't know. If I did, sir, I would tell you." Alex gulped hard. "You know I would."

"Where is West?"

The question made Alex's skin crawl. "West?"

"Don't be daft. I asked where he is." Thomas held the knife to Simon's neck. Simon still didn't wake up. Alex was beginning to wonder just how bad Simon's injuries were—if he'd put up a fight, he would've gotten beaten worse. Simon didn't know how Thomas worked. Alex had never warned him. How could he have?

"West…" Alex slowly sucked in a breath. "He isn't with George?" *Think of a lie! You can't tell the truth now. He'll kill West.* "I think George put him on a mission for the UN, out of the country. Didn't say where."

Thomas' eyes narrowed and he cocked his head. "Out of the country, huh?"

Alex's heart crashed. *Please, God, let him believe me.* He kept his expression sincere, like he was telling the truth.

"Where?" "Might be helping with the European deals? Aiding China? I don't know. I wish I did. He's been AWOL," Alex said, pain throbbing through his body, at least with the drugs wearing off.

"AWOL? What, your little friend went missing on you?" Thomas shook his head. "I need more info."

"I don't have any—"

"Want me to find Jack?" Thomas pressed.

Alex thought of Jack and his girl—Jack had a shot at everything Alex wanted. Suddenly, dying in a basement didn't seem so bad. If Jack got that life, maybe Alex would be willing to die to protect it. *But Thomas isn't testing my life. He'll kill Simon, and Simon deserves to have that life with Rene'. How can I turn the tables?*

"He wouldn't know, either. George doesn't care about Jack and anything West might tell Jack would cause George to lose trust in him." Alex's arms trembled.

"Quite a mess they've got. But I still think Jack would know. He's awfully hard to find. Seems he went underground. You wouldn't know where I could find him, do you? Or do locations suddenly surpass you?" Thomas' voice cut.

"Thomas, I don't want to see Simon hurt. You think I'd lie if I knew the truth?" Alex set his jaw, heat burning under his skin. "You want to kill West to get at George? I'm not the one to stop you. I just don't know where he is!"

Thomas took the knife and lodged it into Simon's left shoulder, expression emotionless. Simon jerked awake, a ragged scream erupting from deep within his lungs. He swung to get away but the chains held him. Thomas kept the knife steady, eyes on Alex.

Alex yelled. "Stop stop stop! I'll tell you!" *God, no, no, no! I can't betray West!* "I'll tell you what I know!"

"I'm all ears, Annie." Thomas didn't withdraw the knife. Simon groaned and sputtered, breaths heavy as he tried to be still. Blood seeped onto his bare chest and ran down his skin. The sight almost made Alex gag.

"West is on a job for the UN and he is out of the country." Alex panted. "I don't know where but I have his contact information. I could call him—"

"And ask him where he is so you can go drink a pint with him?" Thomas scoffed. "Don't be stupid, Alex, I've got a knife, remember?"

Alex gulped hard. *No way out but to give West up... but I can't.*

"Don't tell him a damn thing!" Simon snarled, spittle flying into Thomas' face. Thomas frowned, twisting the knife ever so slightly, causing Simon to roar in pain.

"Stop, Simon," Alex said quickly. "We... we don't have a choice. I can't let you die. West wouldn't want it, either."

Thomas glanced sideways at him, wiping his face. "Stop piping the man's praises. If he's anything like his father, he'll stab you all in the back eventually."

"You're asking me to stab him in the back. I couldn't blame him if he ever did." Alex's voice grew strong with venom. "He's—"

"No!" Simon barked. His whole body shook and blood trickled from his mouth and wound. "Let this ugly freak kill me—but you shut up, Alex! Shut *up*!"

Alex stared at him. No sign of fear or horror lay in Simon's eyes. Just animalistic anger and courage. *He truly means it.* Alex sucked in a breath. *God, forgive me.* "He's at the Canadian border."

"Shut up!" Simon screamed.

Thomas pulled out the knife from Simon's chest and Simon jerked. Blood poured down his chest—Thomas hadn't hit anything vital, but the blood loss would kill him if unattended.

"Finish." Thomas ordered.

Alex gave him the location of a base at the Canadian border. "He's smuggling in more gangsters while the UN is in uproar about the battles over D.C. Y-you can find him there." His voice cracked.

Simon yelled again, breathing hard as he clamped his eyes shut.

"All right. I'll check it out." Thomas eyed Simon. "Answer this next question honestly, and I'll save Simon."

"Anything." Alex whispered.

"What would you do to save the man who proved me wrong and saved your life. The man who is one of the nation's only hopes, unlike you?"

"Anything." The word left Alex's lips like he'd given up his soul.

CHAPTER TWENTY-SEVEN

October 30th, 2027

CINDY ARRIVED AT THE Mexican border in a small helicopter. West's mother was the picture of Southern belle grace and beauty, often wearing dresses, pearls, red lipstick —but seeing her in travel garb and coming off the helicopter like some angel of death didn't unsettle him, either.

Cindy followed West into the building. West couldn't leave the base, so the soundproof walls and sealed door of the building's office would have to work. He had checked it for bugs and would do so again before they began their talk.

Most of the men kept busy and didn't ogle, but Ricardo eyed them from the hall as they passed. His footsteps were silent on the wood floors as he moved away.

God only knows what he's thinking right now. Cindy was never supposed to be here. West had come up with a clever lie that he hoped would cover him—Cindy had private business to handle with West *Some cover story.*

Once they were in West's office, he sealed the door, used a scanner to check for bugs throughout the room, and offered his mother a seat. Cindy smoothed her hair, a strange weariness on her makeup-less face.

She looks like crap. "What is this all about?"

"The game is almost over, West," she said quietly. "You know George will test you soon." "Of course. Is that all —"

"No. No, listen to me." Her voice darkened. "I will give you the name of the Springtown supplier and names of other suppliers for various other townships that will benefit the new government when the war ends. It is ending soon, West."

"How do you know?" Stunned by the first half of her words, he tried to ask a good question instead of demanding the names right away.

"I am a part of it."

West sat on his desk, crossing his arms against his chest. "What does that even mean, Mom?"

"I am a part of it all. And the time is coming, West, to end the madness and restore order. Or else we will lose *everyone* to this war." She shook her head.

Silence. West stared at his mother, the pieces of the puzzle tossing around in his head like a ticket blaster machine. "You... you're helping end the war..." he licked his lips. "You're picking apart the government with the—" *assassinations* hung on his tongue but he clamped his jaw shut.

Cindy's gray eyes narrowed. "Yes."

"For how long?" "Before I formed a covenant with your father." Her hands folded in her lap, Cindy showed no sign of remorse or fear. Just a determination and courage etched deep in the wrinkles of her pale face.

West's chest deflated. "All this time... You... you've been working to stop this..."

"One man can start a war, but it takes millions to end one." She sighed. "I couldn't prevent this civil war, West, but I could prepare before and during to end it. And we are close."

"We?"

"Any soul fighting against the UN is my brother or sister."

"And... you think I..." West looked away, panic rising. Now, of all times, she swooped in? Expected him to join her greater good cause? "Is this a trick?" he asked sharply.

"You would know if it were."

"No, this could be George seeing if I'm loyal—"

"Springtown is under attack, West. George allowed Hochberg, Thompson, Savage, and Bucks to intervene with gang men. George allowed you to save the life of Rene' Fisher, the sister of Brian Jones. Why?"

West slammed a fist down onto the table. "I'm supposed to know why he has broken his MO for the past year?! I'm supposed to understand why he let the boys help the town, why he let me intervene?" His breath came in short, heavy snarls. "I don't understand him! I don't understand what Brian has to do with any of this, what the supplier has to do—I'm completely lost and I cannot be lost because I am the leader, but I am *helpless*!" All the emotion raged in his voice but he didn't hold back. If anyone could handle his fury and his fear, it was his mother. After all, she was the one who had held him when he was a boy, beaten and weeping after countless sessions with George.

Cindy met his gaze. "West."

He turned away, forcing the robot part of him to take over.. "Continue." He couldn't try to sort his own thoughts. Might as well let her go on and overwhelm him some more.

"Flannery is being paid by politicians to disrupt as many stable communities as he possibly can." She continued coolly. "He has demolished one small town in Virginia already. The town had no alliances, completely vulnerable.

"The attacks will also cause uproar in the higher classes. Martial law will cease, West, and people will insist upon voting. Even now, a few argue for votes instead of leaving President Kaden to work." She smirked. "They will not succeed unless we act and make it impossible to continue slaughtering the American people."

"How are we supposed to end a war?" West snapped. "You know Springtown's supplier, but what good is that doing us?"

"If we support the suppliers, protect them, and continue funding things ourselves, we can win. I have put things to play for decades, West, things unseen by anyone. But it will unfold soon. I cannot explain it all yet—I wish I could, son." Her firm voice grew softer. "It is a crucial time. I cannot do it alone anymore. I need your help."

West worked his jaw. *She isn't lying. I can feel it. What she's saying lines up. But even if it is a trap, and I'm doomed, I can still work it out.* Didn't Jack suddenly insist God truly cared? Now was a good time to see if that was true. *As Mom has always said...* aut cum scuto aut in scuto. *Do or die, like the mothers used to say to their Spartan son before the warriors left for battle.* "What do you need?"

She took a slow breath. "I cannot disclose everything. I've watched the powers that be since the beginning, I have carved a way to victory, with God's help, but I need your help. You must be alerted to what is truly going on—in due time. For now, Springtown's supplier is too close to the edge. I would alert him, but if you want—"

"I will." West pushed. "Who is he?"

"Keegan Black. I do not know his ties to the settlement but he has protected them for years." She told him his contact information quickly. "Will this help you?"

"Yes." Gideon would be ecstatic. "You guys really think the nation needs these townships to rebuild?"

She nodded softly. "It might be a dystopia, son, but human nature remains the same. These towns can help rebuild America as it should be."

"How?" West frowned. "By showing others how to? By being men and women who can help rebuild? What if they just wanna stay in their towns?"

"West," she smiled. "They will want their nation back. The fight does not end when the war does."

He knew Mr. Fisher would probably want to help fix his nation. The others would, too. Generally. "Anything else?"

"The Union is angered by the turn of events involving the war, but I'm doing the best I can to settle matters without George knowing." She met his gaze. "George cannot know of any of this. What I ask of you is difficult. I can't explain it all and you are close to your Test."

"I'm in, Mom." West put up a hand. "I'll help you." *I'm a dead man, anyway. Might as well join up with forces who seem to know what they're doing.*

"You're handling this very well." Her eyes had that haunted look in them, the one she'd have when she used to tell West what he could expect to know when he "grew up". He was grown now, and the sorrow in his mother had only worsened.

"The fact you've been the total nemesis of my father all along isn't the worst news I could get today." He sucked in a weak breath. "I don't think you're lying, either." His heart longed for her to be telling the truth. If his mom had been fighting the good fight all along, and hadn't been found out by George, he stood a chance. He could do this. And maybe not alone—maybe he could work with her. His heart hammered. *We could end the war.*

I could kill George.

His phone rang and he glanced down at Jack's number lighting up the screen.

"I have to go to a meeting, West, but—" she paused as if steeling herself. "I love you. No matter what you decide or what happens, I love you."

West stepped over, hugging her tightly. "I can walk you out—""Speak with Jack, I can get to the helicopter." She smiled and left the room.

West groaned, answering Jack's call.

"West! Did you hear about Springtown?"

Tensing at the fear in his brother's voice, West said, "No. What's going on?"

"Thomas Flannery attacked them. Kaleb says he was paid by someone, politician or whatever, but he didn't demolish everything—he took Alex and Simon. He was trying to take Gideon too. They've got a big group, going to rescue them. Have any idea who did this?" Jack rambled on. "Gideon got tipped off by some anon guy. Who would've known about this?"

"I don't know."

"And why would they care if Springtown was protected?!" Jack nearly shouted.

"Jack, breathe. Where are you? Are you at Springtown?" West asked calmly.

"No, I'm with Mels in South Carolina."

"Is she OK?" "Yeah, they're fine. I just got off the phone with Mr. Fisher. The group left to get the others. I can't go, West, I—"

"Stay with Mels. They can handle this. I'll alert George and see if I can help, too." West spoke up. *They? Who's they?* "You just keep me updated if anything changes." "O-OK. I've gotta go, Nate's calling." Jack hung up abruptly.

West looked at the clock, swearing. He had to get out there and work. He sent George a quick message, hurrying out of the office.

Everything had changed. His mother was on his side—the side of the righteous, fighting against George all this time without being caught. Did he believe it? Could he truly trust her?Springtown lay in ruins, Simon and Alex were gone, and one of George's cruelest enemies had something up his sleeve. How was West supposed to win all of this? He couldn't fail the mission George had him on at the border, but everything else screamed for his aid, too.

I have to pull together. Focus on the jobs. I'll speak to George when he calls back. Till then, I work the Alamo.

His mind fell back to Jack. *He said* they.

Mels is pregnant?

CHAPTER TWENTY-EIGHT

November 1st, 2027

NOAH GYLES HAD TOLD them everything—where Flannery's camp was, how many men he had, and what his intentions were. The sixteen-year-old scapegoat's information was vital in their success. Sean was certain Noah wasn't lying. The boy's terror was absolutely genuine.

Nate sat in silence as Kaleb drove the truck full of men. No one spoke. No one probably thought much, either, because if they started thinking, they'd remember. Remember the bodies, the screams, the fire, the fact they'd have to bury comrades when they returned, the fact they might lose more men within the night—

"Nathan," Kaleb said quietly.

Nate didn't respond. He wanted to not exist until he could fight and tear someone's throat out for taking his brother.

"Nathan, I'm not forming this alliance just because George wants possible control." Kaleb's eyes never left the road, the headlights cutting through the blackness like knives.

Nate kept his mouth shut, fists clenching tight.

"I want you to have what I don't. I know you don't believe that. But it's true. Simon and Rene', they've got something. I know it. Fisher knows it. And you, you're a good man, Nathan. I don't know how this war will end or what will happen, not really. I'm not God. I have more knowledge and power than most, but I still can't save you from the world." Kaleb's voice dropped. "But I want to give you what I can, while I can. You don't have to believe me. I wouldn't believe me. But you don't have to stay in my group if you don't want to."

Nate bit his lip, everything in him exploding. "I don't believe you, Kaleb. All my life, you've wanted to give me this right-hand position, you've wanted me to be your soldier, you've wanted perfection—and all the sudden, you're soft? You want us happy? What kinda game is this?"

Kaleb exhaled slowly. "The alliance would keep Springtown safe. I want to help you two be happy, safe, and free. Whether you believe me or not, that's the truth."

"You couldn't tell the truth if your life depended on it." Nate snapped.

Kaleb ran a hand over his face, smearing blood. "You're so much like your mother." A weak laugh lodging in his throat. "I've spent eighteen years trying to drill it all out of you. I wonder what hell could be raged if I let you unleash it, instead?" His voice turned quiet as if a grand idea dawned on him.

He's lost his mind. Probably the shell shock or something. "I'm not your tool.""No, but war uses men as tools, and you might as well be the best one you can be while you can. That's what you wanted, right?" Kaleb shook his head.

Nate gulped. "I wanna end the war. But not as a tool. As a man. Not as a soldier."

"Maybe I didn't screw up so bad, after all."

They drove in silence the rest of the four hour drive.

FLANNERY'S LOCATION WAS A leftover small town but it was a drive-by location—the gangsters abided in a large warehouse and a few nearby apartment complexes, but by the looks of it, it wasn't a permanent base.

Kaleb's men had briefly gotten overhead surveillance by a tiny drone, which hadn't been seen by Thomas' guys, since no activity stirred. Thomas probably grabbed the spot and set up some defenses, just to have a safe place to interrogate Alex and Simon. They probably wouldn't stay any longer than needed, and Gideon could only pray they'd leave Alex and Simon when they were finished.

Gideon wanted to find the whole group of gangsters and kill them off one by one, saving Thomas for last so he could see the humiliation Gideon caused him.

Kaleb and Gideon's men silently prepared outside of the small town. They kept alert for attacks or ambushes but none came. Jordan came with a group of his own, rage etched on his expression. No doubt, he wanted to kill Thomas for taking his son just as much as Gideon. But Jordan kept quiet, listened to Kaleb's plan. AJ came with his small group of veteran bikers, too, and they followed orders without a fuss.

Kaleb's assault was another boxing method—surround the enemy and wipe the edges out first, then infiltrate. If a weak point arose, whoever had the chance would go in, find the victims, and get them out. They'd no idea where Alex and Simon were, but Kaleb stressed the thought that they were probably in one of the buildings. "We don't leave without those boys." Was the last thing Kaleb said.

Nothing more needed to be said. The men finished preparing in less than five minutes. Philip had come, once again throwing caution to the wind, not caring if any of the gangsters got word of him and Danny being alive.

"Gideon?" Percy's voice.

Gideon didn't respond or look behind, swinging his AR-15 around his shoulder, grabbing another knife from the backseat of the truck.

"Gideon," Percy repeated. "Don't get yourself killed. Alex wouldn't want a revenge party."

Gideon met his gaze coldly. "Work the job, Percy."

"*I* am. You're the one making it personal. You'll regret getting emotions involved." Percy snapped.

Gideon didn't respond.

"Gideon, please. I don't want to watch you get torn apart, either."

Gideon glanced at Kaleb. "Ready?"

"Let's roll." Kaleb took the lead and the group moved into town, spreading out, keeping low, making their way to the warehouse. Kaleb had snipers positioned throughout the town, and any signs of suspicious activity would be handled. If Thomas got word they were there early, he and his men would be shot riding out of town.

It took ten minutes to reach the warehouse and complexes.

CHAPTER TWENTY-NINE

November 1st, 2027

SIMON BIT BACK A moan as the thug applied a zip-tie stitch to the wound, sealed it shut, and put another bandage over it for good measure. The man smiled a little as he stepped back.

Thomas looked between Simon and Alex. "Game time," he said cheekily. "Annie, let's go upstairs. Bucks, you wait here for daddy."

The thug unlocked Alex's chains and let him drop to the floor. Alex stifled a groan of pain as he hit hard, drawing himself up. He glared at Thomas.

"Get him some pants," Thomas told his goon, finally sheathing his bloody knife.

Alex forced a few breaths, trying to block out the damp air, the dark corners of the room, the heaviness in the atmosphere that made him shiver. If he let himself, he could see the demons watching, looming, waiting in the shadows, hungry for his blood.

He wondered where the light was, where it was out in the darkness, where it was fighting for him.

Maybe it's in me.

The guy came back, tossed a pair of Army pants at him. Alex hesitated at seeing the camo garment but yanked it on without looking at anyone.

"Remind you of anything?" Thomas asked softly.

Alex glanced up again. "Only that you kill anyone for the pleasure of it. Some hero you are." He knew he should keep his mouth shut. Thomas couldn't possibly know of Brian. *Could he?* If it was one thing he'd learned over the years of con artistry, it was never to let fleeting questions ruin his act.

"Bird of prey, big boy." Thomas gave a small, mocking salute. "Wasn't Gideon's daddy a soldier boy? Army? Navy? Ah, one of those SEALs?"

He's trying to throw me off guard with how much he knows. Alex shook his aching head. "You couldn't play mind games with Gideon now if you tried."

Thomas guffawed. "Aw, but I can and I will. Come on."

"What for?!" Simon barked. "What is it with you guys and mind games? Why do you need to do this?" He tugged on the chains that imprisoned him to the ceiling.

"You'll see. Or you won't. No concern of mine. Let's go." Thomas ruffled Alex's bloody, sweaty blond hair. The touch made Alex's stomach twist and turn. "Oh, and Simon, I'd start screaming for help very soon. Things are gonna get messy." Thomas nudged Alex toward the door.

WHEN FLANNERY LED ALEX out of the cell, every bit of rage kindled within Simon erupted. He didn't scream for help. Wild yells roared from his lungs—and he couldn't stop. He should've breathed and calmed down and made a plan. Good ol' Simon, always making plans, always leading during the heat, always steady.

Not now.

He was stripped, beaten, bloodied. Most of all, broken.

They had taken Alex. His friend. One of his brothers in Christ.

They'll kill Alex... Simon yanked against his binds in vain.

This was all one trap for Gideon to come, for Alex to meet his demise, and for George to be humiliated so Thomas could have the last laugh. Thomas was a psychopath—all of this drama and hardwork, for what?

To disgrace George? Get revenge on Alex? The pieces all had to match to make some bigger picture. But Simon didn't care about the big picture. He was tired of the games. He only cared about his friends' lives. He couldn't let anyone else die.

Simon screamed again, shaking with rage. *What did I do to save Alex? What did I do to stop George from causing so much hell? Nothing. I've done nothing!* Simon slowly pulled himself together. Thomas hadn't left any guards with him. Simon wasn't worth much, and he figured he'd just been bait or something. Maybe Thomas had expected him to talk, or was going to torture him to get to Alex. Simon's head hurt too much to figure any answers. All that mattered was that Thomas had taken Alex and Simon couldn't stop them.

As usual, I'm powerless to help my brothers.

Is this what Jesus felt like? Is this what it feels like to be forsaken? But You say You won't forsake us. What am I doing wrong?

The stab wound ached and Simon clamped his eyes shut. He sucked in a breath. *I know You're with me. I can't do this alone. Save Alex, Lord. Protect the guys when they get here. And... and please, give me strength. I can't help anyone alone but I know... I know that I'm still alive for a reason.*

CHAPTER THIRTY

November 1st, 2027

THE GROUPS SURROUNDED THE town in orderly fashion, thoroughly positioned so that no weak spot remained for Thomas to escape through. The warehouse and houses were eerily easy to enclose, a fact that Nate pointed out to Kaleb. They didn't have time to weigh many other options and were certain that should enemy recruits come and attack from behind, they could handle themselves. The word "retreat" wasn't breathed. Every man there knew full well if things went bad, they'd all die there if they didn't adapt through any odds.

Like Nate, none of them had any intentions to die. Not without one hell of a fight.

The sky faded into soft shades of orange, and red. A cool breeze ruffled Nate's dirty hair. He'd pulled a mask over his face, one of Kaleb's top of the line masks that fit snug and could act as an air filter. This attack would include smoke grenades and gas bombs. Thomas was a dirty fighter and they were prepared accordingly. Nate couldn't wear one of the masks without thinking of when he'd been a little kid, and Hunter first showed him how to wear one. Hunter had always made difficult things fun. He'd chased Nate around the house with a mask on his face and even helped Nate paint a skeleton face onto Nate's small mask. *But he's dead. Simon is all I have. I can't lose anyone else.*

To be a soldier, he was terrified of death.

Before the sun disappeared too far below the horizon, Kaleb, AJ, Jordan, and Gideon made sure everyone was in place. One last time. Snipers. Bombers. Footmen. Launchers. Everyone was ready for action.

Once affirmatives were passed along, the command to proceed the attack was given.

Bombers and launchers began the chaos. Like a beautiful choreographed scene, bombs went off to the east side of the town. Blocking the main road from anyone trying to escape the onslaught.

One. The main road blew up.

Two. Smaller bombs tore up little buildings and sent debris flying.

Seconds passed before they got any sort of reaction from the warehouse and apartment complexes. A few guards started shooting from the perches outside, aiming for anything that moved.

Nate was one of the footmen, or so he called the guys that headed for the buildings on foot while hell broke loose around them. The snipers took out the guards. Noah Gyles had said Thomas had about seventy men at the base. Thomas could've called back up for some great battle, but that was unlikely, Kaleb said. While "the unlikely" was often plausible, they couldn't waste energy in fearing the unknown.

Nate carried a fire launcher. It wasn't as bulky as the original prototypes had been in the early 1900s or 2000s. This fire launcher fit close to his body, had an agile build, and was easy to work. Most importantly, it could fry an iceberg in five seconds. Or, so he was pretty sure, anyway. *I'd like to roast Thomas Flannery alive. Watch him scream and turn to dust...*

His thoughts subsided. All that mattered was the fight. With the snipers covering their backs, Nate moved forward with Gideon and Randy at his sides.

They used fire launchers to kill the first group of men they met at the buildings. They'd set the launchers to a setting that allowed for a heavy dose of smoke, and thanks to the thick dark stuff, the men swarming outside to greet the attack were caught off guard.

Is Flannery expecting this? Is it supposed to be this easy?

Nate didn't trust his gut but it sure didn't shut up.

Phase one ended almost as quickly as it began. The brutal attack and distraction complete, the infiltration started. Or, Gideon started it early, leaving the ground and disappearing to the back of the warehouse.

CHAPTER THIRTY-ONE

November 1st, 2027

MOST OF THE FLANNERY'S men rushed outside through the front exits, fleeing the warehouse. Three men ran straight into Gideon at the back exit, their guns drawn. Gideon shot two down and stabbed the third in the neck before he could shoot. He darted into the dimly lit warehouse.

The thugs raced to attack their assaulters. A few shot at Gideon but he threw a grenade at them. As the grenade detonated, making his ears ring, Gideon attacked two more men. They launched themselves at him, too close to shoot without danger of shooting any of their own.

Gideon sliced his knife and cut both of their jugulars in two swift motions. Another teen jumped on his back, veering Gideon sideways. Gideon flipped him over and onto the floor. He bashed the butt of his knife against the boy's head.

"Move!" The enemies' voices rose in one panicked outburst. They couldn't see through the smoke and therefore, couldn't escape fast enough without getting hacked down. Still, the group swarmed for the doors, trying to shoot their way past the gangsters outside.

Gideon ran for the hallway, hoping to avoid friendly fire. Three men rounded the corner, tumbling straight into his blade, and he knifed the other two. They swung at him expertly but his blade won first.

He pushed on quickly. Percy spoke into his ear comm, "Don't go in there alone, Hochberg!"

Gideon tuned him out. He started opening doors, gun ready. His gloved hands were steady for a man who'd just killed over ten men.

The first two rooms sat empty, the third held a man scrambling to contact someone for help. When the door opened, he lifted his gun, but Gideon shot first. The dead man tumbled and Gideon kept going.

Gunfire and yells continued outside, the warzone barely letting up. Gideon found the basement and started down, gun up. He was ready for any attack or trap that might await.

A yell came from the darkness below.

"*Nate*! Nate, help me!" It was Simon. Gideon didn't run, still unsure what the underground might contain as he started for the sound. No one jumped out to kill him. No one tossed a bomb at him.

There were three doors, but Simon's screaming came from the second. Gideon stepped sideways to it. "Simon?" he said calmly.

"Gideon! Get me down! We gotta find Alex!"

Gideon set his jaw and shot the lock off of the door. He pushed it open, pulling a fold of lock picks from his pants. "Where is he?" he snapped.

Simon hung limply, covered in blood and bruises, a bandage on his chest. Besides him, the cell was empty. "It's a trap, Gideon."

"Which part?"

"All of it. They aren't trying to kill all of us off. It's a cat and mouse. He wanted you, Gideon—he wanted answers." Simon breathed hard as Gideon worked at the locks. "Thomas took Alex for a distraction."

"What—"

"Thomas is gone, Gideon!"

The lock gave. Gideon caught Simon carefully and sat him down. Tugging off his black jacket, he put it around Simon. "Where is Alex?" "Thomas took him. I don't know where."

"When?" Gideon gripped Simon's shoulder hard.

"Gideon, it's been over an hour ago! He knew you were coming. He's gone by now but I don't think he took Alex with him." Simon moaned softly, gripping at Gideon's hand.

Gideon released his shoulder but let him lean against him. "Wait here. Help will come."

"You can't seriously go out there alone. Alex could be anywhere!" Simon choked. "Please, Gideon. I don't know what Thomas has planned but it's nothing good and it's for you."

"For me?" Gideon frowned slightly, then spoke into his comm. "Percy?"

"Chief?"

Two figures appeared in the doorway—Nate and Randy. They were blood-splattered and their masks identified them. Nate ran in, grabbing Simon tight. "Simon, are you OK?"

"Alex isn't here." Simon leaned against Nate. "Thomas is gone."

Gideon tuned them out to talk to Percy. "I need backup outside. Alex isn't here, we have to track him down. I don't know what Thomas wants, but I think Alex is going to be a distraction." *Or a test.*

Percy swore. "We'll be out back."

Gideon turned to Simon. "You guys get out of here."

"Listen to me! We have to find Alex but if you're there, something bad is gonna happen!" Simon hissed.

Gideon hurried for the door—but Randy, the coward, stepped in his way. "W-wait, Hochberg, maybe Simon's right. Something fishy is going on."

"I've got to find my brother." Gideon ran past him.

NATE AND RANDY GOT Simon between them and carried him upstairs. The warehouse was mostly empty now—the fight had been carried outside. The gunshots, screams, and various sounds of explosions rang out and lingered in the air along with the smoke.

They dragged Simon out through the back. Simon insisted he didn't need medical attention, begging them to go after Gideon. Nate didn't push him for explanations as to what was going on. Gideon would find out what was messed up soon enough.

"There you are!" Ben Bordalli ran over like a bat out of hell.

Never had Nate been so happy to see his ugly mug. "Where's—"

"AJ's with your dad," Ben said, gun in hand. "Boy, how many times have I told you, you gotta work as a team?!"

Ben lectured him plenty of times about teamwork and courage. "I got the second part down." Nate snapped, holding Simon tight.

Ben laughed. "Well, let's work on the teamwork part now. The med van is about a mile away now, let's get Simon to it."

"Can't it come closer?" Randy growled.

Simon shook his head. "It's a freaking warzone, guys, I'm fine, give me a gun—"

"You're drugged and weak as a kitten." Ben sighed. "Nate, Randy, get him to the south street, should be quiet that way. I'll cover you."

"Yessir." Nate started helping Randy move Simon along. He'd said yessir without argument, that was teamwork, right?

They moved fast, trying to stay hidden when possible. The fight stayed at the warehouse and complexes. South street was abandoned, of course, with a few random trees and windowless street shops. They had one sniper positioned on a rooftop, but Nate didn't see him anymore, so he quickened his steps.

Simon blacked out from blood loss or drugs, maybe both. Randy stumbled but caught him firmly. "Hurry!" Randy snapped.

Nate pushed on harder.

The gunfire kept ringing from the warehouse.

Another gunshot. Closer. Distinct.

A thud followed.

Behind him.

Nate froze and craned his neck. His stomach dropped. "Ben!"

Ben lay sprawled on the asphalt sidewalk, a gunshot wound pouring blood from his chest. He held a hand over the wound, gun in his other hand as he tried seeing who'd shot him.

Nate pushed Simon at Randy. "Get him to the van!" He scanned the rooftops but didn't see a sniper. He didn't see anyone on the ground anywhere. Nate dragged Ben upright, breathing hard. "Ben. Ben, please hold on."

"Don't worry about me, boy, I'm all right." Ben groaned.

A sob broke through Nate's chest but he shoved it down and dragged Ben along desperately. South street. Med van. Vince would be there, he could fix anyone. He could save Ben. Stop the blood from pouring down the old man's chest.

Another distinct gunshot. It didn't hit Ben or Nate. Nate could only pray one of their own had found the shooter and picked him off.

Nate's footsteps grew too fast for Ben to catch up with. Ben staggered and dropped to his knees, coughing. "Nate —"

"Get up!" Nate nearly screamed. "Get up and move! We're almost there!"

Ben grabbed his arm and let Nate haul him up. They only made it a few more feet before Ben collapsed again. This time, Nate couldn't pick him up again. His hands shook and he swore, trying to use his body as leverage to move the old man up off the sidewalk.

"Look at me," Ben muttered weakly.

Nate held him tight, trying to look past the blood. Trying to look his friend in the eyes. "I'm sorry." There were a million things he wanted to say but never thought he'd regret not saying them.

Ben smiled as if he knew that. "I'm going home, kid. I wanna see you there." Once the words escaped his bloody lips, Ben's eyes slowly stilled, and his chest stopped racking.

Everything went still.

Nate screamed. He screamed and he yelled and he buried his face against Ben's body. The turmoil in his soul was like a sea raging in a small glass cup. Shattering everything and spreading more, more, more. Nate couldn't breathe. He couldn't see past the tears and snot running down his face.

"AJ!" he yelled, only once, because as soon as he cried it, he knew better. They had come to save Nate's brother and they'd lost one. They'd lost AJ's best friend.

Nate leaned his head back and yelled. "Where are you, God? He believed!" But his voice broke and the last word was only a strangled cry in his throat.

CHAPTER THIRTY-TWO

November 1st, 2027

"GIDEON, I HAVE SIGHTS on Alex." Phil's cool voice came from Gideon's comm. He gave a brief location, then, "Approach slowly. We'll scout the area when we have some guys available. Give us a minute. Do not act."

Gideon didn't entirely understand why Philip sounded like someone had killed his best friend. He took a breath and ran on, through the town, staying low and out of easy sights in case someone tried shooting him.

Gideon reached mainstreet. Thomas had escaped before they'd even arrived, but the end of the road had been blown up a few miles down. In less than three hours, the man had done God knew what to Simon and Alex. All that mattered right now was Alex was gone and Gideon needed to find him.

Gideon rounded the corner of a windowless pizza parlor, gun raised and ready. A figure stood in the middle of the road. Obviously, he hadn't been there when they got drone footage.

As Gideon approached the street, Philip's words played in his mind. *"I found Alex, mainstreet."*

Gideon dropped his gun ever so slightly. "Alex?"

Alex turned around slowly, wearing Army pants, small new burn marks all along his chest. He held a small pistol to his temple, his grip shaking so bad Gideon saw it wobble at a distance.

"Stop there!" Alex shouted. "Just... just stop, mate."

"Alex, what are you doing?" Gideon glanced around for someone, anyone, who might be waiting to shoot Gideon when his attention was on Alex.

"Gideon, the area isn't scouted! I said wait!" Philip's taught voice came through the comm.

Gideon pocketed his ear comm. Eyes on Alex, he moved closer down the sidewalk and onto the cracked road. "Put the gun down. Whatever happens because of it happens, but I need you to—"

"No, Gideon." Alex stepped back, legs buckling. He kept the barrel of the gun against his bloody temple. "Stop moving! Listen to me!"

"I'm listening." Gideon clenched his gun tighter. He was just close enough to see the fear in Alex's eyes but not close enough to lunge for him.

"Thomas knows about the suppliers, about you being so vital to the end of the war, he knows about Kaleb's alliance... And he... He's gonna hunt West. He wants to humiliate George and..." A weak, bitter chuckle escaped Alex as he took one more step back. "What better way to do it than this?"

"Put the gun down. We'll figure this out." Gideon moved forward. "You're talking like a—"

"A man has a gun on you, Gideon. If I don't pull this trigger, he pulls yours. People need you. Good people. Innocent people." Alex's voice trembled. "So I need you to look away, Gid." His voice broke.

"I'm not doing anything without you. If this is Thomas' idea of a game, we aren't playing."

"He wants me dead! If I don't do this, you die and I die anyway and the war is screwed and—" Alex's eyes flickered to his left. Movement. Gideon barely caught the small flash of clothing in a doorway to an abandoned corner building.

He kept his eyes on Alex, fury rising. "If Thomas wants to play with George, he'll play with George," he said smoothly. "But you and me, we're not going down."

"He'll shoot you." Alex choked, shaking his head slightly, tears running down his bruised face. "I've seen Faisal kill before, I can't watch you die. I can't watch you die, Gideon." His arm tensed and the gun steadied against his head.

Gideon had never seen him so terrified. Never seen him so peaceful the very next second as he closed his eyes.

A muffled shot went off.

Gideon screamed.

Alex staggered back, the gun dropping from his hand as he gripped his wrist and yelled. "*Gid!*"

Gideon dropped low as soon as he heard Alex's scream.

A gunshot erupted. A moment passed of nothing but silence.

Mind swimming, Gideon ran to Alex and tackled him in a hug. He held tight as Alex sobbed against him, holding his arm that had been darted with a paralyzer. Gideon let go, checking his brother over, speaking quickly. "It's OK. I'm gonna get you home. Where else are you hurt?"Alex wept. His chest was covered with new burns and tiny cuts. The left side of his neck had a new burn mark. Besides those obvious injuries, he'd been beaten, and they'd need an X-ray to make sure he wasn't bleeding internally.

Philip ran over, rifle swung over his back, tugging his mask down. "Med van's coming."

Gideon looked down at Alex, holding him up in his arms. Alex shook uncontrollably and his breathing was quick and shallow. "What the hell were you thinking?" Gideon clasped the right side of Alex's face, steadying his brother. "Don't you ever do something that stupid again or I'll shoot you myself!"

"I-I... I didn't mean..." Alex moaned, eyes clamping shut in pain. "I'm sorry—"

"No, I'm sorry, I should've been here. Shouldn't have ever happened." Gideon glanced up again, heart hammering. Philip went over to the old florist shop, peeking in, gun ready. When he'd made sure the man was dead, he came back out.

Alex groaned and coughed up blood. Gideon held him tight. When he could breathe again, Alex panted, "I—"

"Don't apologize again." Gideon stopped him. "Just relax and breathe. We'll be fine."

"Si?"

"He's dandy."

Alex passed out heavily against Gideon.

NATE DRAGGED BEN'S BODY to the van. He didn't know what else to do. He didn't head back to the warehouse and complexes. The fighting was over now, the world eerily silent, like even the birds dared not make a sound. Darkness wisped throughout the town as night fell.

Nate turned when the van doors opened. Two men carried Simon out and the doors slammed again. The van veered onto the road, heading toward mainstreet.

"What—" Nate paled.

"Bucks is fine," one man said. "Van was needed for another injured guy. Let's get this boy in a truck." He took Simon's unconscious body to a truck, loaded him in the back. "You can sit with him. We should start getting radios and body counts soon. Might need help with the wounded."

Nate squeezed Simon's arm as if trying to gain strength, but Simon wasn't awake. He wouldn't be awake anytime soon. Nate sucked in a deep breath and went to help gather the dead.

After an hour, they'd collected their dead—a mix of Gideon's, Kaleb's, Jordan's, and AJ's, with a total over twenty. Ben was among the dead counted. Over thirty had been injured and they were tended to in vans and trucks.

They loaded the dead into trucks, too. Nate focused on helping the men prepare to leave and didn't let himself stop. Jordan worked alongside him, after checking on his son in silence. Nate didn't know where Kaleb or AJ were —if he were honest with himself, he was hiding from both of them. The two men had never met before. AJ had been more of a father than Kaleb ever had been.

And with Ben dead, Nate was too numb to handle either of them now.

They moved out in the dark, a mini caravan of trucks, headlights, and bikes. Nate ignored everyone and rode with Simon and Jordan, falling asleep near them both.

CHAPTER THIRTY-THREE

November 2nd, 2027

THREE DAYS HAD PASSED since the battle, but West couldn't stop and mourn with his brothers. While Springtown licked its wounds and Alex lay desolate, West had a job to do.

The nation still raged and roared—people wanted to know when Brian would attack, why he hadn't, and where he would. The media didn't shut up and the Union refused to give any information, not wanting the Confeds to get any more insight than they already did. The moles and spies on both sides began meeting their makers: open executions were held whenever a traitor was found.

The Mexican border stood strong. West had done his duty well, even when the world around him tumbled. He knew the time of turmoil would end soon. Gideon had contacted him once to warn that Brian had been out of touch.

Brian was up to something and West couldn't figure out what. He had so much more to understand since his mother had told him her truths. So much more to juggle.

He'd looked into Keegan Black, but found little to nothing. The supplier was a phantom, there was no money trail to be found, but he lived in North California—one of the worst places to abide in. The man might be dead by now. West hoped not—Springtown needed the ghost man. Keegan had done a fair job thus far keeping them alive.

Until Flannery. West had called George the day after the attack and his father had flipped his rocker. "That attack was to anger the media, weaken the nation's hopes, and humiliate *me*. He made that mission personal when he took Thompson and Simon. He's playing with me, Kaleb, and Jordan."

"Why?" West sighed.

"None of your business," George snapped. "We need him dead."

"Who are you going to send?"

"Hochberg, once he can get back to his feet."

"Is that a good idea?" "It might not seem like it but he knows better to make it personal. He's one of the best assassins I've got." George paused for a moment. "Thomas chose Springtown to attack. He was paid, I assume, by someone, but why pick Springtown?"

Is this another test? "He probably found out Gideon had protected the town before and you had allowed it. Or maybe, he knows Springtown is one of the valuable towns to the Confeds, figured he'd stir things up. He could have many motivations." West's head hurt, like a billion sharp edges dragged across every crevice in his skull.

Too many pieces. Too many facts. Too much darkness.

Shut up. Handle it. Every part matters.

"I didn't expect Thomas to arrive for revenge—not now." George growled and flipped the topic smoothly, as if something occurred to him, and it all mattered very little anymore. "I have to go, but I'll see you soon."

The conversation baffled West. He finished his security rounds, checked on the security men and coordinators, prepping the group for the next night's trade through. The trade would be a big one—thirty kids, all smuggled from an American underground ring—and the men trying to take the kids into Mexico weren't known for trustworthy behavior. The thugs were hot-tempered, but West's guys could handle them.

He'd prove himself to George. One last time, probably. George's Test was coming closer.

West ate at the mess hall that night. Not because he liked the food or the company of a bunch of smelly, sunburned men, but because he wanted to live in the mission. As much as he wanted to hide in his room and ponder the challenges before him, this job was vital. Something in his gut said eat with the men one last time. He would probably never see them again.

West sat at a table with Juan, eating quietly, listening to the men chatter in English and their native tongues. He didn't try listening to every conversation. He didn't try to pretend he did. But his presence didn't bother any of the men. Maybe they didn't see him as George's heir, or a killer, or a monster.

You're all of those things and worse.

But they see me...

West forced down some food. How did they see him? Was it all some act? Did any of them truly see him as a good leader? Or an adversary?

Ricardo brought his tray over, sitting beside West, close enough to rub elbows. He kept his voice down, "You look like someone killed your best friend."

Ignoring the venom in Ricardo's voice, West sighed. "Thanks for helping the youngsters earlier. It was some quick thinking you did."

Three young teens had accidentally set fire to the mess kitchen. Ricardo had been the first to see and act, putting the fire out. He'd nearly beaten the boys before other men intervened.

"Don't pacify me, Johnston."

West eyed him. "If you don't want me to pacify you, don't pacify me. You didn't have to sit here." He cast his gaze around the busy tables.

"Why come here?" Ricardo kept his tone low.

"George sent me."

"Why?"

"Because—"

"Cut the bull," Ricardo muttered. "We know that the border was weak but there's something more, isn't there?"

"What do you mean?" Ricardo's paranoia was heightening West's bad mood.

"Everything's complicated with men like you." Ricardo stuffed a big bite of tamale into his mouth. As he chewed it up thoughtfully, he watched West for his reaction.

West didn't budge. "I'm way too tired to try to decipher what you're getting at."

Ricardo fell quiet a long moment. "I need to talk to you in private."

"OK." West shrugged, eating some more of his plain bread. He'd eaten enough tamales and Mexican food to set him for life. "Office at lights out?"

Ricardo nodded and ate the rest of his dinner in silence.

AT LIGHTS OUT, RIGHT on the dot, a sharp knock sounded on West's office door. He opened it, letting Ricardo in. Ricardo was fully dressed and armed, like usual. West locked the door behind him.

"The war is getting worse." Ricardo began. "When it ends, it will end in a bang, not a whisper."

West hesitated. What was he supposed to say to that?

"And you have a great part in it. You are just like your father." Ricardo's lips twisted in a light snarl. "I despise Johnston's impending empire... but," he paused again.

"A *but* makes that all better." West quirked an eyebrow. He bit back any other remark and hid his disgust at being called his father.

"But you have a hand in the nations' greater goods. You can help my homeland. You..." Ricardo licked his chapped lips. "You could get me out of here."

"Out of here?" West crossed his arms against his chest.

"I could be of more use to my nation elsewhere. Do you not need allies?"

"I do, but—"

"Then let me work." Ricardo snapped. "You don't have to like me, and I don't have to like you, but you could let me work. Anywhere, any job."

"What about protecting the border, isn't that homage to your fatherland?" West studied Ricardo's face. His dark eyes were heavy with rage, his lips in a thin line, like he'd a thousand things left to say. But he kept it all tucked away. *Like me.*

"It is but it isn't enough for me." Ricardo shrugged. "I need more. I want to do more. I'm no Johnston," his tone grew biting again, "but if it means I'm useful, I could take orders from one." He lifted his chin, short-cropped black hair and set jaw giving him a regal look. West admired his guts—but didn't trust him.

Do I really trust anyone now? Even Jack is keeping secrets.

"OK." He smirked. "You got a deal."

"What?" Ricardo blinked in surprise before regaining his initial emotionless expression.

"When I leave, you come with me. I'll put you to work. It won't be this easy—won't be near as easy as it's been here. You'll probably die," West said, not a hint of teasing in his voice. What he was saying was true but Ricardo probably knew already.

"*Sí.*" Ricardo exhaled slowly. "Thank you."

West doubted his moral character but couldn't say he wouldn't let Ricardo do what must be done. "Thanks for coming to me." *Maybe I can hand him off to Gideon or something. I don't really need a guy on my side who hates me, do I? He isn't trained or super skilled. But he had the guts to ask me to get him a job elsewhere. Maybe he's trying to run.*

Ricardo gave a terse nod and headed to the door.

"Ricardo?" He stopped.

"Can I ask why you want to fight elsewhere? Do you need money for your family, like Juan?"

Ricardo scoffed, rolling his eyes. "No *familia* for me, Johnston."

"Do you have friends in danger?"

"No. What you see," Ricardo patted his strong chest, "is all that comes with me, sir."

First time he called me sir. Is that progress? "Good." West sighed. "Stay ready to leave. When I'm called, we leave immediately."

Ricardo smirked, leaving the room. West finished up some work before going to bed. He dreamt of Springtown being wiped off the map, of Jack dying in the trenches defending a town he didn't love, leaving a wife and a baby at home. The dream was lopsided but it woke West multiple times. He never could reach Jack in the dreams— he was across the country, chained up in a cell, watching Jack get shot on some little screen across from him. He didn't know why he was chained—George's Test, maybe? Every time he saw the footage, his mind told him he had to reach Jack's family. Protect them. Save them.

And every time, he couldn't break free. He was reminded he couldn't win alone.

He woke up drenched in sweat.

THE NEXT NIGHT, TWENTY minutes after the designated time, three trucks arrived at the Mexican border. West had security keep guns on the trucks, the launchers ready if anything stupid was tried. Every man stood in position, some near the truck, some from the border walls.

The window of the first truck rolled down and the driver's smirked, cigarette hanging from his lips. "Sorry we're late." Underneath the heavy floodlights, West could see the man's glinting eyes and didn't see any remorse whatsoever.

"Open the backs," West instructed.

The man didn't get out. "Do it yourself." He tossed a key at West. West caught it and tilted his head slightly, his instinct to tell the man off. He had a bad feeling the smuggle wasn't going to go smoothly.

He glanced at Ricardo before moving around to the end of the truck. "One truck at a time," he told a guard nearby. Everyone waited and a few came closer with their guns raised, in case it was a set up or the slaves acted stupid.

West unlocked the back of the truck, slid it up, and held his breath as the familiar stench filled his nostrils. Ten boys, all under the age of thirteen, sat quietly in the back. It would be hard for Jordan to rescue these kids since they were being taken out of the US and he'd missed his chance of snagging them before they hit the border. Jordan would carry that guilt—but he'd also hunt them down, though it wouldn't be a fruitful mission.

One of the boys met West's gaze defiantly, his dark, olive skin covered with bruises and some gashes.

"Clear." West told the others to check the two other trucks. He leaned in slightly, whispering, "Come here, kid."

The boy's eyes widened but he jutted his chin and moved closer.

"Take this." West pulled a very small tracking device out of his pocket and before the boy could move, West shoved it into the boy's left ear, securing it. It was too small for the traders to notice, and hopefully the boy would be smart enough to keep it hidden.

The boy froze and the other boys glanced at each other tiredly. West stepped back.

"Chief! *Ambush*!" Ricardo's voice.

Gunshots followed, both from the men in the trucks and the guards from the tower. West slid the truck door shut just before a bullet hit it. West drew his gun and darted for cover, more bullets burning into the truck beside him. He shot the driver who'd given him the key as the man tried to defend himself from within the cover of the truck. The passenger jumped out and shot at the group of guards on foot.

West fired at a man escaping the back of the second truck. The two others hadn't contained children. They'd contained thugs waiting with guns. Their pathetic attempt of rebellion would end with not a soul of them left alive.

West fired again, ducking as gunshots came over his head. Out of the corner of his eye, he saw Juan, running toward the second truck with his gun pumping round after round.

West took aim at another thug as the man tried to hide behind the truck. He fired. The body toppled. The thugs dropped like flies as the snipers on the wall took aim, struggling to shoot around the truck but managing to take out anyone who moved out of cover too much.

"West, move!" Ricardo shouted somewhere to his left. West jerked sideways.

A man approached, shooting at West with all the rage in the world, moving forward like the snipers wouldn't gun him down in a second.

But the gunners didn't shoot the man.

A figure jumped out of the darkness and tackled the thug to the ground before he could reach West. Two gunshots followed.

"Ricardo!" West swore, scrambling to his feet and darting over. The gunfight raged about him but he didn't care about getting shot. He grabbed Ricardo by his shoulders, hauling him off the thug. Carrying Ricardo with one arm like he weighed nothing, West got him back behind the first truck, setting him on the ground.

Ricardo shook in his arms but didn't say a word. West's headlamp moved over Ricardo's body hastily and stopped. Dark blood oozed from a bullet hole in Ricardo's stomach. West pressed a hand to it, shouting for a medic, but doubted any would come.

West leaned closer, trying to cover Ricardo's head as bullets pelted the truck above them. A strange, muffled sound could be faintly heard above the shouts, screams, and gunshots.

He's crying. The sound remained weak and strained. West looked down and clasped Ricardo's neck with his other hand. "You're gonna be fine. Relax. Help's coming."

"Help... never comes..." Ricardo moaned. He grasped West's forearm, shaking hard. "I don't wanna die. I don't wanna die! *Ayúdame.* Please!" His dark eyes raged with pain and fear.

West held him tight, hot blood pushing against his other hand. He'd been shot fatally and they both knew it, but it was human nature to offer vain hope. "Hold on Ricardo. You'll be OK."

"I don't wanna burn, *hermano.*" Ricardo choked past a sob. To be the man with a sharp tongue and burning glares, West never thought him capable of weeping, even in the eyes of death.

"You don't have to if you believe. That simple. Trust me." West didn't know what he was saying. What'd Mr. Fisher said about that thief on the cross beside Jesus? He was losing Ricardo, and fast, so he blurted, "Remember that thief hanging beside Jesus? Just ask forgiveness and you won't burn."

Ricardo's body stilled and his breathing rasped. "I-I'm sorry."

West held him by his shoulder and looked him in the eye till the light faded out. Ricardo's head lolled against West's arm. The medics came then—five seconds too late, and as they tried to resuscitate Ricardo's body, West looked up. The road lay covered with thugs' bodies and his own men. Just like that, the outbreak was over, and men who had been breathing, men with dreams, men with families, only minutes earlier, lay dead.

"Remove our own." He shouted. "We bury them tonight and burn the others."

Juan limped over, gun dropping when he saw Ricardo. In the floodlights, with his hands covered in blood, the man fell to his knees and whispered prayers.

But Ricardo didn't wake. The medics covered him and ran to the next victim in need of help. There was no time for the dead in war.

Juan sat beside Ricardo, body shaking softly. West turned away. He had to establish order—bury the dead, send word to his father, and situate the smuggled kids for the night.

No matter what he did the rest of the night, the burning truth remained at the back of his head. *Ricardo is dead because of me. I'd be dead if he hadn't saved me.* It hurt worse than Ed's death. He just couldn't pinpoint why.

THE KIDS WERE ALLOWED a bunk to themselves, fed, clothed, and put to bed. West made sure of that himself, and no harm came to the children, though their eyes flickered every time they saw movement. The boys went to sleep after a while. Jordan would send men soon to pick them up, pretending to be more traders, though they'd get the kids to an American safe haven.

West went to help bury their dead in the Blocks. The cemetery was large and took up a large plot about a mile from the base. The men called it the Blocks because of how eerily symmetrical it all was. Almost like the old memorial grounds with the white crosses, but instead of white crosses, small gray blocks sat over each grave, some with names, some without.

They'd lost fifteen men in the squirmish. All twenty five of the attackers had been killed and piled up near the Blocks to be burnt.

Once the fifteen were buried, it was near morning, and most of them went to their barracks. West allowed those who'd done major fighting to rest and the others took their positions and jobs.

West went to his office, exhaustion trying to catch up with him. He'd shut off all emotions, except rage, which throbbed through every vein in his body.

He called Gideon, updated him about every detail he'd learned about their missions. He didn't tell Gideon about Cindy's sudden loyalty or her huge move in the shadows. Gideon told him what had all happened at the battle and such, and how his CIA link had been killed, but he hadn't found anything new recently.

"Can you find Keegan?" Gideon asked coldly.

"Yes. I'll do it so George doesn't find out."

"The sooner we can form an alliance with him, the better. He needs to be kept alive."

"The attack on Springtown—"

"Thomas was paid but it was to get at George, so even though we controlled it, Thomas will continue to rampage. If Keegan is alerted, maybe he can help us protect the townships." Gideon grew quiet a moment. "I'm going to hunt Thomas. George gave me the instructions."

West figured Gideon would've hunted anyway. "Right." He sat down, staring at his desk. "How is Alex?"

"Fine." A lie, but West didn't push.

"Did Mr. Fisher accept Kaleb's alliance?" West asked quietly.

"Not yet. They've had no time to discuss much. I haven't pushed anything while I've been here, I've stayed with Alex."

"And?"

"They'll probably maintain alliance but if George ever requests something or pulls something, they'll go down fighting. Kaleb isn't exactly thrilled to be George's candidate for the job." Gideon sighed wearily. "But... honestly, West, I think it just might work. I don't think those two men trust each other as far as they can throw one another, but with the war ending, and us finding Keegan's link... maybe when the war stops, we can restore things. There's so much going on but things will become clear, one day."

West bit his lip a moment. "So much hinges on us."

"We can handle it."

"Strange to think we could help end all of this."

"It's up to us, West. The tiny threads make the bigger picture. Cut those and..."

"Right. Have you heard from Brian?"

"News says he'll be attacking soon, D.C. again probably, with the UN backing. It got loud for a while, it's getting quiet now. The nation's waiting quite anxiously for the war to continue where they can see it." Gideon's tone was heavy with bitterness.

"He'll regret it." West set his jaw. They'd warned Brian not to attack, that he was a puppet in the show, but he'd pushed on anyway. He was harming the nation more than he was helping. The Union and the world didn't see that. Brian was a UN hero and he'd rather die than give that position up. Even if the government he worked for was wicked. Even if the government he worked for wanted his family and hometown wiped off the map.

War was a big picture, but the little pixels, when broken and removed, altered a great deal. If Springtown was in Brian's picture, and he was in the war's picture, things could be changed. If West and Gideon were George's top men, they could change much. If Kaleb, one of the best gangsters in the US, could play the game, he could change the game.

Such little changes, but the war rested on their shoulders. It was all overwhelming and invigorating at once.

Gideon finally spoke, tone hard, "He watched Rene' get tortured without coming for her. I doubt he regrets his stunt in D.C. and I doubt he feels any remorse for his following actions done in the name of his great, honorable cause."

West gulped. "Maybe not, but he's sure making our jobs harder."

"We march on," Gideon said dryly.

West wrestled with his thoughts for a second before asking, "Have you heard from Jack lately?" *Maybe Gideon knows what's going on. He's good at uncovering secrets.*

"Yes."

"How is he? He's talked to me but not a whole lot as of late."

"He's fine."

A sigh, "Thanks, Gideon."

"If you're worried, call him." Gideon hung up.

West closed his eyes. Pictured Ricardo in his arms, bleeding to death, his sobs mingling with the deafening sounds of gunfire and screams. West didn't feel like talking to anyone. Especially not Jack. He left his phone on the table and collapsed into bed.

CHAPTER THIRTY-FOUR

November 3rd, 2027

SPRINGTOWN RESTED SILENTLY LIKE all the life had been drained when they'd buried their dead only a couple—had it been few?—days before. Time didn't exist to Nate. He didn't think it existed to anyone anymore. The town had entered a state of trance survival. Some of Kaleb's men helped rebuild and maintain balance, working what jobs needed to be done while the civilians rested. Most of them stayed busy to keep alert after the first day. They stayed outside, stayed busy, or tended the wounded.

Kaleb and Mr. Fisher spoke together on the second day, after everyone had gotten some rest. Nate listened in, along with a few of Gideon's, Kaleb's, and Jordan's men. Gideon didn't join the meeting—he had been glued to a seat near

Alex since they'd gotten the Aussie on bedrest. Alex didn't eat much and woke up screaming often. Gideon calmed him, usually, and Percy brought him what he needed.

Nate set his jaw, watching Kaleb come into the courthouse meeting room. Jordan sat quietly at the table—the man could've slept sitting up. His face was gray, eyes sunken, hair barely smoothed down. He'd stayed with Simon most of the time but insisted on attending the meeting. Probably figuring Kaleb might snap and he'd have to play intercessor.

Mr. Fisher met Kaleb's gaze coolly and shook his hand. Their chivalry wasn't entirely forced. They'd had each others' backs in the battle, but even though they'd both shed blood to defend each side, neither fully trusted the other.

Nate wouldn't trust Kaleb, either. Didn't trust him. Would never trust him.

But Mr. Fisher had too much at risk not to at least hear Kaleb out, so the leaders of Springtown spoke quietly before they all sat down. The tension in the air made Nate believe they would've stayed standing if they weren't all tired to the bone.

"The alliance would not be imprisonment," Kaleb said firmly. "I know you've no reason to believe me, but my alliance would be to benefit your town. George has no motives for this besides wanting a soft cushion insurance. He doesn't want your men or your submission."

Nate licked his lips. Why was George bothering, then? Was he lying and did want to destroy the town? That didn't seem right—he'd no reason to really care about Springtown and the civilians wouldn't be very useful in his work. It made less sense for him to send Kaleb for this, yet, he had.

Nate watched as the Springtown leaders exchanged brief, weary glances. Mr. Fisher spoke quietly, "We understand. We wouldn't be here without your help. But George being your boss, that raises issues for us, and we cannot trust that this alliance won't destroy us down the road."

Kaleb nodded. "I understand the risks and the what if's involved, sir, but every alliance is like that. George might be my boss, but he ain't the bugger standing here. I am. I make this deal with you, I hold it. I don't make these often. Regardless of George's motives, regardless of what he wants, I'll take care of your town the best I can." There was no venom or coyness to his voice. Just pure sincerity and some annoyance.

Nate glanced at Jordan. Did Kaleb mean any of this? He'd tried to get mushy on the drive to rescue Alex and Simon. *It's just a mask. Just another game.*

Jordan met his gaze, but no traces of anger lay in his eyes. He looked back to Mr. Fisher. "I stand with Kaleb. We stood strong together, Mr. Fisher. Your people may see us as simply thugs, men that cannot be trusted, but we lost men, too, and no trick is worth losing our own. Not to us. We are not trying to force your hand. We would like to help."

Nate wanted to scream. Why did they suddenly care? He and Simon had started this mess. They didn't need their dads to come play pick up.

Mr. Fisher took a slow breath and nodded. "We've discussed it for a while now," the men eyed him as he spoke, "and we will accept the offer on conditions. We need alliances as each time things go bad, they get worse, and we could defend ourselves at first but no longer. That being said..." He met Kaleb's gaze. "If George requests something, or demands us to be killed, we will fight back, no matter the consequences."

Mr. Fisher would die before he surrendered, and Nate figured his men would do the same. They seemingly had no choice right now but to take the risk.

It didn't seem like Kaleb was actually lying. *Jordan knew when he was being stupid and if Jordan agreed with this... No, I can't fall for it, either way.* Nate sighed.

"Understood. If it ever comes to that, you have permission to shoot me yourself," Kaleb said in all seriousness.

Sean stood up a little, haggard and slouched from a shoulder wound. "May I ask something?"

Mr. Fisher nodded but motioned for Sean to sit back down.

"I haven't exactly been up to par as I ought. What will the alliance actually do, if we're taking the risk?" His words were slightly slow, like the painkillers he was on fumbled his speech.

Kaleb gave Mr. Fisher a questioning look before getting a nod, so he explained. "We would send aid when needed. In return, we ask you to let us know of any outside activity you may find, any connections, anything you can give. We won't ask for aid or supplies and we will continue to supply you."

"Seems... lopsided." Sean mumbled.

"We want to help but it isn't a charity," Kaleb said. "Your information will help us, you'd even have the ability to leave and go with us on certain missions or such, to see the nation, but nothing is required. I can handle this treaty. It will keep your town alive. If it goes bad, you guys don't want it, whatever happens, we can end it."

Nate nearly chewed his lip off. Kaleb had lost his mind.

Most of the men and leaders agreed to the alliance quietly. Nate watched as Mr. Fisher shook Kaleb's hand, his jaw set. He probably just wanted to go home, hug his wife, sit with his kids, make sure Simon wasn't being bothered by the little girls who insisted on playing doctor with him. Instead, Mr. Fisher had to run a town, protect people who caused issues.

Simon might love the town, but Nate didn't see the attraction. A home was nice, maybe, and Mrs. Fisher's home cooked meals were to die for, but he'd take the gang any day. The gang was predictably unpredictable—hold your own, most couldn't be trusted, protect your brothers but only if you were safe first. A town was more like a family—a good family, where you could love and get hurt, defend and be hated. He didn't trust the town. He didn't trust safety or love or anything resembling what Mr. Fisher had.

"Don't we have to name it?" Sean asked groggily. "The alliance, I mean?" Another officer nudged him to shut him up.

Kaleb smirked. "How's the Grim Alliance sound?" Mr. Fisher studied him for a moment, as if searching for any disdain and finding only morbid humor. "I don't have anything better and my daughter isn't here to pick a good name."

"Grim Alliance it is." Jordan stood up, hiding his new limp.

"Let's go home." Mr. Fisher adjourned the meeting.

Nate watched Kaleb walk away. A part of him wanted to go after him, get some truthful answers. But he watched Mr. Fisher and Jordan leave the room. He'd rather rest with them for a while, see Simon, and see if the men spoke of their own concerns before he voiced his to Kaleb.

SIMON SQUEEZED RENE'S HAND tightly but couldn't bring himself to watch her face fall as he said, "As soon as we're healed, we're going back to Paradise." It was the first time they'd been alone since he'd been brought to their farm home, and he didn't want to ruin it, but she deserved to know.

"What? Why?" Rene' shook her head. "There's no need —"

"West could take the Test any day now." He licked his lips. "And Jack can't be there."

"What?" Her voice dropped. "Why not?"

"Can you keep a secret?" "Of course."

"Jack's getting married and his girlfriend is pregnant so he has to move her and take care of them and all that. He really can't leave last second to help West survive if the Test goes bad." Simon glanced up. *There. I played a Spencer Anderson and spilled everything.*

Rene's eyes widened with concern. "His girlfriend is pregnant?"

"Yeah." Simon groaned. "Her and Abi are both expecting at freakin' fantastic times."

"God'll take care of them." She didn't let go of his hand, holding it tightly. "What about West? You guys have to go back *why* exactly? You could go help from here."

"Our base is closer to where we think George might test West—at his estate." Simon sighed. "Anyway, we don't wanna draw any more attention to Springtown than we have already. If a bunch of thugs camp up here for too long, it's dangerous. The leaders," he smirked a bit at the title, "decided some of each group will stay, mostly guys from Kaleb's gang, to defend you guys. No more guys than necessary and they'll bring lots of weaponry with them when they come back for good."

Rene' took a shaky breath. Her whole world was being rocked, and he just wanted to hold her, but he didn't dare move. His wound ached too bad and he honestly wasn't sure if she'd like affection right now. Her clenched jaw made him wonder if she was angry. Probably so.

"Right. I know," she mumbled. "So that means you're going to help West when the time comes."

"That's part of the plan."

"And what if George hurts you? Kills you? He won't like anyone interfering, Si, that's crazy dangerous!" She glared at him.

"I know but we've gotta. West needs our help." Simon shook his head. "We'll be fine. No matter what George does."

"It's the same Test that Jack's dad died from, isn't it?" Rene' dropped her gaze, voice tight.

"Yeah, but West'll pull through." He put an arm around her slowly. When she didn't pull away, Simon relaxed a little bit more. "We'll come back. You're not getting rid of me that easy."

"When?" She frowned.

"I don't know if Nate wants to move into the town, or if Mr. Fisher would allow it so fast... But maybe for Christmas? We have a few more jobs Kaleb needs our help with but that oughtta be it."

Rene' pulled the blanket over them snuggly. "West deserves that kinda love, Simon. You're a good guy for giving it. I don't think he expects this kinda thing from anyone."

"He doesn't. Guy thinks he's a monster, like Gideon. Maybe we can show 'em different." He almost melted when she leaned her head against him.

"Yeah. God will show them, anyway, and we can try," Rene' said. After a moment of silence, she whispered, "Si?"

"Hm?"

"After what Thomas did... Are you all right? It's OK not to be."

Simon focused on what it felt like to have her in his arms. Safe, calm, like they ought to be. He briefly wondered what it'd be like if the world wasn't hell. He could take her out for dates. *But if the war never happened, I never would have even met her.* "I'm OK. Me and God kinda had a little meeting in the cell. I could've come out way worse. And less handsome." Though he teased, he truly didn't want to talk about what had happened. Rene' had been chained and harmed once— she'd know better than to push. Simon didn't want her worrying.

"Yeah?" She sighed.

"Yeah... I'm a stubborn Bucks man but I'm... slowly learning that I don't always have to have the answers to, well, do the right thing... or help others. I'm not always in control," his voice wavered briefly, "but God is. So that's enough. Y'know?" He hoped the conversation was over. Rene' must've sensed it because she smiled up at him gently and nodded.

"I know."

Dax came into the room, feet dragging. He'd been quiet since his accident but hadn't let himself stay down for too long, despite his parents' and grandparents' insistence. He sat beside Rene' and lay down on the couch, too, falling right asleep.

Simon smiled. "I could get used to this." He closed his eyes and let himself drift off. He didn't have nightmares of any of his fears or worries about the torture, the town, Thomas, anything. He dreamt of a new house down the road, with a barbed wire fence, and a mutt playing with all of Rene's nieces and nephews in the grassy yard.

THE TOWN DIDN'T STOP but Rene' didn't leave the house often. She kept up with the town's progression and decisions through Lee. Lee had remained steady, even after his best friend had gotten injured, they'd lost one boy, and his group had vehemently stood with the gangsters. Danny had done the best he could to earn their trust and it was working.

According to Lee, the town was working to be stable again. The injured stayed at home or the hospital. A few doctors and medics from Kaleb's group helped the hospital staff. As had been decided, many of the fighters had left, though a few remained, and more would return with supplies and weapons.

They would form a defense system for Springtown, camp at the border in a section of woods unattended, in an effort to protect without upsetting the township. Many people voiced concerns of the men being rowdy, stealing, or harming their daughters, but in the end, they'd take the chances and keep alert.

Lee finished explaining and leaned against the counter top. "I think the worst is over. Just need about a week of rest, then we should all be good to roll," he muttered.

Rene' hugged him tightly. "Get a shower before dinner, try to relax a bit, OK? Things will be OK." Her voice was tired but she meant that.

Lee nodded and squeezed her shoulders. "OK." He headed to his room to grab clothes.

Rene' finished up dinner, lost in thought. Ever since the battle, being in the medic cabin and helping the wounded, she'd broken down only twice. Once, when she'd woken up from falling asleep near Simon, hearing screams he didn't hear. She cried and cried against him, but he'd prayed aloud the whole time. The second time, she'd been alone, bathing, and seeing the scars on her thighs had flipped a switch she hadn't meant to touch.

The memories, PTSD, all of it, would have to wait. She had a family to care for. She had duties to tend to. She had nieces and nephews who needed her strength. Even though she wouldn't allow herself to process the pain yet, she pushed closer to God. Her doubts, her fears, her guilts, they all seemed smaller now. Quieter. Like she was managing to find faith, even the smidgest bit of it, that helped drown the darkness out.

Rene' didn't want to let the darkness take over. So she clung to the strange peace God offered, that through hell, she could breathe.

She prayed for the same sort of peace for her family. Lee didn't deserve to face gruesome battles or drag his friends out of foxholes. Henry and Terri ought not have to fear for the lives of their innocent children, and Henry ought not have to lay in bed with a bullet wound. Rene's parents deserved peace and happiness, some island off Hawaii, for God's sake. Yet, God allowed them to live in the middle of hell. What for? She didn't understand any of it.

Maybe she didn't have to. Maybe fighting for what was right would be enough.

"Rene'?" Simon's voice, quiet from behind her.

She turned around, scowling. "You shouldn't be out of bed!"

"I got stabbed. I didn't get tied to a buoy in the ocean for a week." He smirked cheekily. "It's been, what, four days? If I don't move a bit, I'll get fat off you and your mom's cooking."

"I don't think you're capable of getting fat." Rene' rolled her eyes. She grabbed plates from the shelves.

"Are you saying I'm handsome?" Simon gathered some forks, not reaching too much and moving stiffly.

"I'm saying—"

"—that my body is like Superman?"

"I don't think Superman is capable of getting stabbed," Rene' teased.

Simon made a face. "Ouch. Sharp words from someone who is supposed to love me."

She blew him a kiss and set the table with him, taking a tired breath as her family flooded into the house. Mrs. Fisher had gone to help gather the kids with Terri for the big family dinner. The kids washed up, Mr. Fisher came inside, and they sat down to eat. Sean was five minutes late, hair disheveled and shirt untucked as Rene' let him inside.

"Sorry," Sean said sheepishly. "Cat nap got away from me."

"You needed your rest. Come sit down," Mrs. Fisher smiled, getting him a hot plate of food and biscuits. They ate and talked quietly but nothing of the war, the town, the injured, or the dead. By the end of the meal, Mr. Fisher looked more relaxed, Sean went to crash on the couch, and Lee played with his nieces. Paisley grabbed Nate's hand and hauled him into the bedroom to play dolls. Nate hadn't had the guts to tell her no, though he was white as a ghost when Rene' watched Paisley close the door behind them, imprisoning Nate.

Rene' helped Terri with the kitchen, but Simon sat at the table and chatted with them, drying plates as Terri handed them. He assured them it didn't hurt to help a little. "Can't make it worse," he said.

Terri rolled her eyes, mumbling, "Men."

Simon caught it and winked at Rene'. "I love it here."

AFTER A WEEK OF resting at the farm again—a tradition Simon couldn't shake, apparently—Kaleb, Nate, and Simon left. Simon wasn't thrilled to leave the farm. He didn't want to work for Kaleb for another whole month at the least, but it'd been part of the agreement, and they had to be ready if West needed them.

Simon watched the world roll by as Kaleb drove them away from Kentucky and toward Paradise. He dozed off and on, almost wishing the trip were longer. He woke with a jerk when they finally stopped.

"Home sweet Paradise," Nate said bitterly. "Not a problem along the way. Guess the homeless knew better than to jump at a Savage." He clasped Simon's shoulder and helped him inside their house.

Graham was waiting for them, eyes wide as they came inside. He hugged Simon gently, weary of his wound, not letting go. Simon held him and squeezed his shoulders, saying, "It's OK, kid. I got good news."

He lifted his head, eyes red from crying. "Huh?"

"I talked with Mr. Fisher." Simon grinned, tired to the bone but filled with new excitement. "He said you could come to Springtown!"

Graham's eyes grew wider. "H-he what?" he stumbled over his tongue. "I can?!"

"Easy there," Nate chuckled, locking the door. Kaleb's truck rumbled as it drove out of the driveway outside.

"Yep." Simon ruffled Graham's hair. "We've got about a month worth of work, but after that and West's Test, we're heading back. Maybe for Christmas. You could have Christmas in Springtown, kid!" Every bit of Simon wanted to paint a grand picture of the event for Graham to savor, but truth be told, he wasn't too sure what Christmas would look like.

Graham grinned, speechless. He hugged Simon again. "Thank you! Thank you!"

Simon's heart burned with love for the boy. "Just hang tight till then, OK?"

Nate smirked and squeezed Graham's shoulder. "Who knows? Santa might bring you something."

Graham rolled his eyes but went to help Nate get dinner finished.

Simon went to the bathroom, splashed cold water on his face to wake up a little. He hoped he wasn't getting Graham's hopes up for nothing. Would the town bother to celebrate Christmas? Graham deserved Christmas light adorned buildings, endless hot cocoa, caroling, wagon rides, all the fun things Simon had done as a kid. Back when the world had been all right, and his dad, even his mom before her death, had treated him like a precious gift. Graham had never had that kind of experience.

Simon let himself remember the times he and Nate had celebrated Christmas. With no mothers, it really had never been the biggest funfest, but it had been bittersweet in its own right. Jordan had paid more attention to the holiday: he'd gotten them gifts, always what they wanted, made sure they ate that day and had free time to relax. When Hunter had been alive, he'd gone out of his way to help Jordan give the boys a good day. Kaleb never cared about Christmas, never gave Nate any gifts, never put up decorations.

They were grown now. But Graham wasn't grown. He had a few years left of holding on to wonder.

Simon studied himself in the mirror, taken back by the dead look in his own eyes, the paleness in his cheeks, the blackness under his eyes. Maybe he could use some wonder, too. *God, thank You for getting us home. If You could have mercy a bit longer, help us win. Help me get back to Rene'. Help Graham get a taste of the life he deserves.*

And above all... Forgive me.

CHAPTER THIRTY-FIVE

November 17th, 2027

THREE VANS RUMBLED AWAY from the Mexican border and headed for their destination in Colorado. Since the attack, no more mistakes had been made. West should never have failed to begin with, and he would carry that weight with him to his grave. Still, George hadn't been angered, hadn't tortured West as punishment. Instead, George had chuckled and said West was growing into his role just fine.

Those words hadn't left West's head since he'd said them.

This is what I wanted, isn't it? To become a monster and end him, once and for all? West wanted George dead.

He didn't want to end lives for his cause—how different was he from George if he did that?

That's war, good or bad, men must die for the truth.

West grabbed a shower, finished work, and went to his office. He needed more time to think. He needed time to breathe. The men looked up to him for guidance. They trusted him, even after he'd gotten their friends killed.

In August, only a few months ago, though it seemed like eternity, he'd been ready to be a monster. He'd been full of furious zeal to conquer his father, alone and without his brothers, if that's what it took to protect them. But now? West wished sometimes he was the dead man getting tossed into a hole in the ground.

He sucked in a breath, sinking onto his cot. *God, I'm the one becoming a monster—and I can do that. If You need me to go to hell to scrub even a little hell off earth, I will.*

West closed his eyes. Pictured Ed and Ty, the two brothers perched on the hood of their truck, laughing at some stupid joke West had made once. They'd had faith, pure and steadfast, and Ed had died. All those years of being their friend, it left West with a hunger. A hunger for a God that cared. A father who wiped his tears away and lifted his spirit up, instead of striking him down and drowning his hopes.

I can't ask God to have mercy on a monster. That's what I chose to do and I can't turn back.

West had a place in the UN, the gangs, the people. The people feared and respected him. West had control and power—but he didn't want George's empire. The only choice he had was to end the war, kill George, unite the people.

He sprawled out, pulling the cover across himself. Months ago, he'd had little clue how to end the empire besides, somehow, killing his father after he'd earned his trust by becoming a beast. Now? The war was far more than what he'd expected. It was up to him, and a few others, to end it, and not only end it, but begin immediate rebuilding.

The townships, the survivors, the slaves, the spies—so many variables. Cindy couldn't just pick off every corrupt politician or UN leader. Not everyone would get assassinated. A part of him hated Cindy for dropping him the truth without a solid plan and no explanations behind what was happening.

Though West had tried to contact Keegan with the info Cindy had given, the trail died. Gideon figured Keegan had been killed or covered his tracks. Either way, he and West continued the search for the enigma.

On top of all of this, Gideon's hunting Thomas. He will get himself killed going against Flannery alone. If George wants Gideon on the job, maybe he'll back him, protect him. But if Gideon still gets hurt, I need to help. Somehow.

West moaned softly. He needed more versions of himself. He needed *help*. But he was the helper, the one working to fix everything else.

West drifted off just as his phone beeped. He fumbled for it, answering. "Hello?" "Get ready to go, a chopper is coming to get you now."

West sat up in bed. "George?"

The line went dead. West's body surged with adrenaline and he got up, grabbing his clothes. Peace—or was it surrender?—enveloped him as he prepared to leave and take the Test.

THE MANSION WAS THE same as when West left it—giant and dark. He followed George inside, eager to leave the frigid night behind him. George hadn't spoken a word since picking West up from the private airport. The drive home had been silent. West figured it was all part of the Test—try to get West's nerves fried before any torture began. Getting West out of bed and moving across the county in a night was just another way to mess with his head.

West followed George down the halls, downstairs and deep into the basements below the estate's structure. The underground was the only part of the estate West truly didn't entirely have mapped out in his head. He'd never been allowed into it besides one basement room, which he'd gotten locked into plenty of times. The rest of the underground was foreign.

George leaned his face against a small block in the wall. Four tiny metal prongs stuck his forehead, jawbones, and under his chin. An eye scanner flashed over his eyes. The identification process only took a moment and appeared painless. West licked his lips, knowing one day, when the mansion was his own, he'd have to do that. For now, he stuck close to George and followed him through as the sealed door slid sideways and closed behind them again. They reached a door, the basement George always tossed West in for punishment, but for the first time in West's life, they kept going.

The underground was brightly lit and white—almost reminding West of a hospital, but without the strange smells and scary people. George turned a few corners of the maze and finally stopped in front of another white door. West watched him unlock it using a key card on the lock. Key cards were a tad outdated but the types George used were advanced.

George stepped into the small room and flicked the lights on. More bright LED light flooded the room. A metal table sat in the center, a white safe box stood near the wall. Four holes in the ceiling corners made West think of the gas chambers he'd seen.

"Take a seat." George ordered.

West obeyed, eyes on George. George didn't open the safe. He turned to face his son, his expression emotionless besides his heavy eyes.

"The Test is the final covenant between me and the elect worthy of my trust and capable of successfully following my instructions and accomplishing missions for the greater good of my empire." George spoke with a cold voice. "This empire will become yours, West. When you take the empire and rule the nations, you will remember this day as the moment you were born again."

West didn't move a single muscle.

"The Test will try every part of you. Your mind and your body will be tested, and if you come out alive, you will not only be the next leader, but you will be as excellent as I am."

You've never gone through this test. If anything, your elect are braver than you. "Yessir."

"Let's begin." George chained West to the metal table by his wrists and ankles. West stared up at the white ceiling and bright lights. George removed a needle from the safe, filled it with a black liquid, and injected it into West's left forearm. It stung for a brief second before a flood of pain seared through West's bloodstream, traveling through his body and burning the whole way.

West focused on breathing, in and out, staying calm. His mind briefly wandered to all of the burdens he carried, all of the troubles he had to face—the townships, the gangs, Keegan, Thomas, Cindy's new plans. Would George torture him for truth? If he died, what would happen to the others? He forced the thoughts away as George continued to speak, in a more mechanical tone. The poison racing through his veins made it a slight challenge to keep up with George—but right away, he knew what George was doing. George was trying his mind, telling him lies, challenging his ability to decipher truth from fiction or bluffs.

CHAPTER THIRTY-SIX

November 17th, 2027

"GID?" ALEX GROANED, TRYING to sit up in bed. The smell of something burning wafting through the cabin he called home. If Gideon had to fend for himself when it came to food, the man would starve. It'd been weeks, but the burns on Alex's chest and the fractured bones in his rib cage left him a wreck. He slept more than usual and struggled to do simple things—like sitting up. Alex took painkillers to ease the pain and help him breathe easier but despised the process of healing. It made him feel weak, powerless.

Especially when he was needed elsewhere.

Gideon still didn't answer. Alex dragged himself to his feet tiredly, ignoring the throb in his chest, and went into the kitchen. A bowl of soup—he hoped it was supposed to be soup—boiled over the pot, burning onto the electric stove top. Alex moved the pot over, careful not to burn himself. He shut the stove off and opened the windows to let the freezing air in and the smoke out.

Alex stepped outside, suppressing a cough because the pain would be horrid if he dared. He nearly ran into Gideon, grunting. "What—"

Gideon lifted his head, phone to his ear. His eyes were dark as he shook his head slightly.

Alex froze in his tracks, blood rushing from his head. He clamped his jaw shut. What did a bloody shake of his head mean? Was someone dying? They'd gotten some injured after the fight, sure, like Preston and—Alex stopped his thoughts mid sentence. *It's West.*

Gideon hung up, dialing another number.

"What—"

"West left the border. George is giving him the Test."

"Who told you?" Alex licked his lips.

"Hunter Savage."

Alex blinked once. Twice. He pinched his arm a little.

"It's not a dream. Hunter's alive and he's going after West."

"But... but... bloody hell! Hunter *died* taking the Test!" Alex hissed, grabbing Gideon's arm. "Are you sure it's him? Is it a voice manipulator? It could be a trap, a part of West's Test—"

"It's Hunter," Gideon said, voice low. "I made sure of it."

Alex stared at him, mind whirling. "Did... anyone know...?""No one knows he's alive except George." Gideon shook his head. "I'm calling the others and we go in as back up, like we planned, you and me at a distance so George doesn't know I don't deserve the mark anymore. Go get dressed." He knew he couldn't convince Alex to stay home so he didn't bother trying.

CHAPTER THIRTY-SEVEN

November 17th, 2027

HOURS WORE ON. WEST was sure it'd been hours. Maybe days. The metal table bit into West's back like a thousand little teeth tore into his flesh. The poison—all three doses of it—made it impossible to focus on anything besides the agony. The lights filled his vision, blinding him, burning his skin.

West struggled for every breath. George spoke still—menacing words full of venom. Despite the agony, West heard George's voice, just couldn't differentiate between George and the hungry demons that filled the room.

"Jack is dead. Killed on the way to a safe haven with his lovely new wife, Mels, isn't it? You promised to protect him."

"Ed's in that lake—we tossed him in. The friend who loved you and tried to serve his God was left to rot."

"Your mother invented the Test, you know. She couldn't wait till the day you took it and became my right-hand."

"What would Richard say about you? Your uncle said you wouldn't grow into the man I wanted. We showed him, didn't we?"

The poison raged and West cried out in pain. He couldn't let himself believe any of the lies, not even for a moment.

The pain almost became his lifeline—the only thing proving his heart was even still pumping.

He saw strange things—memories, most of them, small flickers of reality mixed into the darkness. Ricardo, bleeding out in his arms. Gideon, killing a man to protect West, back when they'd been teenagers. Jack, laughing and wrestling with Ty as Ed tried to make them stop before they broke the only couch their shack contained. At first, he held onto every memory he could, but they faded fast, replaced by illusions.

Gideon, getting shot down trying to save someone from a burning building—a child? Jack, crying at a grave, the tombstone out of West's vision. Spencer, holding Randy's limp body and screaming at the sky. Mr. Fisher, on his knees before his demolished town.

West yelled. Used his own voice to somehow block out the images that crept into his mind like a sickness taking over.

The demons fought harder, as if giant, sharp claws probed at his mind and heart, tugging and ripping him apart. There wasn't anything he could do to fight the voices, the screams and laughs in his ears. Or the pain.

Too much.

He moaned and opened his eyes. George stood over him, but he'd shut up, his dark eyes wide.

I don't want this. God, I don't want this. A voice in his head whispered. *Give up. You can't save any of them, anyway, so give up now. Better be dead than be like your father.* West sucked in a ragged breath, looking down at his bare chest. His arm veins were black, throbbing beneath his skin. *I was bred to be a monster. I can't change. I couldn't be anything else if I wanted to.*

I'll fail them, all of them. I'd rather die now than let anyone else die because of me.

George laughed softly. Said something. Probably some other lie or jab or word of venom to break West down—but West couldn't hear him over the demons. Not anymore.

Faces filled his mind, faces of the men he'd killed, faces of innocent children lost because he'd been too late. *Help me. God, help me.* The words crawled into his mind but he grabbed onto them. Shaking on the table, sweat pouring down his skin, he groaned but couldn't get the words out.

God, I'm sorry. I'm sorry!

He shouldn't have tested God. Maybe this was his punishment for never heeding Ed and Ty's words. *I'm sorry. I shouldn't have tested You. I need Your help. Please. You know I've done the best I can but I can't do this.*

Something pushed down hard against his chest. He opened his eyes but George wasn't touching him. Like two big hands against his torso, the weight grew heavier, making it hard to breathe. He gasped for air and stared at the ceiling—nothing. No creature trying to strangle him that his eyes saw.

But there was something unseen.

Something hungry.

Something furious.

Something trying to stop him.

It comforted him enough for him to hold on a little more.

GIDEON ALERTED JACK AND Spencer first thing before packing up and driving out with Alex. He called Simon and Nate when they were on the road. Simon couldn't believe his ears. Gideon didn't explain who told them about the Test. He confirmed that while the Tests were done all over the US and never in the same place, West was undergoing the trial at the Johnston estate, just like they'd hoped. Jack wasn't able to come due to some complications with Mel's health.

Spencer brought Nabeel and Bo along for the ride. Every one of them was fully aware that if they did have to intervene, and George found out they were trying to disobey orders—they were doomed. Dead, maybe. Tortured, probably. Kicked out of the gang? Well, that depended if option one was executed.

Simon sincerely prayed that West would make it. That they'd all survive, somehow. Who knew? Maybe they could really go haywire and kill George.

Nate drove in silence, speeding along the road, the GPS guiding his way. They'd never been to the Johnston's mansion before. Simon hoped this wouldn't be the first time, either. "Nate?" "Hm?"

"I know you're still mad at Jack, but it isn't gonna do any good." He hadn't brought it up much since Jack admitted he'd chosen family over the gang. Nate didn't talk about it when he did. Tonight, they needed to talk. Simon wouldn't let things fester anymore.

"No?" Nate asked dryly.

"Nate, come on. He made some mistakes, yeah, but we all do."

"He made stupid *decisions*."

"You can't hate him forever." Simon pushed. "I mean, at least he warned us. He didn't leave West out on the hanger alone."

Nate scoffed. "How compassionate of him."

"Do you hate him for choosing family?" No answer.

"Because you're also fighting for me, right? I care about Rene'. What if we got serious, would you ditch me, too?" Simon's voice grew tight with annoyance. He knew Nate never would but he was tired of Nate being bitter over things they couldn't change. "You've gotta forgive Jack some day, Nate. It's eating away at you—"

"No, it isn't. I am in control, I am the one working the jobs and protecting my brothers. I am not the one with an issue. So get off my back, Si." he said, bitterness dark in his eyes, "I don't need him. And if you guys stopped counting on him, we'd all be safer."

Simon clenched his fists, anger raging in his chest. "Everyone has reasons to hate anyone if they tried, Nate. But God—"

"If God doesn't want us to hate, that's not my problem. I'm protecting my family. God would respect that, yeah?" Nate rolled his eyes and pulled onto another road.

"Vengeance is God's. That's going to bite you one day." Simon licked his lips, fighting back all the things he wanted to say. Why couldn't Nate get off his pride and egocentric high horse? "Yeah, Jack's failed you a lot, but hating him is just gonna hurt you."

"Don't see how."

"Nate, I can't lose you." Simon forced the words out nice and calm. "I am not gonna force you to have faith in God... or love Jack like a brother... but I'm asking you to try and let go." *Even though he can't let go without God. Are You hearing my prayers, God? I know Nate has to choose change but... I'm getting desperate here.* "It... it's what Ben would've wanted."

Nate's knuckles went white on the steering wheel. He didn't have a sharp reply. Hopefully, the mention of Ben was enough to make him think twice about Simon's words.

CHAPTER THIRTY-EIGHT

November 18th, 2027

WEST SLIPPED CLOSER AND closer to the edge between reality and oblivion. He screamed and fought for hours, days, time still didn't exist. Nothing existed but the pain. There was no sort of sanity he could grab hold of.

There was nothing. No one. Only darkness and black poison in his veins.

One instant, he opened his eyes long enough to see George standing over him After seeing the tears streaming down George's face, West closed his eyes again to ward off the illusion. Reality was far from him.

He fought hard and long, every minute dragging by as he pushed against the darkness. He clung to the idea that God might forgive him. The demons surrounding him grew angrier. They didn't want him to change. They'd rather he die than stop kneeling. But he'd rather die than keep listening to the voices scream inside his head.

The illusion shifted. The demons dragged him down into deep, murky waters. Water clawed at West's eyes, poured down his nostrils and throat, filling his lungs like tar. He fought at the water, trying to swim up, but he couldn't. Deeper he sank, down, down, down.

The water held him, comforting, silent. His screams died in the water.

He breathed in. Water rushed into his lungs again and the salty water washed over him like acid, but the pain was blissful. It felt right, somehow, as if the peace suddenly flooding his body could only be known seconds before death.

Dead. The word grazed through his weary mind.

Eternity.

The pain was vanishing.

Hell.

God, don't take me. Please.

But he'd gone too far. The water pushed against every inch of his body, anchoring him to the black depths. He opened his eyes just long enough to see the faces of big, grinning creatures—demons, he knew, but never wanted to see them.

West breathed in, again, once more, till he could no more.

God, forgive me.

"HUNTER? ARE YOU THERE?" Gideon asked quietly, holding the phone to his ear. He still had a few hours of driving left before reaching the mansion, assuming no one attacked along the way.

"I am." Hunter's Texan accent reminded Gideon of Jack. Strange to think after all those years, Jack's father was very much alive. And very much a slave to George. "You boys keep a distance when you get close. I'll call when I leave."

"And if you don't?"

"Can't call if George kills me."

"Right." Gideon glanced at Alex before watching the road again. "You're certain West won't just come with you and leave?" He knew it was a childish question. West couldn't leave after he took the Test, if he survived, especially not now. They were too deep in the shadows. The shadows needed West up front and center. It was best that way, though it would probably end in West's demise.

"I'm certain. You and I both know he's central to the plot of the whole damn world." Hunter let his voice go wry. "I've gotta go. You boys stay safe."

Gideon gulped hard. It wasn't the time to be sentimental, but he had missed hearing the man's voice. *If Dad were still alive, he'd be awfully glad to see him right now. Probably punch him and get him a beer later.* But his dad was MIA, and that meant dead. Though Hunter and Jeremy would have been quite the unstoppable force in the apocalypse. Gideon hoped he and Alex could do as much as they might've.

"Gideon?" Alex asked quietly.

Gideon shoved his phone away. "Thinking."

"I'm sorry." Alex glanced at him, eyes heavy. "Hunter's going in?""Yeah."

"I pray this is a good idea."

"Even if it isn't, we're pretty good at making bad ideas work out." Gideon smirked, pushing on the gas pedal a bit more. Of all the crazy things he'd done, Gideon figured this time topped quite a few. *Just hope West lives to tell the story.*

CHAPTER THIRTY-NINE

November 18th, 2027

TWO STRONG, GENTLE HANDS gripped either side of West's feverish neck. He felt a small nudge to his cheek. It was the first thing he'd felt since slipping into a strange trancid state—dead. He'd been dead.

Hadn't he?

A voice followed, panicked, strained, "Breathe, son, that's it. Open your eyes. Please." The voice was familiar but didn't sound right.

West forced his eyelids open but they weighed like bricks of iron. He moaned but that burned his sore throat, causing him to swallow, causing his head to pound at the movement of his muscles.

"Easy does it, boy. I'm giving you the antidote now." Another voice. George. West's whole body hurt too much to identify a small prick of a needle.

George rubbed West's arm. "There it is. Breathe in, boy. You did it. You passed the Test."

West stared up with half-closed eyes and shook.

"Now back away from him." Another voice, the voice from before. Colder. Rougher. Just as familiar.

"You said it was over." West wanted to yell the words at his father but they came out as broken, choked moans.

"It is," the voice repeated. "Why don't you explain, George?" "West should rest right now. The antidote hasn't kicked in properly." George didn't move his hand from West's neck.

"I said explain." The voice dropped lower.

West craned his neck to see past George. His heart hammered against his aching rib cage. *Nothing is real. It's another illusion. Another test. A game.*

Hunter Savage kept his gun leveled at George's head, a shiny, military grade weapon West had only seen in photos. Hunter stood tall, clad in black military grade clothing, his short-cropped brown hair streaked with gray. He watched George without meeting West's gaping gaze.

Maybe it was a part of the hallucinations.

Maybe Hunter wasn't actually there and West was imagining him again.

George licked his lips, released West's neck. "Explain what, exactly?" he asked haughtily.

Hunter stepped closer, almost nonchalantly, as if he had total control of the situation. Didn't he know security could come in at any moment? West rubbed his aching head. *You'll wake up soon.*

George Johnston, the leader of one of the world's largest mafies, flinched as Hunter came closer. "All right," George snapped, throwing his hands up.

West pushed himself up a little, the chains that had bound him lay on the floor, his wrists bloody. He didn't bother looking at the rest of him. "What..." he mumbled groggily.

"This isn't part of the Test," George said coolly. "Hunter never died."

"I'm so glad you cleared that up, I wasn't sure there for eight years." Hunter smirked.

Hatred burned on George's face as he studied West. He worked his jaw. "Hunter survived the Test."

"With flying colors, I might add, like SEALs do," Hunter said.

West stared at Hunter, clenching and unclenching his fists in pain. A part of him wanted to reach out and touch him. He couldn't sit up, much less stand up. *And he has a gun. He might not be trustworthy.* His thoughts were blurred but that one stung.

"I decided I needed a phantom," George continued, voice tight, eyes on the gun aimed at his head. "Kaleb and Jordan were good leaders for the world to see but Hunter was a trained killer."

"Soldier." Hunter corrected.

"*Soldier.*" George smirked.

"Keep going, George. West deserves to know. There's clarity in his eyes now." Hunter still didn't look at West when West glanced back again.

Why won't he look me in the eyes? George continued. "I told Hunter that if he did not remain dead to the world, I'd let harm befall his family. He would be more useful to the world as a ghost—and he has been. Until recently, I gave him his life back. He is free to return and reveal himself to his family. But he didn't." George smoothed his hair back with one hand, a vein in his neck bulging. "I gave him the best way at protecting all of you. Don't look at me like I'm the monster."

"You took my life from me." Hunter didn't budge.

West stared at the gun in Hunter's hand. "I... I don't understand." Wasn't a total lie. He might've heard George's pathetic explanation, but he still had no idea what was going on. "Hunter faked it?" *Wrong words.* "George made you play dead so you could kill a bunch of people?"

Something flickered in Hunter's dark green eyes. He met West's gaze for a nanosecond before looking back at George. "Yes."

"Hunter here has killed more terrorists and corrupt political leaders than he cares to admit," George chuckled.

He's staring one down right now and hasn't pulled the trigger. Yet. West cringed and struggled upright, moaning in agony. He clutched his chest. "You... you didn't have to... do that, George... It's been—"

"I'm well aware of how many years have passed of this gig, West. One day, you will understand. Some missions have limited variables. I removed the largest one of all. Family. He could protect you each better in the role I gave him and he benefited the world—"

"I can speak for myself, George." Hunter interjected. "I've been your silent puppet for far too long."

George gave a mocking smirk. "Go ahead."

Hunter kept his gaze focused on George and his gun never wavered. "I'm sorry, West."

No explanation. No reasons as to why he'd let them all believe he was dead, even if George had explained, it wasn't enough.

West rubbed his sweat-soaked hair, shivering.

"I was there sometimes," Hunter's voice was quiet, heavy. "Just sometimes. The times you were alone and suffering—some of those times, I was there."

West's mind flashed to different instances, landing on a time in July. George had given him another torture trial and West had handled it well. Till he'd staggered home and broke a beer bottle all over his kitchen floor. When he'd woken the next morning, the mess had been cleaned and a bottle of strong painkillers sat on the countertop. "In July..."

Hunter just smirked. "Your memory's sharp for someone who just went through the Test, son."

Son. West gulped hard. Hunter had used to call him that, often. *Please, God, let this be real.* A part of him was terrified to believe it was, even now.

Hunter continued, "When Kaleb stabbed Nathan— closest I ever came to blowing cover. I followed the boys to AJ's."

"AJ knows?"

"No." Hunter shook his head. "No one knows, West. No one."

"You've just... been at the edge of our lives then?" West strained the words out. "Lied to us? Did George's dirty work?" Anger radiated his words.

Hunter met his gaze this time. His eyes were empty. West didn't remember seeing them that way. "I did. I'm sorry."

"You... you should have told us." The dumb words were all West could muster to say to Hunter without screaming or crying.

George scoffed. "Why do you think I did what I did? He couldn't have worked properly with a family dragging him down and guiding his moral compass."

West looked down at his broken body, closing his eyes. "Is it over?" His voice fell hollow. *Good.* He was stronger when he was empty. But his chest raged and tumbled with pain, regret, and sorrow. He wanted to stand up, hug Hunter, the man who'd been the closest thing to a father he'd ever had. He wanted to find Uncle Richard and say "I survived it, I won't become George, please, see me."

He couldn't do either of those things.

"It is," George said, squeezing West's shoulder gently.

"You almost died, West," Hunter spoke up. "I couldn't let you die."

"As if that sentiment makes up for the years you left him alone?" George scowled. "I would never have let my son die. I have let other Tested die, but *never* West. Never my own boy."

West looked between George and Hunter. *Who do I believe? Would George let me die if I were weak?* "Was the Test over when you gave me the antidote?" "Of course. You passed." George smiled. His eyes gleamed with pride. Something else lay there, too. Almost like the eyes of that demon staring him down in the depths.

"Why did you step in, Hunter?" The name almost choked West. All the years he'd been gone, West hadn't mentioned him unless speaking of the Test in which, supposedly, he'd died.

"I couldn't take another second risking George hesitating. I couldn't wait around in the mansion till he dragged you upstairs." Hunter never lowered the gun. Maybe he was going to shoot George, just waiting for the opportune moment. West almost longed to hear the gun go off. "I made a lot of mistakes, boy, but I won't be making the same ones again."

What did he mean? West licked his lips, head aching. "But I passed?" He hadn't gone all this way, wasted his whole life making George proud, just to be seconds off from triumph. He'd rather be dead than allowed to pass without undergoing the Test in whole.

"You passed." George waved a hand. "No doubt about it. You can rest now. You return to the border tomorrow."

West's head whirled. "Hunter...? What will you do?"

"I have a lot of wrongs to right," Hunter said, eyes down the barrel of the gun.

George tensed but smirked. "Oh, put it down. Security knows not to kill you. Go on and see your family. It took you long enough to decide you would."

West heard the hint of strain in his father's voice. *George is afraid?* "Where are you going, Hunter?" Hunter frowned slightly. "I'm going to Jack. He's struggling to get his girl somewhere safe."

"Perhaps Springtown could offer sanctuary," George cocked his head. "Good luck, Hunter. Till next time." The last words were a soft threat. West immediately looked up as if expecting the gun to go off.

Hunter didn't drop the gun, glancing at West, his eyes still empty. "You hold on, son." He backed up out of the room and vanished. No alarms or security alerts went off—West doubted they'd even gone off before. Hunter had broken into George's mansion without getting caught. Or maybe he'd been let in. West thought the latter unbelievable but he'd ask later.

George called for guards a few minutes later. West slowly got feeling back into his body. The pain diminished but his skin remained threaded with the blackness in his veins. It faded, as if the antidote ate it up and got rid of it. Head aching, West allowed the guards to lift him up and carry him upstairs.

I passed the Test.

And so did Hunter.

CHAPTER FORTY

November 19th, 2027

THE GROUP TURNED BACK since none of them were needed. West was staying. Sure, Nate had counted on it, but it still stung. It wasn't right. *West deserves freedom. We all deserve freedom.*

As he drove, Nate remembered Kaleb's words on the way to battle. Had he meant any of that? Did Kaleb genuinely want to protect Springtown, or was it a ruse?

Nate had already failed Simon and Alex. They'd both been taken, tortured, used against the town and George like puppets. Gideon had permission to hunt Thomas— what about Nate? Why hadn't George spoken to him since? Just because he wasn't a trained killer didn't mean he couldn't get the hang of it. He wanted revenge.

Dirty revenge.

Nate shifted his hands on the steering wheel. Simon snored softly and the rock music on the radio blocked him out.

Kaleb said they could be free, that they could settle in Springtown. Only, they couldn't. Life would always be crazy, they'd always be fighting for their lives. He'd no hope that would change but he still had to fight.

Warriors don't belong with families. He didn't want to risk Simon like Jack had risked West. Another family simply wasn't worth that extra risk.

Ben hadn't had family left. His ex-wife had disappeared after the war, and when he'd found her afterwards, she'd made it clear she wanted absolutely nothing to do with him. AJ didn't talk about it much, but from what Nate gathered, Ben's marriage had broken because of his job in the military. They hadn't had any kids from what Nate knew.

Nate had made himself scarce when AJ found out about the death and when he told the veteran biker group. Nate hadn't wanted to watch anyone else learn the news. He didn't want to see anyone mourn.

Nate set his jaw and willed himself to hold it together. He'd cried enough already.

I should have been nicer. I should have made sure the old man knew I cared about him, even though I smarted off and didn't listen and flipped him off a few times. I should have told him before that I loved him.

But Ben was gone, in heaven, since he believed in all that.

And Rob left the same way. I cared about him and never showed it.

Nate sucked in a sharp breath, turned the music up a bit more. Focus on the mission. But he had no mission, not really. Gideon hadn't even told him how they knew West was alive—he'd been eerily vague of what had gone down during that Test. Was West OK?

And what about Jack? He couldn't come because of Mels. Nate really didn't know how dangerous having a baby was. *It lasts like, twelve months, doesn't it? Had Rene' said nine months?* Rene' had said, too, that it could be dangerous. She hadn't specified how.

Nate didn't love Jack, or Mels, and didn't have time for babies, but he hadn't really thought of the dangers they might face outside of gangs and crimes. Jack could handle all of that and protect Mels. He was good at taking care of those sorts of dangers. But what if trouble came in a different form?

Let karma work. He ditches us, we ditch him.

That thought didn't settle right. Ben had said something about cutting Jack slack, hadn't he? It seemed only right to give it a shot. *For Ben.* He licked his lips for a moment. Glanced at Simon, who slept soundly. Nate picked up his phone and dialed Jack's cell.

It rang a few times, then, "Hello? Nate?" "Hey."

A surprised silence. "H-hey, Nate. Everything OK?"

"You could call it that. Gideon call you?" "Yeah. Yeah, he did. West is OK." Jack sounded disjointed. Like something was wrong.

"Are you OK?" Nate frowned.

"Yeah. I'm fine. Um, listen, I'm taking Mel to Springtown. Just got off the phone with Mr. Fisher and he said come on ahead. Uh, after that, I can come help you guys finish up the jobs Kaleb has for you, if you need." Jack continued, but still didn't sound right.

"Don't worry about it." Nate frowned. "We'll call if we need you." *Why on earth would he go to Springtown? What happened to the safe haven?* A small sliver of disappointment rose in his gut. Simon deserved to move there first, not Jack. Jack had helped with supplies, but Simon had done the most for the town.

"OK. Thanks, Nate. For... for everything." Jack managed.

"Don't mention it." Nate sped up a bit on the road. They were getting close to Paradise and the sooner they got there, the less he had to talk to Jack. He hadn't wanted an emotion-fest phone call.

"Right... um, I'll let you go, I guess."

"Good luck."

"Thanks. And, Nate... I'm sorry about Ben."

Nate's jaw tightened, heart aching as he tried to control his voice. "Thanks. Gotta go. Just wanted to see if you'd heard about West." He hung up quickly. *What's eating at him? Maybe guilt. I hope it's guilt.*

But something told Nate it was something else. Something worse.

Once Nate pulled into Paradise, waving a bit at the guards, he relaxed. Simon stirred, moaning, sat upright. His dark hair stuck out and he rubbed at his scruff. "I'm gonna shave," he mumbled.

"How many painkillers did you take, man? You can't wake up without blurting the first thing you think of." Nate sighed.

"A lot of them. And Rene' said she liked it. I'm getting tired of it. Can we go to Kaleb's? He messaged me before the ride, said to meet him there..." He checked the clock. "Well, thirty minutes ago, but, better late than never."

"Guess so. Message Graham, let him know we'll be late." Nate yawned and drove toward Kaleb's house across town.

Simon texted Graham, getting out once they parked in the driveway. Kaleb's car was in the drive, but so was another car. Nate blinked in surprise and headed to the porch.

"Who's that?" Simon didn't bother keeping his voice down.

"Don't know." Nate knocked but the door was unlocked, so he shrugged, pushing it open.

Two familiar, furious voices filled the living room. Nate faltered in the doorway, gaping at Reese Burns and Kaleb arguing. Reese Burns was one of the best fighters the US fight domes had ever known, and unlike many, his handler extended great freedom. Kaleb had kept tabs on him for years now, knowing he was a valuable token to have on his side.

They rarely, if ever, met up.

Kaleb stopped and glanced over. "You're both late," he said flatly, as if the argument wasn't still going.

Reese smirked at Nate, looking the same as the last time Nate had seen him back at the Shack in May. Reese towered over most men with his big, muscled body, more scars than skin. He always had shaggy black hair and a beard. Only thing that'd changed since last time was a brand new shiner and his left arm was bandaged. "Hey, kids."

Simon stared at them. "What are you doing here?"

Kaleb glanced at Reese expectantly, crossing his arms against his chest. "Go ahead. I called them here for a reason. Start from the top."

"You guys know about the wars and the news, right? Big deals being made in the UN, Brian flunking D.C. but trying again sometime soon, all that jazz?" Reese asked tightly. "You get your sources from Kaleb, not the news, yeah?"

Nate nodded. "Duh."

"While the world is watching the politicians and the battles rage on live television, we've got bigger problems."

"Great..." Simon sank onto the couch.

Reese took a deep breath. "The government is kidnapping people from the human trafficking systems. Sex slaves, fighters, you name it, they're disappearing. Kids from Africa and Asia are swarming into the US but most of 'em don't even reach the domes or the sex rings."

"Why not? What's the government taking them for?" Simon studied Reese, frown etched deep on his pale face.

Reese shook his head. "They're creating hybrids, messing with genes, DNA, all that movie BS. Trying to create machines, monsters, anything they can to benefit the UN. They're using innocent people to do it."

Nate bit his lip. "We knew they were doing this stuff. What's the difference now?" "It's been years and it's gotten worse," Reese snapped. "Those towns getting wiped off the map, it ain't always gangsters doing that. The government locates weak spots and swipes the towns. They put the men into the trenches and use the women and kids. It's freaking sick but no one's stopping them. It's like medieval times behind the curtains but the news swears we're still a civilized nation." Reese laughed bitterly, dark eyes narrow. He eyed Simon. "One of your guys asked me to find Springtown's supplier, kid. I didn't, but I've known about the experiments—just didn't know they were targeting towns. Springtown is at risk." Simon blanched. "They would target Springtown..?"

Kaleb broke in. "Reese came for our help. He has a group of fighters in a small, poor dome, he thinks the gov will target it soon. He needs them to be retrieved. I think it is time we step into the government's plans and break things up a little." His tone held no emotion, fully business.

"I don't have anyone else to ask for help." Reese glanced at each of them. "I'll owe you, I'll give you anything." Heavy words, coming from one of the best fighters, a man known for merciless fights and never begging. "But I need help saving these men. After that, I can escape the domes, or go in as a little birdie, whatever you need. I don't know how this war will end but the gov can't keep dehumanizing people."

Kaleb nodded simply. "We'll help. Gideon's on the mission to kill Flannery, but since you spoke the matter over with him, he's aware of the updates."

"D-did we find the supplier for Springtown?" Simon broke in.

"Not sure," Kaleb sighed. "They have an alliance now, Simon. They will be protected."The idea of the town getting demolished by the government, the women and children getting prodded and poked with needles like the old sci-fi movies Nate watched as a kid, made him nauseated. When did fiction become reality? How was he supposed to stop the unfathomable?

Simon rubbed his head, voice shaky. "OK. When do we do the retraction?"

"Beginning of January," Reese said quickly.

"Not too soon, then." Nate gulped back relief. "We can handle it."

"We begin planning," Kaleb said, holding up a hand. "But none of this is spoken to another living soul. Ever. This information is enough to get any of us killed. Understand that?"Simon nodded, standing. "We have no choice, if Springtown's endangered."

Nate studied Kaleb but Kaleb never met his gaze. In a tight, low voice, Kaleb continued, "This is big, boys. Real big. I'm letting Jordan in on it but we don't need to screw around. I trust you both to be able to handle it."

"We can." Nate didn't hesitate. He'd waited his entire life to hear those words. If Kaleb trusted him, Nate wouldn't let him down. Not this time. Not with Nate's family at risk.

Even if there's something wrong about this, something that doesn't make sense, something that Kaleb is hiding. I'll figure it out.

SIMON SAT UP WITH Graham that night, watching some 90s sitcoms on the portable TV, munching on some fruit. Graham dozed off and on beside him. Nate watched them a moment, then headed to the kitchen to get himself a drink. A knock on the front door stopped him.

Simon glanced over, frowning. "It's kinda late...?"

Nate peeked outside. "It's Abi." Robert's widow, her baby bump starting to show if Nate looked hard enough, which he tried not to do.

"Open the door, man, it's cold and she's pregnant!" Simon chided.

Nate unlocked the door and opened it. "Hey. Something wrong?"

Abi, a tall, thin woman with black, curly hair and big brown eyes, offered a weak smile. She tugged her coat— no, Robert's old coat—around herself tighter. "No. Just wanted to talk to you."

"Let her in," Simon said.

Nate stepped out of the way quickly. "Sorry. Come on in." He rubbed his temple, too exhausted to deal with her, but he didn't have a choice.

Abi stepped in, smiling at Simon. "Hey. Glad to see you in one piece."

"Thanks. Want something to eat? Drink?" Simon sat with Graham asleep nearby so he didn't get up. Obviously, he meant for Nate to play hostess. Or host. Whatever it was. Nate closed the door and locked it.

"I'm fine." Abi shook her head.

"Lemme grab a beer. Uh, for me, not you." Nate led her into the kitchen. He never talked to the woman, even before Robert died. "You can skip the small talk. What's up?"

She bit her lip, glancing down. "I wanted to talk to you about Robert."

"What about him?" Grabbing a beer from the fridge, Nate popped the cap and sat down across from her.

Abi took a slow breath, eyes filling with tears. "Robert always figured he'd die on the job. We weren't unprepared. N-not really. Um," she gulped, pulling a thick envelope from her coat pocket. "Robert had a few people he really cared about. You were one of them. This... this is yours. Please, don't open it till I leave."

Nate hesitantly took the cream-colored envelope. It had Robert's handwriting on the back, one word: *Nate*. "Uh...

thanks...?"

"Robert loved you," Abi whispered. "He *adored* you. He tried time and time again to soften Kaleb's heart toward you. I... I don't know if it happened. I don't know if Kaleb ever listened to him. Robert wanted you to love him, like a big brother. I know it's too late now... but... but maybe one day, maybe we could have one last chance." Abi wiped at her eyes, tears streaming down her dark-skinned cheeks.

"He believed?" Nate sat the envelope down, not wanting to open it, ever. He had cared about Robert. Just a little. The idea the man had returned that feeling—more than a little? *I messed up. I messed up big time.* He took big gulps of his beer.

"Yes," Abi choked. "He did."

"That's good." Nate didn't want her crying. "I'm sure he's happy now." *Like Ben. And Ed. And all the other sorry buggers who have died along the way—they're safe, happy. Dead.*

Abi smiled through the tears. "I... I want you to know that I'm here, Nate, if you ever need anything."

"If you need anything, I'm here, too," he said firmly, hiding his utter surprise at her words. He barely knew her. Why was she so nice? Was it a hoax? *C'mon, Nate, she's a grieving widow. She just wants to extend the same compassion Robert had for me.* How was he supposed to react to that kind of kindness?

Abi got control over her tears and stood up tiredly. "I'd better go." She squared her shoulders. "Thanks, Nate. You stay safe, OK?"

Nate thought of the plight of the nation, the gang wars, the Grim Alliance, and recently, the plan they'd created that night to save the fighters. "I'll stay safe," he lied.

Once Abi left, Nate grabbed the letter and opened it.

"What is it?" Simon growled from the couch. "Read it in here."

Nate stepped into the living room, gulping hard as he read it to himself first. It was Robert's neat cursive, dated over six months ago.

Hey Nate,

I scraped by long enough without taking care of my dues and all, so I'm writing this letter in case I bite the dust, I don't leave everything unsaid. You and I don't talk much. We took one job and it didn't exactly warm our hearts, huh? But I don't blame you for hating me. I'd hate me, too. It wasn't right for me to get close to Kaleb when he treated you wrong. Randy and I both know it isn't right. Guess it's why we try so hard to make it up to you. Not that we have. Sorry for that. You deserved better, always did, always will. I don't know if Kaleb will change, I honestly think so, and I pray so every day. If he does, please, give him one last chance. He does love you. I promise you, he does.

There should be 20k in this envelope. Enough to buy you a pony and some candy. Don't blow it all in one place. I know money ain't exactly as good as it used to be, but I didn't have much else to leave you.

Lastly, Nate, I'm sorry. I've written this letter countless times and can't put it any better than that. I'm sorry. I love you. And I pray that I get to see you again. I really do.

Till next time,

Robert

Nate stared at the letter, read it again. Simon was talking but Nate drowned him out, ears ringing.

"Nate, what is it?" Simon repeated. "What's wrong?"

"A letter from Robert." Nate glanced into the envelope. "And twenty thousand dollars."

Simon eased out from beneath Graham, eyes wide. "What's the letter say?"

"Just..." Nate licked his lips. *No, no, no, this isn't right. Hate, anger, those things protect me. Nothing in this letter is true.* "He apologized."

"For what?" Simon's eyes grew pained.

Nate told him quietly but shook his head. "It's not... not true."

"But it is, Nate!" Simon grabbed his shoulder tightly. "It is true. Robert and Randy love you. Always did. Kaleb does, too, and maybe he's a freak, but he's trying. He's doing this Springtown gig for us, man. I know it's risky to believe but... I believe him."

Nate pulled away. "It's a trap!"

"What if it isn't?" "Everything will fall apart!" Nate snarled. "One day, somehow, we'll still lose *everything*!" The words flew out before he could stop them. "I tried warning you! I tried telling you that loving Rene' and the Fishers was asking for pain. I tried warning all of you. This is what happens when you don't listen!" His voice rose as he waved the letter in Simon's face, spit flying. "You lose people!"

"And if we all listened to you? If we didn't choose love, even if people died? What kinda life is that?" Simon grabbed Nate by his shirt collar. "That isn't a life worth living!"

It's safe. "It's what warriors do!"

"No! Warriors don't fight to protect their hearts, they fight to protect someone else's! Love isn't safe, Nate, but without it, no risk matters." Simon shook his head, voice firm but low. "You're afraid you'll get broken again."

Nate jerked free, fists clenching. *He's right. Let him be right. Stop fighting.* But he couldn't. "Someone has to stay alert, stay strong, protect all of you."

ANGELA R. WATTS

Simon released him, clamping his eyes shut and turning his head away. "Fine." He stepped back over to Graham and sat beside their friend.

Nate went to his room, locked the door. *Why can't I do anything right? Why can't they understand that me being cold is me protecting them?* He collapsed into bed, aching for another beer but too tired to get one.

Robert is dead. Ben is dead. They loved me. And I failed them.

He clamped his eyes shut. *I can't make the same mistakes again. But loving someone, and not being cold, and... and trusting them... it's a risk. Too much of a risk.*

CHAPTER FORTY-ONE

November 20th, 2027

RENE' WAITED AT THE border with her father and Lee, the dawn enveloping the Kentucky landscape, a cool breeze biting her cheeks. They'd faced worse winters, back when they'd no supplies. God had gotten them by, and now, they had more than they'd dreamed of. Rene' tugged her jacket tighter and glanced up at Mr. Fisher. Her father carried the world on his shoulders but was slowly learning to surrender more to God. She found comfort in that—if he could, she could, too.

Even if it took time.

A familiar supply truck crept toward the border and stopped. It carried precious cargo—but not supplies. Jack and his fiance, Mels, were coming to stay. The town wasn't happy about the arrangement but Jack promised he could help. As far as they knew, he worked with Gideon and Kaleb, not directly with George. He'd made it clear to them that he could pull his weight.

Jack rolled his window down, gulping a little as he smiled at Mr. Fisher. "Hey, sir."

"Glad y'all made it safe." Mr. Fisher nodded. "Follow us into town, all right? You guys are camping up with the Tanford's, till we get another place ready."

Rene' stood close to Mr. Fisher but smiled at Mels, who sat in the passenger seat. Mels was a beautiful Cuban, her brown eyes heavy with exhaustion, a big blanket wrapped around her. The sight of the expecting mother's concern bit at Rene's heart.

"Yessir. Thank you." Jack licked his lips and rolled the window up again.

Rene' got into the truck with her father. He sped onto the road and Jack followed close. Rene' watched the road before them, muttering, "Think we'll be OK, Dad?"

"Of course." No hesitation, no fear. Only some tiredness Mr. Fisher could shake with a third cup of coffee once they reached the Tanford's.

"Think Mels will be OK here? And her baby?""Definitely. If it's one thing you ladies know how to do, it's take good care of moms and kiddos." He glanced over, smirked, and focused on driving.

Rene' curled up a bit, silent till they reached her best friend's house. Jack helped Mels inside the garage, which was heated and had been made into a small room area for them. Mr. and Mrs. Tanford welcomed them gently. Mr. Tanford handed Mr. Fisher a big mug of coffee.

Rene' went to Bethany in the cozy kitchen, hugging her tight. "Hey."

"Hey, girl," Bethany said, squeezing before pulling away. "Coffee?" Bethany had always been the night owl. Rene' pulled late nights but preferred early mornings, before the sun could shake her and remind her the day had started.

"Please." Rene' sighed, tightening her ponytail. "They're all settled, I guess. We can't stay long. I've gotta help with chores."

Bethany poured two coffees and Rene' portioned some sugar in. "I can't wait till the animals start milking."

Rene' chuckled. "Feel like a colonial maid?"

"Without the handsome minute man." Bethany teased dramatically.

"You'll have Ty soon." Rene' sipped her coffee, leaning against the counter, listening to the adults' voices coming from the open garage door down the kitchen hall.

Bethany blushed. "Rene'!"

Rene' smirked at her best friend. "What?"

Bethany drank some coffee and sat down. "Moments like these... I know God's got us. Y'know?"

Rene' nodded, focusing on the warmth of the coffee as it filled her belly. "Yeah. I know." And this time, no doubts lay behind her words.

CHAPTER FORTY-TWO

November 20th, 2027

WEST SAT IN HIS office at Alamo in the dark. The past two days had been a blur. He'd gone straight to the Alamo after the Test and hadn't had any time to properly recuperate. West had blocked it all out—in a strange sense, becoming numb to the reality of living since the Test had ended and Hunter vanished again. But he still faced the graphic nightmares.

It was eleven PM and he'd been back for two days. The men accepted him back—in fact, they'd actually missed him during the time he'd been gone. No trades had occurred and nothing terrible happened—they just wanted a leader. *They want me.*

A pity it wouldn't last much longer. West had a legacy to own, an empire to build. But he was on the verge of losing his mind. The Test had weakened him in mind and body. West knew he'd need to rest but he had no time to do so. Not now. He had to push on. His mother, his men, all of the world depended on him.

What about Hunter? He's alive. After all these years, he's alive and he can help us.

Gideon finally messaged back, the words glowing softly on the screen: *"I received an answer from Big Hero."*

Big Hero was their nickname for Keegan. They'd thought him dead when he hadn't responded to West before. *"And?"*

"He's the man."

So he had been supplying Springtown. West snatched up his phone, dialing Gideon. As soon as the assassin answered, West snapped, "What did he say? Why didn't he answer before?"

"Keegan's alive, but he had to go off grid. Someone got too close. He wouldn't go into detail. In response to our little request... he agreed." Gideon spoke steadily. "He'll keep us in the loop from here on out if we do the same. He wants updates—if spies or moles are in the Confed lines, he wants to have heads up, help the South have some footing."

"He's a rebel Confed?"

"What, you think he was the type of guy to have tea with President Kaden?" Gideon snarled.

West paused, noting that Gideon's attitude had soured since Alex's kidnapping. "Anything else?"

"I think Keegan is one of the Good Samaritans. I doubt he has greedy intentions. Our call was short but we should be good to roll. Not bad progress, even if it took us too long to get."

"Least we got it," West muttered.

"How's your end?" Gideon asked. "Feeling any better?"

"Bucket of roses." The Test had drained him of body strength and mental alertness, but as a leader, he could show no signs of weakness.

"Basket of roses," Gideon corrected.

"Shut your—"

"Brian still hasn't acted. I'm a bit concerned, West. Not striking back hard is having severe drawbacks. The Union doesn't have much hope left—they want full annihilation. How can Brian fight that when the media is feeding such a brutal strike?"

"You're asking the wrong man." West took a slow breath. "But if Brian wants dirty, we play dirty, too."

Gideon's end went muffled. Then, "West, I've gotta go. I'll call you back." He hung up.

West rubbed his temples, downing a few painkillers. He held the bottle in his hand, letting his mind wander to the times he'd found himself in situations where it'd almost been like an angel had been there, watching over him. *It was Hunter the whole time. Protecting me. Helping me. Now, it's my turn to make George flinch after he made me break.*

I'll make him bleed. I've got the Test under my belt, I've got George's trust, I can finally end him.

West didn't have to work alone anymore. He'd no actual reason to not believe Cindy was on the good team. He'd do his mother's work and, standing in the light, they could work in the shadows. They could end the Second Civil War.

West took a shaky breath. If anyone knew how to break apart the government from the inside, it was Cindy. She'd been doing it for years.

But if I die first? Even after all the torture sessions and trials George put him through since he was young, nothing had left him feeling like the Test. *Am I dying?*

West shoved the thought aside, though he heard Ed's voice in his head, *"I know, if it came to it, I'm ready to die. When you accept Jesus, you accept that."*

Am I ready to accept that? I told Ed I was starting to believe. When he died, I shut off. Couldn't entertain the idea of believing in a God who let him die.

Am I ready now?

He closed his eyes, shoulders shaking. *I almost died in the Test. Maybe I was dead. I don't know. I was terrified. Where would I have gone? Hell? I've killed, I've stolen, lied, I'm black with sin. There's no redemption for a man who chooses to be a monster.*

Is there?

West's phone rang. He answered weakly, "Hey, Jack."

"West, thank God, I've been trying to call you all day. Um, we've moved into Springtown. Mels and me. I need to tell you something. I know it's late... Um, I was gonna do it in person but I've gone long enough."

West ran his tongue across his teeth. He wanted to stop him, flat out tell his brother he knew about the baby, but decided against it. "OK?"

"West... Mels is pregnant. I'm so sorry I didn't say anything sooner. I-I panicked, man. Big time. There's no excuse. I-it isn't a big deal, I should've said something. I didn't know what to do. I made a mistake. Lots of them. And I'm trying to make up for it. But... but that's why I didn't come, West, and I—"

"Stop there," West said firmly. "No reason any of you should've come, I told you that when I first left."

"I should—"

"You're my brother, nothing changes that. Your family comes first. You take care of Mels and the kid. Leave the rest to me."

"That's not fair," Jack snapped. "We've never worked alone, West, we're always there for each other and I messed it up."

"Get off your high-horse." West sighed and leaned back in his chair. "If it makes you feel better, I've got plenty of others helping me."

A pause. "Yeah?"

"Yep."

"How are you feeling? You sound terrible."

"I feel terrible, but I'll be fine soon enough."

"West, please, be careful. You've got big missions but we still need you."

"Don't get mushy on me." West refused to let himself feel the same sorrow. West locked his pain up inside, somewhere far away, so he didn't have to think of the months that had passed without any personal contact with his brother.

"Ty misses you, you know. He prays for you every day. So... so do I." Jack steeled his voice once more.

"I think the prayers are doing something."

"You told me you believed when you left... you still do?" Jack asked softly.

More or less, but West couldn't get into the gritty details then. "Yeah." This time, the peace that came over him wasn't a lie. He'd wrestled with God for weeks but his answer was clear now. God had already shed His own blood as ransom. It wasn't vain hope anymore. It was the only thing West had to give him the strength he needed to defeat the world—the God who'd already defeated the world was on his side. *That's what Ed used to say, anyway.*

"Get some sleep, man. I'm here if you need to talk. You sound like you're falling asleep," Jack said, sounding choked up.

"On it, big guy. Goodnight." West hung up, shoulders sagging. "Well, God... Guess this means I should pray. Hand my life over. Repent." He closed his laptop, crashing into bed. West's broken, bruised body didn't move another inch. His lungs ached with every breath. His head pounded and throbbed, the painkillers doing little to ease his tension.

Defeated. He'd passed the Test, but he was completely weakened, broken, and his mind was on the verge of breaking.

God, You were there, weren't You? You let me live. I was almost dead, surrounded by demons hungry for my blood, and You woke me up.

He drew a heavy breath. *I don't want to die, but when I do, God, I want to see You. I want to have the peace Ed had. I don't deserve it, but he swears he didn't, either.*

And like I told Ricardo... the man on that cross next to you didn't deserve it, either.

The Bible is all real. It isn't just stories. I know it's all real, even if I don't know what else is real anymore.

West didn't want to talk aloud and his eyelids drooped, but he mumbled weakly, "God, forgive me. I've ignored it long enough. I've been bitter over Ed long enough—I watched Ricardo beg for forgiveness before he died, and I can't ignore it anymore. So... I'm sorry. I... I want to serve You. That seems to mean I've gotta be a monster, but I'm trying to do good. You want that, right?" *Heartfelt, West, really moves God to tears, I'm sure.* But he was too tired to pour his heart out to God. Instead, he bared his soul, quietly, too exhausted to stay awake.

I'm afraid and I need You. Do You accept me?

He fell asleep and didn't get any answer.

CHAPTER FORTY-THREE

December 21st, 2027

CHRISTMAS IN SPRINGTOWN PROVED quite beautiful, even if it was nothing like Simon expected. With little funds for anything grand, the town hadn't planned on any sort of major festivities. Maybe a few family meals, caroling and dancing in the park, things that didn't cut down on the supplies. Most everyone had put up their artificial Christmas trees in their homes, or chopped down fresh ones to later use as firewood, decorating them with sentimental ornaments but no lights.

The gangsters had different plans for the town's Christmas.

Jack organized the extra supplies—food, blankets, but more than necessities. The thugs brought in trucks that carried toys, gifts, even fireworks. Simon and Nate, with Graham sleeping between them, drove one truck. They crossed the border, heading toward the courthouse. Rene' wasn't able to make it, but Jack, Mels, and the Tanfords would be at the courthouse.

The four trucks stopped outside the big brick building. Jack hurried over to the truck in front, a grin on his face as he greeted Gideon. Jack had grown a beard and courtesy of his flannel shirt and jeans, looked like a real country lumberjack. Simon chuckled and got out. Graham woke with a small jerk and followed Simon like a dog.

Gideon's expression was cold and he looked over the waiting crowds of civilians uneasily. Jack and Mr. Tanford took charge—the trucks would be unloaded into the courthouse. Since most of the supplies were gifts—Gideon assured them some more would come later in time for the holiday—they'd organize them all later.

Simon wasn't sure any of the adults would get much besides a new shirt or a pair of mittens, but the kids would be given clothes, and Gideon's men had gone all out in finding toys, like Jack requested. Bikes, dolls, toy trucks, it was all there, unloaded by joyous parents who couldn't wait to give their kids a tiny piece of heaven.

Bethany worked alongside Ty, carrying boxes inside with him. Simon noticed Ty acted different around her. Since Ed's death, Ty had gone quiet, but around Bethany, he almost shined.

"Why don't you go on?" Nate whispered at Simon, following him to the back of their truck. "You can't grab much, anyway." "I'm healed—"

"I'm trying to cover for you."

Simon smirked. "It's fine. I'll unload a bit." He helped but grew more eager every passing moment. Was Rene' happy? Had she missed him? She'd messaged him that she had often—but what if she wasn't happy to see him? What if she were secretly angry with him? *Can it, Simon. You're freaking out like a love-sick pigeon.*

He went over to work beside Gideon and Alex. Simon had been cooped in the cab with Nate for too long. Alex chatted quietly with Sean—Alex wasn't lifting much and had a slight paranoid look about him, but he spoke kindly. Sean tried to ease his nerves. Simon always knew when Sean was playing big brother. Alex didn't relax any, but he probably liked the social interaction. Simon couldn't imagine being stuck with Gideon all the time, especially since Alex was a believer, and having to put up with an assassin's grim pessimism sounded exhausting. Living with Nate was bad enough.

Gideon carried the boxes inside and kept silent. Simon followed his footsteps, sighing. "You could focus in, you know," he whispered. "It's Christmas. Everyone else has forgotten about the battle... You should try to, too."

"The ones who lost loved ones are remembering their dead now more than ever." Gideon didn't look back, setting his box onto a pile.

"The holiday always has mourning. But we can all still hang onto the good," Simon said tightly. "Alex is alive. I'm alive. A lotta guys died and it hurts like hell, but you walking around with a scowl on your face and a death plan in your head? That's not helping anyone." He dropped his voice. "Alex is walking on eggshells. So breathe in, slap a smile on your face, and pretend to be a domestic man for a while. For Alex's sake."

Gideon stared at Simon like he'd grown two heads. He clenched his jaw a moment, muttering, "You're right. Thanks."

I just told Gideon freaking Hochberg off and he thanked me? Christmas really is a time for miracles. "Uh... you're welcome." Simon tossed his head.

Gideon's shoulders sagged slightly for a moment and then, drawing himself back up, he smirked. "The fact any girl could love you boggles my mind." He turned around but nearly ran into a woman and stepped back, his fists clenching instinctively.

She raised her eyebrows, black hair pulled in a low ponytail. "Sorry, sparky."

Gideon took the box she was holding, gaze lingering for a nanosecond before he turned and put the box up.

Simon smiled at her. "Hey, Chloe." He tried being chivalrous to the town members, often unsure as to which ones liked him and which ones despised him. Chloe smirked back, so he figured she was one of the nice ones.

"Thanks for helping all this work out," she said, a bit awkwardly, as if trying to find the right thing to say. "It means a lot to me. To all of us. Especially the kids."

Gideon glanced over. "Don't mention it."

"Well, I already did." Chloe nodded. "Y'know, with the Grim Alliance and all, people need to be reminded that you guys don't want our heads on silver platters by the time the war is over. You're not cannibals." Her eyes glinted like she'd told a joke.

Simon smiled good-naturedly. "Yeah. Thanks."

She glanced at Gideon one last time before hurrying down the hall.

"She's one of the survivors, right?" Gideon asked, following Simon upstairs again, but Chloe had already vanished.

"Yep. Kinda... kinda crazy, but really nice. She's friends with Rene'." Simon didn't like labeling anyone crazy, but Chloe sure wasn't the town's version of normal. Rene's family found her endearing, so Simon figured he'd decide the same soon enough.

"Remind me why you like it here?" Gideon whispered.

"Oh, come on, you guys need healthy female interaction, trust me." Simon paused. "Anyway, when was the last time you talked to a girl off a job, anyway?"

Gideon shrugged, raising an eyebrow. "Does it matter?" "Your social skills are rusty." Simon gestured behind them. "You gotta learn how to talk to people who aren't trying to kill you."

"I can," Gideon said. "Just don't see the reason to—"

"For Alex, remember? Try to be normal for the week. George gave us time off—so instead of seeing it as a trap, see it for what it is. A luxury. Kaleb swears it's just a week off, nothing dirty." Simon nudged him. "Stop thinking so much."

"Coming from you, that's iconic."

"Shut up."

RENE' LISTENED TO HER mother and Terri talk eagerly about what surprises they had in mind for the kids' Christmas. The big pine tree in the living room sat proudly, and Rene' drew in a deep breath, letting the scent of pine needles and boiling venison stew fill her nose. In such small, busy moments, she tried freezing the feeling.

The feeling of being home, with the kids playing in the living room, all anxious for their Papaw, Dad, and uncle to return from the supply drop. The feeling of not only being safe, but having hope.

She finished stirring the stew and glanced over, smiling, "Biscuits almost ready to go in?""Almost." Terri scooped out the dough onto the two trays. "I hope the guys hurry back, it'll get cold."

"You sound like Mom," Rene' teased.

"Well, she *is* a mom." Mrs. Fisher squeezed Rene's shoulder gently. "She's allowed to sound like one." Mrs. Fisher started singing a Christmas carol, and the kids joined in from the living room. Their off-key singing made Rene' chuckle.

Rene' rinsed out one of the measuring bowls in the sink. Two trucks pulled down the dirt driveway, catching her attention. "They're here!" She called.

The kids darted for the door. Henry sat on the couch with Dax, still confined to resting, thanks to his wound.

Mrs. Fisher shooed Rene' out of the kitchen. "Go see Simon. We can finish here." She winked and turned to help Terri.

The trucks parked in the barnyard out front. Rene' ran after the kids, insisting they got coats on before they went out, warning them of getting a cold. Paisley and Jaycee obeyed but Lily ran out, tackling Mr. Fisher's legs as he headed over.

Sean got out with Mr. Fisher, laughing as he ruffled Lily's hair. Simon, Nate, and Graham crawled out of their truck, all quiet, but Simon's face lit up when he saw Rene' at the door. "Rene'!"

Everyone was safe. Everyone was home.

Rene' ran off the porch. Simon met her halfway across the barnyard and wrapped his arms around her. He squeezed tight.

"Simon! Are you OK? How's your chest?" Rene' poured the questions out, but with her face squished against his body, doubted he'd heard her concerns.

Simon didn't let go and didn't speak. Instead of asking again, Rene' relaxed against him, burying her face against his jacket. She took a deep breath, closing her eyes.

This was real. Not a dream. Her family being home, safe at the end of the nation as they knew it, with the guy she loved holding her like she might vanish. It was a gift, not one to be held with fearful hands, but one to hold on to with all her might.

"I missed you, too," she choked.

Simon pulled back a bit, smiling, pushing her hair back. "I'm so sorry—"

"All that matters now is that y'all are here, so let's focus on that," Rene' whispered, squeezing his arm. "Wait—you shaved?"

He laughed, the slight gleam of tears in his eyes vanishing. "You said it made me look like a grizzly bear."

"I said a *scruffy* grizzly."

"I wanted to soften the blow to my ego, but, thanks." Simon kept his right arm around her.

Mr. Fisher herded the kids inside. Nate and Graham followed Sean inside. Graham kept his head down but Rene' caught a glimpse of his eyes—wide, taking in every detail, like he'd never seen a farm, or a family, before. *He probably hasn't.* Rene' squeezed Simon and led him into the farmhouse.

If Simon and Nate had never taken such a giant, rogue risk to help our town... We would've never met, never lasted as a town, never formed this wild alliance... We would never have had the chance to help anyone outside our town. Not Onya, not the girls I helped at the sex trafficking ring. Not Jack and Mels. Not Dan and Phil. Not Noah. Not Graham... She shoved the painful thoughts away quickly.

Instead of considering the "what ifs", she'd praise God for the "how it is". He'd worked it all out and would continue to do so. God gave them all hope. A chance. Another day to be together.

And Rene' would cherish every moment.

As they began setting the table for dinner, everyone talking, the rest of the guests arrived. Gideon, Alex, Dan, Phil, and AJ. Danny and Phil came inside like fish out of water. Danny stuck close to Lee, walking with a slight limp from when he'd been hurt during the forest fires. Phil stuck with Gideon and Alex in the living room. AJ looked relieved to have time with his dear friend Mr. Fisher again.

The table wasn't large enough for everyone to fit, so the kids ate on the living room floor, and everyone else found any available spot. Graham sat with the kids, enthralled by them. Lily loved the attention and offered him some extra peas off her plate.

Rene' watched them all, heart full. Gideon and Alex had been invited by her father, and while Gideon kept to himself, Alex seemed to have fun. He talked, laughed, relaxing. Rene' prayed for him as she ate her food. She also prayed that Bethany's family, along with Jack, Mels, and Ty, who was still healing from his slight battle injuries, would have a good night, too.

Simon came over, sitting beside her on the couch. "Kinda crazy, huh?" he whispered, grinning.

"Which part? The part that Nate's actually carrying on a good conversation with Henry, or the fact Gideon just laughed at Sean's pun?" Rene' whispered back, leaning closer.

"The fact a conservative, Christian family invited a bunch of thugs into their home and everyone is actually loving it. But, yeah, what you said, too." He winked and dug into his meal.

"God's love does crazy things." Rene' took another bite and savored the deliciousness, eyeing Simon. *He's alive, looks like he's gotten some good sleep, and he's happy. I could live in this moment for a long time.*

Simon glanced down at her, eyes softening. "Yeah. It does."

ALEX WATCHED THE KIDS play on the living room floor. Dinner had been cleaned up—Phil and Lee took over the kitchen, giving the ladies a chance to rest. Henry and Terri sat together on the couch, baby Aiden in Graham's arms as he sat beside the parents. The teen watched Aiden with big eyes and tried to make him smile. When Aiden laughed, Graham practically melted.

Simon squeezed his shoulder, smirking, "He likes you. Told you he would."

Alex smiled, glancing at Gideon, who sat on the floor beside him. Alex found the room full of people to be a bit overwhelming, but the good type of overwhelming. For once in years—maybe a lifetime—he was in a house full of love, friends, family, people who genuinely cared about him. It made it hard to swallow when he thought about it, so he focused on everything else, instead. He watched Rene' and Simon talk quietly, then they headed outside. He watched Mr. and Mrs. Fisher, how kind they were to their grandkids.

The people who ran the town had shed compassion on gangsters—and this was one of the outcomes.

I've always told Gideon we'd have a future. We could have hope. But it's... starting to happen, Lord... And it's strange.

Mr. Fisher got up, went into the kitchen, and Alex followed him. "Mr. Fisher?" he asked softly.

Pouring a cup of black coffee, Mr. Fisher glanced up with a smile. "Want some?"

"Oh, no, sir, thanks. Uh, I wanted to thank you for inviting us. All of us. It... it means a lot, sir." Despite his best efforts, Alex's voice grew thick, and tears burned his eyes. Mr. Fisher's approval, his compassion, it meant the world to Alex, but should he show it?

Mr. Fisher squeezed Alex's shoulder, wary of his injuries, but speaking softly, "You men have done more for this town that we can thank you for, Alex. This is your home. No matter what."

Alex started to speak but nothing came out. He glanced down, working his jaw.

"And I'm no soldier, but I'm here if you ever need to talk about what happened, Alex." Mr. Fisher's voice was low, strong.

Alex clamped his eyes shut. Did he dare talk about it? He knew he couldn't talk anything over with Gideon. Not yet, not with Gideon in a blood-thirsty hunt for Thomas. "I... I wasn't afraid. I *was* afraid. But... but at the moment... when I was going to pull the trigger, I had *peace*." Mr. Fisher knew what had happened, but Alex hadn't told anyone this part. He needed to.

Alex glanced up quickly, but Mr. Fisher just listened, no judgment on his face. "I... I know that peace is something a Believer should always have. But I struggle with it, sir. I was scared out of my bloody mind the night before the attack. I thought Thomas was gonna kill me. Then I had to trap Gideon and... I wasn't afraid of dying. I knew what would be saved if I pulled the trigger." Alex's shoulders shook and he opened his mouth to finish, to say something meaningful, but all that came out was a muffled sob.

Mr. Fisher put his arms around Alex, like a solid rock for him to lean on. Tears streamed down Alex's face as he gripped the older man tightly. The stress, fears, and pain of the previous month fell off his shoulders in waves. *I had peace, God. I'm sorry I don't have that much courage all the time but I'm trying. I'm bloody trying.*

ANGELA R. WATTS

Mr. Fisher didn't say anything. He didn't have to. He just held him in the kitchen and let Alex cry like the warrior he was—a fighter who needed a father to remind him that the battle was far from over. And that it was already won.

———————

SIMON AND RENE' SAT on the back porch steps underneath the big moon. They watched the stars, pointing out some satellites, and while the nighttime world was pretty, Simon was too distracted to take it all in. He glanced back down at Rene', sitting so close to him he could feel her body heat through her jacket. He'd missed her more than anything. Being safe and sound with her was almost surreal.

Squeezing her hand, he said, "So how have you really been?" Texts and phone calls could only tell so much, even if they had kept up with each other daily.

Rene' leaned against him. "Trying to process everything. I made a list, y'know. It's really long. I carry it with me, when I get a moment, I bring it out to pray over something. It gets... messy up here." She tapped her head.

"Could I see the list?" he asked, almost too afraid to ask.

Rene' pulled away a bit, digging into her jeans pocket, pulling out a piece of notebook paper. "Uh... sure." She handed it to him wearily.

He studied it, feeling like he'd been given a priceless artifact. The list took up both sides of the paper, the top titled "Road Thus Far + Prayers".

"Believe me, there's more where that came from." She smirked but there was a heaviness in her voice.

Rene's handwriting was chicken scratch, but he made out most of the writing.

Pray for the Confeds to hold down the cities and the Union to surrender.

Pray for Brian to stand down.

Pray for Jordan's group and anyone else to stop the human trafficking rings.

Pray for my friends and family, their health and safety and happiness.

Pray for the Union President to come out of hiding.

Pray for the Confed President to gain control.

Pray for West to stay safe.

Pray for the supplier of Springtown to stay alive, let us thank him, even if we don't understand what's going on.

Pray for everyone to benefit from the Grim Alliance and not let it be a trick.

He glanced up, frowning. Rene' met his gaze and quickly looked back down at her hands, rubbing them together. "What?"

"The alliance will work out," Simon said softly. "Kaleb... He's a good guy... I mean, he's a jerk, but this isn't something he's doing just to appease George. This matters to him. Not sure why, but it does, so it will be fine." He folded it back up, not having the heart to read any more.

She pocketed it, squaring her shoulders. "Yeah. Just wish we had more answers."

Simon put his arm around her, looking out across the horse pasture. "We'll figure this all out. God's gotten us this far—and whatever isn't made clear here on earth, it'll make sense when we're dead." *I might be dead sooner rather than later after helping Kaleb and Reese. If George found out what we're doing, we'll bite the dust. I don't understand why Kaleb's letting us in on something so dangerous when he's been so weird and protective, but You know, God. And I gotta do this for the sake of Springtown.*

Rene' eyed him. "You OK?"

"Yeah, sorry. Just easy to get lost in the tangled web." He took a slow breath as she leaned against him, her small hand tightening on his. *God, I don't want to lose her. Every odd is against us all right now, it seems that even with the help You've given us, it's still easy to be afraid we'll lose. Give me faith. Please. I need to be strong for Rene'.*

"Yeah. But we've got each other, we've got family, friends, alliances, too." She laughed again. Simon loved the sound of her laugh. "Better than nothing."

"Yeah, it is."

"We can face anything." Her voice was soft, like she was trying to convince herself.

Simon cupped her cheek and tilted her head up, meeting her gaze. She didn't pull away. "We can. No matter what happens, no matter who comes against us, we'll make it through."

And he kissed her.

He didn't think at all. He didn't know what to expect. Instead of hitting him, or shoving him off, Rene' kissed Simon back. He pulled her close, losing all sense of situational awareness. Until the soft sound of a child giggling came from the farmhouse door behind them.

Simon pulled away, glancing at Paisley. She grinned underneath the porch floodlight, whispering, "Mom said come get you guys for dessert, but I see you've started without us."

Rene's jaw dropped. "Paisley! You're *eleven*! Where did you learn—"

Paisley stuck her tongue out and ran back inside.

Simon glanced at Rene', mind scattered. *I kissed her. She kissed me back.* "Guess we should, um, go inside."

Rene' tucked her hair behind her ear. "Yeah..."

He led her back inside, sat beside Nate on the floor. Rene' went to help Mrs. Fisher and Terri get the kids cookies. Simon met Mr. Fisher's gaze and smiled softly, praying Paisley hadn't blurted the news to the whole house, but everyone carried on, so he doubted anyone knew.

Except Nate.

Nate leaned over, whispering in his ear, "So, did you make your move?"

Simon struck him in the gut, just subtle enough so no one noticed.

"Ah. You did. Thatta boy." Nate smirked and went over to Graham, who still held the baby, and started chatting with Philip.

Simon was too happy to be bothered by Nate's smug attitude. He watched the room full of family and thugs, heart hammering. Not in his wildest dreams had he thought this could be possible—but he supposed if God wanted something, there truly was nothing stopping Him. There was nothing stopping any of them. After years of thinking he had to choose the gang, or choose his father's group, or choose family, maybe he had been wrong. Maybe families could learn something from gangs, and maybe gangs could learn something from families.

Together, they could survive the war.

The perfect moment was interrupted when his phone rang. He nervously excused himself, stepping out into the cool air to answer it. "Dad?"

"Hey, Si," Jordan said softly. "I know you're probably busy with the party, I just wanted to say I love you."

"I love you, too, Dad." Simon glanced back at the house. "And in case you needed to hear this from your sarcastic, pain-in-the-rear-end son... We're all gonna be OK."

CHAPTER FORTY-FOUR

December 21st, 2027

JACK AND MELS CAME over after their dinner with the Tanfords, but Gideon didn't have much to say to the man. Not since the gangsters had pulled a mutual "don't talk about war or death unless entirely necessary". Gideon didn't want to ruin anyone's good time. He just wasn't capable of ignoring the world's problems in order to enjoy himself. But Alex needed the down time, the rejuvenating atmosphere of a rejoicing town that welcomed them all as alliances instead of mere thugs.

Gideon didn't need that kind of acceptance. It was all the same to him. The town could change its mind about them in a second. All that mattered was they did their job in the end.

As usual, he kept his back to the wall at all times. The crowd of people in the Fisher farmhouse was beginning to overwhelm him. It was strange, seeing the men he had fought alongside, bled beside, and killed for, in such a downright joyous setting. He had never seen Jack so happy, and Mels was absolutely tickled pink by baby Aiden. Terri said she'd become a second aunt to the kids since they had moved in. While no one else thought twice about the statement, it lingered in Gideon's head.

His whole world was, in this setting, flipped over.

Jack was capable of having a family. While Gideon had been aware of this, it messed with his head to see it happen.

Alex was capable of having a father figure who cared about him. He had a relationship he'd wanted for years. thanks to Mr. Fisher, a role Gideon could never fill was now taken.

Philip, the cold-blooded sniper, was laughing and teasing with Lee and Danny.

So much to take in.

Too much.

Too many faces.

And what about the missing faces?

What of West? Ed? Clint? Everyone they'd lost along the way. Every poor soul who hadn't gotten any invite to a dinner? Gideon ran a hand through his hair and stood up, making his way out of the house, avoiding bumping into people like avoiding tiny bombs in a minefield.

The fresh, cool night air hit him as he stepped outside, closing the door behind him. Gideon went out to the horses, his heart hammering. Now was hardly the time to let his nerves get the best of him. He had to hold it together—for Alex, like Simon had said. He needed to be normal. Just for a week. He could do that. Couldn't he?

Short breaths. He focused on breathing deeper, but the breathing technique didn't help. He leaned against the wooden fence, clamping his eyes shut.

Monster.

Cold Eyes.

Look at you, playing another con, playing the part of the heroic gangster who can fix all of their problems. You can't even protect Alex.

When you hunt Flannery down, and you kill him, these people will see you for what you are. A killer, a monster, worthy of nothing but death, certainly not worthy of love.

A monster in a house full of love couldn't escape unscathed. Gideon couldn't handle it—and he could hardly fake handling it.

Still, if he didn't kill Thomas, Thomas would kill West. Gideon would tell West about Thomas' intentions of West's demise and George's humiliation, but not until

West had his wits about him. He was still recovering from the Test. More bad news would break him right now.

Something warm bumped his neck. Gideon jerked back, opening his eyes to stare back at a horse. The palomino snorted but didn't back off.

Gideon straightened. "You're Rene's horse. Sugar, I think," he mumbled, shaky hands releasing the fence.

Sugar put her big head over the fence and gently nuzzled him again. Gideon frowned, running a hand over her forehead. The mare didn't move, huff, or bite him. She stood still, letting him stroke her again and again. Despite his slight dislike for horses, peace fell over him. "Voices get hard to ignore sometimes," he whispered. She didn't respond, of course. A horse couldn't talk. *Seems like they can understand, though.*

The backdoor opened and Gideon lifted his head, watching Sean come over. Sean stuffed his hands in his pockets. "Hey. Everything all right?"

"Yes," Gideon said, pulling away from Sugar. She kept her head there, as if waiting for him to change his mind. His tight chest had eased up and forcing a smile for the Irish officer was surprisingly easy this time, unlike the hundred times earlier that day.

"Kinda overwhelming in there, huh?" Sean patted Sugar's neck.

Gideon just nodded.

"Family's like that." Sean gave Sugar one last firm pat.

Gideon was too tired to hide all of his surprise. Sean smirked, "What? Bad news for you? It's true."

"You have no idea what you're saying," Gideon said flatly.

"I do." Sean crossed his thin arms across his chest. "You wanna know why we took the alliance, Hochberg? We took it because we know you guys. We know you all went through hell to have our backs when it could've bitten you in the rear end. Yeah, the alliance could go bad, but we trust you guys. And ya know something? You trust us, or you wouldn't be here."

Gideon set his jaw tightly. "And?"

"And..." Sean sighed. "And, thanks, for everything you've done, all of you. I'd like to return the favor sometime."

"Don't worry about it."

"I hear you're going after Flannery," Sean said quietly. "If there's anything I can do to help, let me know," his tone grew hard as ice.

Gideon nodded, unsure as to why Sean would care so much. "I can handle it."

"I know. Offer still stands."

Gideon smirked. "Noted. We should go back in." His nerves back under control, he followed Sean inside, just in time to hear Mrs. Fisher telling an embarrassing story about Terri. The Fisher family was crazy, Gideon decided, but he sure cared about them.

He cared about them enough to keep contact with Keegan Black and help the man protect Springtown once the war was over. It'd be over soon, and he'd no intentions of letting Springtown fall to the wayside when the triumphant government took over.

Catching himself, he shook the thoughts away and went to sit by Alex and AJ. *God... I fit in here about as well as a snake in a wolf pack, but thanks for the chance to see what I'm fighting for. I might be a monster, but I know You have a job for me to do, a job to protect innocent lives, and I promise You, I'll do the best I can.*

He was jerked out of his reveries when Mrs. Fisher suggested they all sing Christmas carols. To Gideon's chagrin, everyone pitched in, singing both holiday tunes and worship songs. Gideon knew very few of them, but watching them all sing together gave him a sliver of hope. He remembered when he'd been brought back after his mark and woke up to Alex singing *It Is Well.*

For once, Alex didn't sing alone. Gideon didn't join in, but he listened and tried to thank God for the things he didn't yet understand.

THE NEXT MORNING, IT was business as usual, the town both prepared for Christmas and spoke of the upcoming events. Since the gangsters had bunked up in town as their defense system, news of the war—real news, and not the nonsense that the Union government allowed the radios to air—was constant. Rene' found it overwhelming, but it helped give the people of Springtown a solid sense of understanding.

The war, indeed, was ending.

But Brian Jones had fallen off the map. People waited, tried to understand why he hadn't attacked, tried to make sense of the fact the Union groups attacking were all failing. Where was Brian? Why hadn't he done anything?

To the world, Brian Jones was a Union General, and they painted him the fool or the hero. To Rene', he was the brother who had taught her how to swim, how to tie her shoes, how to sketch with charcoal pencils. The same brother who had left her to die in a torture room.

Rene' closed her Bible, praying hard for her family, nation, and her brother, but tears ran down her cheeks. It was almost lunchtime. She'd help make food, feed the kids, and the men would get home from the town hall meeting. Or that's what she called it. They'd all gathered to discuss politics, plans, goals, all of the heavy matters that didn't dissolve just because Christmas approached.

Rene' bit her lip. *Please, God, guide us all. I know You'll protect us, no matter what, but help us become strong, so when the war ends, we can do more than just survive. It seems we have some part in Your plan. With us being targeted so often, with Keegan protecting us, and now, even George allowing alliance... something is happening. Big or small, let us be ready for Your will.*

THE NEXT DAY, RENE' went to the courthouse with Lee, Alex, and Simon. Alex wanted to meet Noah, the scapegoat that had done so much of Thomas' dirty work. When Lee pointed out the boy only seemed to relax around Rene', Alex asked her to come along. Lee drove them in silence toward the courthouse.

Rene' fought off a shiver as they went inside and out from the cool winter air. The town was warm, secure, and ready for winter, all thanks to God, gangsters, and hardworking town members.

Lee went to the cell downstairs, unlocking it with a key one of the officers gave him. Noah posed no threat. He sat on a cot in his cell quietly, never speaking unless spoken to. He lifted his head when Rene' stepped in.

"Hey, Noah." She smiled. "How are you feeling?""Fine." It was hard to tell if he was telling the truth.

"It's almost lunch, so we won't keep you long. Um, Alex Thompson is here. You've heard of him, right? He wanted to talk to you... He knows what it's like being hurt by Thomas." Rene' spoke gently, not hesitating so that Noah didn't get wild ideas and panic. "He wants to help." Noah looked past her with wide eyes, his breath hitching. "I-I told you guys everything!" "He isn't here to hurt you. He's here to help." Rene' stood firmly between Noah and the slightly ajar door. "Alex is a friend."

"A coward doesn't have friends," Noah whispered. "Make him... just make him go away." Alex poked his head in, voice soft, "Please, mate, I don't want any info. I was about your age when Thomas had me. Younger. I had the same job as you." His voice was steady but raw, making Rene's insides ache.

Noah didn't move, clutching the edge of the cot with both hands. "I don't want to talk."

"I want to help, Noah. Is there anything I can get you?" Alex asked gently.

Noah hadn't even asked to leave the cell. He also didn't ask to go mingle with anyone. If he was a mole, intending to send information to Thomas, he wasn't getting any. Philip had said he doubted that—Thomas tossed weaker members like Noah aside. He'd probably just left him behind for dead, not for further information.

Noah dropped his head as Alex spoke. "No sir."

"No one here will hurt you." Alex shook his head, staying in the doorway. "We'll be deciding what to do with you, but listen, Noah, you can stay with me. Please, don't run. Don't do anything stupid. You can come live with me, I'll keep you safe."

Rene' glanced back at him in surprise. Had he talked that over with Gideon? She studied Noah again. The boy's shoulders sagged. *He's terrified, God. Please, help him. Let us help him.*

"You'd just hurt me like the others. You're... you're one of Johnston's." Noah shook his head, grimey curls bouncing.

"No, Noah. I wouldn't hurt you. Please, just give me a chance. I can keep you safe. I wouldn't ask you to do a single thing to endanger yourself ever again." Alex stepped closer, sincerity written all over his face. "I know how you're feeling right now. Please, let me help."

Noah finally lifted his head again, his eyes dark with tears, chin trembling. "OK. I'm screwed anyway. I'll do what you want."

Alex froze. "I can help you start over, like I did."

Noah licked his lips, obviously struggling to hold it together, jaw clamped shut. Rene' wished he would talk to them. How long had he held everything inside to fester? Would he take this chance at hope?

"If I could help you, could you leave this all behind?" Alex whispered.

Noah's eyes closed and he nodded weakly. "I'd leave it behind."

"Then I'll help you."

A man came with a platter of food. Alex stepped back, speaking quietly, "We'll see you, Noah. Thank you." He disappeared.

Rene' took the tray and handed it to Noah. "It'll be OK, Noah. Thomas is gone. You're gonna make it through this." She wanted to help him so badly.

Noah sat the tray onto his cot with shaking hands. Silent.

Rene' left him, going into the hall with the others, following them upstairs. Outside, Alex and Lee started talking about Noah, but Rene' hardly noticed. Down the sidewalk, Quinn stood, hands in his coat pockets, watching her.

Rene' frowned but before she could do anything, Quinn turned and walked away. Rene' got into the truck with Simon, thoughts whirling. Quinn, like every other able-bodied, had fought in the battle. Did he still think all they were doing was for nothing?

Nothing we do is in vain. We'll make it through this. We won't just survive, we'll rejoice in the fire.

CHAPTER FORTY-FIVE

December 22nd, 2027

"IT'S BEEN ONE HELL of a year," George muttered, pouring himself a large drink. At his favorite, well-furnished warehouse, at the heavily stocked bar, he sat across from Guns, relaxing with his comrade.

"Don't let a successful six months fall away simply because Flannery entered the picture again," Guns sighed, downing his whiskey. "Gideon can handle Flannery. That man will never humiliate you like that again." The footage of Alex being used as bait, holding a gun to his head and fighting tears like a babe, had spread throughout the gangs —just as Thomas wanted. He'd had the trap taped and spread like wildfire, all in the petty hopes of trashing

George's bombproof reputation, but mostly, just to jab at his old master, George.

"When Gideon finds him, I'll carve that J into his back a second time, then put a bullet in his head." George seethed. "I'm sure he has motives, probably wants more money and power. But he is a wild card... he'll do things simply for vengeance. That makes a man dangerous, when their running force is based solely on emotions."

"Well, his are based on both," Guns said cheekily. "Those are fun opponents. Loosen up. Have some fun with him."

"I have no time for games. Not those sorts of games. He betrayed me. I'll have him killed. No sense in buying into his hunt." George waved his hand. "I have bigger plans at work. He's just a thorn in my side."

Guns laughed bitterly. "Ah, the words of wise men." He poured himself another glass. "How's West?"

"Manning Alamo. I'll be moving him soon. I'm proud of him. Even Hunter's surprise visit didn't sway him." George leaned against the countertop. "Hunter's still in the shadows. Only Jack knows of his existence, as far as I can tell."

"Hunter is afraid of what Kaleb might do." Guns licked his lips, smirked. "But the alliance was a nice touch."

"Stop rubbing it in."

"Oh, come on, now."

"Any word of the next attack?" George shoved the topic aside.

"No. Jones has been a closed book. The Union's attacks in the West proved pointless. Both sides are low on supplies but... well, you and I both know some people are supplying the Confeds and the suppliers to the Union are being picked off like flies."

"It must be stopped." While his empire would reign, even if the Confeds won, the UN would be difficult to deal with if the Union lost the war. George hated their whining as it was.

"I'm doing my best. Would you like to change places?"

George rolled his eyes.

"That's what I thought," Guns smirked. "Everything is under control."

George pulled a cigar from a case on the counter, lighting it. "Our empire will begin soon." All of the decades of planning, scheming, paying politicians, building his mafia—it would all pay off soon. Nothing could stop him. West was his heir, the Union rolled over at his beck and call, the UN trusted him, everything fit in his hands.

Guns laughed and lifted his glass. "You can have the empire. I'll take the war."

EPILOGUE

December 24th, 2027

CHRISTMAS EVE. BRIAN COULD remember Christmas time with his family, years and years ago, in a country town, with a big pine tree in the living room and his siblings shaking the gift boxes underneath when their parents weren't looking. Life had been beautiful back then. Brian hadn't known anything but love and freedom.

Those two things were gone now, like ashes in the wind.

This Christmas, he had men bleeding out and dying in muddy trenches, fighting their own brothers. He had teenagers coming from all over the nation, begging to fight just for some shoes and food in exchange. He had the UN breathing down his back, ordering him around as if the men behind desks knew how to run a war better than he did. He wanted them to all come out in the battlefield, see how much they knew then.

Everything rested on his shoulders. Everything.

He had failed to recover D.C.

He had failed to stop the media from running rampant with every second of sickening footage they got.

He had failed to kill the terrorists that raged the US.

Brian rubbed his temples, taking a slow breath. He didn't tire of the war, but the war grew tired of him. The Union had strength left, yes, and he held onto hope they could win. But wars could swing to either side of the pendulum. The rebels were suffering due to lack of supplies in the winter, but thanks to the lack of aid from his own government, so were Brian's men.

There are calculations in the madness. But the odds stacked against him. He hadn't expected the rebels to gain such ground. Someone—more than one person—was working in the shadows. People within their own government leaders were helping the Confeds. There was no other explanation Brian could find. He hadn't the time to warn any of the UN leaders, nor did he know if anyone else knew and was handling the situation accordingly.

His major concern now was to regain D.C. without much government aid. The greedy leaders were stingy with assistance, money, and supplies.

Brian watched the holographic laptop play the news coverage—rumors, fear mongering, nothing more—and shut it off. Outside in the frigid Maine night, his men were camping in thick tents, working hard to stay warm. He pulled his jacket tighter, swearing at the Union leaders under his breath for their ill-supplying. And their arrogance. And their news coverage. He could end the war if they stopped playing the world's politically correct games.

Something Mr. Fisher—his step-father, the man who'd raised him with a heart of gold—used to say came to his head. *"Some men are built for war, and sometimes, war builds men." Which one am I? Does it matter anymore?*

Brian stood up. He could end it all. He could be a hero for his nation.

What was truly stopping him from flipping off the entire Union and UN, and ending the war in a way no one, not the world, government, or gangs expected?

Nothing.

His wife and kids were safe in government housing. His men, all of them, would follow him through hell and back.

Brian picked up his secure phone, licking his chapped lips. There was something else he had to do, first. He typed in a phone number he knew by heart, waited as it rang once, twice, three times.

A soft, tired female voice came over the line. "Hello?"

She sounded older. Stronger, somehow.

"Who is this?" she mumbled groggily, a flare of irritation to her voice.

Brian smiled. "Hello, little sister."

TO BE CONTINUED...

THANKS FOR READING THE GRIM ALLIANCE!

The story continues in The Mercenary's Deception!

If you'd like to support the book, please review it on Amazon and share the word about it on social media!

If you want to get the inside scoop on my new releases, sign up for my newsletter on my website!

ACKNOWLEDGMENTS

I thank God for leading me, holding me when times get hard, and teaching me how to fight. May all the glory go to God!

Thanks to my parents, for guidance, love, and feeding me when I forgot to eat. I wouldn't be who I am without you two. Thanks to my siblings and nieces and nephew, for not only supporting me, but tethering me to reality. You guys rock.

Thanks to the Z Team. Y'all's support means the world to me. Thanks for the good times and karate madness.

Thanks to my bestie, Sydney, for cheering me on and always being there.

Thanks to my beta readers and street team. You guys helped make this novel better.

And huge thanks to the dude who lives next door. (Stop judging my driving skills, though.)

Lastly, thank you, dear reader, for reading this novel. If you enjoyed it, Amazon reviews are like espresso coffees for authors. We really appreciate Amazon reviews, needless to say.

ABOUT ANGELA

Angela R. Watts is the bestselling author of The Infidel Books and the Remnant Trilogy. She's been writing stories since she was little, and when she's not writing, she's probably drawing or working with her amazing editorial clients. You can join her newsletter or connect with her on social media.

https://angelarwatts.com/

Printed in Great Britain
by Amazon